THE HEIR OF EXILE

Note from the Author

The Heir of Exile can be read as a standalone fantasy novel, though I generally recommend reading the central Seeder Wars trilogy first, as this book contains major spoilers for books 1–3. That said, new readers and those already familiar with my Seeder Wars series will have very different experiences as they take on this journey, either discovering things alongside the main character, or gripping the edge of their seat at times because they're privy to more details than she is.

Regardless of which type of reader you are, I hope you enjoy Leah for all she is, even with her faults!

*

Sign up for my newsletter for updates on upcoming publications, promotions, and bonus content! (Including a FREE download of "Son & Soldier: A Seeder Short Story" at JHouserWrites.com)

Book-related merch can also be purchased on my author website!

Content Warning

Select scenes and topics in this novel may be more difficult for some readers. These topics include: violence/death, discrimination, suicide, abuse of minors, and sexual assault.

In most instances, these topics are brought up in passing or simply implied. None of the above listed situations are shown graphically on page. My intention is never to glorify or justify harmful behavior, even if a fictional character doesn't get it quite right.

~J. Houser

Pronunciation Guide:

<u>People</u>

Beata: bay-AH-tuh

Boman/Bomen: BOW-man

Camry: CAM-ree

Eleana: el-ee-AH-nuh

(Leah: LEE-uh)

Elonta: ee-LAWN-tuh

Guillen: GUY-en

Kaylah: KAY-luh

Kyas: KAI-us

Rian: ree-ann

Tobias: toe-BYE-us

(Toby: TOE-bee)

<u>Places & Things</u>

Boloru: bowl-OR-oo

Guenjalis: gwen-YAWL-iss

Selen: SELL-en

THE HEIR OF EXILE

J. HOUSER

The Outer Rim
Boman Lands
Grand Sea
Seeder Territory
Ivy Kingdom
Capital City
Boman Lands
Ivy Palace
The Green Lands

Prologue

BEATA LAY IN BED, restless as the sun peeked through the windows. She smirked. It was still so majestic—life in the palace. The stained glass was intricate, the ivy-lined ceiling magical. Pondering the dreams and plans that had been set in motion, she drew a deep breath.

"Mmm, you're awake," Soren said in a groggy voice, wrapping his arm around her.

"You are *astonishingly* perceptive." She rolled over for a kiss.

He grinned. "How are you doing?"

She wrinkled her nose. "I've been better."

"I know what always makes *me* feel better." He nuzzled her neck.

She laughed. "Yeah, well, I don't think that cures maternal sickness. Pretty sure that's what caused it."

"Damn right it is." He moved over, straddling her.

She sighed, gazing into his stunning green eyes. "I don't really feel like it right now."

He pursed his lips. "What was it you said when I asked you to marry me? 'I'll do what you want, be what you want.' You gave me an oath."

They stared at each other for a moment before she replied. "Yes. That's what I said. And I'll stick to that. I didn't say no. But that doesn't mean I can't be open with you and give you a chance to pretend like you're considering my feelings now and then."

He rocked his head back and forth. "Mmm, maybe that's true." He leaned forward, giving her another kiss. "We should talk, anyway."

"What about?"

He rested his hands on her stomach. "You … and the baby. And what we'll do if they take on the palace again."

Beata raised her eyebrows. "You've tripled security. You've dismissed or killed half of the servants and guards to weed out the disloyal ones. You're still worried?"

He shrugged. "You know me. I like to have plans."

"I intend to stay here. By your side. You don't have to worry about my loyalty."

"I don't want you here if it happens. Your aides have been instructed on where to take you if we're under attack."

She scowled. "I'm not running away like a coward."

"I'm the king, dammit."

"And I'm the queen."

His eyes narrowed. "You're a queen because I made you one. You don't control the Vines."

She resented that reminder, staring into his cold eyes. His position of authority was just as precarious as hers. "I'm a queen because *we* made me one. It might have been your idea, but we *both*," she lowered her voice, "did things we can't speak about to get here. Don't talk down to me."

He nodded in thought. "I won't budge on this one. Not when it comes to my child."

"*Our* child."

His jaw clenched, and a signature spark rose in his eyes. "You'll leave as I order you to."

She'd never been afraid of his temper. "This kingdom needs a united front."

He raised his voice. "Did I stutter?"

She closed her eyes, breathing deeply. Hopefully it would never come to that. Soren's plans were well thought out. "I'll follow your orders."

His smile returned. "That's what I wanted to hear."

Her lips formed a hint of a grin. "I love you."

"I love you too. I always knew I was picking a strong girl. You just have to remember our deal." He leaned forward again, nibbling her ear. "Now, should I stay in bed, or should I find out if one of the new maids wants to see what it's like to please her king?"

Beata wasn't even fazed by that threat. She knew the man she'd married. He'd never devoutly promised to be faithful. But when possible, she always preferred to keep him happy and closer to her. "Stay with me."

Chapter 1

LEAH LOVED TO SHOP, though not in the same way her peers did. Not with a gaggle of gossipy girls, browsing through the pretty things and emptying their parents' bank accounts.

Leah loved it for the thrill.

Pulling down her hoodie sleeves, Leah glanced around to make sure the coast was clear, then picked her target. She placed her hands on the edge of the store shelf, where they could clearly be seen by someone passing by or a hidden security camera. Not as easily spotted were the vines she extended from her wrists. Green vines peeked out, as thick as her pinky, lined with several small leaves. She reached them forward, grasping the small trinkets she was aiming for on the shelf below, and reeled them in, smoothly tucking them into her sleeves. With her vines fully retracted, she moved her hands to her pants pockets and let the items slide down her sleeves.

She grinned and walked to the next aisle. The rush always lasted from the moment she picked her first target, to the moment she unloaded it all in her bedroom. Every time. Without fail. She didn't even really care for half of the items she'd take.

Spotting her next targets—bottles of nail polish—she followed her usual routine. One of the bottles tipped over, and she focused on flexing harder, picking it back up. Her deformities had some perks, but a good grip wasn't always one of them. She tucked away the first pair of polishes and sized up the other colors, deciding if she wanted to add any others to her collection.

A sudden pain in Leah's ear took her by surprise. She clenched her teeth in anger.

"Put them all back!" the woman hissed while pinching Leah's earlobe.

Leah stood stiff, scowling. "I don't know what you're talking about."

"Don't be a brat. I saw you do it. Empty your pockets. Now."

Leah rolled her eyes. "Fine. If you promise not to tell Mom." She glared at her Aunt Cheryl.

Aunt Cheryl glared back. "I don't keep secrets from your mother. Would you rather face her, or the cops?"

Leah sneered. "Would you rather me walk out with a few items, or have the cops find out about our family of freaks?"

Cheryl pinched and twisted her ear harder.

"Ouch!" Leah reached into her pockets. "Fine." She dumped her pilfered treasures onto the shelf, and her aunt released her ear, giving her a shove in the direction of the store exit.

They marched out of the store without purchasing anything, not saying a word until they got in the car.

"Buckle your seat belt!" Aunt Cheryl was always uptight. She hated Leah, and she hated the world. Sometimes it seemed she even hated her own sister, Leah's mom.

Leah buckled her seat belt. "None of the stuff I had was even that expensive. The store writes off that kind of stuff without a second thought."

"You're a disgrace," Cheryl muttered without taking her eyes off of the road. "Just like your father."

Leah looked down at her lap. It was a complex insult. Cheryl had made it clear she'd never been fond of Leah's dad. She seemed to blame him for things her own mom didn't. Why that was, Leah never knew.

But Leah smirked a little at being compared to him. They so rarely talked about him. All she knew was her dad had been a good man. A man who had loved her and her mom, worked hard, and been ambitious. And died far too young, in a tragic accident at work before Leah was born. And that she'd inherited his stunning green eyes. That was all her mom would ever tell her.

Fighting a frown, and the ache of never having met him, she kept her smile. She'd imagined a million times what it would have been like to grow up with a dad. She'd always painted a picture of what their relationship would have been like. He would have been the kind of dad to step away from demanding work to play with her, to talk with her. He would have been there to stand up for her when she'd needed it, and to provide more stability in her childhood.

"Did my dad know about our deformity?" Leah asked, running a thumb across her wrist.

Cheryl pursed her lips. "Never mind him. We just moved to a new city. Why is that?"

Leah gazed out the window as they passed unfamiliar buildings. "Because you and Mom like to see new places?"

Cheryl threw her a dirty look. "Or perhaps it's because you don't know what it means to stay out of trouble! Do you want to move again already? Then get caught shoplifting again. Sneak a boy into your room again. Get kicked out of school again. Have someone other than me spot you using those things. Might as well stop unpacking if you're going to do this."

Leah shook her head. "You and Mom use them, too. Don't pretend you don't, when you think I'm not looking and you're multitasking."

Cheryl huffed, braking at a stop sign. "We might extend them in private. That's a completely different story, Eleana!"

Leah rolled her eyes again, and stared out the car window for the rest of the ride.

Stupid family secrets. Stupid rules.

***

As they pulled up to their house, Leah sighed. Her mom was already home. Both she and Cheryl worked full-time, on different schedules, so Leah was always supervised when she was home. They treated her like she was a baby, or a psychopath or something. Sixteen was plenty old enough to be left alone. She could admit to herself that she hadn't exactly done anything to *earn* their trust, but maybe if they backed off a little, she wouldn't act the way she did. At least not as often.

Navigating her way through a maze of boxes and furniture, Leah took a sharp left after the living room, heading down the main hallway, straight to her room. She sat on her bed, staring at the bright orange comforter. As much as she pretended it didn't bother her, she hated moving again too.

A soft knock on the door announced what she'd known was coming—the lecture following Cheryl's tattling. "It's unlocked."

Her mom opened the door, disappointment painting her face. While Leah had her dad's eyes, she shared her mom's short thin nose and jet-black hair.

"Hi, princess," her mom said.

Leah bit her lip, her head cocking to one side. "Hi."

Her mom entered the room, closing the door behind her and sitting on the edge of the bed. "Why'd you do it?"

Leah tucked her knees up, hugging them. "You wouldn't have to ask that question if Aunt Cheryl knew how to keep her mouth shut."

Her mom scolded her with her eyes. "Aunt Cheryl is keeping you out of trouble. And this isn't about her. This is about *your* behavior."

"She hates me."

Her mom frowned. "She doesn't hate you, sweetheart. And … we owe her a lot. You need to be nice to her."

Leah gritted her teeth. "Whatever." Whenever her mom was physically and emotionally present, she was there for Leah. Despite all the trouble she'd gotten into, her mom usually believed her. Except when it came to Aunt Cheryl. Then again, Aunt Cheryl never threw her most venomous insults in front of Leah's mom, never laid a hand on her in her mom's presence.

"So, why did you do it? You have an allowance. You could have bought those things."

Leah shrugged, avoiding eye contact.

"And using your vines in public?"

Leah bit the insides of her cheeks.

"Sweetheart, we're just trying to keep you safe."

Leah's eyebrows bunched. "Is that it? You think a mob's going to come after us because we're a little different? Because it seems to me it's less about safety, and more about being ashamed of yourself, and your own daughter."

A disheartened look crossed her mom's face. "Eleana, I'm not ashamed of you. It's … complicated. Some things should be kept private."

Yeah… Private. Suck it up.

"Can you please just try to behave and make some friends here? I'm so tired of moving."

Leah stared at her mom, then went back to looking at the bedding. *Make friends? When we'll probably just move in a few months anyway?* She traced the flower pattern on the comforter with a finger. She'd screwed up a lot. But not *all* of the moves were her fault. Sometimes, they'd pick up and leave without any explanation at all.

"Princess? Sweetheart?"

Leah met her mom's gaze.

"I love you—you know that. And you're bright. You could have *so* many friends, if you'd try a little more."

Leah shook her head. "Friends that I can't allow to know the real me, right? I'm pretty sure I could join a circus. That would make some good money, and then I'd have plenty of friends that are freaks just like me."

Her mom sighed, rubbing her temple. "You're not a freak. I love that you have something special about you. I know you don't understand my opinion on this, but I'm *absolutely* not ashamed of your vines, or you." She rested a hand on Leah's. "And what's different about you, physically—that doesn't define you. If you want people to know the real you, let them see how smart you are, how sweet you can be … when you want to be."

Leah gnawed on her bottom lip. "I'll try to do better."

Her mom gave her a half-smile. "That's all I'm asking. Now…" She tapped Leah's knee. "Since Aunt Cheryl returned empty-handed, and we don't have any groceries, how about we order something in? Celebrate a fresh start? Anything you want."

***

The first day of school was never fun. Especially when it was Leah's first day at a new school that had already been in session for three weeks. When 'Eleana Edwards' came up on each roll call, she had to inform her teachers she preferred to go by Leah. And she tried her best to stay positive, but it didn't come easy.

At lunch, she found a half-empty table in the cafeteria and sat down by herself, digging into her small basket of fries. She hadn't even eaten two bites before a pair of girls approached. They claimed seats across from her without even asking if she'd wanted them to.

"Hi. You're new, right? I'm Jackie, and this is Tina."

Leah finished her bite, looking the two of them over. They both donned bright smiles—a brunette and a blonde. She didn't need a pair of Mary Sues to pick her up as a charity case. Without a word, she stood, grabbed her tray, and walked away.

Finding a door to the outdoor courtyard, she took her tray outside. It was a beautiful day, and she loved the outdoors anyway.

Near the far corner, Leah spotted an empty table and sat down to finish her meal in solitude. While she picked at her food, her mom's plea sounded in her ears: she should be trying to make friends. But she wasn't a pathetic loner, and she *wasn't* desperate.

Though, she did enjoy eavesdropping on a table of guys sitting behind her. They were a bit raucous, but it was entertaining.

"You guys still coming over tonight?" one asked.

"Yeah, you can count on me."

"Of course we can. His crush is gone." A different voice snickered.

"You're an idiot. I barely knew her."

"Take it from a bowman that's lived here his entire life: don't waste your time with the green-eyed girls. You never know when they're gonna get sick and have to leave for the rest of the school year."

Leah furrowed her brow. *What's wrong with girls that have green eyes? And are they seriously making fun of sick girls? Is that supposed to be a jab at eating disorders or something?* She adjusted her position to see the guys out of the corner of her eye. None of the trio were particularly distinctive—all brunets, average height and appearance.

"Yeah, well, I'm a bowman too. But if I was actually interested, that wouldn't stop me. I could see them when I go back home." He took a drink from a soda can. "I'm just saying, I barely knew her. It's not like we had a thing."

"Sure you did. You're a momma's boy," one teased with a smug grin.

"Momma's boy?" He raised an eyebrow.

"Yeah. She's a green-eye, right? You've got a soft spot for them."

Both of the other guys instantly looked perturbed.

"That's not cool, man."

The guy the teasing had been aimed at spoke again. "Screw you, Tanner."

Tanner rolled his eyes. "Come on, Marcus. Learn to take a joke."

"You thought she was cute, too." Marcus scowled. "Don't be a dick."

Tanner shrugged. "I can appreciate a pretty face without wanting to date her. I'm old school."

Marcus sat straighter, narrowing his eyes. "How old school? Why are you even here? Socializing with the likes of us?"

Tanner frowned. "I did *not* mean that. You know I'm not like that. My parents never would have let me come here if we thought that way."

Should Leah be minding her own business? Yes. But these guys were … weird. Intriguing. She left her tray, turning and sliding into the empty seat at their table. They all looked surprised at her uninvited appearance.

She rested her chin on a fist. "What's wrong with girls that have green eyes? I happen to think they're beautiful." She batted her lashes to show off her favorite feature, making a point.

All three guys immediately donned smirks. The one whose name she hadn't heard yet—the shorter of the three—did a poor job of stifling a laugh.

She squinted at him. "What's your name?"

"Jake."

"Well, Jake," she stole a fry from his tray, "did you know only two percent of the population has green eyes? I'd say that's pretty unique." She bit into the room-temperature fry.

His smile grew. "Fun fact. A statistic I'm sure is true for *some* parts of the world."

She shook her head. "Worldwide."

He still wore a contented grin. "Okay."

"So?" She lifted her eyebrows.

"I'm Marcus," the one sitting opposite her said. His hair had a bit of a curl to it. "And who are you?"

She faced him. "Leah."

"Don't worry about these two idiots. They didn't mean anything by it."

Jake and Tanner shrugged.

"Right…" Now it was awkward, with them clamming up. She wasn't going to move back to her table, and she wasn't going to head back inside for the rest of lunch. She twisted to grab her lunch tray and continued eating with them. "So … I just moved here. What's there to do in this city?"

Jake took a bite of his hamburger. "Mmm, that's a question for me." He pointed a thumb to himself. "These two are both new here this year."

"Really?"

"Yeah. I'm foreign exchange this year," Tanner said. His hair was a lighter brown than the others.

She detected no accent. "Where from?"

Jake grinned. "Yeah, Tanner. Where from?"

Tanner rolled his eyes. "Canada."

Leah smirked. "*Very* exotic."

He scowled.

"What about you, Marcus?"

He stabbed at his side salad with a fork. "Oh, I'm spending a year with my grandparents."

"And what brings you here?" Jake asked.

Leah wore a grin of her own. "My mom didn't approve of my friends or extracurricular activities in our last place."

Tanner smiled. "Sounds like fun."

Jake raised an eyebrow. "Sounds like trouble."

She looked at Marcus, curious whether he had an assessment as the bell rang.

He took another swig of his soda. "Sounds like it's time to head to class."

Chapter 2

LEAH STOOD AT STUDENT PICKUP, waiting for Aunt Cheryl to come get her at the end of the day.

"Hey. It's Leah, right?"

The voice belonged to none other than her new acquaintance. "Yeah. Marcus, right?"

He nodded, tugging on the straps of his backpack. He wore a dark grey crewneck t-shirt. "I hope you weren't offended by what the guys were saying earlier. It's more of an inside joke than anything. They don't actually look down on people with green eyes."

"Good to know."

He smiled. "Yeah. Kind of a stupid thing to judge someone by."

She chuckled. "Yeah. That would be."

They stood awkwardly for a little while, teenage giggles and chatter, and cars driving by, filling the silence between them.

"So … no car?" he asked.

"Nope. My aunt picks me up. You?"

He shook his head. "Grandparents."

"What did you guys mean when you were talking? You and Jake said something about being bowmen?"

Marcus smirked. "Oh, you heard that? Eavesdrop much?"

She shrugged. "The conversation was interesting enough, and you weren't exactly whispering. So, what does it mean?"

He scanned her face. "What do you think it means?"

She scoffed. "I'm the one that's asking, right? I don't know. Are you talking, like, bows and arrows?"

He looked down, scuffing the sole of his shoe on the cement. "Yeah. You're right. Jake and I, uh, both like to shoot bows."

"Doesn't that make you archers? Is bowmen even the right term?"

Marcus swatted a hand in the air dismissively. "It's a nerd hobby, anyway."

"No, I think that actually sounds really cool." She tilted her head slightly, looking into his brown eyes. She'd never met anyone who knew how to shoot a bow. "Would you mind if I came sometime to check it out?"

His cheeks reddened. "Yeah, we could totally do that."

She smiled. "That sounds like way more fun than hitting a movie theater in a new town. What's your number?"

They exchanged numbers right before Aunt Cheryl arrived in her red sedan.

"Cool. Text me." She smiled again, tucking her phone in her pocket, and hopped in the car.

"How was your first day?" Cheryl asked. Her voice was neutral despite the perma-scowl wrinkles on her face.

Leah rolled her eyes. "Like you care."

***

Leah sat at the small desk in her room, snacking on sour-cream-and-onion potato chips, sorting through her homework.

"Hey, sweetheart. I'm home." Her mom appeared in the doorway.

"Hi. How was work?"

Her mom opened her eyes wide. "Adult jobs ... *full* of thrills."

Leah chuckled. Her mom had worked a number of jobs over the years. She didn't complain about any of them all that much, nor was she enamored with any of them. Her current job in this new city was as a receptionist at a car rental.

"How was your first day of school?"

Leah closed her textbook. "It was school."

"I see you're doing homework?"

Leah twisted in her chair. "I'm not a *complete* failure, you know."

Her mom frowned, tilting her head forward. "I never said you were."

Leah returned her focus to her American History papers.

"Make any new friends today?"

She mentally ran through her day. "Yeah. I think so."

"Someone I'd approve of?"

Leah laughed. "Yeah. Pretty sure he's a Boy Scout."

"I'm glad to hear it. Want to come help me make dinner?"

Leah clamped the bag of chips closed. "Sure."

They stood in the kitchen, Leah's mom stirring a pot on the stove, Leah picking through a bag of spinach for salad.

"So, you said your new friend is a boy? Are we talking boyfriend potential? Or boy that's a friend?"

Leah sniggered. "I'm definitely thinking the latter. What about you? Any dashing suitors at your work?"

"Oh, you know me. I am not looking to date. I don't need anyone in my life other than you."

Leah frowned, leaning back against the counter. "But is that healthy? I mean it when I say I wouldn't hold it against you. You deserve to be happy."

She wished her mom would go to therapy, would talk about her problems. Would even allow Leah to go to therapy. But they'd put that idea to bed years ago. Her mom had resolutely declared that therapists were useless. They just turned your own questions back on you and meddled in people's business when they ought not to.

Her mom faced her with a forced smile. "No one in this world could compare to your father. I'm really not interested in dating right now."

Leah bit her lip. "Why won't you ever talk about my dad?"

Her mom dodged eye contact, looking at the tile floor. "I talk about him."

"You've never even told me his name or shown me a picture of him. Do you know how weird that is? Sometimes I feel like he was a one-night stand and you're just ashamed you don't actually know who he is. And if that's the truth, I'm old enough for you to say so."

Her mom scowled. "Don't you dare think that of me, of us. We were legally married. We dated for *years* before we got engaged. And I've told you—we lost a lot of things in that house fire when you were a baby. I'm sorry I don't have more for you."

"Okay," Leah whispered.

Her mom lightly rested a hand on Leah's arm. "Princess, I know you want more. And someday, we'll talk more about it, alright?" She closed her eyes. "Just … not right now."

Leah sighed, trying to move on from the topic of perpetual vagueness. It hurt, after all these years, that her mom still hadn't gotten over his death. That it was too painful to talk about him.

After dinner, Marcus texted to see if Leah had Friday evening free to go shooting, and they set a time. It brought a smile to her face, giving her a fun new experience to look forward to.

***

The next day at school, Leah considered where she'd sit at lunch. She could try to make more friends, but that required effort. And caring. She took her lunch straight out to the courtyard, and sat at the table she had the day before, by herself.

The trio from the day before sat at their table again. Marcus glanced at her a couple of times. "Do you want to sit with us, Leah?"

She waved her hand while finishing a bite. "No, I'm good."

He shrugged. "Okay."

She thought it over again, then picked up her tray and joined them. "So … will you be there Friday, Jake?"

He was visibly confused. "Friday?"

Marcus cleared his throat. "Oh, um … yeah. We're going to go do archery. Leah and I talked about how you and I like to shoot, after she overheard us talking yesterday about being *bowmen*."

Jake smirked. "Sad to say, I'm otherwise engaged. Love a good bow and arrow." He slapped Marcus hard on the back. "And my skills could *never* compare to this guy's. He's a regular Robin Hood, this one."

Marcus shook his head, looking Leah straight in the eyes. "That's a major exaggeration."

Tanner laughed. "No, it's not. He's *seriously* impressive!"

Marcus threw him a dark look. "Shut up."

Leah grinned at their teasing. Now she *really* wondered how talented he was at the sport.

***

By the time Friday rolled around, Leah was definitely looking forward to her first time at an archery range. It was a nice break from homework and unpacking. Marcus swung by to pick her up, briefly meeting her mom and sharing the range's address before being allowed to take Leah.

Marcus looked all sorts of nervous on the drive out to the archery range. "This'll be my first time coming here. You know, since I'm new in town."

She nodded. "Cool. How many years have you done archery? I don't think I've known anyone that shoots."

"Oh, really? Yeah. I guess it's not that popular. Pretty cool little niche though, right?"

She smiled. "I guess we'll see."

An electronic bell dinged as they walked in the front door of the archery shop, and an employee quickly greeted them. Leah surveyed the area while he guided them to the counter. In the main lobby area, well over a dozen round racks were crowded with bows and clothes, most of the clothes camouflage or neon orange. Hanging high on the walls were different styles of decoys, targets, and a few mounted taxidermy animals—not exactly Leah's cup of tea. Looking past the products for purchase, she caught a glimpse of the shooting range. At the end of a long room lit by overhead fluorescent lights, bales of hay had been stacked to the ceiling. A number of targets were secured to the bales.

"Yeah, we're wanting to rent some bows to shoot," Marcus said.

"Right this way." The employee directed them to a sign behind the counter, and quoted prices. "Do you have a preference?"

Marcus's hands were shoved in his pockets, his arms rigid. "I left mine at home. I'm not sure what the best rental equivalent would be."

"What's your weight?" the man asked.

"Um … one-fifty?"

The man smirked. "Right… You say your bow's at home?"

Marcus cleared his throat. "Yeah. You know, it's *her* first time. Maybe you could recommend a good option for a first-time shooter?"

The man kept grinning, facing Leah. "Alright, now, it's up to you. We have a lot of nice compounds, but I'm of the camp that believes a beginner should start with a recurve." He pointed to a row of more basic-looking equipment—these bows were made of wood. "Simpler to start off with."

She shrugged. "Then we'll go with that."

The man turned back to Marcus. "Would you like to go the same route?"

"Yeah. Sure. Why not?"

They pulled the string back on a couple of bows each, landing on something that gave a comfortable resistance. The employee went over the rules of the range and set them up with all sorts of other rental accessories. He tried to explain some of the basics, but Marcus thanked him and said they could handle it from there. "It's really not that hard," he told Leah.

She let him go first. His first shot went wild, finding its place in a hay bale absolutely nowhere near the target. "Just takes a little getting used to. You know, using one that's not mine." The second shot had him clenching his teeth and grasping his arm where the string had hit it.

"Hold your arm straight, kid," a white-haired man shooting nearby called out. "And wear your armguard. Gonna hurt like the dickens if you do it that way, especially being double-jointed."

Marcus rolled his eyes, taking a little more time to aim and shoot a couple more arrows. Neither hit their mark, but he had a nice red spot where the string had gotten him again.

Leah fought a smirk. He was clearly a fish out of water. But he figured out where the aforementioned armguard belonged, strapping on the piece of leather he'd tossed on a folding chair behind him, onto the developing welt.

"Choose an anchor point and stick with it," the older man called out.

Marcus shook his head, his nostrils flaring. Leah frowned. It was kind of fun to watch him suffer, since he'd obviously lied. But he was a nice guy; maybe he deserved a break.

She slipped on her armguard. "How about I take a turn?"

"Yeah." He set his bow down. "Maybe I'm just nervous with everyone watching me."

Leah picked up one of the other accessories they'd been given— a leather finger guard. Her arrows had neon-green and orange plastic fletching instead of feathers. Picking one up, she rested it in position on the bow, clicking it onto the string with the plastic nock at the end. She placed her pointer finger on the string, above the arrow nock. She then rested her middle and ring fingers underneath, as the employee had briefly demonstrated, the leather guard separating her fingers from the string. Closing one eye, she carefully pulled the string back; there was a springy resistance. Once it was pulled all the way back, she did her best to line up the arrow with her target.

As she released her grip, the string snapped forward, and her arrow launched across the room. From yards away, she thought she could hear the rip of paper as it punched through. She'd hit the target. Kind of. The arrow jutted from the bottom right corner of the paper her target was printed on, not actually having hit any of the rings.

She tried again and didn't do much better, until she asked for a few pointers from the elderly gentleman so eager to help. She asked Marcus if he wanted to go again, but he declined. By the end, her arrows were still scattered, but they were forming tighter groupings with more practice. She insisted Marcus try again with one more round before they took off. He reluctantly obliged, redeeming himself with a couple of decent shots.

They approached the counter to return their equipment and pay. Marcus had tossed his target in the trash after retrieving it; Leah held hers to take home, marking her first experience with archery.

She reached for her wallet.

Marcus held up a hand. "No, I've got it."

"You sure?"

"Yeah, I'm good."

The employee grinned as he took the bows over the counter. "We've got affordable lessons, if you two are interested."

Marcus pressed his lips together. "Thanks. How much was it for tonight?"

Leah smiled. "Hey, I'm going to use the restroom before we head out." She turned the corner and stopped to eavesdrop once the employee started talking again.

"Word to the wise? If you're going to lie to impress a girl, do a bit more research if you're going to pick something like archery. Or take her to something a little less complex, like bowling."

Marcus huffed. "Yeah. Thanks."

"Oh, yeah. And in case you two want to come back: your weight? You were pulling thirty-five pounds back there; your girl was pulling thirty."

Leah stifled a laugh and headed to the bathroom, folding her target and slipping it into her back pocket.

Returning to the lobby, she found Marcus browsing the different displays of equipment. She leaned in close. "Looking to add to your collection?"

He jumped and spun, smirking. "Yeah. Definitely."

She bit her lip and laughed. "Let's head out."

They got back to the truck and buckled up.

"So … not an archer?" She raised an eyebrow.

His face was red. "Picked up on that, did ya?"

She laughed again, and he joined in this time.

He rubbed his forehead. "I'm sorry. That was stupid. Hands down my worst date. I mean, not that you, obviously, you know, just… I promise I don't usually lie."

She pursed her lips. "Is that what this was? A date?"

His eyes shot up to meet hers. "No. I mean. No. I don't know why I said that. Obviously just a hangout."

She shrugged. "We can call it a date if you want to."

He rolled his eyes. "I know how to get a proper date, thank you very much. I don't need you calling it one out of pity."

She rubbed the knee of her jeans, feeling awful about this train wreck of an evening. "Date or not, how about ending it with frozen yogurt? My treat."

He smiled at the olive branch. "Sure."

They sat down to eat their frozen yogurt in a shop bustling with families and couples.

"So … why did you lie?"

He held his bowl against the welt on his arm. "It's … complicated."

"What does that actually mean, then? Bowman?"

"It's a nickname, really." He stabbed at his dessert. "Just another inside joke."

She picked out a spoonful of fruit boba, allowing the juicy spheres to pop in her mouth. "But you're not going to tell me? Lots of inside jokes. Is it a perverted guy thing, and that's why you're not telling me?"

He shook his head. "No. Not at all. Just don't worry about it. It's stupid. Seriously."

Hmm. "Okay. So, let's talk green eyes. The guys said your mom has green eyes?"

He rocked his head side to side. "More or less."

"And you have brown eyes, so that must mean your dad has brown eyes."

"No. Actually, my dad has blue eyes."

She hesitated, having learned a thing or two about genetics and eye color. "Green and blue eyes are recessive traits. Sorry to tell you, but…"

He wore a soft smile. "It doesn't matter. I'm adopted."

"Oh. Okay. It was about to get awkward if you didn't know that." She chuckled. Her tone got more serious. "Either way, sorry to hear that."

He furrowed his brow, swallowing another spoonful. "Why would you apologize?"

"Well … I just know that can be a sensitive topic for some people."

Marcus shook his head, scooping another bite of his frozen yogurt. "My parents love me. I'm really okay with it."

"That's enough for you? Do you have any memories or information about your birth parents?"

He drew a deep breath, looking down at his treat.

"Sorry, I really shouldn't ask."

He wrinkled his nose. "It's fine. Is it enough?" He met her eyes. "Most days. I don't remember my birth parents, and I have no desire to ever meet them."

She nodded pensively. "I guess I'm curious because I never got to meet my dad. He died before I was born. It's always just been my mom and aunt and me."

He gave her a sympathetic frown. "Sorry, that sucks."

"Yeah. Luck of the draw, right?"

Marcus sat up straighter. "Well, anyway … what about you and your hobbies? You were … vague."

She'd been right about him being a Boy Scout if he'd been that embarrassed about a little white lie over archery. "I don't think it's your style."

He gave her a dimpled smirk. "Alright, we both get to keep some secrets. Fair enough." He pointed his spoon at her. "But … fun fact: I'm actually decent at throwing knives."

"Intriguing. And we didn't do that tonight, instead of that shameful display at the archery range, because…?"

He chuckled. "Because I was already committed to *that* lie."

"Here's a free tip." She raised her eyebrows high. "You suck at lying, almost as much as you suck at archery. And that's saying something. Stick to the truth, Squeaky Clean."

He widened his eyes. "I can promise you that."

Their playful banter was interrupted by a call on Leah's cell. Her mom.

She sighed, picking it up. "Hi. Yes. Sorry. We'll be back soon. Chill. Love you too."

She rolled her eyes after hanging up. "Sorry, my mom is a tad overprotective." It wasn't like she hadn't already texted her mom to check in at the archery range, per her mom's usual paranoid requirements…

"No worries. Let's head out."

Marcus drove Leah back to her house. "Sorry again," he said while putting the truck into park.

"Don't be. It was still a lot of fun."

"Cool. Well, since this is *not* a date, I'm going to stay here and *not* walk you up to the door."

She smiled. "Have a good night. See you at school."

Chapter 3

LEAH'S MOM FURROWED HER BROW upon her return from the frozen yogurt shop. "You know the rules, Eleana."

Leah threw her hands into the air, sitting across from her in the living room. "I know. I'm sorry. You're the one that tracks my phone, anyway. Why I even have to check in with you is beyond me."

Her mom rubbed her temples. "I shouldn't *have* to track your phone. I should be able to count on you letting me know when your plans have changed!"

"We went out for frozen yogurt afterward. It's not a big deal."

"Maybe not to you. But I have my rules to keep you safe!"

Leah raised an eyebrow. "To keep me safe? Is that it? Or is it because you don't trust me? Although, even *if* you trusted me, I have a feeling you'd still monitor every last detail of my life. It's not about safety. It's control you want."

Her mom shook her head. "You may not like my rules, but you're afforded plenty of freedom. Maybe *too much* freedom."

She glared at her mom. "I already said I was sorry. It was an innocent mistake. Can we be done now?"

Her mom slumped back in her chair. "Yes. Go."

***

Leah beat the guys to the lunch table on Monday. They were already in the thick of a conversation as they joined her.

"Come on, man," Tanner said. "It would be really cool to attend. Just think about it."

"No." Marcus furrowed his brow. "And it's *super* awkward that you would even ask."

Leah nibbled on a french fry, curious about the topic of the day. "So … what's this exciting event?"

Marcus opened a can of soda. "My older brother's getting married."

Leah looked at Tanner, surprised. "You're inviting yourself to a *wedding*? Isn't that weird? And why? Weddings are boring." She dipped another fry in ketchup.

Tanner leaned forward. "Hear me out. The bride's side is going to have hardly anyone there, anyway. I could totally blend in. And there's going to be some pretty big names attending! I'm just saying, it would be cool."

She took a swig of water. "Big names? Like actors and musicians, or boring politicians?"

Marcus shot a dirty look at Tanner. "It doesn't matter. You're not invited."

Tanner appealed to Jake. "C'mon. You have to agree with me on this."

Jake shook his head before shoveling a huge bite of pizza into his mouth. "Not my thing. Sorry."

Tanner huffed and dug into his lunch as well.

"Why isn't the bride going to have many people attending?" Leah asked.

Marcus looked down at his tray as he answered. "It's a long way for them to travel."

She picked up a fork for her side salad. "Then shouldn't the wedding come to them?"

"It's … complicated. My mom has a thing with her health. She can't really travel, either."

Leah gave him a sympathetic frown. "Sorry, that sucks. Kinda rock and a hard place, huh?"

"Somehow, I think they'll all survive," Tanner drawled.

They moved on to another topic as they plowed through their meals. With a few minutes left, Jake perked up. "Hey, I almost forgot. How did archery go this weekend?"

Marcus and Leah exchanged a small grin.

"It was great!" Leah exaggerated. "I was *really* impressed. You guys were right."

Tanner and Jake looked at her in full disbelief. Marcus's grin grew to a smirk as he focused on his tray.

Tanner clicked his tongue, stacking the garbage on his tray. "Why do I have a hard time believing that?"

Leah put a hand to her heart. "I'm not even kidding. Really talented. And frankly, the best date I've ever been on."

Marcus's eyes shot up, narrowing.

She bit her lip, reaching across the table and stroking the back of his hand. "Best kisser, too." In the split second it took his face to turn beet red, she winked and grabbed her tray, standing up. "But maybe I've said too much. I'll see you guys later." She sauntered away, suppressing a laugh.

***

At the end of the school day, Leah waited for Aunt Cheryl to pick her up again.

"Why did you do that?" Marcus asked as he approached.

"Do what?" she asked with a grin.

"Lie. About everything." He gave her a disapproving look.

She laughed. "Because sometimes it's fun to stretch the truth."

He rolled his eyes.

"Come on, Squeaky Clean."

He glared. "Don't call me that."

She gently nudged his arm. "I didn't mean anything by it. I was just having fun."

"Whatever." He pulled out his phone, scrolling through messages.

She frowned. "Are you really mad at me? I didn't lie about having fun on Friday. I meant that."

He met her gaze. "Fine. Whatever." He returned his focus to his phone.

She gave him a warm smile. "You're kinda cute when you're flustered. We'll talk tomorrow? I'll let the guys know I was joking."

He sighed as his grandma pulled up in a white minivan. He shoved his phone into his pocket. "Yeah. See you tomorrow."

***

Leah smoothed things over with Jake and Tanner the next day so things were less awkward by the time lunch ended. At the end of the day, she sorted through her locker, packing her backpack.

"Hey, so this is your hallway, huh?" Marcus said, stopping to chat.

"Yep. Guess you found me."

"I was just passing by, but I wanted to say thanks for—"

While she was paying attention to Marcus, one of her books on the top shelf tipped over. Without even thinking about it, she extended a vine to balance it before it tumbled from her locker.

"What the freak, Leah!" he whispered, eyeing her wrist.

She panicked, having slipped and been caught. Another screwup. Another move across the country. Her heart raced. "I don't know what you think you saw, but you're wrong." She scowled. "And I'm not a freak!"

His eyes narrowed. "I never said you were." He glanced around, continuing in a whisper. "But you can't just pull out your vines in public like that. Not around humans!"

She read his face while rubbing her wrist. *He… This doesn't make any sense. He actually knows about the deformities? And… If there was one* thing Leah hated more than moving and making new friends, it was feeling stupid, being out of the loop. "You're right. I should be more careful."

He cocked his head. "Ya think? Don't screw it up for us."

She shook her head, still trying to understand his reaction. "Yeah. Sorry."

He narrowed his eyes again. "Why have you been pretending this whole time?"

"What do you mean?"

His tone reflected growing annoyance. "Like you're not one of us. I know we all have to blend in, but come on. Pretending you don't know what a bowman is? And why weren't you at orientation over the summer?"

"I, uh … was sick. And … visiting family." She studied his expression, still *absolutely*, *positively* clueless about what Marcus was talking about.

"Yeah, but lying the whole time? I thought you were kidding about enjoying it, but I guess I was wrong."

He seemed to know more about her than she did about herself; this was an opportunity she might not get again. "I promise, no more lies. I was just seeing how long I could go before you found out. Like you lying about archery." She smirked to lean into the lie. "Don't be mad because I'm more convincing than you."

His expression softened, and he chuckled. "Touché." His face lit up. "This is really cool. I'm guessing it's okay if I tell the guys? Then we don't have to be so secretive."

"Um… Jake and Tanner?"

"Yeah, of course." He continued to whisper. "We had a seeder girl in the group at the beginning of the year, but it sucked that she had to go home so soon once her bloom started."

Leah slowly nodded as though she knew what any of that jargon meant. "Yeah. Sure. Or maybe let's wait to talk about it at lunch tomorrow, okay?"

***

The whole ride home, and that evening, Leah was distant, lost in thought. She wasn't alone. It wasn't just some weird genetic defect that only ran in her family. She'd scoured the internet and had never found anything to explain the freaky secret she shared with her mom and aunt. The only thing she'd been able to pin down was that the leaves resembled ivy plants, but no medical diagnosis was listed online, and her mom had insisted they didn't need one.

But Marcus had clearly seen the growths, and even called them 'vines' like her mom did. As if they were even … *normal*. With her mom as touchy on that topic as she was about Leah's dad, Leah wasn't about to broach the subject with her again. The fact that she had a group of peers like her in that weird way… She needed to get as much information as possible.

The particularly unsettling fact that weighed Leah down … was the way Marcus had talked about humans. As if *he and she* weren't. She shuddered at the thought. Not only was she making friends with weird and quirky guys … but maybe with *crazy* guys. But … how crazy could they be, if they were just like her?

***

The next day at lunch, Tanner beat everyone else to the table and started normal chitchat with Leah. Not much later, Marcus and Jake joined. No one said anything about the hallway incident from the day before, but Marcus flashed Leah a couple of knowing smiles. Halfway through lunch, he must have tired of waiting for her to bring it up.

"So … Leah … any news with you?" He challenged her with his eyes, sipping from a water bottle. "Anything to share with the group?"

Jake and Tanner looked at her in anticipation. Her face warmed. She genuinely didn't know what to say. "Oh. I thought *you* wanted to be the one to tell them."

Marcus grinned, keeping his voice low. "She's ivy."

Jake lifted his eyebrows. "You're kidding me."

Tanner beamed. "Nice! Add one to the scoreboard for Team Ivy."

"Not a bowman?" Jake asked.

Marcus shook his head.

Note to self: Marcus and Jake are bowmen, whatever that is. Obviously not archers… I'm … ivy, like the leaves on my vines…

Marcus continued, "I caught her using vines yesterday. *In school…*"

Jake gave her a chastising look. "Not cool, Leah. You're lucky it was one of us that caught you."

"Yeah. Sorry. I'll do better."

"Give her a break. It's like second nature to use them sometimes," Tanner defended. He glanced at her. "I mean, still … don't get caught. I barely even use mine at my host family's house."

Jake cocked his head. "Why did you hide it from us this whole time?"

She grinned. "To see how long I could get away with it."

He busted out laughing. "Seriously the best prank I've seen in the Garden Club. The sheer terror on poor Marcus's face at having to put on an archer act—that was *priceless.*"

Marcus rolled his eyes.

"No kidding," added Tanner. "Leah *totally* could have been in covert ops back in our parents' day. She's convincing."

Marcus uncomfortably side-eyed Tanner. "Is that supposed to be a compliment? What kind of person wishes the war was still happening?"

Tanner threw a hand up. "Of course, I don't mean that. But come on, even the *queen* was a master of covert ops!"

Marcus narrowed his eyes in obvious disgust. "This. This is exactly the kind of reason I'd *never* invite you to the wedding. She's not exactly proud of that! But you act like it's something to hero worship." He stood up, grabbed his tray, and walked away.

Leah sat still, not sure what to do. Nothing made any more sense now than it had when the conversation started. Ivy? Bowman?

Queen and covert ops? She wanted to go after Marcus, but had absolutely no idea what to even say. Instead, she picked at her fingernails, waiting to hear what the other two would say.

Jake sighed. "Tanner, you really need to stop it." He also took his tray and left.

Leah pursed her lips. "Well, that was fun."

Tanner huffed. "Word of warning? Those two are a bit touchy. I'm not racist. I'm just saying, some bowmen think we're all out to get them or something. But honestly, just because they're both Ivy Kingdom, I mean, it's not the same. Right?"

She studied his face, swallowing hard. *All these words. Racism?*

Luckily, Tanner didn't expect an answer. "Jake's family are expats and barely even go to visit. And with Marcus's family being mixed… I get that they've had persecution, but…" He shook his head. "Anyway." He smiled. "I'm doing all the talking. I'm excited to learn more about you."

She was speechless, her mouth dry. "Um… What do you want to know?"

He shrugged. "I don't know. What part of the kingdom are you from?"

She took a sip of water. "South."

He peeled back the film cover of his mixed fruit cup. "How far from the palace?"

"Oh … um … I don't know, really. Pretty far south."

"Cool. I'm north central."

After a few more questions she had to give vague lies to, the bell rang.

"Hey, we're doing a Garden Club hangout tonight at Marcus's place. You down?"

"Garden Club?"

He chuckled and pointed at her. "You're good. I still can't believe you had us all fooled."

She stood to join him. "What can I say? I've got skills."

He grinned. "I'd love to learn more about all those mysterious skills and extracurricular activities of yours. It's nice having a girl from back home at this school."

She blushed at his obvious flirting. She may not have understood the hodgepodge of information they'd spat out, but she gathered Tanner might be the only one of the group really like her, with the vine growths. "Yeah, I should be able to make it."

Chapter 4

MARCUS GREETED LEAH WITH A SMILE. "Hey, glad you could join us! Come on in."

She warily walked into his house, unsure what to expect from this 'Garden Club.' When they'd texted about it, he'd said she didn't need to bring anything. She wasn't really interested in growing plants, though she figured, like most things with these guys, it probably stood for something else.

"You don't have to worry about being yourself here," he said. "My grandparents are both human, but they were host parents for my mom during her seeder youth. They understand all the green-folk stuff."

"Cool." She nodded. *Wish I did…*

He led her to the family room, where the other guys were already hanging out. They sat on a long leather sectional in front of a large entertainment center. Tanner had his feet on the wooden coffee table.

"You up for games, Leah?" Tanner asked.

She shoved her hands in her pockets, shrugging. "Sure? What kind?"

"Xbox."

"Yeah, I'm down. As long as you don't try and drag me into a D&D group, I'm down."

Tanner and Marcus laughed, glancing at Jake. Jake rolled his eyes.

"That's Jake's thing," Marcus said. "He got a human group together; he's trying to convince us to join."

"You might find it fun, if you'd give it half a chance," Jake defended.

"Anyway…" Marcus said. "Help yourself to the snacks, and just chill." He gestured at a folding table set up to the side, loaded with chips, cookies, a veggie tray, and various drinks.

Leah sat down, and Tanner handed her a controller, but not with his hands … with his own set of *vines*. He caught her eye, smirking.

"Using vines during the game is *cheating*," Jake warned with a pointed glance at Tanner. "Sometimes we have to remind Tanner."

The entire evening was a pretty standard hangout. Games, chatting about school, and only minor mentions of the inside secrets she was trying to learn about. A bit disappointed, Leah decided to try her luck, focusing on something Marcus had once said.

"Since I was late moving here, did I miss anything in orientation?"

"Not really," Jake said. "It's just a recap of all the prep courses you take before coming over as an exchange."

That isn't helpful in the slightest. "I guess I just want to make sure I don't forget anything important."

Tanner counted on his fingers. "Let's see… Don't get into trouble, don't break human laws, don't get discovered."

She smiled. "Like using vines at school?"

He winked.

"Honestly, you really had me fooled," Marcus said. "You seamlessly use electronics and everything."

"Yeah. Electronics are nice to have, right?" she replied as casually as she could manage. *What kind of place do these guys come from that doesn't have electronics?* She'd started to wonder about the possibility of aliens, but that required spaceships and stuff... She wanted nothing more than to have it all laid out for her, and was tempted to confess she was out of the loop, but she couldn't do that. It didn't feel right. She privately scoffed at the irony. She didn't want to feel like an outsider … to a group of outsiders.

"I haven't been here that long, but I can already see why your brother's marrying a human and moving to the human world," Tanner kidded before crunching into a chip.

Marcus chuckled. "Yep, that's *exactly* why he's marrying her and leaving the Green Lands. It's all so he can use the internet and game on a daily basis."

Green Lands? That … sparked something. Something she'd almost forgotten from her childhood.

***

After returning home, Leah retreated to her room and tried to think of everything she could remember about the Green Lands. It was such a silly thing, really. Her mom used to tell her about a beautiful and strong princess, bedtime stories about majestic mountains and magical people. She'd called the paradise just that—the Green Lands. *It can't be a coincidence.*

Leah toyed with the idea of bringing it up to her mom that night, but couldn't get herself to do so, not right after hanging out with the guys. If there was one thing Leah needed, it was the freedom her mother gave her, despite the phone tracking and frequent checkups every time Leah wasn't at school or in her mom or Aunt Cheryl's custody. The level of freedom Leah currently enjoyed had been bought over the years, despite all of her mistakes, by the healthy amount of guilt her mom carried about them having to move so much, and because she refused to talk about Leah's dad. Associating the Garden Club with something her mom had kept from her all these years didn't seem like the best way to keep her freedom to hang out with the guys.

The next morning, Leah was deep in thought, running a brush through her hair.

When home, Aunt Cheryl usually kept to her room in the opposite corner of the house, and might not have even picked up much about Leah's friends or her comings and goings. Even so, Leah wouldn't risk braving the waters with her, either.

"You almost ready?" Aunt Cheryl asked while tossing her purse strap over her shoulder.

"Yeah, I just have to pack my bag."

"Hurry up." Aunt Cheryl left the bathroom doorway.

Leah tucked her hairbrush in its drawer.

"Leah… What is this?" Aunt Cheryl's voice was low, sharp, threatening. She reappeared at the bathroom doorway, holding up one of Leah's notebooks. Her face was fierce, a look Leah had seen before. That was the look she'd given Leah once in elementary school—right before they started to pack up and move.

Swallowing, Leah tried to hide her panic. She hadn't realized Aunt Cheryl had left to go shove her school things in her backpack, and that Leah had left a notebook wide open on her desk. All over the top of the page were doodles of 'The Green Lands.'

"That means nothing. You shouldn't be going in my room." She stood rigid, terrified.

"Eleana! What's this about?"

She started to sweat. "It's nothing. Seriously. Let's go." She tried to snatch the notebook back, but Aunt Cheryl held it out of reach in the hallway. "We're going to be late." Leah stepped forward to leave the bathroom, but Cheryl shifted to block her.

"I'm not going to ask again."

Maybe I should have just asked the guys.

She glared at Aunt Cheryl. "You're crazy. It doesn't mean anything."

Cheryl grabbed a fistful of Leah's hair, practically shoving the notebook in her face. "Is that where you heard this phrase? School?"

Leah winced at the pain as her breathing picked up. Maybe she could lie and pretend she'd meant to somehow write 'Greenland' the country, but that was a pretty weak claim. "No! No. It's nothing. I just… I remembered bedtime stories Mom told me when I was a kid."

Cheryl's eyes narrowed. "And why would you remember that all of a sudden?"

"It's a writing assignment for English. Memories from our childhood!"

Cheryl released her grip with a skeptical stare. "Forget about *stupid* fairy tales and places that *don't* exist. Write about learning to ride a bike like a normal kid."

"Okay. Fine. Can we go now?"

After another moment of staring her down, Aunt Cheryl tore out the page with Leah's doodles and part of her math homework, crumpling the page and pocketing it. She picked Leah's backpack up, cramming the notebook in without any care that she'd bent back several pages, and shoved the backpack at Leah.

After Leah flung it over her shoulder, they made their way to the car. Leah kept glancing at Cheryl's pocket. What would Cheryl do with that paper? Show it to Leah's mom as proof they ought to move again?

On the ride, Leah kept her eyes on the window, rubbing her sore scalp as they drove to school in silence.

They pulled into the drop-off line. "You're not lying?" Cheryl asked.

"Why would I lie about an English assignment?" Leah asked as though she were confused. It was a sad excuse, especially given the doodles hadn't even been in her English notebook, but it was the best she could think up at the moment.

Cheryl pursed her lips. "Forget those stupid stories, and don't even bring it up with your mother."

So she's not going to tell Mom? "Fine. Done."

***

"You okay?" Marcus asked at lunch as Leah mindlessly stabbed at her Caesar salad.

"Yeah. Of course." She forced a smile.

She looked the guys over as they chatted. They were her only hope to figure out what she really was. After the bell rang and they dispersed for classes, she chased after Tanner.

"Hey. Question for you," she said.

"Yeah. What's up?"

"I was wondering if you wanted to hang out sometime." She bit her lip. "You know, just the two of us."

He grinned. "Yeah. Sounds like fun. Have anything in mind?"

She shrugged. "Just talk … and chill. I'd say we could hang at my place, but my mom and aunt are always home."

"Yeah. We can work something out."

***

They were set to meet up that Friday, but then it happened again— sticky fingers. Well … more like sticky vines. At least this time it was her mom who caught her and not Aunt Cheryl. She was now grounded, stuck in her stupid house for anything except school.

Leah sorted through her bedside table drawer, where she always stashed the pilfered things she'd successfully stolen under the radar and had actually decided to keep. Her mom and Aunt Cheryl of course didn't know about this collection, and her mom didn't search her room that often. Even then, the plastic basket full of lifted goods was usually hidden by a few books she laid on top of it.

Small glass bottles clinked against each other as she raked her hand through her collection. For a girl who didn't paint her nails often, she sure owned a lot of nail polish. 'Owned' in a very loose sense of the word, since she'd never purchased a single one of them. She sat on her bed, starting on her toenails. *This sucks. All of it.*

All of Leah's lifelong—and new—questions ran through her mind. She shouldn't have risked stealing this time. Cheryl and her mom were getting more vigilant every time they would allow her to go shopping with them. And instead of hanging out at Tanner's, she was a prisoner at home.

Once her nails dried, now sporting a coat of azure blue with a holo glitter topcoat, Leah got ready for the night. Peeking into her mom's partially opened door, she spotted her mom writing in a journal. She wrote in there a lot. This time she seemed deeply lost in thought, wiping away a tear.

"I'm heading to bed," Leah said.

Her mom stopped writing, setting down her journal and gently covering it with a pillow. "Okay, princess."

Leah frowned. "I'm sorry."

Her mom sighed. "Are you sorry you did it? Or are you sorry you got caught?"

Leah looked down at her feet, wiggling her sparkly toes. "Both?"

"What's bothering you, sweetheart?"

"Nothing."

Her mom cocked her head. "You sure? It's not like there's an exact science to it, but I've noticed you tend to have more troubles when you're stressed."

What could Leah say that she hadn't said before? They'd already hashed and rehashed it all.

"I'm fine. Really."

Chapter 5

AFTER TWO WEEKS, LEAH'S SENTENCE had been served. She'd missed out on a couple of Garden Club hangouts, and she was itching to get out of the house. More than anything, she was looking forward to one-on-one time with Tanner. Alone, she could get to asking more questions. He'd been giving her flirtatious glances the last two weeks at lunch, too. She wasn't mad about it. He was cute enough, even if he was a bit arrogant.

He picked her up, and they went back to his place. She didn't want to go anywhere public, so they could be more open with their conversations.

He welcomed her in. "So … this is my place for the rest of the school year."

"Nice house." She scanned the front room. It was tidy, bright, and looked like it could have come from a magazine. "You get along with your host family?"

"Yeah, they're cool."

She hadn't noticed any other cars parked outside. "Will I be meeting them?"

"Oh, um… It's just going to be us. My host parents took their kids out to a movie."

She raised an eyebrow. "Really? Are they okay with me being here?"

He grinned. "You didn't want to hang out at your place because of your mom and aunt, so … I thought…" He cleared his throat. "Well, anyway, yes. They know I have a friend over."

She smirked—did they know the *gender* of that friend?

He led her down to the basement family room. "Want anything to eat or drink?"

"Some water, maybe?"

He filled them each a glass of water, and they sat down on a plaid sofa.

"So, what did you want to talk about?" he asked.

She mindlessly stabbed a decorative pillow with her finger. "Just … stuff, you know. Green Lands and all that."

"What about it?"

"I don't know. What do you miss from there?"

He furrowed his brow. "Hmm. Haven't really been gone that long to miss a ton. I mean, obviously the lack of ambient energy, right?"

"Yeah. Of course."

He frowned. "Are you homesick?"

"Maybe a little."

He set his glass down, lounging more comfortably on the couch. "What I've been wondering, though, is that you said you live with your mom and aunt?"

"Yeah. Since I can remember—just my mom and Aunt Cheryl and I."

"So … are you just here for the one year?" He ran a hand through his light-brown hair. "They're sacrificing a whole school year so you could come study in the human world? Or what? I thought that was weird instead of just connecting with a host family."

"Oh, that? We move a lot. They like a good adventure." She shrugged it off, taking another sip of water. "I didn't think it was too weird."

"No. I mean, that's cool. I had to *beg* my parents to let me come."

She set down her glass of water too, shifting to face him more directly. "I have a weird question for you."

"Okay?"

"What all do you use your vines for?"

He glanced at his wrists, poking his vines out a bit before retracting them. "Same as anybody else. Just, you know, multitasking … catching you when you fall, wrestling… Why?" He rubbed his chin, a playful look on his face. "Do you have any fun extracurricular activities you use yours for?"

"Hmm… Well, I *did* get grounded recently…"

He perked up. "I wondered about that…"

"I … well…" Her face grew warm. "It's a bad habit." She fidgeted with her hands. "My mom thinks I'm a klepto, but really it's just a teensy bit of … shoplifting … now and then."

He pressed his lips together, nodding. "Interesting hobby."

She wrinkled her nose. "I guess maybe not the best use of them, huh?"

He grinned. "I don't think I'd have the guts for it. But I'm not gonna lie, that's kinda hot."

She raised her eyebrows. "Hot, huh?"

He reached over, stroking her arm. "When I found out you were also ivy, well, I mean, you're cute. I *really* want to kiss you."

She bit her lip. It was not at all the reason she'd come over, but she wasn't a stranger to a good make-out session. "I'm not opposed."

He scooched over, giving her a couple of soft and sweet tester kisses. There was some decent chemistry there. It became apparent rather quickly that he was also experienced.

He drew closer, sliding his hands to her waist. Her hands landed on the nape of his neck, pulling him in. In his enthusiasm, Tanner leaned into her, slowly bending her back.

She preferred to have more control in the situation. Putting a hand to his chest, she pushed him back against the couch, lips still locked.

Pulling away, she gave him a grin and caught her breath as she straddled him. He smirked and drew her in, his hands on her lower back.

Hot and heavy was on the menu.

Until he moved a little too far outside of Leah's comfort zone for a first make-out session.

He started to move his hands up the back of her shirt.

Without skipping a beat, she arched her back. "No." She leaned in again for the part she was thoroughly enjoying.

Tanner didn't get the hint. Before she knew it, vines extended up her shirt, undoing the clasp on her bra with quick and expert precision. She leaned back, pinning his head against the wall with her hand on his throat.

"Did I stutter?" She glared at him, clenching her jaw, her chest rising and falling with each breath.

He smirked, unfazed. "C'mon. I'm not saying we have to go all the way. But … you know, if we're going to make out…" He glanced down at her chest, and then back up. "Might as well spice it up with some vines. We were talking about extracurricular use, right?" He gazed into her eyes while moving one of his vines again, slipping one of her bra straps off of her shoulder.

Beyond pissed, she extended one of her own vines. Grasping it between both hands, she pressed it against his throat. "You think that's funny? You want to play with vines? I said no! What part of that is so hard to understand!"

The harder she pressed and the angrier she became, the quicker his expression faded from cocky to panicked, to furious.

Tanner shoved her off his lap, onto the floor. Caught by surprise, it took Leah a moment to recover.

"You psycho!" he belted.

He clutched his throat. As he removed his hand to look at it, she understood his anger. Blood was smeared on both his throat and hand.

Her eyes grew wide, darting between his neck and the wrist her vine had already retracted into.

"Get out!"

Her heart thumped wildly in her chest. *I cut him?* Her stomach lurched at the sight of the bright red blood. She certainly hadn't planned on going so far as to slit his throat! "I'm sorry. I … didn't know… I didn't mean to…"

He slapped his hand back up to his neck. "Did I stutter, Leah? Get the hell out, you psycho!"

She scrambled to her feet, barely able to take her eyes off the blood. "I'm sorry, really, you have to believe me."

He seethed with anger, pointing to the staircase. "Out. Now!"

Her breath shuddered as she ran up the stairs and left out the front door. Not knowing where she was going, Leah marched down the street. She rubbed her wrist, pacing once she stopped at the end of the street. Shaken, confused, and without a ride, she called the only person she thought she could trust.

"Hey, what's up?"

She started to cry. "I need your help."

"Umm … yeah. Are you okay?"

She whimpered. "I hurt Tanner. I didn't mean to. I need a ride. Can you come?"

"Is he okay?"

"I think so. I just—" She sniffled.

"Where are you?"

"I'm down the road from his house." She glanced at the crossroad signs. "Fourth and Elm."

"Okay. Stay put. I'll be right there."

***

In the ten minutes it took for Marcus to borrow his grandparents' minivan and arrive, Leah rehooked her bra and gathered herself emotionally. He pulled up behind her, and she hopped in.

He looked her over. "You're sure Tanner's alright?"

She rubbed her wrist again. "I honestly don't know. I think so. He was standing and everything." Her hands were even shaking. "He kicked me out."

"Okay … well, we'll assume he's fine, then. Are *you* okay?"

She twisted her lips. "I don't know. I… Can we just … talk for a bit?"

"Sure. Do you want to go back to your place?"

That was a resounding no. "Maybe just a frozen yogurt parking lot or something? Then I can text my mom where I am, and she won't suspect anything."

He raised an eyebrow. "Suspect anything?"

"Just … please?" She wilted. "I want to get away from here, and I'll explain everything."

Marcus nodded. "Alright." He turned the key in the ignition, and they drove away without another word.

***

Leah bit her nails, staring out the window as they drove in silence. Once Marcus parked, she texted her mom the change in plans and location so it would match up to her phone's tracker.

"What happened?"

She faced him, her nerves still tightly wound. "I cut him. On accident. With my vines."

Marcus raised his eyebrows in surprise. "What the heck were you doing?"

She pressed her lips together.

"Or … maybe I shouldn't ask that."

She rolled her eyes. "It's not a big deal. We were making out."

He cleared his throat. "Yeah, maybe I don't want all the details. I didn't realize you guys were…"

"Oh, give me a break. We're not. It wasn't even a date. It was just kissing. Don't judge me."

He put his hands up in the air. "Go on."

"He, well … anyway…" She shook her head. "It wasn't anything I couldn't handle."

He furrowed his brow. "Tanner did something while you were kissing that you had to *handle*?"

She chuckled. "It sounds dirty when you say it *that* way. I wasn't *handling* anything. Just forget that part, alright? He pissed me off."

"But … are you okay?" Marcus asked cautiously.

She scowled. "I can take care of myself. I didn't call you for help with that. Let's move on to the part where I *literally* cut his neck with my vines. I *promise* I didn't mean to. You have to believe me. I didn't even know I could."

He nodded, his face skeptical. "I'm just a bowman … but how do you *accidentally* cut someone? And not realize it's possible?"

She gnawed on her lower lip, taking a deep breath. "Because I grew up thinking I was a human with a freaky genetic defect. I have *no idea* what half of the crap is you guys are talking about. I don't know what a seeder or bowman is. I don't know where the Green Lands are. I don't know any of it."

He studied her face in silence. "So, you want me to believe you were lying about lying?" He cocked his head. "Leah, you're a bit hard to keep track of."

Her shoulders dropped. "I'm not lying this time. Can you please just explain what I am and what the hell is going on?"

"I… Well … I still don't get it. How do you not know? And why wouldn't you have just asked us?"

"My mom and aunt have always lied to me. I thought my vines were just weird growths that ran in our family. But when you caught me… I guess, I felt stupid not being in the loop when you guys acted as if *not* being human is something normal."

He gave her a scrutinizing glance. "You've lived your whole life in the human world, not understanding what it is to be an ivy?"

"That about sums it up."

He ran his hand through his hair. "I gotta be honest. That's weird. Most ivies who have permanently moved are here because, well … they're racist or elitist. And sore losers when they lost the war. But … they hide their true nature from the human world, not their kids."

"My mom isn't racist!"

He paused. "You've never heard her say 'seeders' or 'bowman' or anything like that? Or referencing green eyes? It doesn't have to be about skin color to be racist."

She spoke firmly, more than annoyed at his accusations. "No. Never."

"Bowman wasn't even a label that was used until after the war ended. She never makes fun of people for their differences or disabilities?"

"No! She's the one always telling me our physical differences don't define us."

He put his hands up. "Okay. I believe you. Maybe, I don't know… Maybe she got so fed up with all the chaos that she's trying to leave all aspects of our realm behind." He shrugged. "Even then, most ivies who move away end up coming back. The energy of the realm is something we all crave."

Leah leaned her head back, exhausted with all the lies. Both hers and her mom's. "Right now, I just want to know the truth."

He glanced at his phone. "There's a lot to explain. How much time do you have?"

Chapter 6

MARCUS DREW A DEEP BREATH. "Where to start? The Green Lands—it's our homeland. It's another realm located on this planet."

"Where?" Leah asked.

He chuckled, running his hand across the steering wheel. "Honestly, no one really knows. It could be an island; it could be a hidden valley somewhere. It's surrounded by an outer rim of incredibly tall mountains that no one has ever been able to get past. Even by flying. Pretty sure there's an energy barrier there, as well. It keeps it safe."

"Then how do you go there?"

"Only way in or out is rifting." He clarified when her expression twisted in confusion. "Like energy doorways. It's so beautiful, too."

"What else?" This was her chance. No more lies. She needed to know it all.

"There are two races. Seeders and Ivies. You're obviously Ivy. Within each race, you'll find bowmen like Jake and I. It just means we're born into Seeder or Ivy families, but we're pretty much your standard-grade human—no vines, no powers." He gave her a warm smile. "That's B-o-m-a-n, singular. No W. No arrows. It stands for 'Botanical Human.'"

She nodded, happy to finally put that piece of the puzzle in its place.

"My mom's a Seeder. That's why I'm adopted, because Seeders, Ivies, and humans can't have kids together. Anyway, back in the old war days, Seeders had to hide their daughters in the human world until high school, when their powers came in. It's complicated, but my mom understands what it's like to not know what you are your whole life."

Leah licked her lips, taking it all in. "Interesting. It would be cool to talk to her sometime. Are your parents planning on visiting while you're here?"

"Well … my dad might. But … Seeders are complicated. They're the more powerful race, but they have lots of limitations. My mom *literally* can't leave the Green Lands. It has to do with their strong connection to the energy of the realm. That's why the wedding's taking place over there." He shifted in his seat. "Well, the main wedding. They're doing a human ceremony over here, too, for the bride's family. It's pretty exclusive which humans know we even exist."

Leah soaked it all up like a sponge. "Tell me about Seeders."

He thoroughly described them—their culture and abilities. They were a floral race that lived more simply, in wooden cottages and homes, had kids in batches—*twenty-four* at a time—and could fly, able to transform and wield energy differently than Ivies. They even had more abilities and strength than the Ivies. Just like Ivies, Seeders could conceal themselves in the human world if they wanted, walking amongst humans with no way to really be detected.

"And Ivies. Like you … well, there's the vines. Like an extra appendage. As you … unfortunately … discovered, you can flex the leaves to be rigid, sharp."

She still couldn't believe that. "I wish I'd known."

Marcus's voice was kind. "It's okay. You'll sort it out. He's lucky you didn't poison him. He didn't seem dizzy or anything, right?"

"Poison?!" She read his face. "Um … should we check on him?"

He waved a hand dismissively. "No. It's not lethal to Ivies. And I think you have to be pretty intentional on that one. But yeah, you can administer chemical compounds through those leaves. Like numbing, or even plant fertilizer."

She looked down, rubbing her wrists. As if she hadn't been a freak before…

Marcus explained basic Ivy culture, how it was ruled by a queen and king.

"And Bomen, where do you fit into it all?"

"Here, there, and everywhere." He chuckled. "Lots moved here after the war, like Jake's family. But back home, Bomen live in our kingdom, in the Seeder nation, and some in their own colonies. Lots of variety."

"You guys talk about this war a lot."

His mouth hung open. "There's a lot of baggage there. Over two hundred years at war. It finally ended, actually, around the time you and I were born. You know, people still have prejudices and differences of opinion, but it's nothing like what our parents grew up with."

She leaned her head back, mulling it all over. "Thanks. For being understanding, and honest with me. It means a lot. Gives me a heck of a lot to think about." She bit the insides of her cheeks. "I really want to go check out this place now. You said there are portals. How does that work?"

"Seeders and Ivies have different abilities for rifting. But honestly, people pretty much exclusively use the cave networks now. They're monitored, and you have to have a passport." He frowned. "I'm not so sure you can visit without your mom's permission, and without going through the legal process."

She picked at her fingernails. That wasn't going to happen. Not if her mom had spent Leah's entire life concealing that part of her.

"Well, anyway…" She blew out a puff of air. "I don't know what I'm going to do about Tanner. He was livid. And I don't blame him."

Marcus shrugged. "You're going to have to be honest with him, like you were with me."

Every ounce of her pride revolted against that idea. "I hate looking like an idiot."

"You don't." Marcus pointed at her. "But just telling him you didn't mean to, without him understanding where you're coming from, is like a human scratching someone's eyes out and saying they didn't realize their fingernails were capable of doing that."

She choked back a laugh at the comparison. "I get it."

He nodded. "Should I take you home?"

"Yeah. Let's do that."

Minutes later, Marcus pulled up to Leah's house and parked the van. "You going to be alright?"

"Yeah. Just lots to process."

He toyed with his keys, which still dangled from the ignition. "Tanner can be a real jerk sometimes. You're sure you're alright about him, too?"

She smiled. "You're really sweet. I'm good."

Was she good? Kind of. She'd dealt with worse than what Tanner had just done. She'd learned to numb the side of her that acknowledged what had just happened.

What would she do about it anyway? Tell her mom? This wasn't Leah's first make-out session gone bad. She had a type. Her mom would be there for her, just like she'd been before. The problem was … her mom's version of 'taking care of things' usually involved moving far away and starting all over again.

And then there was Aunt Cheryl. Under the thick layer of denial Leah laid down in her heart, Cheryl's biting words nipped at her. Leah was a slut. It was her fault. It wasn't like Tanner had pinned her down. It wasn't like Leah hadn't jumped at the opportunity to make out in the first place.

"Do you want a hug?" Marcus asked.

She grinned, taking in his kind face, his curly hair. "I'm not really a hugger. But maybe I could use one tonight."

They both got out of the van, and she met him on his side. He pulled her in for a perfect tight squeeze. "Are you going to talk to your mom, now that you know?"

She swallowed hard. Tanner? The secrets of the Green Lands? They'd moved for less. "I don't know if that's a great idea. We'll see."

He pulled back from the hug. "See you Monday?"

"Yeah, of course." She cocked her head. "Thanks for being a great friend, Marcus."

"You're not such a bad friend yourself." He rocked his head back and forth, shoving his hands in his pockets. "When you're honest."

She blushed. "No more lies. I promise."

"I appreciate that."

Leah ambled to her front door and unlocked it, all the while lost in thought. Marcus drove off only after she stepped inside.

"You returned with a different friend than the one you left with?" her mom questioned once she entered.

Leah huffed, weakly gesturing at the front door. "You've met both of them. Just friends. Calm down. We were at Tanner's house, then went out for ice cream, and Marcus volunteered to take me home."

"Alright. I'm going to head to bed, princess." Her mom smiled and strode back to her room.

Leah also smiled as she went to her own bedroom, mulling everything over. 'Princess' was such a juvenile pet name. Sometimes it annoyed her. But in a lot of ways, her mom's nickname for her was also sweet and indicative of their relationship.

Despite all the moves, and drama with Aunt Cheryl, and their arguments … her mom was a good mom. Leah never doubted her love.

But why the lies?

***

Monday at lunchtime, Marcus searched out Leah in the cafeteria. After he found her, they stood in line together, selecting their food and getting caught up.

"How was the rest of your weekend?" he asked.

"I guess as good as it could be?" She grabbed a carton of milk from the refrigerator.

"I half expected you to call or text again." He made eye contact. "You can reach out, if you need to talk."

"Thanks. I'm good." She glanced at the cafeteria doors. "Though … um … I think I'm going to eat lunch on my own today."

He bunched his eyebrows. "Why?"

Really? "Tanner? I don't know that I'm ready to go through that yet."

Marcus shook his head. "Then let *him* sit somewhere else. If he … well… I don't know what all happened. But I'm just saying, what you did was an accident. I hardly doubt whatever he did to piss you off was." He picked out a banana from a bowl of fruit, placing it on his tray. "Jake and I would prefer you be there. Or if you want, I wouldn't mind leaving those two and coming to sit with you somewhere."

She appreciated Marcus's willingness to back her up. "I'll come sit with you guys. We'll see how it goes."

Jake was at their table by the time Marcus and Leah arrived. She trained her eyes on the door to the courtyard to see if Tanner would show his face. A few minutes later, he peeked through the door, tray in hand. The moment their eyes locked, he turned and went back inside. She thought about it. *Why put it off?* She excused herself and went after him, leaving her tray behind.

"Tanner!" She caught him before he found a new place to sit in the cafeteria.

"I'm not really in the mood to talk," he said.

"Please. It's important." She blocked his way, sparing a glance at his neck. He had three regular-size bandages on it.

He wouldn't make eye contact.

"I promise I didn't mean to do that. I can explain. But," she looked around, "somewhere more private."

He rolled his eyes. "Fine."

They walked into an empty hallway and sat on the linoleum floor.

"You went too far," he said, setting his tray on the floor next to him.

She glared. "We both did. Don't pretend you weren't in the wrong."

He met her gaze, his head tilted to the side. "Yeah, but seriously? Cutting me?! You just had to say 'no' another time, or get off of my lap. It's not like I was … *forcing* myself on you."

She scowled. "I shouldn't have to say 'no' two, or three, or four times for you to get the message!"

He swallowed and looked down. "No. You're right. It won't happen again."

"I seriously hope not. And it definitely won't happen with me. That was a onetime thing. I never meant anything by it."

He shrugged. "I didn't either." He looked up, raising his eyebrows. "But seriously. What you did went too far, too. That was—"

"An accident." She wrung her hands. "I've been lying to you guys because I felt stupid for not knowing. I was raised human. I didn't know I was capable of that."

He squinted, studying her face. "How's that possible? We all learn to use them super young. Like … learning to walk."

Ugh. This conversation all over again. "My mom lied to me. Yeah, the vines were just kind of part of me. But other than basic reaching and grabbing … I didn't know. I didn't know *any* of it until I had Marcus explain it to me after I left your place."

Tanner fidgeted with his hands, seemingly nervous. "Marcus knows what happened?"

"Not everything. He knows we got in a fight. And I hurt you on accident, and was freaking out." She took a deep breath. "I needed a ride and answers." She didn't want to rock the boat more than necessary, and she *could* have a temper. She'd been expelled before after standing up to an ex-boyfriend who had used her. Granted, she hadn't known she harnessed Ivy energy that could make her stronger than these human guys, but she probably wouldn't have cared at the time, when she'd kneed him in the groin so hard he'd fallen to the floor, and hadn't gotten up before she'd stalked off. Just one more thing that had forced one of their many moves for a fresh start.

Maybe this time, she'd just let it go. Pretending Aunt Cheryl didn't exist usually served Leah better than standing up to her. Why should it be any different with this situation? And frankly, Tanner may have taken things too far, but he might have more information Leah craved to know about who she was.

"Can we just … be friends?" she asked. "Move past this?"

He averted his gaze. "Is it going to be awkward with the other guys, and all of us hanging out?"

"Only if we make it awkward."

He slowly nodded, picking up his tray. "Let's see how it goes."

They walked back out to the courtyard together. Jake and Marcus were having a discussion. Marcus's eyes followed Tanner and Leah to the table.

"What's with the bandages?" Jake chimed in without wasting a second.

"Shaving. Had to get a new razor," Tanner said, lowering his head to look at his food.

Marcus glanced at Leah before turning his focus on his own tray.

Leah forced a smile. "Jake, how was your weekend?"

Chapter 7

LEAH HAD ANSWERS. BUT NOT ENOUGH. After the reality of the Green Lands and green folk settled in, the fact that her mom had kept something so essential from her screamed out. She considered trying to force her mom's hand, confronting her with the truth, but she didn't want to face Aunt Cheryl's fury. And doing so, revealing that she'd found the truth, might mean another move. Away from her friends, away from those who gave her such important information.

One night as she was preparing for bed and saying good night to her mom, Leah spotted her doing something she'd seen her do many times over the years—writing in a journal. A journal Leah sometimes wondered about—who wouldn't want to know what was said of them? But now, she wondered if there was something hidden in there, compelling enough to break the tenuous trust they had between them.

And how to read it without her mom finding out…

With either her mom or Cheryl almost always home, Leah didn't have much luck in trying to snoop. She bided her time, trying in a few snippets of minutes alone to search for where her mom even stashed it. After a few close calls of getting caught in her mom's room, Leah at least knew a few places it *wasn't.*

Eventually, the day came. Right after Cheryl left for work, Leah got a call.

"Hey, princess. I'm so sorry, but I'm going to be late getting home today. They really need me here, and I'm going to be a couple of hours late."

"No problem. I'm just doing homework."

"Okay. There's leftovers in the fridge, and I expect you to stay home. No boys. No trouble. I'll know if you left."

"I'll be good," Leah drawled. *I have absolutely no plans to leave home tonight.*

With two hours to herself, she entered her mom's room, and continued the search. Eventually, she looked in the closet. Her mom had a pair of medium-sized safes, and Leah worried she might be out of luck. Making sure no stone was left unturned, she carefully shifted things around on the shelves, taking care to return them to their original places so her snooping would remain unnoticed. As she moved one of the safes, two journals tipped over, having been tucked behind it.

Jackpot!

She took them both down, carrying them to her mom's bed to peruse. Flipping through the pages, Leah glanced at the dates at the top of the pages, also noting that one of the books was only half-full. The full one started with a date that preceded her own birth date. She decided to start there.

"I don't know what to do. Other than wait, and worry, and write. I should have stayed. We should have slowed down, been more patient. Or maybe I'm wrong, and we should have been more aggressive…"

"No one's come. I sent out Amy to get news three days ago, and she hasn't returned. We might have to move to a new location. If things are bad… If she was caught… I can't sleep…"

"I sent Ada over to find out the state of the kingdom. It can't be good if we haven't received word. He was supposed to send for me when it was safe again. I can only imagine the worst…"

"I can't bring myself to even write it. Then it makes it real. But the truth is … he's gone. He'll never get to meet his own child, his heir. This baby will never have a father. And it's all Kaylah's fault. That traitor will do nothing but undo all the hard work we put into our proud kingdom. She's always been jealous, weak, and making friends with the wrong sorts. I told him we should have killed her right away. Damn it, he should have listened! But now she sits on his throne, destroying everything his family worked for. What we worked for. That bitch killed the love of my life, and I have nothing left…"

In a daze, ravenously reading each new entry, Leah paused a moment, running her finger over a portion of that last entry. The page was wrinkled, the ink smudged. *A tear.* She read on.

"I felt the baby for the first time today. How is it the best things can bring the most pain? I'll do anything to keep it safe. But it reminds me so much of him. Sometimes I tell myself that if our people turned things around, ousted Kaylah from the throne, I could take my place again. Maybe, just maybe, the day Soren's heir takes his place, I could have some sort of closure. But I know that's false hope. And even if we got our kingdom back, I don't know how I could ever rule without him by my side…"

"It's a girl. I think he would have loved that it's a girl. She has his eyes…"

"Eleana…" Her mom's voice startled her.

Leah glanced up from the pages. Expecting anger on her mom's face, she was instead greeted with a look of profound sorrow.

"Sweetheart, you shouldn't be reading that."

Leah glared. How many years had she felt like an outcast, had been clueless as to why they'd moved around so much? "You shouldn't have been lying to me my entire life!"

Her mom lingered in the doorway, shaking her head. "It was to keep you safe."

"You said my dad died in a tragic accident at work! You don't think I deserved to know the truth?!"

Her mom's eyes narrowed as she raised her voice. "He died far too young. That was tragic. That was devastating!"

"You left him to die!"

"Don't you dare, Eleana." Her voice shook. "I loved him and would have died by his side. I was loyal to him and always will be. He *ordered* me to leave. If I hadn't, I would have faced execution right next to him, and you never would have been born to even have this conversation!"

A tear rolled down Leah's cheek. "You could have done *something…*"

Her mom spoke softer, defeated. "Me and what army? It ended as quickly as it began. Your father was ambitious, but his dreams were too big."

"And now, what? We're just going to live as outcasts for the rest of our lives? You think he would want that?"

Her mom marched to the closet, pulling down one of the safes. She set it on the bed and opened it. "You want your birthright? You want to be a real princess?" She gestured at the open safe. "Here you go. You can have my old tiara. That's all we have left."

Leah studied the sparkling accessory; it was simple, but stunning. Golden ivy leaves intertwined with precious gemstones. It was beautiful, but that wasn't the point. She looked up, scowling. "I don't care about any of that. If what he was doing was best for your people, you shouldn't have given up so easily!"

"The moment I go back to that realm, my life is forfeit. I'm never going back. And neither are you."

Leah held up her wrists. "We don't belong here!"

Her mom erupted into tears. "Eleana! This is not up for debate. Sometimes you have to know when to give up hope. No, we don't belong here. But we don't belong there, either. You and I—we don't belong *anywhere!*"

Leah looked down at the journal, with so many pages still left unread. A tear of her own landed on the page, and she snapped it shut. Without another word, she got up and stormed out of the room and into her own. Slamming her door, Leah launched herself onto her bed, sobbing.

Her dad hadn't died. He'd been murdered.

***

After a good half hour, there was a soft knock on Leah's bedroom door. Her mom slowly opened it when she didn't respond.

"Can we talk?"

"I guess so." Leah sniffled, grabbing a tissue from her bedside table and sitting up.

"Princess, I'm sorry I didn't tell you earlier."

Leah glowered. "Don't call me that anymore."

Her mom joined her on the bed. She reached over, tucking Leah's hair behind her ears. "You'll always be one to me."

Leah rolled her eyes. "Were you ever going to tell me?"

She pursed her lips. "Of course. And maybe I should have earlier, but I wasn't really sure when. I needed to know you could keep it secret. At this point, I was waiting until your eighteenth birthday."

Leah considered her friends… None of them were old enough to have been involved in the war that had ended her dad's life, but their parents would have been around then. Truthfully, she didn't even want to know where they stood with it all. She couldn't lose her new friends, not her only other ties to the homeland she'd never known.

"Do you and Aunt Cheryl have any friends like us at all? With the vines?" She wanted to ask several more questions, but realized she needed to continue to seem ignorant about other things Marcus had told her.

Her mom frowned and shook her head. "Doesn't mean we haven't run across some. But … it's dangerous. They might be like us—having left after we lost the war. But they might not share that opinion. And if they went back and reported us… Eleana, now that you know, you need to help Cheryl and me keep us safe. I'll go over some basic things, and if you see or hear them, you need to let us know right away."

Leah hid a frown. "We'd have to move, right?"

Her mom nodded. "Where we're from, people can blend in like humans, but there are a few different traits to look for…" She described Seeder appearances like Marcus had, down to the glowing green eyes. She brought up some of the same terms: green folk, Green Lands.

"I remember you telling me stories about the Green Lands when I was younger."

Her mom quietly rubbed the fabric of her dress pants. "I shouldn't have. I was still foolishly clinging to hope."

"But we can talk more openly about it all now, right?" Leah asked, yearning in her voice.

"It's still really hard to talk about." Her mom's tone and demeanor echoed that of a woman who had never fully healed. "How about I tell you more about your father?"

Leah beamed. "I want to hear it all."

They snuggled up next to each other, and Leah leaned her head against her mom's shoulder.

"He was so handsome. Dark brown hair, those stunning green eyes. A smile that lit up my day. We met fairly young, at a party. I was fourteen, he was fifteen."

"Was it a fancy ball, or something like that?"

"Not a ball, but a medium-sized gathering of some youth near the palace. I was lucky he picked me." She chuckled softly. "He was actually being kind of a jerk, trying to show off for the girls. He liked that I didn't put up with his crap. Gosh, after that, we saw each other as much as we could."

Leah thought back to the journal. "Why couldn't you have at least told me his name growing up?" Soren—it sounded kingly.

There was a long pause before her mom responded. "I couldn't risk anyone finding out." She whispered, "And I couldn't … bring myself to dishonor him or his memory by giving you a fake name."

That made sense. "When did you know it was love?"

"Hmm… I don't know, sweetheart. He was passionate and goal-oriented. He had my heart pretty early. I didn't get to see him much for three years, though."

Leah smiled, imagining their cute love story. "Why didn't you get to see him?"

"He was doing assignments for his uncle here in the human world. They were really close, and worked together on their attempts to end a ridiculously long war. His sister killed him, too—their uncle. That's where things really started to fall apart."

That was like a punch in the gut. "His sister? The one you wrote about, Kaylah? His own sister killed him?"

"Yeah, his younger sister," her mom whispered. "They never got along."

"That's horrible."

Her mom drew a deep breath, poking the comforter. "Yep. And last we checked, she's still in charge."

"Why wouldn't the people have gotten rid of her by now?"

Leah's mom scanned her, then opened her mouth, hesitating. "I won't lie to you. Your father wasn't perfect. Not everyone agreed with his views or his tactics. But it was war. Things were messy. You can never make *everyone* happy."

Leah nodded pensively. "I'm sure it's complicated." Her mom hadn't written much about the specifics of the war in her journal, at least not in the portions Leah had just read. It wasn't like her mom had been writing a history lesson all those years ago.

But Leah couldn't resist thinking of what little information Marcus had given her about the war, and the guys hadn't talked a ton about it, but they'd said things in passing back when she was clueless about everything. She couldn't remember enough to know what to make of the situation. And she didn't want to question her parents, but it sounded like the Green Lands realm was relatively peaceful now… "What's the realm like now?"

Her mom bobbed her head. "Well, a war that spanned over two hundred years is now over… So, there's that…"

"That sounds like a good thing…" Was her Aunt Kaylah really so bad if she'd ended such a long war?

"I wouldn't go that far," her mom said. "Seeders—the enemy, the only other race in the Green Lands—are massively overpowered, especially now. Their territory is now twice the size it was when your father and I ruled, and they can now freely walk about our lands whenever they want."

That made Leah uneasy. Would tensions rise again? "Do you think they'd attack again?"

Blowing out a long breath of air, her mom considered. "It's hard to say. Honestly? Probably not. People have become complacent, despite the fact that half of Ivies lost their jobs when the war ended, and Kaylah threw them into financial disaster. They're lazy."

Leah didn't know what to make of it all. She'd never found American History that interesting, and she couldn't make much of a judgment call about a realm she'd never stepped foot in. Her confusion must have been apparent, because her mom spoke again.

"Seeders drove our people from our lands centuries ago. Look at it this way: the human world is much, much larger than the tiny realm we come from, our little corner of this planet. In how many human nations do the indigenous people coexist with their colonizers? They're not in open war, but that doesn't mean there's not resentment, that wrongs were righted."

Leah nodded again. Her parents had obviously fought to the best of their ability, and this Kaylah had only brought peace by giving in to the Seeders. Just as her heart ached for the father she'd never met, it ached for the homeland she'd lost.

She wanted to brush away the heavy topic for now to allow herself time to ponder it. "What was it like, being a queen?" She smiled. It was still so mind-blowing. Just as much as finding out about her identity as an Ivy, imagining her parents as actual, real rulers of a nation was so crazy.

"I'm sure in peacetime, it would be a heck of a lot more enjoyable. It was stressful. But we were also newlyweds," she gently poked Leah in the arm, "and discovered *you* were on the way, so that made it all worth it."

Leah's smile grew. "Did his being a prince have anything to do with your interest in him?" She batted her eyelashes.

Her mom grinned wider. "I'd be a liar if I said no. But it definitely wasn't just that. We were meant for each other. He loved me. He loved you, too." She leaned over, giving Leah a kiss on the head.

Leah's mom entertained her with a few more stories about their courtship. Before her mom left the room for the night, she addressed one more thing.

"I know you and Aunt Cheryl don't get along, but please try to work things out." She looked down at her hands. "She's not really your aunt. She's one of my aides who helped me escape." She frowned. "We owe her our lives. She's the one who's gone back to check on the state of things. She was there to help me through your birth. Human doctors would be clueless when it comes to Ivy births." She met Leah's gaze. "Eleana, she owes us nothing. Be grateful."

Leah nodded, whispering, "Okay." Before her mom left, Leah thought to ask, "If you knew then, what you know now, that this would happen, would you have done things differently?"

"Absolutely," she replied wistfully.

After settling in for the night, Leah lay restless in bed. She loved being able to form a mental picture of her dad. And being royalty … still a shocker. But the betrayal, her mom's heartache—they didn't deserve that. Leah might not be able to take back her dad's kingdom, or secure her mom's position to do things differently, to be successful in a kingdom they could be proud of. But she had to be able to do *something*. Her mom was held back by fear—she was broken.

But Leah—she was angry. The more she thought about it, she wasn't content to give up the world she should have had a place in, while the traitorous woman who had taken her dad's life sat on his throne.

65

Chapter 8

LEAH GOT READY FOR SCHOOL the next day. As usual, Cheryl met her at the bathroom as she finished, trying to speed her along.

"Cheryl?"

"What?"

Leah frowned. "I talked with my mom last night, and—"

"She said as much."

"I didn't realize what all you've done for us."

Cheryl's reply dripped with sarcasm. "Is that a hint of actual gratitude?"

Leah clenched her fist in an attempt not to roll her eyes. "Yes. I wanted to say thank you."

Cheryl scoffed. "Well, I didn't do it all for *your* spoiled ass."

Always such warmth and love. "Right. Do you miss the Green Lands?"

"Of course I do."

"Could you teach me how to get there?"

Cheryl scowled, shaking her head. "You're out of your mind. You think we've spent all this time in the human world for you to just pop in and be discovered?"

Leah sighed, putting in a pair of stud earrings. "It sounded like my mom wasn't very far along when you left. Would they even know to look for me?"

"That's not the point. I'm not risking our lives for a spoiled brat like you."

Leah stood taller, squaring her shoulders. If Cheryl had been one of her mom's servants, that meant she'd been loyal to her dad as well, the king. "You don't think my dad deserves justice?"

"He got what he deserved." The words rolled off her tongue venomous and cold.

Leah's heart ached, the tears from the night before threatening a reprise. "Why would you say that?"

Cheryl's eyes narrowed. "He was young and foolish. He took risks and failed. And now we're stuck *here*, away from the family and realm I grew up in. This is all *his* fault!"

Leah couldn't look her in the face; she instead slipped past Cheryl to pick up her backpack. "I'm ready. Let's go." Cheryl would be no help in getting to the Green Lands. But she wasn't the last person on the list who might be able to help.

***

Weighed down, still forming her decision, Leah skipped grabbing any food, and went straight to the Garden Club's usual lunch table. She was the first one there, and to her luck, the next to arrive was Tanner.

"Hey, I've got a favor to ask of you," she started in without a proper greeting.

"What's up?" Fortunately, things were mostly back to normal between the two. Not that she didn't often think about how much of a jerk he'd been, but they did a good job of pretending nothing had happened, for the sake of avoiding awkwardness in the group.

"Could we meet up sometime? I have more Ivy questions. Not so sure Bomen could help me."

He shrugged. "Sure."

She gave him a casual smile. "You're awesome, thanks."

Marcus and Jake joined the table with their usual greetings.

"Not eating today, Leah?" Marcus asked, picking up his plastic fork.

"Mmm … not hungry."

He arched an eyebrow. "You okay?"

She pursed her lips, thinking about it. Could she mention any of the new information she'd learned? No. Who knew what their parents thought… Like her mom had said—wars were messy. Whether or not they'd agreed with her dad's reign, drawing attention wouldn't be good. Though, she internally smirked—she could have been a real princess. What would these guys think of that tidbit?

"Yeah," she finally responded.

"Well, that was a long pause for a 'yeah,'" Jake poked fun.

She chuckled. "Yeah, I'm okay. I didn't say I was *fantastic*."

***

Tanner and Leah met up at a nearby park after school, per her request. As with every outing in her life that wasn't at home or school, Leah texted her mom the plan and location.

"What did you want to talk about?" Tanner asked as they walked side by side on an asphalt path.

"A little of this and that. Our powers and culture," she said.

"Sure. Shoot."

"Who are the current king and queen?"

"That would be Queen Kaylah Elonta and her husband, Eric. He's a human."

Leah nodded. *So, she's still there.*

"Does she have any siblings?"

"Yeah. She has two younger brothers—"

Would they be like her dad?

"—and she had an older brother, but he died in the war. Lots of drama with that one."

Trying to hide a frown, Leah nodded again. "Why do you like the queen?"

He shrugged. "From the stories I've heard, she's pretty badass."

Leah clenched her teeth. *As if murdering is something to praise.*

"And I mean, she's a queen. It might be a small kingdom, but royalty is still pretty cool."

She relaxed and internally smirked at that. If he knew who Leah really was, practically a princess, with them having made out—he'd eat that up.

"Gotcha. And this part is kind of awkward for me to be asking you, but I don't have anyone else I can ask."

Tanner side-eyed her. "Okayyy?"

"Just, self-defense… How can I hurt people?"

He laughed. "Sorry, but the way you worded that. 'How can I hurt people.'"

She rolled her eyes.

"I mean, you understand the sharp leaf thing now."

"Yeah, I practiced a little with that last night. I think I understand how it works now, with the flexing. But I'll need to practice more."

He held up a finger. "I'm not a test dummy."

She huffed, tucking her hands into her pockets. "Wasn't asking you to be."

"Other than making them sharp, the other main thing is poison. But I couldn't teach you about that—that's a girl thing. And you'd need a proper teacher."

Ugh. This is stupid. And getting me nowhere. "Am I capable of killing a person with my vines?"

His face scrunched uncomfortably. "When did this escalate from self-defense to killing someone? You kinda scare me sometimes."

She tried to laugh it off. "Come on. I just want to make sure I don't hurt someone on accident again."

He rubbed his neck. "Yeah … probably good to be careful…" He cleared his throat. "I can show you vine manipulation techniques sometime. Maybe before the next Garden Club at my house? No, uh … extracurricular activities this time."

She smiled, grateful they hadn't burned their bridge. "I'd really appreciate that."

"Yeah. No prob. You can't enlist in the army nearly as young as you used to be able to, but my dad served back in the day. Granted, the way they teach history, it sounds like *everyone* was enlisted." Tanner bent down, plucking a dandelion and popping off its head. "Anyway, he showed me some moves."

Questions kept coming to her mind, kept pushing her, prodding her, like the barely there breeze blowing at their backs. "Which side did he serve on?"

Tanner grimaced. "That's not really a polite question to ask, you know? Kind of touchy for people."

She bit her lip. "Sorry. I'm not really familiar with everything, remember? But I'm guessing by your reaction that he fought for the king that lost?"

Tanner looked down, shrugging a single shoulder. "Yeah. Not something you really talk about with others, though. I definitely wouldn't bring it up in Garden Club."

She nudged him with her elbow. "Your secret's safe with me." She couldn't decide if she was grateful to hear of someone who had supported her dad, or bitter that he was one of the troops who had surrendered, who had abandoned her dad and allowed him to die.

Nearly reaching the end of the path, Leah sat down on the grass, and Tanner followed after her. "What about getting to the Green Lands?" she asked. "How do we do that?"

"We have a cave network."

She already knew that wasn't an option—no passport. "Marcus said something once about Seeders and Ivies having different abilities with that, about opening a portal of some kind?"

"Yeah, that—rifting. Technically, we rift in the caves. But we can rift through trees, too." He blew out a puff of air. "At least we *used* to be able to," he drawled.

"What changed?"

He pointed at Leah. "That's one thing I definitely *don't* agree with the queen on. We used to be able to practically come and go whenever we wanted." He gestured at the park around them. "Any tree. Anywhere. No passports. No security checks. But not long after she got into power, she banned it."

Leah bunched her eyebrows. "That sucks."

"Right! And it's not fair. That's something unique to us, as Ivies. Seeders can still rift in their unique way. She didn't stop *them*. Granted, I doubt many do, but it's not like they can't." He glanced around as if to check that no one was nearby. "Some people would call her a weed-lover, not that I'd personally put it that way…"

"What does that mean?"

He cringed, leaning over to retie a loose shoelace. "You know, pretend you never heard that. It's… If the other guys heard me say that, they'd pummel me. Not exaggerating. My point is, the queen's best friend is a Seeder, right? She used Seeders to help her win the war—they got to keep their rifting practices. Her husband is a human—they weren't even capable of going through rifts until she let them in. But who's looking out for *our* rights?"

Leah shook her head, her gut heavy, her ears warming. This was the kind of confirmation she needed. This queen was no saint—she was oppressing her own people. She needed to go.

Leah was trying to be rational, not just be ruled by her emotions, but the evidence was stacking up. Her dad deserved justice. And his people deserved better. "Sounds like you're not too fond of humans? Or just humans being over there?"

Tanner waved a hand. "Humans are fine. I don't have any problems with them in their own world, but they used to not be able to enter the Green Lands. Do you know how vulnerable that makes us now that they can? What if we became public? If people came to experiment on us? To destroy our lands like they have their own paradises in the name of tourism or growth? It's not right. It should only be Ivies and Seeders over there."

Leah considered Tanner's words, running her hand along the grass. "You make a fair point."

"Yeah. Like I said—not her finest policy."

"So, there's no way to rift over there at all? Other than the monitored caves?"

"I've heard some people in certain jobs might get special permits. But no, not really. The only time we're allowed to tree-rift is in emergencies."

Hmm… "What if I needed to leave? What if I had an emergency? Would you teach me?"

His mouth opened, but nothing came out for a moment. "I, uh … don't feel comfortable with that. What I've been taught is only theoretical, and you have to have specific location names to know where to go … there's a lot of rules and stuff."

She made eye contact. "Come on. Please?" She could really use this.

He averted his gaze, plucking up a few strands of grass. "I'm not trying to be a jerk. But … I'm going to have to say no. It's illegal. If you want to be taught, you should ask your mom."

Leah clenched her teeth, frustrated. She had three options— threaten him, and she wasn't there yet; give more information about herself, and perhaps he'd cave, but she couldn't be sure it was worth the risk; or try to convince him in other ways … the kind of ways he'd definitely enjoyed before, but they'd agreed to not go there, and it wasn't guaranteed to work. That third option made her particularly sick to her stomach.

With a mix of hope and guilt, Leah recalled previous conversations in the club between Marcus and Tanner. There was still one more option. Her last option. And truthfully, her best option.

The queen would be attending Marcus's brother's wedding.

And Marcus had no plus-one.

Chapter 9

LEAH WASTED NO TIME ENACTING her plan the next day. After lunch, she quickly and quietly asked Tanner if the queen or her brothers had any kids. It dawned on her the queen might be attending Marcus's brother's wedding because they were somehow related. Even if Marcus didn't know it, Queen Kaylah was Leah's aunt. A horrible waste of space, but technically her aunt. And Leah needed to make sure she wasn't trying to date a cousin; just the thought of it made her gag. Luckily, Tanner confirmed the queen and her younger brothers didn't have any kids yet.

Leah grabbed Marcus's attention as they waited for their rides at the end of the day. "Hey. I was wondering if you wanted to go on a date this weekend. Teach me knife-throwing?"

He raised his eyebrows, clearly surprised. "A date? Or hangout?"

She grinned. "I said the one I meant."

"Um…" He averted his eyes. "Well…"

Okay… So this might not be as easy as I thought. Did I misread his signals? I thought he had a bit of a thing for me. He's the one that called our first hangout a date…

"Will … it make things awkward?" he asked. "With you and Tanner?"

"Oh, that? No." She shook her head. "Definitely not. We've discussed where we're at. Just friends. It was a onetime thing. Didn't mean anything."

"Okay…" Marcus hesitated.

Unless he's judging me *for it… Great!* "Do you think it's weird? I didn't think you guys were that close," she added.

He scoffed. "You know where we stand with that. We'd never be friends back home. The only reason we tolerate each other is because it's nice to have people from back home who understand green-folk stuff."

"So, that's a yes?" she asked with some pep in her voice.

"I just…"

For. The. Love. Seriously? Take the bait. It isn't that hard.

She shifted her weight to the other foot. "I didn't expect you to have to make a pros and cons list… It's just a date…"

He loosed a breath. "I just thought we were doing the friend thing."

She tilted her head, looking him in the eyes. "You're a great friend. You're kind, and considerate, and funny." She tapped his shoe with her own. "You're also cute and sweet. I'm just saying … we could give it a chance." She hadn't planned for his resistance, hadn't rehearsed the compliments. They flowed naturally; they were genuine.

He gave her a soft smile. "Yeah. Of course. I don't know why I'm making a big deal of it. Friday?"

"Cool. I still can't drive, so are you able to borrow a car from your grandparents? I'll pay for dinner?"

"Yeah. That works. And I'll sort out the knife-throwing."

Cheryl pulled up. Leah grabbed one of Marcus's hands, giving it a gentle squeeze and making eye contact again. "I look forward to it."

***

Leah smirked, thinking of the archery fiasco as she waited for Marcus to pick her up. He had no reason to lie about his knife-throwing skills. Her smirk faded as she thought back to the notebook she'd started, hidden in her room—her plans. *How do you assassinate a queen?*

She had five months until the spring break wedding. That should be plenty of time for her to win Marcus over, get an invite to the wedding, and figure out how she'd actually be able to kill someone. She wasn't crazy, or some superwarrior. She was a regular teenager. Kind of.

The notebook included a pros and cons list. The reality of what she was planning was … terrifying. Successful or not—killing *anyone*, especially a queen, wasn't an action to take lightly. She didn't want to go into this based on rash emotions, but the dad she'd yearned to know all her life had been taken from her. By someone who, based on more than one account, didn't deserve to be there and was making things worse. And it wasn't only justice for her dad. Leah would be helping out all of the Green Lands, and her mom, herself, and even—not that she cared much—Cheryl. In the end, if all went as planned, Leah would have until the last minute to decide. Plan, prepare, and if she couldn't make it happen for one reason or another, she'd return home, and everyone would be none the wiser.

A knock on the front door pulled Leah from her thoughts. *Worry about that later. For now, have fun and get things started.*

She opened the door. "Hey."

"Hey. You ready to head out?" Marcus asked with a warm smile.

"Sure thing," she replied, tucking her hands into her back jeans pockets.

They hopped into his truck, heading to a new Greek restaurant Leah had picked out.

"You're looking sharp," she said. She could swear he was wearing the same cologne he had at their archery night fiasco, too.

"You don't say." He cleared his throat. "Is that a reference to knife-throwing?"

She laughed. "No. I didn't spend all afternoon coming up with that one."

He threw a quick glance her way as they approached a stop sign. "You look nice, too."

"Phew! I'm glad I don't look *mean*."

He chuckled.

They enjoyed good conversation over their dinner, just like they had in the last several weeks of their friendship.

Leah figured she might as well start with some hints. "I didn't realize the hummus would have so much garlic. That could be an end-of-the-night killer."

He blushed, not responding or making eye contact.

Trying to date Marcus was going to be a new adventure. Not wholly shy, he was still reserved in some ways. And like she'd called him before … squeaky clean.

They ended up going back to his house for the knife-throwing; he had set up a couple of targets in the backyard.

"I'll show you first, and we'll go from there?" he suggested.

"Sounds great."

Marcus pulled out a set of specialty knives, standing several yards back from a wooden target. Grasping his first knife, he raised his arm. He launched the knife with controlled force, and it soared through the air, finding its mark in the target with a firm *thwack*. She smiled at his confidence as he threw five more, each finding its place on the target.

He retrieved the knives and approached Leah, a smile creeping across his face to match hers.

"Maybe a *smidge* more impressive than your archery skills." She winked.

He teemed with pride. "I've had a lot of practice. My dad taught me." He handed her the knives. "There's lots of different styles of throwing knives. Some of my favorites are back home, but these are nice."

She looked them over and felt their heft.

"Do you want me to give you tips, or just take a shot at it first?" he asked.

"I'll give it a go first."

Leah tried her best, knowing she wouldn't master it right away, just like archery. Only one of the knives barely stuck into the wood. Most of them smacked against the target before falling amidst the rest with a *clang*. She gathered them up and returned to his side. "I'd say I'm a natural."

He laughed again, clutching his hands to his chest. "I'm in awe."

She grinned. "Alright, I'm your humble student. Teach me your ways."

"It's all about force and form," he said. "You gotta throw it like you mean it, but do it in a controlled way. So, throw a little harder. If needed, you can also adjust how far back you are."

She nodded, taking it in.

"And when you go to throw it, don't flick it with your wrist. Let it *glide* from your hand," he coached.

Figuring she could layer the hints and have some fun, she asked, "You don't want to do that cliché guy thing where you stand behind me? Putting a hand on my waist and another on my hand to show me proper technique?"

He stared at her, a shy smile peeking through. His throat bobbed. "Probably not the smartest idea to stand that close to a girl when she's learning to fling sharp objects."

Leah giggled. "You may have a point." She glanced down at the knives in her hand. "And a sharp point, at that."

He chuckled as she took her place in front of the target again.

She tried a couple more rounds, getting a little better with more advice from Marcus. He took another turn as she watched. She couldn't help herself—she couldn't stop smiling, admiring. His biceps flexed with each toss. He was assertive, confident, and in his element. She liked this side of him.

Leah's smile faded as she swallowed hard, her guilt threatening to ruin her casual fun moment. She was using him. This wasn't just a date. It was part of a plan. And not just for an invite to the wedding. Her notebook had a page listing *all* the ways she might be able to kill the queen. She had five months to learn how to use her vines, and to learn any other feasible options for success. Who knew … maybe throwing knives might be an option? She wasn't going to dismiss any possibilities.

Marcus gathered the knives and smiled at her, walking back to the throwing point. She gave him a half-smile back.

Could she really kill someone? This was crazy. *Who does that?*

But she wasn't just a regular human. And this queen wasn't just some useless politician. She had denied Leah and her mom the life they could have had. *Should* have had. This woman had stolen her dad. He deserved justice.

Leah watched Marcus, frowning. He'd never done anything to deserve being used. And she genuinely loved spending time with him. She fixated on his curly hair, his physique, his…

This is bad. I just have to focus on my goal…

But … there's nothing wrong with actually enjoying being with him, too. I can keep them separate.

***

At the end of the evening, Marcus dropped Leah off back home. With this having been a proper date this time, he walked her to the front door.

These are always so excruciating…

He shoved his hands in his pockets. "I had a lot of fun."

"Me too." She hummed playfully. "Even more fun than archery."

He let out a breathy chuckle. "You and I remember that event differently. You had fun; I was being tortured."

She grinned. "You brought that one on yourself."

"I won't argue on that account."

She drew a deep breath. *Time to seal the deal.* "How do you feel about kisses on first dates?"

He pressed his lips together. "I'm going to have to say no this time."

Her heart sank. *What's that supposed to mean? 'This time.'*

"I thought … things went well."

His mouth opened, but nothing came out. He closed it and cleared his throat. "I have a date with someone else tomorrow. I just don't feel like it would be right."

"Oh…" *That sucks.* She scanned his face. "Can't blame her. You're a great guy."

He bit his lip, slowly nodding.

"Oh… You did the asking." *Was this a pity date?*

He frowned. "I'm sorry. This is awkward. I should have said something. I literally asked her, like, an hour before you asked me."

Every ounce of Leah's pride screamed to cut the line. Sure, there was chemistry there. But she was *not* the type to chase a guy. If they didn't like her for who she was, they weren't worth pining over.

But there was more weight to this potential relationship than others she'd been in before. She couldn't just ask to be invited to the wedding. Tanner's interactions had made it incredibly clear that Marcus wouldn't take someone who seemed interested in the queen, in being a social climber. Leah needed this.

"I'm guessing asking you if you want to go on a second date would be awkward, then?" she asked. "Since you don't know how tomorrow will go?"

He rubbed the back of his neck. "Let's talk Monday?"

"Sure." But she couldn't lose him. *What if he enjoys tomorrow more?* She internally gagged. *I don't fight over guys. I'm not insecure like that.* "Then maybe this is weird, but I want to put it out there, anyway… the Sadie Hawkins dance is in two weeks. I think we'd have fun." She paused for a moment. When he didn't jump at the opportunity, she added, "But no pressure. I just wanted to put it out there."

He pulled his keys back out, fidgeting with them. "We'll talk?"

"Yeah. I'll see you Monday. How about a hug?"

He smiled. "I'm down with that." He pulled her in for a squeeze. She happily took what she could get. And he was a great hugger.

***

The weekend was absolute torture. This was all so foreign to Leah. Guys were simple. Dating was simple. Sometimes, she just wanted to kiss without strings attached. When she wanted something a little more substantial, she could flush out her type and get into a relationship easily enough. If they weren't sure about wanting to date her, they were out. If they didn't want what she had to offer, they weren't worth the investment or energy.

But this was far from simple. She agonized the entire weekend. Not texting Marcus. Wanting desperately to know what the other girl was like. If they were having fun.

She pouted as she watched a movie with her mom, picturing Marcus teaching his date to throw knives, too. What if he kissed her, having decided he liked her better?

Leah moped, imagining him inviting the other girl to his brother's wedding. She had to be a human. Would he do that? Could he? Based on what Marcus had told Leah, revealing the Green Lands and green-folk secrets to humans was a very serious step, not taken lightly. But he had months to grow close to the mystery girl. And it wasn't like humans weren't allowed into the Green Lands at all… Just like green-folk teens came to the human world as inconspicuous foreign exchange students, a few humans in on the secret were allowed to spend an exchange year in the Green Lands, too…

Leah frowned as she stuffed a spoonful of peanut-butter-cup ice cream into her face, straight from the carton. He *clearly* already liked the mystery girl better, because he'd actually asked her. Maybe Leah could break them up in time for him to still give her a chance and invite her.

Oh my gosh, I am not that girl. I'm not desperate. I'm not pathetic.

But it wasn't just about wanting to date him. It was about the end goal. Maybe she could get lucky, and he'd take her as his plus-

81

one just as a friend? Whether or not he had a girlfriend? She couldn't count on him deciding to do that on his own. And she'd only ever have one shot at asking him. If he didn't take the suggestion, that trust would be severed. That was only a last resort. Leah's anxiety rose as she envisioned her limited options.

Calm the heck down!

***

Leah happily joined her mom on a shopping trip to get her mind off of things. With a stern warning from her mom, Leah went to another part of the store in search of a couple of items on their list. But … she was itching for another nice distraction. Strolling near the makeup wipes, she figured she might treat herself with something small … like a lifted lipstick or two. She picked out colors and made sure the coast was clear. Starting to extend her vines, she hesitated. She quickly retracted them with a sigh. If she got caught, got grounded—it would jeopardize the big plan. And Squeaky Clean probably wasn't the type to understand her hobby.

Leah let out a long puff of air, returning to meet her mom.

Her mom raised her eyebrows in accusation. "That took a little longer than I expected for two things."

Leah scowled, placing the list items into the cart and turning her pockets inside out. "I was just looking around." She cupped her hands over her boobs. "Nothing stashed here, either."

A man in his seventies was shuffling by them. He gave them an uncomfortable glance, cleared his throat, and moved along.

Her mom lightly swatted at her arms. "Stop that!" she hissed.

Leah put up her hands in innocence. "Better than a strip search in the middle of the store. Just trying to make it clear I'm being good."

Her mom closed her eyes, pinching the bridge of her nose. After a second, she actually started to chuckle.

Leah furrowed her brow in confusion.

Her mom opened her eyes, reaching over and smoothing Leah's hair. "Just … in another time, in another life, I'm imagining the shock on the face of your father's entire family. His heir, groping herself in front of strangers in the cracker aisle in the, well, *here*, wearing a t-shirt and jeans."

Leah frowned. "Sorry." She'd never be who her mom wanted her to be.

Her mom matched Leah's frown. "I didn't mean it like that, sweetheart." She gently put her hand under Leah's chin. "Prim and proper, or just as you are, I love you. And they would have, too." She lowered her hand, her expression full of longing for a future they'd never have. "I could have spent your youth teaching you the proper fork to use, or putting you in classical dance lessons, or any number of things. But that's not who we are, anymore. You're free to be you." She grinned. "Though, we should maybe keep the self-groping in public to a minimum."

Leah busted out laughing.

"The next time an old man walks by," her mom added, "he might have a heart attack, and we're trying to keep it low-key."

"I'll try my best."

Her mom gave her a soft smile. "That's all I'm asking. Now, what else is on our shopping list?"

They turned back to the cart, and Leah hooked her arm through her mom's. "I think we need more ice cream." She paused a moment. "And I wouldn't hate it if you taught me about different kinds of forks."

Her mom hummed wistfully. "I could do that."

Chapter 10

MONDAY FINALLY CAME. *Longest weekend ever.*

Leah was a bundle of nerves as she approached their lunch table. Marcus gave her a tiny smile. It had been nice sharing bonding time with her mom, but Leah could only stay distracted for so long.

The rest of the meal, Leah and Marcus didn't look at each other. A few minutes before the bell would ring, Leah piled up the garbage on her tray and stood. "I'm going to get some fresh air before lunch is over."

Jake glanced around. "We're eating outdoors. This isn't fresh enough for you?"

She playfully chucked a plastic spoon at him. "You know what I mean. Stretch my legs. See you guys later."

"Okay if I join you?" Marcus asked.

Her stomach did a leap. "Yeah." She'd hoped he would pick up on that. She'd dreaded the idea of waiting until after school, with the possibility of being interrupted by their rides arriving earlier than wanted, or even worse—having the conversation over the phone.

They took care of their trash and trays, strolling out onto the school lawn.

"How was your weekend?" he asked.

"Like any other weekend." *Except for the torture.* She gave him a smile. "Except for a pretty cool Friday night."

He returned her smile, and they walked in silence for a while. "I guess I should say something."

The tension was killing her.

"I, uh… Well … she's a nice girl, and … she asked me on a second date."

Leah glanced at him out of the corner of her eye, trying to play it cool.

"And I said yes."

Her heart sank. He'd never wanted to date her, after all.

"But…" He rocked his head back and forth. "I swear I'm not, like, *that guy*… I just… I want to try a second date with you, too." He winced. "Is that weird?"

She shrugged. "We could give it a try." Normally, she'd have given it a hard pass. He wasn't a trophy to win, and she wasn't a player in a game. But she needed this. As much as she appreciated her mom's efforts to allow Leah a normal life, Leah couldn't let that nagging feeling go—that she didn't belong here, that the queen needed to answer for her crimes. If anything, growing closer to her mom made Leah want to do this even more.

"And she knows," he said. "Not like I'm being a creepy jerk, keeping this from either of you." Marcus stopped, facing Leah. "But … if you still want… I'd love to go to the dance with you. No matter how things go, I know I'd have a lot of fun with my friend." He gave a hopeful smile. "But I understand if you don't want to, or don't want to commit to it, now that you know, well, you know…"

Leah drew a contemplative breath. This was a good sign. Whether or not the other girl had asked him to the dance as well, Marcus was still keeping Leah close. "Let's plan on it. I didn't want to go with anyone else."

His face was bright and happy. "Sounds like fun. And thanks for being cool with all of this."

She swallowed and nodded. "Yeah, of course."

But cool with it, she was not. It was a full week of doubting herself.

Friday night, Marcus picked Leah up, putting her out of her misery. They grabbed a bite to eat at a local pizzeria and enjoyed a game of bowling. She couldn't resist admiring his figure again in the dark jeans he wore, and he'd caught her glancing once. She was pretty sure he'd checked her out once or twice, as well. She'd picked out an outfit accentuating her best features, after all.

The end-of-the-night door scene was just as awkward as the last, with the exception of Leah wondering whether there would be a kiss. He gave Leah another of his signature hugs and thanked her for another fun night.

She pursed her lips. "I'd tell you to have a good weekend, but I kind of hope it's not *that* good."

He gave her a shy look acknowledging the awkwardness of the situation. "We're still on for the dance, right?" he asked.

"I'll be there."

***

Monday came around. Marcus had gone on his second date with the other girl, too. Leah was going out of her mind, imagining him being so indecisive as to ask for a third date with each girl.

Instead, he said nothing.

Leah returned home from school, frustrated. After Cheryl left for work and her mom came home, Leah decided to try rehashing another strategy to make it to the Green Lands.

"I got to thinking about something you said." Leah dipped her toes in the water, carefully. "That Cheryl goes back to check on the state of the Green Lands now and then?"

"Yes," her mom said, unpacking groceries in the kitchen.

"How does she do it?" Leah folded up an empty plastic bag. "Like … how's it even possible? You never explained that to me."

She knew good and well it was somehow done through trees, but her mom had avoided anything on that topic.

"You don't need to know that."

"But no one over there knows what I look like, right? I wasn't even born by the time you left." She folded another empty bag.

Her mom shook her head, opening the produce drawer and placing a fresh pack of celery inside. "Not worth it." Her tone carried a firm finality.

"You expect me to *never* even see the place?" Leah's frustration grew.

"It's not safe for us."

Leah huffed. "You can't stop me forever. What if I go off to college and spot someone like us? Maybe *they'll* teach me how to get back."

Her mom frowned, closing the fridge door. "Sweetheart, please." She sighed. "Maybe we can revisit this conversation when you're eighteen."

Leah rolled her eyes, shifting gears. She thought of the current Ivy policy of emergency tree rifting. "What if someone comes for us, and I need to get away? Isn't it important to have options?"

Her mom rested her hands on her hips. "And you think the Green Lands is the answer? Even if you found a way to get over there … where would you go? I'm sorry it was taken from you, but that's not your world. It may never be."

Leah's well of hope was drying up. She remembered with perfect clarity the night she'd discovered the truth about her dad—her mom had said they didn't belong *anywhere*. That ached more deeply than her mom understood. It hurt. Once, when she was twelve, tired of being a freak and having to hide it, she'd taken scissors and a knife to her vines. Despite tugging a bunch out, hacking it off, then doing it a few more times until she literally passed out—they grew back the next day. The realm of the Green Lands was part of her, whether or not she wanted it to be.

In one last attempt at getting anywhere, Leah continued her focus on safety. "Fine. No Green Lands. What about our abilities? If I need to keep myself safe, is there anything else I'm capable of doing?" She knew about the ability to sharpen her leaves … from experience now, and the ability to poison. Tanner was going to teach her some techniques with her vines, but Leah was willing to take anything she could get.

Her mom remained silent, sizing her up. "We're always home to keep you safe. And that's why we have you notify us of your plans and give you mace, for when you're out with friends." She pressed her lips into a thin line. "But I suppose it's time I teach you a little more, for your own safety." She held up a finger. "But this is only in an absolute emergency, because once someone sees your vines… Just, be careful."

Leah nodded. "I will be."

***

The next day at lunch, Tanner was picking on Jake. "I doubt you even realize what you're missing after living over here so long."

Marcus was glaring at Tanner, obviously growing tired of the conversation.

Leah was too. "How about you shut up and get over yourself, Tanner," she scolded. "You're the one who chose to come here. You could have stayed home. There's nothing wrong with Jake living here." She huffed. "And some people don't get a choice, do they?" She stood and stomped off.

Marcus followed after her. "Hey, wait up."

She jutted her thumb over her shoulder, gesturing to the courtyard they'd left behind. "Remind me why we hang out with him."

Marcus twisted his lips. "You okay?"

She slowed her pace to walk with Marcus. "Yeah. Of course. Why wouldn't I be?" She crossed her arms.

"I just wasn't sure if that was you telling Tanner off 'cause he was a jerk to Jake, or because of … you know, your mom keeping you out of the loop."

She shrugged. "Can't it be both?"

"Yeah. It can be." A moment of silence punctuated their footsteps on the green lawn. Marcus swung his arms with nervous energy. "Sorry for not getting back to you yesterday about where we stand."

She braced herself for bad news—as much as she could, what with only mildly caring in the moment.

"I, uh, told her I wasn't interested in a third date."

A small smile grew on Leah's lips as the news gave her a ray of hope. "Thanks for letting me know." She stopped to look at him. "Where does that leave us?"

"That leaves us at the dance this Friday, right?"

***

Sadie Hawkins was casual dress, but Leah made sure to get a little more dolled up than usual. She wore her favorite pair of jeans and a black top—sleeveless, with a rhinestone swirl near her waist. Wearing her hair up in a ponytail, she finished her ensemble with a deep red shade of kissproof lipstick.

Marcus picked her up, complimenting her outfit. Leah's mom mortified her by taking pictures despite it not being a formal dance.

"Sorry you're always the one having to drive," Leah said as they got into his grandpa's truck.

Putting the truck into gear, he looked over his shoulder and backed out of the driveway. "I really don't mind. I spent a ton of time this summer learning so I could have some freedom and blend in."

"What's school like over there? Do you guys have dances?"

"We study some of the same stuff. Obviously some things like history are different."

More often than not, lately, her mind kept wandering to this mystery realm, to the Green Lands. What would the history books say about her parents? She wasn't stupid; she knew they would speak ill of them. With the woman who'd ousted them still in control, she could choose the propaganda fed to her people.

"As for dances," Marcus continued, "we've got them, but nothing like they do here. And the music is all performed live."

Leah nodded in approval. "That sounds cool."

Being an informal event, hardly any attention was paid to decorations in the school gym, but the obligatory disco ball and light show were included.

Not long after they arrived, Marcus introduced Leah to a group of his other friends. She hadn't made more at this school since her arrival. They danced with the group, and she loved how carefree Marcus was during the fast songs.

The first slow dance came on, and he offered his hand. She slid her arms around his neck, pushing him to dance closer, with both his hands on her waist. She loved this, how conversation flowed between them. Their playful banter, their shared secret of being green folk. Her heart pounded as she glanced at his lips.

After a couple more fast songs, and with the stifling heat of the school gym becoming unbearable, they headed out to the open courtyard, to their usual lunch table.

"This DJ's not too bad," she said.

"Yeah. Good songs for dancing."

They sat side by side on the small table, breathing in the cool air, and planting their feet on one of the seats.

"What do you want out of this?" he asked.

She turned her head and smiled. "I thought I was pretty clear about wanting to date you."

"But are we talking about a relationship, or friends with benefits?"

She frowned, looking down at her shoes. "You're judging me. Because of Tanner."

He sighed. "No. Though, I'm still a little worried it'll make things weird in the club. But I just want to make sure we're on the same page. We're not the most obvious couple, you know?"

She met his gaze. "I don't care what Tanner thinks. And I didn't think you did, either. If he has a problem with it, then … well, that's *his* problem. As for obvious couples, does that matter?" She furrowed her brow. "I like spending time with you. I'm attracted to you. Isn't that why people date?"

"Yeah. And I like spending time with you, too." He gave her a shy smile. "And I'm attracted to you, too. You look really great tonight. I don't remember if I told you that already."

She grinned; he had. Though she doubted she still looked *that* great with a bead of sweat running down the back of her neck. "Then let's give it a go."

"Okay. You and me. Exclusive?"

"Yes."

"Then I'm in."

She smirked wider. "Does that mean you'll finally kiss me?"

He chuckled. "I think I can manage that." He shifted a little, getting a better angle. Leaning in, he offered up a sweet, simple kiss. He pulled back, getting lost in her eyes.

She studied his face. There was a spark there, with room to grow. But after the way he'd made her wait, she wasn't going to let him get away with a tiny kiss like that. She leaned closer, moving a hand behind his neck, and caressing his lips with her own. He returned the kiss with mirrored enthusiasm, but stopped short of a heated make-out session.

When they pulled apart, he bit his lip. "You're not shy, are you?"

She laughed. "Not when it comes to something I want."

He drew a deep breath, rubbing his knee. "How's this going to work with the club? Should we say something at lunch?"

She leaned against his shoulder, breathing in a hint of cologne. "Mmm… I think that would be awkward. Let 'em figure it out on their own."

He extended a hand, offering it palm up. "Like when they see us holding hands?"

She slid her palm onto his, intertwining their fingers. "Exactly."

He gave her hand a squeeze, kissing her on the cheek. Another couple came out to the courtyard, interrupting their solitude.

"Are you cooled off enough?" Marcus asked. "Wanna get back to the dance?"

She took her hand back, hopping off the table. "Let's do it."

***

At the end of the night, Marcus dropped Leah off at her house. She'd finally get a proper end-of-the-night drop-off with him.

"Thanks again, for saying 'yes' to the dance. And for giving us a chance."

He grinned. "I'm already glad I did. On both counts." He held her waist and didn't hesitate to give her a goodnight kiss.

Leah went inside with a smirk on her face. The front room was dark, and a sudden noise made her jump.

"Does that mean he's a boyfriend?" Cheryl asked.

Leah blew out a breath of relief, a hand over her heart. "Scare me half to death, will you?" She huffed. "Yes. We're dating," she muttered.

"You know the rules."

Leah threw her hands in the air. "I planned to tell her just now. We only made it official tonight." The rules were stupid. Friends, boyfriends, friends with benefits—the moment her mom or Cheryl saw more than a hug from a guy, they wanted to know *every* detail of his life. She had to admit that they at least gave her *some* level of freedom with all of their concerns—it could be worse. She shook her head at the hypocrisy, though. When she'd asked her mom about how her dad had proposed, her mom wouldn't give a play-by-play of the event. They'd dated for four years, and her mom described him as 'aggressive' and 'passionate,' and 'affectionate' but also 'not really romantic.' It was pretty clear they hadn't exactly been innocent and inexperienced.

Leah peeked inside her mom's room. "Home from the dance. Dating Marcus. Interrogate now, or in the morning?"

Her mom sighed, sitting on her bed. "Let's talk in the morning. How was the dance?"

Leah leaned in the doorway. "It was good."

Her mom gave her a single contented nod. "Okay, then... Have a good night, princess. Um ... sweetheart."

"You too."

Leah wiped off her makeup and brushed her teeth. After tossing her clothes in the dirty hamper, she climbed into bed in a fresh pair of cozy pjs. She mused on the kissing from earlier that night. Marcus didn't seem that experienced, but not completely new to the practice. Their first kiss had been basic, though the door drop-off was evidence of them finding their groove.

Chemistry wasn't going to be a problem. Keeping her lies straight might be.

She'd already formulated a backstory for Marcus, one that omitted any hints of being a Boman or knowledge of the Green Lands. She just had to remember it, and make sure he kept up the guise anytime he might be around her mom or Cheryl.

Leah's phone chimed, and she opened the message.

<Thanks for a great night. Let me know if you want to get together this weekend.>

<I'd love to. Free tomorrow?>

<Free all day. Just some homework to do.>

<Ditto. I'll bring mine over?>

<I look forward to it ;)>

<Sweet dreams.>

Leah set her phone down but didn't smile. Like a moth to a flame, Marcus was falling for her plan. How could she ever truly enjoy this relationship when she planned to use him? She was the flame on a destructive path, and he was going to get burned in the process.

Maybe not. She rationalized that she could still enjoy it. Using him to get to the queen was merely an option on the table. She wasn't so delusional that she couldn't see the plan would be nigh impossible to pull off. Not knowing the venue, or the timeline of the wedding events, or how many guards… With so little actually known, her desire was a long shot, at best. For now, she pacified herself with the thought of enjoying her time with Marcus, while it lasted.

Chapter 11

THE NEXT DAY AT MARCUS'S PLACE, the new couple hit their homework first. They got plenty distracted, chatting and making jokes as they worked. After finally completing it all, they went to the backyard for more knife-throwing. After a few rounds each, they cuddled on a rocking bench in the backyard.

He held her tight. "Gotta admit, I like having a girlfriend." He quickly added, "Not that I haven't had one before, just, you know, having one here."

She enjoyed the warmth radiating from his arms. "I'm a fan."

"I think it's kinda funny. I come all the way to the human world for school, and end up dating a girl from back home."

She drew a deep breath. "Actually, we need to talk about that."

He faced her, raising his eyebrows. "Uh-oh… We need to talk? Not my first relationship, but maybe my shortest…"

She rolled her eyes, then stole a peck on the lips. "I'm what you call green folk, but I'm not exactly from 'back home,' am I?"

He frowned. "Yeah, sorry. Didn't mean anything by it."

"It's fine. I just want to make sure we keep my mom thinking I don't know about green-folk stuff. I may have fudged a few details about your family."

He squinted. "You still don't think you could come clean with her about knowing?"

She shook her head. "No. Trust me. It wouldn't go well."

He shrugged. "Okay. We'll make it work." He traced a zigzag pattern on her knee. "I already have a cover story, you know. I guess we didn't know each other that well before you discovered my secret, but each of us has to memorize a story to keep details of our realm hidden from humans."

She nodded, feeling stupid for not thinking of that. "Yeah…" She winced. "I kinda already told my mom one I made up last night. Your cover story doesn't happen to include your parents being a nurse and a doctor, does it?"

He scrunched his nose. "Not so much. But we'll make it work. My mom can heal, and my dad likes to fix things … so it's close enough to remember." He poked her leg. "Why'd you pick doctor and nurse?"

She gave him a warm smile, grabbing his hand and interlacing their fingers. "You've met my mom as my *friend*. But not as a boyfriend. You just lost twenty points."

"Dang it. How many points are there?"

She gave him a toothy grin. "Twenty."

He looked at the sky, forming a fist with his free hand and shaking it dramatically. "Noooooo!"

She giggled, happy to be there, happy things were going her way. If they could pull this off, there would be no moving, and things could proceed as planned. And in a way, Marcus had passed his first test—he was willing to bend the truth to what she needed. This might be *exactly* the loyalty she needed to get her to the Green Lands.

Marcus smiled, once again focusing on Leah. "In case I need more than respectable jobs for my parents to earn points, maybe I should teach you how you increase your luck in our kingdom."

She raised her eyebrows, fully curious, though hesitant, given the hint of mischief on his face and in his voice. "Luck is good. Do tell."

He cocked his head. "It's two parts." He paused.

"Okay?"

"So, the first part is this." He leaned closer, slowly pressing his lips to her neck.

She couldn't hold back a bright smile.

"And the second part…" He pressed his lips to her neck again, blowing a huge raspberry.

Leah jerked her head away, bursting into a fit of laughter and smacking his hands off of her. Marcus joined in with a hearty chuckle.

"You are *such* a dork!" She couldn't stop laughing as she rubbed away the tickle from her neck.

Marcus put on a serious face, placing a hand over his heart. "Leah, that's an *integral* part of our culture——who we are. Now we'll both have good luck for a week. I'm hurt you're not taking this more seriously." He feigned devastation. "This is special."

"BS. I don't believe that lying face for a second!"

He smirked, shrugging. "I guess we'll just have to see how the next week goes."

She playfully narrowed her eyes.

His face softened, as did his voice. "I'm really glad we started off as friends."

Guilt washed over her. She didn't deserve to enjoy any of this. Not when she had ulterior motives. A battle ensued on her face, her heart tugging her muscles into a frown while her mind forced as genuine of a smile as possible to remain.

He squinted ever so slightly, reading her face.

She quickly wrinkled her nose, rubbing it. "Sorry, fighting a sneeze."

His smile bounced back. "Bless you."

She couldn't handle another lie that day. The truth was easier right now. "I really like you."

"Ditto. Do you want to stay for dinner and maybe watch a movie?" he asked.

She gave him another kiss. "I'm having way more fun here than I would be back home."

"I'm having more fun than if you were back home, too." He moved in for another longer, more involved kiss.

***

The Garden Club was set to meet at Tanner's house the next week. As promised, he met with Leah earlier than the official start time. She'd been nervous about spending time alone with him again, but the human family that hosted him as a foreign exchange student was upstairs this time.

Seemingly having learned his lesson, Tanner carefully showed her some basic fighting and protection forms he'd learned from his dad, from his days in the Ivy army. She appreciated being that much closer to having viable options for her plans. Combined with the basic poison and protection techniques her mom had reluctantly taught her, Leah had even more tools at her disposal now.

"Thanks again," she said, taking a glass of water from Tanner. "Before the other guys arrive … I figured it might be good to give you a heads-up. Marcus and I are dating."

Tanner lifted his eyebrows, nodding. "Okay."

"Is that weird?" She wiped the condensation from her glass, the ice cubes tinkling against each other.

He took a sip from his own glass, his eyes widening. "Are you asking me to rate your relationship?"

She glared. "I think you know what I mean."

He tentatively held up a hand. "You do you. We agreed that was a onetime thing, right?"

"Yeah. Thanks for being cool about it."

Not much later, Marcus and Jake arrived. Leah had told Marcus ahead of time that she wouldn't need a ride. The group decided to watch a movie. Leah sidled up next to Marcus, and he offered his hand. She loved that; it had been a while since she'd had a real boyfriend, and he was so sweet.

She caught Tanner's knowing glance a couple of times. Halfway through the movie, Jake got up to use the bathroom. Leah spotted a spark of realization in his eye on his return.

The group knew, no drama—she wouldn't have it any other way.

***

A month passed, and things were good. All the balls Leah was juggling were in the right places. She and Marcus were great as a couple. She was staying out of trouble, and her grades were even better than normal.

"Happy birthday," Marcus said as he handed Leah a wrapped gift. They stood in the driveway after eating at her house.

"Oooh, thank you." She started to unwrap the heavy rectangular present.

"It's, uh … maybe kind of a stupid gift." He blushed. "I wasn't sure."

She beamed. "I love it!" She leaned in for a kiss, holding her brand-new set of throwing knives.

"Good." He grinned. "I figured it was very 'us.'"

He wasn't wrong. It was definitely still one of their favorite activities together. Her technique was slowly improving.

"Is it me, or did your mom almost seem to even like me back there?" he asked with eyebrows raised.

She chuckled. "I told you she doesn't like anyone I've dated. But you've definitely won some points with her. You're keeping me out of trouble, and I get all my homework done on time."

He inched closer. "I do enjoy a good study date."

She grabbed his shirt, pulling him in the rest of the way. "Me too. Especially at *your* place, where we have more privacy."

He laughed.

"I'll see you tomorrow?" she asked.

"First, I wanted to ask you…" He pressed his lips together. "Well, I'm assuming, since we're dating… But I wanted to be sure we're on the same page… Would you want to go with me to—"

Finally! The wedding. Just needed some more time.

"—winter formal?"

Internally she groaned, but quickly recovered with a smile. "I'd love to."

"Awesome." He gave her a brief smooch. "I better head home."

"Okay. Thanks again for my present."

***

Things were going great. Until they weren't. Just a week later, after an argument with Cheryl, Leah slipped. Since she'd been caught, her nail polish collection didn't grow.

"I won't budge this time, Eleana," her mom said, taking her anger out on the vegetables she was chopping for dinner.

"Please! I'll do *anything*."

Her mom shook her head. "A month. No dance. No friends. I'm tired of your excuses and this behavior! You would think that when you realized who you were, who your father was, you would've come to your senses."

Leah frowned. She'd been doing *so* well with Marcus unknowingly keeping her in check.

"Your father would be so disappointed. His daughter, his heir—a common thief and a liar."

Leah's eyes stung with tears. It was true. She didn't even know why she'd done it.

***

"Thanks for chatting with me," Leah said as Marcus strolled with her on the soccer field during lunch the next day.

"Of course, what's up?"

She took her hand back, sliding it into her pocket. "I can't go to the dance."

"Why not?"

She couldn't look at him. "I'm grounded. She won't budge."

"Seriously? How long? What happened?"

She huffed. "A month."

"Ouch. Why?"

"Doesn't really matter." She rolled her eyes. "It was stupid."

When she finally looked at him, he studied her face.

"Just … homework…"

He furrowed his brow. "Why would it be a whole month for not doing a homework assignment?"

"Just… It doesn't matter."

He let out a frustrated sigh. "It matters if you're lying to me, Leah. I don't believe you. What's the real reason?"

She wilted, her heart dropping. "Why is it a big deal?"

"It's a big deal if you're lying to me. You promised you wouldn't lie to me again."

She shook her head. "You don't want to know."

"Try me." Marcus crossed his arms.

She bit the insides of her cheeks. There was no way she could get out of this one. And there was no way he would understand. "She caught me stealing," she mumbled under her breath.

"What?"

"My mom caught me stealing."

His eyes grew wider, reading her face. "What did you steal?"

"Why does it matter? It was just small stuff, from a store. It was stupid." She looked down at her feet. "I've been doing so good."

"That means you've done this before?"

Great job, Leah. Keep digging. She met his gaze, her shame complete. "Yes. But I promise, I'm done. And no more lies."

He shook his head, his jaw agape. "This is crazy, Leah. How can I even believe you?"

"I'm sorry! I'll do better. And I'm sorry about the dance. I really am."

He scowled. "You think I care that much about the dance? I came here for *one year* of human-world exchange. And yes, I wanted to spend that time with my girlfriend. But I'm pretty sure her lying to me and being a criminal is a little more important!"

"I don't know what you want me to say! I've made mistakes. I'm going to do better. You've been a good influence on me."

His tone and expression were unforgiving. "Why do you even do it?"

She kicked at a rock on the grass. "I don't know. It's just a bad habit."

He glared. "Biting your nails is a bad habit. Shoplifting? Not so much."

Her eyes welled with tears. "I started 'cause… I don't know. It was something I could do with my vines, when all I knew about them was that they made me a freak. And then, all the moves…"

"That sounds like an excuse."

"What do you want from me, Marcus? I'm being honest right now."

He ran his hands through his hair. "We should take a break."

"You mean break up?" Her heart threatened to do just that. "Please, give me another chance. I swear."

"I didn't say break up… Just … take some time apart…"

Her shoulders were limp, her hopes deflated. "You're my best friend."

"Then maybe you should take some time to figure out your priorities." He read her face. "We'll see where we're at when I get back from Christmas Break."

She looked down, sniffling. "Fine."

***

Leah had thought it was rough waiting two weeks for Marcus to choose to date her in the first place. Waiting an entire month for him to decide if he could stand to be around her was going to be unbearable. She'd meant every word. She wasn't going to steal again. Or lie. At least she *wanted* to mean it.

Not sure of Marcus's plans, Leah couldn't show her face at their usual lunch table for the two weeks left before Christmas Break. A couple of days into those two weeks, Tanner came looking for her. He found her sitting alone; she still hadn't made more friends. She'd always been the type to commit more fully to smaller groups of friends. More people meant more investment, and more people to lose.

"There you are. The table's a little boring with just me and Jake," Tanner said, sitting on the linoleum beside her in the hallway.

She didn't look at him as she took another bite of her pizza. He'd confirmed Marcus was keeping his distance as well. She sulked. Marcus was probably off with his human friends. Maybe even rekindling things with that *other* girl. It was just a waiting game for him to call things off altogether, realizing he could do much better.

"You coming to the club hangout this week?" Tanner asked.

"I'm grounded for a month." Leah set the slice of pizza down, wiping her hands on her jeans.

"Oof. That sucks. You and Marcus were going to go to the dance, right?"

Yes. Please rub salt in the wound. "We wouldn't be going together right now, anyway."

"Gotcha... His absence makes more sense. Thought you two up and ditched us for good."

She held back tears. "Well, we'll see how we feel about things after Christmas. I might leave you guys as just the original group." *And be forced to start all over. You'd think I'd be used to it by now.*

He sat there, not saying a thing.

She needed to talk more, and Tanner already knew this secret. "He knows about my shoplifting. Guess he wasn't a fan."

Tanner smirked. "He's vanilla. What did you expect?"

She scowled. "Shut up." They'd only dated a little over a month, but Marcus was the best boyfriend she'd ever had. He'd respected her, and never pushed her to go farther than she was ready to. He was funny and sweet.

"Sorry." Tanner frowned. "I didn't realize you guys were that close…"

They weren't supposed to be. Marcus was supposed to *think* they were. He was supposed to fall for Leah. Invite her to the wedding. Give her the opportunity to make things right for her family. She was supposed to have fun with Marcus while accomplishing her goals, not fall for him.

***

Leah respected Marcus's request to not contact him while they took a break. It killed her when they caught each other's eyes while waiting for their rides after school. The only time she couldn't help herself, she texted him another brief apology, on the night of the dance. He didn't respond.

It was the worst Christmas she could remember. Perhaps second worst; it had been horrible having to pack up and drive cross-country one year. But this one was a close second—being stuck with Cheryl, who hated her, and her mom, who'd imprisoned her and put a wedge between her and Marcus.

Leah had more than enough time to herself to think about things, especially during the two weeks of Christmas Break. She wanted to be with Marcus. She couldn't imagine being at that school without him. That meant she needed to change. Another misstep, and her mom might decide it was time to move on again. Leah wouldn't be stealing again. It wasn't worth it.

She opened her bedside table drawer, full of her pilfered goods. She stared at the bright collection of nail polish and accessories, supplemented by a random trinket here and there. The deed had already been done. But more than a useless New Year's resolution, she needed a fresh start.

Leah threw away every last stolen thing in that drawer, and emptied it completely. Instead, she placed a single object inside—her set of throwing knives. She closed the drawer, slowly exhaling. Then her eye caught on the notebook she'd been taking notes in—an assassination plan. She'd tucked it between her mattress and the bedside table.

What kind of lunatic even thinks this way? She chucked the notebook in the trash, staring at it with a frown. She couldn't do both. She couldn't be happy and honest with Marcus, while using him to fight for the memory of a dead man. Justice wouldn't bring her dad back.

But … she hadn't actually done anything wrong with the notebook. Perhaps it was just a cathartic release, writing those things in there. It was a way of expressing her grief. She wouldn't actually carry out those plans. What kind of sane person could? Maybe she wasn't completely off her rocker. Perhaps she was just rushing into it all.

She pulled the notebook out of the trash, clutching it in her arms. Even if Marcus invited her to the wedding, it wasn't like she *had* to do anything to the queen. Maybe she'd just enjoy the chance to see what her home realm was like, and feel out the situation. The queen was still young. If Leah's dad hadn't gotten proper justice after seventeen years, she could wait another year, until she was at least eighteen.

Leah put the notebook in the drawer, accompanying the throwing knives. She took her trash to the outside can and drew a deep breath, moving on.

Chapter 12

WITH BOTH HOPE AND FEAR, Leah awaited a text from Marcus at the end of Christmas Break. The day before school started back up, it finally arrived.

<Just got back into town. Up for a walk?>

<Name the time.>

Marcus came over, and Leah greeted him at the door. No hug. No kiss. Just shy half-smiles and hands shoved in pockets. They shared awkward glances as they started out on the sidewalk in front of her house.

"I really missed you," she said.

He nodded ever so slightly. "I missed you too."

Her hope cautiously grew. "Before you say anything else, I have something I want to show you."

"Okay."

She reached into her pocket. "Hold out your hand."

He obliged, and she placed a bottle of bright red nail polish and a receipt in his hand. He raised his eyebrows. "Not really my color."

She gave him another half-smile. "I bought that yesterday. It's the first nail polish I've ever bought with my own money. I threw everything else out."

He nodded and handed it back.

"I'm really sorry," she said, sliding the bottle and receipt back into her pocket. "For being an idiot, for being a horrible person. And for lying to you."

The sharp, chilly air accentuated his long exhale in a cloud of vapor. "I had a lot of time to think. And … the question that keeps coming back to me is: how am I supposed to know you're not hiding things from me again?"

She took a minute to consider his question. It was valid. "I don't know. All I can do is make a promise. And follow through." She still couldn't be forthcoming about her family secrets. Doing so would endanger lives—they weren't hers to tell.

He bit his lip. "Then let's just take things slow. Give it another go."

She wore a genuine smile. "Really? Thank you! That means the world to me." She gazed into his eyes. "So does your friendship. And … boyfriendship."

He chuckled. "Boyfriendship?"

Oh, how she'd missed his goofy chuckle, his sweet eyes, his soft heart.

They strolled a bit further. "Not that I'm doing myself any favors by asking, but can I ask why? What do you see in me?" She'd given that question a lot of thought during their break. Especially with their relationship having been capped at mild making out and cuddling, combined with her screwups, she was genuinely both elated and surprised he hadn't broken it off completely.

"Well, it's no surprise I find you attractive. And then there's the kissing." He winked. "But being back home gave me a lot of time to hang out with family and appreciate what you and I had. What we have. My parents are best friends. I think it's important to be with someone you can laugh with, that you never run out of things to talk about with when you're together," he shrugged, "that you can work through hard times together with."

Her heart melted in agreement. She wanted nothing more than to kiss him, but reminded herself he'd said they'd take it slow.

"Honesty is really important in my family," he said. "Don't betray my trust again."

She nodded, her heart in turmoil. She didn't want to betray him. And she wanted to meet his family, who he obviously loved. She desperately wished her parents could have had a chance, that their family could have had that kind of chance, to grow together. "I won't."

He offered his hand, and she willingly took it.

"I want to hear all about Christmas Break in the Green Lands," she said. "And about your family."

"Mmm. Christmas in the Green Lands. Well … it doesn't snow there, so no snowmen. As for religion and observance, it's all across the board. There's a larger variety represented in Seeder culture because of the way they used to raise their kids. Ivies know what Christmas is, but there aren't a lot who observe human holidays."

She loved hearing more about this place she yearned to see for herself. "Your dad's an Ivy Boman, and your mom's a Seeder, right?" She thought back to the injustices Tanner had talked about against their people, that the new queen loved Seeders more than her own kind. "Is it hard for your parents to be together?"

He nodded. "They've been through the wringer. They got married around the end of the war."

She studied his face as they walked. He loved his parents. She imagined him being like his dad—kind and wise. His mom … well, even if she was a member of the race that was part of the problem, it wasn't like *every* Seeder had to be bad. She'd obviously shown good taste by marrying an Ivy, and by settling in the Ivy Kingdom, even with the problems brought on by the new queen. "They *chose* to live in the kingdom, right? It's not like they're there against their will or anything…"

He looked both ways as they stopped at a crosswalk. "No, they like living there. They're both closer to his family than hers. And when they got married, it wouldn't have been safe for him to live in the Seeder nation anyway, with him being a Boman."

That was sickening to hear. *What do Seeders have against Bomen?* If Jake and Marcus were decent representatives of their kind, Seeders should be ashamed of themselves. More evidence that Queen Kaylah didn't deserve Leah's dad's throne.

While Marcus had given Leah the basic rundown on Seeders and their powers and culture, discussion with her mom had helped clear that picture up a bit more. Marcus had initially told Leah that Seeders were the more powerful of the green-folk races, and Leah's mom had confirmed that when discussing how the war had ended, how Queen Kaylah had won by turning on her own people, using the force of the Seeder army against Leah's dad. It stung a little that Marcus hadn't truly addressed the monsters that Seeders were, that he spoke of them in such a neutral way. But then again, she couldn't expect him to hate his own mother. Leah had to remind herself that just like humans, and their religions and political parties—it was impossible to judge them all the same. In every group, both good and bad could be found. If anything, it sounded like Marcus's mom was a pioneer of sorts—a visionary—for leaving her kind to marry Marcus's dad.

Leah squeezed Marcus's hand tighter. "Your mom sounds smart."

"She is. Is it weird if I say you remind me of her a bit?"

Leah batted her eyelashes, recalling their first meeting when Tanner had teased him about his mom. "The green eyes?"

He chuckled. "Not quite. Did I ever tell you her eyes are actually brown? They're only green when she shows them with her Seeder energy. I just meant you remind me of her because you can be tough, but sweet. And you go after what you want."

She grinned. "Not always."

He lifted an eyebrow. "No?"

"No. Like right now, I really want to kiss you. But I'm not going after it. Because you want to go slow." She met his gaze, not expecting … but hoping…

He hesitated. "Give it some time," he said softly.

She could be okay with that.

***

It didn't take long for the couple to get back to their regular routine. Another month passed, and Valentine's Day was right around the corner. Marcus and Leah sat in his family room, cuddling after watching a movie.

"Is this your favorite kind of movie?" she asked. "Sci-fi?" She shifted, lying down on the couch and resting her head in his lap.

He took a strand of her hair and tickled her nose with it. "I don't know. Don't have them back home. Seems cool enough."

She smiled, swatting his hand away. "It's funny to realize the truth is sometimes stranger than the fiction in movies and books. I mean … Green Lands? Secret societies and botanical beings?"

He grinned. "If you could do anything at all, no constraints, what would it be?"

It didn't take long to find her answer, though the way her grief slammed into her took her by surprise. She fought tears, frowning. "Honestly? Meet my dad."

Marcus's carefree expression did a one-eighty; he frowned with compassion. "I'm sorry." He rubbed her arm. "I wish there was something I could do for you."

She studied his face. Nothing would bring back her dad. But if she could get a glimpse of his kingdom … with or without killing his traitorous sister…

Leah sat up, locking eyes with Marcus. "Thank you. That means a lot to me. *You* mean a lot to me." She leaned in, gently caressing his lips a couple of times. Her heart beat faster, her mind running a mile a minute.

Marcus's grandma had just left to go pick up her husband from across town; he was having problems with their truck. Marcus and Leah were alone.

She leaned back, studying his face again. Maybe she wanted to thank him for being such a sweet boyfriend. Or push him along to invite her back home—to the Green Lands, to the wedding. Or maybe she wanted something to help console her empty heart. Or something that just felt good. Maybe … she wanted them all.

Leah pressed her lips against his, baiting the hook with a hint of tongue. Marcus didn't take long to get the picture, deepening the kiss into one more passionate than any other they'd shared before. She shifted onto his lap, straddling him. He slid his hands to her hips, and she moved hers down, grabbing the bottom of his t-shirt, and slowly pulled it up. Parting lips for a moment, she got it up over his head, tossing it to the side and smiling.

He was breathing as hard as she was. "You're, uh…" He swallowed and struggled for words.

She smirked. "I'm what?" He didn't tell her to stop, so she continued. She nibbled his ear, and trailed kisses down his neck and chest.

His chest rose and fell. "I, uh…"

"Yes?" She straightened, locking eyes once more. Then reached down, unbuttoning and unzipping his pants.

He took a sharp breath. "I think we should stop."

She stopped, resting her hands on his bare sides. "You don't want to?" She furrowed her brow.

His eyes exuded passion. "Oh, I want to."

She cocked her head. "Is it, like, an Ivy/Boman thing? Are things different?"

He bit his lip. "Well … yeah, there's kinda stuff … but that's not why." He closed his eyes. "Can we have this conversation with you not on my lap?"

She gave him a soft smile, knowing full well the agony he was enduring in the moment. "Yeah." She moved over as he buttoned and zipped his pants back up, then grabbed his shirt and tugged it back on.

"Maybe we just need to talk about this," he said. "I was raised to … you know … wait until I'm older, more committed."

Leah pursed her lips, nodding. She'd hoped for more, but couldn't be too surprised by his confession.

"Not that I'm judging you for being different in that way," he added.

She nodded again. "Yeah. Whatever you want."

He looked down with a pensive expression. "Whatever *I* want? What about what *you* want?"

She sweetly ran a finger down his forearm. "I thought I was making that pretty clear."

He smiled and shook his head. "I mean us. I'm only here for a few more months. Do you know what you want?"

She picked at her nails, taking her time to answer. She didn't anymore. Her goals and desires all contradicted each other.

"I'd be willing to come visit you over the summer, and during school breaks," he offered.

She met his eyes, smiling. "Let's plan on that."

"Okay. Should I take you home when my grandma gets back?"

"Yeah, I guess so."

They played a board game until she returned, mostly in silence, then borrowed the van.

As they neared her house, Leah couldn't help but ask, "Does that mean you're a virgin?"

"Would it matter to you if I was?"

She shrugged. "Not necessarily. Would it bother you if I wasn't?"

He put the van in park, facing her with a smile. "Not necessarily."

She gave his hand a squeeze. "Good night, Marcus."

"Good night."

Chapter 13

LUCKILY, THINGS WEREN'T TOO AWKWARD after their heated encounter. Leah and Marcus picked up where they'd left off—a great friendship, homework dates, Garden Club, lunch at school, and sometimes going out for something more fun together. More excited and nervous than she'd been before about a dance, Leah looked forward to junior prom. Unlike senior prom, held closer to the end of the school year, their school put on junior prom before spring break.

She went dress shopping with her mom and almost settled on a beautiful burgundy one, but decided last-minute on a forest-green ball gown—it felt more fitting for her journey that year. Her mom loaned her some real diamond earrings, and Leah put extra effort into curling her hair. With perfectly smokey eyes and her favorite brand of kissproof lipstick on, she glanced in the mirror, making sure she was all set.

Her mom stood at the bathroom doorway, a hand on her heart. "You really do look like a princess. Just missing your tiara."

That was a gutting reminder. They *actually* owned a real tiara. How many girls could say that? And how many moms said their daughters looked like a princess, while knowing they actually could have been one?

"I'm sorry I'm not what you and dad wanted."

"We wanted you!"

"I just mean, you know… I don't do a lot to make you proud. And I'll never be a real princess like you wanted me to be."

Her mom pursed her lips as her eyes welled up. "We're doing the best we can, right? I will *always* love you." She wrapped her arms around Leah, giving her a tight hug.

The doorbell rang, breaking them apart. Leah wiped away a tear of her own and drew a deep breath.

"You've got your purse?" her mom asked.

"Oh, yeah." Leah strode to her room, grabbing a little clutch with a thin metal chain, and throwing it over her shoulder.

"Just a second." Her mom stopped her before she answered the door. "Not that I'm giving my approval, or that a human could get you pregnant, but you have protection, right? Just in case?"

Leah tried to hide a grin. If only her mom knew. Marcus had clarified that an Ivy Boman could still knock her up. Seeder Bomen were sterile. Powers or not, Ivies didn't have nearly as many biological restrictions as Seeders did. And Marcus had already turned her down, and wasn't likely to be ready for that anytime soon. "We're good."

Marcus beamed when she answered the door. They exchanged a corsage and boutonniere. Her mom took pictures, and they went on their way.

"You look *stunning*," Marcus said as they got on the road.

She bit her lip, looking him over in his tux. "You clean up pretty nice yourself."

After an extraordinary Italian dinner, they arrived at the hotel where junior prom was being held. They walked in, arms linked. Without hesitation, after leaving her purse at the check-in, Leah pulled Marcus onto the dance floor to get the night started. After some time, Tanner and Jake found them, accompanied by their dates.

They claimed a table together and enjoyed punch and chatting. The two other girls left for the bathroom; Leah opted to stay with the guys.

"I don't need to go with them and gossip about you guys, when I could stay here and gossip about *them* with all of you."

Marcus smiled, giving her hand a squeeze. "But it's not a horrible idea. I think I'm going to follow their lead." He stood up, pursing his lips. "I mean the men's room, not women's. And this nose doesn't need powdering." He winked at Leah.

She watched him walk away, admiring how he looked in his tux.

"Does that mean we gossip about Marcus, too?" Jake kidded.

Leah shifted her gaze to Jake, stretching her arms out on the table toward him. "You and Emily are cute together. You guys have gone out a couple of times, right?"

He grinned, tugging on the sleeves of his suit jacket. "Yeah. She joined my D&D group. She's pretty cool."

"That's awesome." Leah faced Tanner. A knot in her stomach told her she shouldn't give much commentary on Tanner's date. Not after their past. "Brittany's in my history class."

Tanner nodded. "Cool. She's nice."

Leah picked at her nails.

"So how long is it for you and Marcus, now?" Jake asked.

Leah focused on her hands. It depended on whether you counted their month apart. She decided to include it. "Four months."

"You guys are good together," Jake said.

"I'm going to get Brittany and me a refill," Tanner said, standing up.

Jake was still clueless about what had transpired between them, and about the fact that Leah had lied about her knowing she was green folk, that she'd been raised as a human. Jake genuinely wasn't the kind of guy to pry or judge, and she hadn't wanted to confess to yet another person that she'd grown up in the dark about her own identity, and that she'd lied to the group.

After Tanner walked away, Leah returned her attention to Jake. "Thanks. I really like Marcus. Does Emily have girlfriend potential?"

He gave her a goofy grin. "I was gonna bring it up tonight."

She cracked her knuckles, her mind struggling with a thousand questions she'd wanted to ask in a thousand different ways over the months.

"Why did your parents decide to move away from the Green Lands?" she asked. Supposedly, all green folk could sense the energy that flowed in the realm—it was a part of them. Bomen didn't feel it as strongly as Ivies or Seeders with powers, but they could still perceive the lack of it.

Jake cocked his head, a look of confusion covering his face. "Well … my mom was pregnant with me already before the war ended."

That meant nothing to Leah. They sat in an awkward stare-down. She pulled from a tidbit Marcus had once told her: Bomanism was rare. Unless a Boman was born to a Boman parent, the chance of an Ivy randomly being born as such was exceptionally uncommon.

"Sorry if that's an awkward question. I honestly haven't met a lot of Bomen back home, you know." She hoped it came across authentic.

Jake shrugged it off. "Yeah. Just, it was dangerous for us in our kingdom, you know? Things were unstable when Queen Kaylah took over. People took advantage of Bomen. My parents got out the first chance they were given."

That had to have been so hard, to give up their home. She could only imagine her mom, also pregnant, fleeing at the same time.

"I'm glad they made that choice, so I could meet you."

He gave her a sweet smile, accented by a single dimple.

She dared to push a little further. So many questions loomed, but she'd never wanted to give away her family secrets, or jeopardize their safety. And she didn't want it getting back to Marcus, ruining her chances.

"How much do you know about Marcus's friends and family back home?" she blurted.

Jake scrunched his eyebrows. "I don't know. Probably less than Tanner." He shrugged again. "You know—he's private about his family."

Exactly. "Do you know why the queen is going to be at his brother's wedding?"

Jake's eyes narrowed. "You really don't know?"

There was that feeling again… Stupidity, being out of the loop.

"Why don't you just ask him yourself?"

She glanced down at the table. "I don't want to scare him off."

"Why would that scare him off? You're not dating him to get in the limelight, right?"

She looked at Jake, biting the insides of her cheeks. "No. Of course not. That's exactly what I'm afraid he might think, though."

"Well—"

Marcus was approaching, returning from the bathroom. "Never mind. You're right. I'll ask him myself. Pretend I never said anything."

Marcus sauntered up behind her, massaging her shoulders. He leaned down. "Want to dance some more? Or do you want to sit for a little longer?"

She moaned. "I'll stay in this spot for the next hour if it means you'll keep massaging."

Marcus laughed, and Tanner returned to the table with a couple of punch cups.

"You know what? Let's dance." She kicked her heels off under the table. "But I'm done with these shoes for the night."

Marcus stepped to the side, holding out his hands to help her up. "Sounds good. I promise not to step on your feet."

She raised a skeptical eyebrow, grinning.

"Okay. I promise to *try* not to step on your feet."

She chuckled. "Deal." They left the table, hand in hand, as the other girls returned.

He held her close as a slow song came on. She knew what the answer would be, but figured she'd still ask. "Did we have any plans for after the dance?"

"We?"

"I just … you know…" It *was* prom.

He hummed knowingly. "Wanted to see if I had a room key in my pocket?"

She bit her lip. "Just checking."

"I'm not planning on it. Not that I wouldn't mind some kissing." A shy grin formed on his face as his hands pulled her in even closer.

"You're cute when you blush," she said.

His gaze was piercing. "You're cute when you anything."

She smirked, standing tall and giving him a peck on the lips. "I'm really glad you were my first friend at this school."

"And I'm really glad I gave us a chance."

She nodded, her smile fading. "And thank you, for a second chance."

His cheerful expression dropped. "That's past us, right?"

"Yes."

He smiled reassuringly. "I noticed you're wearing black nail polish tonight. Very dark and mysterious for prom."

She was surprised he'd noticed that mundane of an accent to her ensemble, though given the topic, it wasn't like she'd explicitly shown him a black nail polish with accompanying receipt. "My mom and I got a mani-pedi together."

He nodded.

"I've been good. I promise."

He kissed her forehead. "I'm glad to hear it."

She leaned her head against his chest. He was still checking on her honesty. She didn't need him questioning her motives for wanting to go to the Green Lands, to the wedding.

As the dance floor cleared and the evening grew late, the Garden Club and their dates arranged to meet up for milkshakes.

On the drive over, Leah stared out the truck window, lost in thought.

"What's wrong?" Marcus asked, putting the truck in park.

She pulled out her phone to text her mom their location. "What do you mean? Nothing's wrong."

"You were practically chewing your fresh manicure off the whole way over here. Did I say something? Or?" He raised his shoulders.

She looked over at him, frowning. "Nothing you did."

He furrowed his brow. "Then what is it?" He took her hand, shifting to face her.

Off-the-wall assassination plot aside, it was eating away at her that he hadn't even asked her if she would be his date for the wedding. She'd assumed Green Lands weddings were similar to human ones, that he could take a plus-one to his own brother's wedding.

She sighed. "It's more of what you *didn't* do."

He pursed his lips, rocking his head back and forth. "I thought we agreed to wait. I didn't think—"

"I don't mean sex."

He searched her face. "Okay. What didn't I do?"

She paused. "I don't want you to judge me. I don't want you to think I'm like Tanner."

His eyes narrowed in obvious confusion.

"Why haven't you invited me to your brother's wedding?"

He perked up, sitting straighter. "We seriously haven't talked about that? Of course, I want you to come."

She instantly donned a smile. "Really?"

He gripped her hand tighter. "Yeah. It's, uh, the second Saturday after spring break, and—"

"Wait," she said. "I thought it was *during* spring break. Are you talking about the one here?"

Marcus cocked his head. "Yeah. You're talking about the one in the Green Lands?"

She rubbed the back of his hand. "Yeah. The one your mom can attend, the one all of your side of the family will be at."

He pressed his lips together.

She frowned again. "I keep wondering if you'd be ashamed because, if they know my mom is weird about Green Lands stuff, or about, you know … the … stealing thing."

He shook his head, his voice soft and kind. "No, that's not it at all. I haven't told them about any of that."

Her heart felt lighter. "Then why?"

"Because you can't go. You don't have a passport. And…" He stroked her palm with his thumb. "You say you go after what you want, but you're too afraid to even bring it up with your mom, to try getting a passport."

She freed her hands, running them across the fabric of her skirt. "I have." She had no choice other than to lie. It was only a partial lie. "I tried bringing up the Green Lands after I met you guys. I remembered her telling me stories as a little kid. It … didn't go well."

Marcus's face was painted with confusion. "So, she's known I'm a Boman the whole time? Does she not approve?"

"No. That's not it. And she doesn't know about any of the club. And it needs to stay that way." The pain of Cheryl grabbing a fistful of Leah's hair was enough of a sore spot to be believable. "My mom was livid when I even mentioned it. She wants to put that world behind her."

Realizing she could lace the half-truths with another truth he could latch on to, she added, "She finally told me how my dad really died. It was in the war you guys have talked about. It was really hard on her." She regretted saying it out loud, now fighting tears. She hoped, like Tanner had said, that it was too much of a taboo to talk about sides, so she wouldn't have to lie more.

Marcus took her hands again and rubbed them. "I'm sorry. A lot of people died in that. Both of my parents barely made it out." He frowned, his eyes sad. "That still leaves us without a passport."

"I know. And if it were just about visiting the Green Lands, I could wait until my eighteenth birthday to apply alone." She shrugged. "I just didn't want to wait that long to meet your family."

A look of adoration crossed his face. "I would love nothing more than to show you off at the wedding."

She swallowed hard. "I wouldn't need a passport if I could tree rift."

"That's illegal." He squinted. "Did Tanner tell you about that?"

"I know. That's what he said." She read his face. "I got to thinking about how my mom and I have flown before, and she's forgotten her ID. She lets the TSA agent know she's forgotten it, and they interview her, then let her get on the flight. I thought maybe we could show up and say I realized the night before that I'd lost my passport, or something like that." She averted her gaze. "But I know how you feel about lying."

He scratched his arm. "Maybe we could try that? It's not fair you've been denied your homeland your entire life."

Her heart filled with hope. "Really? You'd do that for me?"

He smiled warmly, confidently. "My dad has some pull. He'll be on this side to greet my grandparents and me."

She matched his smile. "You don't know how much this means to me. I know we have to peg down a story, and logistics, and I have a billion questions. But I…" She shook her head, then planted a kiss on him.

He grinned after stealing one more. "Of course. But don't thank me yet, we still don't know if they'll make the exception."

She nodded. "I understand. If they don't, I could get a ride home, right?"

"Yeah. But I hope it works out." He caressed her face, pulling her in for a decent kiss.

Chapter 14

MARCUS AND LEAH STROLLED INTO the ice cream shop; their group was already sitting and chatting. Jake's arm around his date gave Leah even more cause to smile. They must've had the talk about becoming an official couple.

Jake glanced at his watch. "Supposed to make out *after* ice cream, so you don't make your friends wait." He smiled.

Leah rolled her eyes. She and Marcus showed very little PDA in the club, not wanting to make things awkward. "We were talking." Which was true, for the most part.

Tanner looked directly at Leah, and laughed. "*You?* I'm *sure* that's true."

All the joy from Marcus's wedding invitation drained from her face. Tanner's meaning might be misconstrued by someone who hadn't been there, but his arrogant tone and smug grin told Leah all she needed to know. Leah wasn't the kind of girl to *possibly* be capable of sitting in a vehicle and just having a conversation, was she? Not by his estimation. Not when she'd so willingly made out with him the first time they were alone, when she'd sat on his lap, when *he'd* taken things too far.

She hugged herself, her mood soured by his pointed mocking. The double standard. If she'd done the same to him, he'd proudly own up to their make-out session. Instead, she was the slut? She glanced down the restroom hallway. "I'm going to the bathroom."

Marcus placed a hand on her back, stopping her. "Do you have a problem, Tanner? Do you have something you want to say?" He'd apparently picked up on Tanner's meaning as well.

Tanner looked between the two of them, holding up his hands. "Just having fun."

Marcus glared. "Have fun with someone else."

Leah shifted so Marcus's hand was no longer on her back. "Calm down," she snipped, trying to avoid a public conflict.

Jake was already raising his eyebrows at the tension.

Marcus clenched his jaw. "Do you want to go somewhere else?"

"No," she whispered. "Just take a chill pill. I'll be right back." She left for the bathroom, calming her breathing, attempting to focus on the good news of the evening, the almost-perfect dance.

By the time she returned, now fully recomposed, Marcus had joined the others, sitting down. Everyone was chatting except for Marcus. He was slumped in his seat, scrolling on his cell. She gave him a reassuring smile and a squeeze on the shoulder before sliding in next to him. He put away his phone. "Ordered your shake for you. Hope you don't mind."

"Mmm, depends on what you got me," she said playfully.

"Peanut butter cup. Right?"

She grinned. "You know me." She placed a hand on her chest. "Heart and soul."

He perked up. The group soon enjoyed their treats, critiquing the décor and music from the dance. Tanner avoided direct discussion with both Leah and Marcus.

After polishing off their shakes, Leah and Marcus said their goodbyes to the group and walked out to his truck. "Hold up," she said, before either of them got in. They watched and waved as the others took off. "Come on. Back seat."

He stood in place. "I don't know that I feel like kissing a whole lot right now."

She scolded him with her eyes. "We can't just talk?"

"We can talk in the front seat." He tilted his head to the side.

She took his hand. "I just want to talk. You and me. No barriers."

He opened the extended-cab door, allowing her to get in before going to his own side. "Okay."

"Why did you say anything to Tanner?"

He scowled. "We both know what he was alluding to."

It wasn't like she hadn't suffered from her number being written in a bathroom stall before, after hooking up with the wrong guy. "Maybe. But all you did was make it worse."

"How's that?"

"I told Tanner you didn't know anything, so it wouldn't make things awkward in the club. And honestly, you really *don't* know anything about what happened that night."

Marcus looked down, scratching his arm. "Does he still like you? Has he hit on you since we've been together?"

"No! And even if he did like me, I don't care." She stared at him. "Hey."

He met her gaze.

"For all of my faults, I'm not a cheater. I would never do that to you."

"I know. I believe you. Doesn't mean he wouldn't try something."

She furrowed her brow. "You're getting mad about a *hypothetical?*"

"No. I just—" He ran his hands through his hair. "I don't know. You're right that I don't know what happened that night. I would feel a lot better if I just knew."

She fidgeted with her hands. "That's not really any of your business. That was before we started dating."

He pursed his lips. "I know that. But I know something happened. And I can't just forget that. Every time I see you two sitting next to each other…" He paused. "I would just feel better knowing *what* he did."

She shook her head. "What is with this possessive side?"

"It's not possessive!" Marcus snapped. He rubbed his face. "It's not. It's just … couples take care of each other. I know you say you don't need my help. But I *want* to help. What's so wrong with that?"

"It happened before we were together! What gives you the right to know about every guy I've kissed, or done anything else with, before you?" She shifted in her seat. "Unless it matters more to you than you're letting on," she whispered. "You said it didn't matter that much."

He frowned. "You have a past. I get it. But we eat lunch with him—every day. We hang out with him—every week. It's different. And you keep saying it all happened before us, but what he did tonight," he pointed to the building, "was not before us. That was aimed *right* at you and *right* in front of me."

"I'll take care of it. And I really don't think he'll be a problem anymore." Leah had given it some thought back in the bathroom. Tanner had originally only shown an interest in her after finding out she was an Ivy. "I think he's just annoyed he can't be as free about who he is with human girls."

Marcus rolled his eyes. "Won't be a problem anymore? For you? Or for anyone?"

She glared. "He learned pretty quickly how I felt about things once I *cut his throat*. Remember that part? And what are you, the morality police?"

"What's that supposed to mean?"

She pinched the bridge of her nose. "It means I want to go back to how happy I was with you before we went inside. Please don't do this."

"Don't do what? Care about you?" He huffed. "You're okay with me helping you come to the wedding, but I can't help when he pulls a dick move like that? *You* get to choose when I'm allowed to help?"

"Yes. That would be respecting my wishes."

"Fine. If I see you getting mugged, I'll wait until I have your consent to help out."

Her ears were warming in her anger. "Who's being the dick now?"

He opened the truck door, getting in the front seat and turning the key. She buckled up, stewing in the back seat as he drove to her house. Once he parked at her house, neither of them moved.

"Is this how we're ending our prom night?" she asked, still upset, though aching at the wasted evening.

"It seems like this conversation should have ended before it began."

She got out, also moving into the front seat. "I get that you want to know everything. I do. But not everyone's so open about their pasts and struggles, Marcus. Sometimes, people want to sort through it alone. Or just … do their best to forget about it."

Frowning, he nodded. "I just don't know how to step back from it. I can't not care."

Leah gave him a half-smile. "That's because you're the most caring person I know. We just have to figure out where to draw the line." She fought off memories of experiences she'd give anything to have never endured. "It honestly doesn't bug me that much, what Tanner did. At least not anymore." She picked at her nails, sick to her stomach, dead inside. "I've had guys do worse. And you can't fix that, either."

Marcus read her face. "I'm sorry. For anything that's happened to you."

She shook her head, a tiny smile forming. "What are you apologizing for? You didn't do it. You couldn't have stopped it."

He silently bobbed his head. "I know. And you shouldn't feel like you have to tell me."

"It's probably not as bad as you're imagining with Tanner." She grinned. "You and I have been closer to getting in trouble than he and I were."

Marcus gave her a shy smile.

"Yeah. Look at that. Squeaky clean."

He rolled his eyes, his smile growing.

"I promise. It was just kissing. He got handsy. I said 'no.' I had to repeat myself. Like I said, I've had worse."

Marcus's smile faded, and he gave her a look of resigned acknowledgement. "Okay."

"And what are you going to do now that you know more? Go pummel Tanner?"

He cocked his head. "I'm guessing you're against that."

She poked his hand. "A little bit. We already worked it out. I think tonight was a fluke. We were just off tonight."

He blew out a puff of air. "I'll try to be chill."

"Thank you." She rested a hand on his knee. "I was really excited to start planning for the wedding. Let's not allow Tanner to spoil things for us."

He slid his hand to hers, interlacing their fingers. "Deal."

"How about you walk me to the door and give me one of those signature hugs of yours?"

He smiled. "Am I turning you into a hugger, after all?"

She laughed. "Not on your life. I only like hugs from *you*."

They got out of the truck, and he pulled her into a perfectly tight squeeze. He really did know how to do the job.

"Marcus?"

He pulled back. "Yeah?"

"I'm really glad I met you. I mean it. With how often I've moved over the years, I … don't always make the best friends right away. I don't always connect with people." She played with a button on his shirt. "I've never actually had a boyfriend this long."

His smile could melt an iceberg. "It's not about the quantity. It's about the quality. The right kind makes things work." He gave her one more short squeeze and a kiss on the forehead. "We'll talk tomorrow?"

She nodded. "Wouldn't have it any other way."

Leah ambled inside the house, letting out a long exhale from the ups and downs of the evening.

"No making out at the door?" Cheryl said. "Must've already shacked up with your boyfriend in a parking lot somewhere?"

Leah scowled. She was used to them spying on her. She was used to Cheryl's insults. But tonight, of all nights? "No. Not that it's any of your business."

Cheryl scoffed. "Isn't that the only way you manage to keep them around?"

Leah gritted her teeth. "What the hell do you know? You're just a bitter old maid too afraid to move on with her life."

Cheryl glared. "You are the most ungrateful—"

"*Go to hell.*" Leah's voice was low and threatening, carrying with it a thousand unspoken curses she'd wanted to mutter over the years. "We don't need you anymore." Before Cheryl could lash out again, Leah turned, striding down the hall to her mom's room.

"I'm home," she announced with all the perk she could muster. Cheryl's bedroom door across the house slammed shut.

"Were you good?" Her mom glanced up from her journal.

Leah pursed her lips. "I think most human moms would first ask how the dance went."

Her mom smiled gently. "How was the dance?"

Leah rocked her head back and forth. "I'd give it four out of five stars."

Her mom nodded. "And were you good?"

Leah rolled her eyes, cracking a smile. "Yes. Like I told you, Marcus is a Boy Scout." After providing a few more details about the dance, she headed to the bathroom to shower.

All cleaned up and in fresh pjs, Leah glanced at her phone, opening a text from Marcus.

<Sorry again for being an idiot. Hope you sleep well. CU tomorrow?>

She wore a soft smile. <Not an idiot. Just caught up wanting to be Prince Charming. ;)>

<Maybe I am. Does that make you my Princess?>

She chuckled. <More than you know :P On for tomorrow. Sweet dreams.>

Setting her phone down on the bedside table, Leah glanced at the bottom drawer. Opening it up, she grabbed her set of throwing knives for the next day. The only other thing in there stared at her until she picked it up. *Seriously, what kind of person plots an assassination?*

She flipped through the pages she'd written on. Her heart ached at her list of reasons for why the queen deserved to die.

But it won't bring him back. Move on.

Leah frowned, tearing out the pages, crumpling them up, and tossing them in the garbage.

She was going to the Green Lands to visit her homeland. To attend the wedding. If and when the time came for her to meet the murderous queen again, she'd have more than vague plans about how to kill her. She'd find a way to make her hurt. But that wasn't what this trip was about.

After crawling into bed, and turning off her lamp with a click, Leah fell asleep with a smile on her face.

Chapter 15

AS PLANNED, THEY HUNG OUT at Marcus's grandparents' place the next day. "You're sure we're good?" Marcus asked as they pulled into the driveway.

"Would I still want to come over today if we weren't?" Leah asked.

"Okay." He smiled. "Let's have a good day."

They made their way to the backyard, throwing a few rounds of knives, then sharpening them. Hungry for lunch, they went inside to make sandwiches.

"Wheat?" he asked, undoing a twist tie.

"Yes, please." Leah reached into the fridge, grabbing mayonnaise and mustard. She went back for the rest of the fillings, having trouble finding the lunch meat. "You guys usually have ham, right?"

Marcus came up behind her, placing his hands on the fridge. "Yes, there on the left." He leaned in, caressing her neck with his lips.

She turned. "Did you hide it so you could corner me?"

"You know me. Plotting and planning." He winked.

"Yes. You're the *most* mischievous person I know."

He beamed. "I'm such a scoundrel. What can I say? I can't help myself. I think you're pretty *cool.*"

She lifted her eyebrows. "Is that because I'm standing in front of an open fridge?"

He busted out laughing. "Yes." He snuck a kiss, grabbing the lunch meat and backing away.

"You are so punny." She grinned.

"I do what I can." He laid out the pieces of bread, spreading on the mayo. "Enjoy the lunch meat, you'll learn to appreciate it after a week in the Green Lands."

"Right. Vegetarians." She opened the lunch meat and layered it on the bread. "Thank you, again. I'm really excited."

"I'm excited too. You'll love it there. And I think my family will really like you."

"You *think* they will?"

He threw a teasing glare. "I know they will."

"I'm sure I'll like them too. But I'm going to have a million questions to get ready."

He grabbed a bag of chips, picking up his plate. "Let's get to it."

They sat down in the family room, eating and chatting. "Who all will I be meeting?" she asked.

"*Lots* of people. It won't be your usual scene."

"Yeah. Kind of nervous. Sounds like a pretty big shindig if the queen is going to be there." She dared to probe more, now that she had the invitation. "I understand it's a pretty small kingdom compared to some human ones, but … does she attend a lot of weddings?"

He shrugged. "It's not like I track her schedule." He took a bite, looking down at his plate. "My parents have connections. I don't really like to talk about that kind of stuff."

He always did that—he was happy to talk about his parents, but only vaguely. "Okay. It's not like I'm going there to meet *her.* I'm there to be with you. You know that, right?"

He met her gaze. "I know."

"Good. But … I've never been around royalty. So, you're going to need to coach me so I don't screw up. I don't know anything about what to wear, or customs, or geography. Any of it." She fought a grin, thinking about taking her mom up on formal dining etiquette lessons. "I guess I shouldn't say I don't know *any* formal customs. A particularly smartass Boman once taught me about a custom for good luck." She threw a chip at him.

He wore a toothy grin. "You didn't have any bad luck that week, did you? Maybe that's going to be the ticket to getting you back home."

She refused to let him win, refused to smile or laugh.

He raised his eyebrows. "Or do you need one now?" He slowly leaned over, lips puckered, aiming to give her neck another raspberry.

She held her ground, raising her hands as if she knew karate. "No."

Marcus grinned again, leaning back. He picked up the chip she'd thrown, chucking it back onto her plate. "Here. You lost this."

She grabbed it and crunched down on it defiantly. "So. Back on topic. Is it taking place at the palace?"

He shook his head, kicking his feet up onto the coffee table. "No. But it'll be at a pretty big manor."

They talked for a couple of hours, discussing how the week would go. Marcus's grandparents would drive, as they were also attending. She'd meet his dad at the rifting cave. The cave they'd arrive at in the Ivy Kingdom wasn't far from his home. He'd planned on taking the whole of spring break for a visit. They had two days before the wedding, then more family time after that.

"If you need to go home early, we can arrange that, too," he said. "Um … even if we can fudge the truth to get you over, how are you going to hide this from your mom?"

She swallowed hard. "Don't worry about that one. I'll figure it out." It was better he didn't realize the lies she'd be piling up.

He frowned, hesitant. "Okay. I just … don't want you getting in too much trouble."

She scooched closer, leaning against his shoulder. "I'll be fine. This will be worth it."

He kissed her on the head. "I'm excited. I bet my mom will *love* getting you all sorted with a beautiful dress and everything."

"Right. Can't exactly carry much through a rift, right?" She drew a deep breath. "Will there be many Seeders there?"

He rested a hand on her leg. "I guess you haven't met one yet, huh? There should be a decent amount at the wedding."

She frowned. The enemy of her dad. The ones Pretender Queen Kaylah had sided with to steal the kingdom. But … Marcus was close to his mom. She had to be a decent Seeder, and it only made sense her family would be invited. "Why did your parents settle in the Ivy Kingdom? You said it wasn't safe for your dad as a Boman in the Seeder nation?"

He gently traced a finger up and down her leg, between her knee and midthigh. "Well, Bomen Lands didn't exist when they got married, and they're almost exclusively home to Bomen, anyway. Not that my mom wouldn't be allowed to live there, but it wouldn't be as comfortable. And she's not as close to her Seeder family as others might be. They're a lot closer to my dad's Ivy family."

Leah smiled, her anticipation building to meet them both. "Tanner once said pretty much everyone was in the old war. And you said your parents fought?"

"Yep. That was another reason they stayed in the kingdom. War's ugly… They wanted to help the kingdom with all the aftermath."

"Yeah. War's ugly," she whispered.

Marcus's grandpa, Brad, poked his head in the family room. "We're getting dinner going. Will you be staying, Leah?"

"If that's not a problem?"

"Never is."

She leaned forward. "I wouldn't mind helping. I cook with my mom all the time."

"We might take you up on that sometime. We're all set for now, though, thanks."

Marcus took the opportunity to wrap his arms around Leah as his grandpa left.

"Is this the house your mom was raised in?" Leah said.

"No. My grandparents, well … there's been some family drama. It's kind of complicated. But my grandma moved shortly after my mom rooted in the Green Lands."

Leah gave a breathy chuckle. "Complicated families—I get that."

***

The next Monday rolled around, and Leah walked through the high school hallways with a spring in her step. She was going to visit the Green Lands. She was going to experience the energy, her culture, all of it. And with the person who made her the happiest.

That joy faded as she spotted Tanner at his locker. Her frustration bubbled up, and she decided to have a word with him. She marched up, kicking his door shut. It was perhaps a *little* dramatic.

He raised his eyebrows. "Wow. Moody much?"

She glared. "Why were you such a jerk after the dance?"

He sported an insincere frown. "Did I ruin the mood for you and Marcus? Did *he* end up with bandages?"

"You're not funny. Why are you even bringing that up?" She squinted. "It's not like you want to date me."

He shrugged. "Maybe I just realized you and I would have had more fun together on prom night." He smirked. "A girl like you, you've probably screwed a dozen guys." He glanced around briefly, lowering his voice. "But none of them your own kind."

She slammed him against his locker. "What I do with my life is *none* of your business. Sorry there's not another Ivy for you to enjoy screwing. But you and I will *never* have anything again!"

He rolled his eyes. "I don't need you or the stupid club. You're not very exciting now that you're dating Mr. Boring, anyway."

"Screw you, Tanner." She clenched her teeth. His smug look was too much to resist. She balled her fist but stopped short, instead shoving him against his locker again. "Bring it up again and we'll find out if a kick to the 'nads hurts you as much as it does a human."

He picked up his backpack. "You *are* psycho. Go take care of your boyfriend's 'nads and leave me alone." He stalked away before she could do the damage she desperately wanted to do.

***

Unsurprisingly, Tanner was a no-show for lunch. Leah was still in a sour mood. She wished she hadn't confronted him after all. Leah, Marcus, and Jake sat around their usual courtyard table, recapping their weekends.

"I'm happy for you and Emily." Leah forced a smile. "Too bad she doesn't have the same lunch hour as us."

"Yeah." Jake shrugged. "Especially if Tanner's going to be a no-show."

Leah and Marcus exchanged a look.

"So…" Jake said. "What was all the tension about the other day? Or am I going to be the only one in the dark?"

Marcus focused on building his hamburger.

Leah bit her lip. "Just a disagreement. He, um … might not be spending time with us anymore."

Marcus looked up with questioning eyes.

She averted her gaze, taking a sip of water. "He told me this morning that he wants to focus on human interactions for the remainder of his exchange year."

Marcus remained silent, slipping a hand under the table to squeeze her knee. She rested a hand on his. In the end, they were all going to be better off without Tanner.

Jake took a bite of his burger, shrugging again. "I won't cry any tears if he wants to hang out elsewhere."

***

Leah was finally calming down. Her past wasn't perfect. She'd made bad decisions, one of them being having done anything with Tanner. But her mistakes didn't define her.

She was doing her best to pay attention in English class, until she was called to the office. *Great. This is never good.*

"Ms. Edwards. Take a seat." The vice principal pointed to a black pleather chair in her dark and stuffy office.

"Yes, ma'am." Leah's stomach was in knots. She'd had her fair share of office visits over the years.

The VP crossed her arms. "I've had a report of you being involved in a physical altercation earlier today."

Leah fidgeted with her hands. "I, um … just had a disagreement with someone."

The VP raised her eyebrows. "A disagreement that involved you shoving him against a locker?"

"Is that what he told you?"

"'He' being Tanner Holgrum?"

Leah looked her in the eyes. "Yes." This was low.

"I spoke to him, too."

'Too'? So someone else reported it?

"But I'd like to hear things from your side."

Leah bit the insides of her cheeks. "He was being a jerk. We argued. I lost my temper."

"You have nothing else you'd like to add?"

Leah rubbed her wrists. How many times did girls like her get dismissed, especially after waiting to report something? How many times had her mom jumped straight to moving because she was trying to protect Leah? They owned their own furniture dolly, for heaven's sake. "Nope."

The vice principal sighed. "Your transcript shows a lot of moves, and a few problems along the way. Is there anything else you'd like to talk about?"

"Nope."

"I'm trying to help you."

Leah matched her gaze. "I don't need help. I'd like to get back to class, unless there's something else."

"This is your first offense here. If there's nothing else you'd like to add, you can return to class. You'll have in-school-suspension for the rest of the week."

Leah's jaw dropped at the prospect of being cooped up in detention during lunchtime. "ISS? I didn't even hurt him!"

"It's violence against another student. Unless you have something else to add, you're dismissed, and I don't want to see you in my office again."

Leah clenched her jaw. "Yes, ma'am."

Marching back to class, Leah fumed. People needed to keep their noses out of her business. She should have made it worth her while and actually punched or kicked Tanner like he deserved. Just before she reached the classroom, her phone vibrated.

The text was from her mom. <I'll be picking you up today. Be at pickup right away.>

Oh crap.

Leah promptly made her way to student pickup after classes.

Marcus found her, wrapping an arm around her. "Hey, beautiful. How are you doing?"

She blew out a long breath. "I've been better."

He frowned. "Do you want to talk about what happened with Tanner?"

She scrunched her eyebrows. Had Marcus somehow been involved with her visit to the office? "What do you know about it?"

"Nothing… You mentioned you talked to him."

She closed her eyes, shaking her head. "Right. I, um…" Her mom pulled up in her blue hatchback. "I'll talk to you later?"

He gave her hand a squeeze. "Sure." He bent over, looking in the car. "That's your mom and her car. Not your aunt today, huh?"

Leah gave him a quick kiss, her heart dropping. She hadn't genuinely worried about her mom forcing them to move for a while. But was she overreacting about the ISS? She'd already had three shoplifting strikes in this city…

Leah decided to give Marcus a quick hug as well. "I…" She ran a hand through his handsomely curly locks. *I need to calm down.* "I'll talk to you later."

Chapter 16

LEAH GOT INTO HER MOM'S CAR with a gulp. After a moment of silence, she decided to be the first to speak. "Why are *you* picking me up today?"

Her mom's jaw clenched as they drove down the street. "I would like to wait until we're home to have this conversation."

Leah's breathing picked up. "Are we moving?"

Her mom didn't respond.

She endured the rest of the ride in painful silence. Once they got home, walking to the front door felt like walking down death row. Surely this wasn't all about the ISS… But maybe it was the last straw after the shoplifting…

Leah panicked—the notebook pages in her trash can. Had she taken out her trash? Had her mom? Had she discovered her plans and now knew that Leah had exposed herself to green folk? A thousand fears ran through her mind.

"Sit down!" her mom ordered once the front door closed. She tossed her keys onto the coffee table and crossed her arms. "Eleana." She shook her head, balling her fists.

Leah kept her mouth closed.

"Why do you think I'm upset?"

Leah shrugged.

"I had to leave work early today. Because of you. I got two phone calls. *Two!*"

Leah furrowed her brow. "Two?"

Her mom plopped down in an armchair, burying her face in her hands. "Let's talk about the school office call first."

Leah bit her lip. "He deserved worse."

"In-school-suspension? You hurt another student. Why?"

"He was a jerk."

Her mom cocked her head. "Everyone who disagrees with you could be classified as a jerk, right?"

Leah scowled. "He…" Her mom knew she'd had trouble with guys before, though just the tip of the iceberg. Leah struggled to get the words out of her mouth. "Even *you* would have approved of more than me shoving him."

Her mom softened, frowning. "What did he do?"

"I don't really want to talk about it. I'm fine. I'm just saying … he deserved it."

"Did you tell the vice principal?"

"That's none of her business."

Her mom sighed. "Life would be easier if you would allow people to help you."

Leah locked eyes with her. Wasn't it her mom who had said therapists were useless, that she needed to learn to take care of herself? Wasn't she the one who had kept secrets from Leah her whole life because she was afraid? "You're not the most talkative, either."

Her mom looked down. "Is Marcus causing any troubles?"

"No! You've met him. He's a good guy."

"You two have been dating for a while. And you spend a lot more time over there than you do over here. Maybe it's time I met his grandparents."

"No. Why?"

"Is there a problem with me meeting them?"

Yes. They know I'm an Ivy and don't realize it's a secret... "Of course not. I just don't need you making it weird. I'm perfectly safe over there. And Marcus is a good influence—you know that." She sat up straighter. "What have my grades been like? And ... I haven't had *any* problems at the store since he threatened to break up with me over it before Christmas."

Her mom nodded. "Even then, I wish you two would spend more time over here."

"We can, if that's what it takes." Leah wrung her hands. "But his grandparents are retired, they're always home. We never go in his room. We know the rules."

"Fine. For now." Her mom sat back, crossing her legs. "Moving on. The other phone call I got today."

This one was the mystery. Leah couldn't even begin to guess.

"Take a look around."

Leah glanced around the room. There was nothing too spectacular in their living room. The decorations were simple from her mom having grown tired of packing and unpacking things over the years. Though Leah *did* notice a couple of items missing. Most notable were Cheryl's coat and purse, absent from their place on the coatrack. Leah had assumed, or perhaps just hoped, that Cheryl was under the weather, forcing her mom to come pick her up. But she wasn't there... "Okay?"

"Cheryl took a job over two hundred miles away."

Leah's heart froze. "You just said... Marcus... I don't want to move yet!"

Her mom's face became stern. "We're not. She made it *very* clear she no longer wishes to live under the same roof as *you*."

Leah crossed her arms. "Good."

"That's not something to be proud of, Eleana!"

"Why not? She was always mean to me! You can only turn a blind eye so much." A scowl covered Leah's face. "She hurt me, and you never did anything about it."

Her mom glared. "Don't pretend you're an innocent little angel."

Crestfallen, Leah fought tears. "I'm not. I never claimed to be. And I get that she was your servant, and you felt like you owed her something, but she wore out her welcome a long time ago."

Her mom threw her hands in the air. "Our lives are full of compromise. You know that. We don't belong here. She was my last connection to our home."

A tear fell from Leah's eye. "*I'm* your last connection, right?" Her voice trembled. "You and me, we don't need anyone else."

Her mom frowned. "Of course. I didn't mean that, princess. It's just…" She shook her head. "You don't understand how much we really needed the money she brought in."

Leah sniffled. "Well, I… I can give up my allowance. I can get a job."

"No. It's not that simple. I'll agree to the allowance. And I'm going to see if I can get more hours from work. But we've managed things like this for *years*. How am I supposed to work so much *and* watch out for you?"

"I'm old enough to watch out for myself. I'm safe with Marcus. I'm safe at home and school."

"And you've been listening to make sure no one from the Green Lands is in your school?"

Tanner wouldn't do anything in retribution, would he? He knew she was keeping secrets from her mom. "Yes. I've been listening. We're fine."

"We'll see how things go for now." Her mom stood, holding out her hand, palm up. "Two weeks of grounding."

"Why?" Leah whined. "Because you have to work more? I—"

"Because both of your problems could have been handled better."

Leah was done with the conversation; she never won this part of the fight, anyway. She pulled her phone from her pocket. "Can I at least tell Marcus?"

"You'll see him at school."

Leah wilted, handing it over.

Her mom tapped away at the screen, as she had on more than one occasion before. She wouldn't dare leave Leah without a phone for safety's sake, but she *could* activate a parental setting that suppressed most of the functionality of the phone, only allowing approved numbers to be called or texted—those of herself, Cheryl, and 911. "And since Cheryl and her car are now gone, you'll be taking the bus for now." She handed Leah's phone back to her.

Leah shuffled to her room, a mix of emotions. Maybe she shouldn't have pushed Tanner. No, she should have *punched* him and made it worthwhile. She prayed her mom could get more hours so they wouldn't have to move to find a better paying job. She considered the irony of how she could steal things to help with expenses, but she'd only be punished more for it.

***

Leah was less than thrilled to wake up even earlier to take the school bus for the first time in her life. It was noisy, dirty chaos.

She'd never been allowed social media accounts like her peers. Leah now finally understood the reasoning behind that decision—it wouldn't do well to have pictures of King Soren's exiled heir floating around the internet. But even then, Leah was used to texting Marcus, or looking up videos on social media without actually having an account. She kept rubbing her pocket, longing to turn her phone on and wipe away the world around her. Instead, it was like a brick against her hip, only good for emergencies and tracking.

The bus got to the school with barely enough time for her to stop by her locker, allowing no time to chase Marcus down. She tried dropping by his locker when she could between a couple of classes, but missed him. She reported to ISS as ordered, feeling the prisoner vibe through and through.

It was only between her last two classes that Marcus tracked her down at her locker. "Hey, what's up?"

She let out a sigh of relief, pulling him into a huge hug. "Gosh, am I glad to see you. I tried to find you earlier."

He pulled back, squinting. "Something happen to your phone? Missed you at lunch."

She pursed her lips. "ISS this week."

He raised his eyebrows. "Do tell."

She threw on a forced, cheesy smile. "I may or may not have gotten physical with Tanner."

He frowned. "Did you tell them what happened? Not that I even know what happened, but I'm sure he more than deserved it."

She grabbed his hand. "He did. But don't worry about it. He didn't show at lunch again, right?"

Marcus shook his head. "But they still suspended you?"

She twisted her lips.

He sighed, tucking a strand of hair behind her ear. "Next time he does something, I'm taking care of it. You can be as mad as you want."

She swung their joined hands. "We'll see."

He bent down, giving her a kiss. "For the record, if you had let me handle it, it wouldn't have happened on school property." He placed his hands on her arms, rubbing them reassuringly. "That explains lunch, but why haven't you been answering my texts?"

She swallowed hard. "Grounded for two weeks, no phone. Well, no phone service. It's locked."

"Seriously? Because of ISS?"

"Yeah, that's part of it."

He slowly pulled his hands back, tucking them in his pockets. "What's the other part?"

She shook her head, deflated. "It would be really nice to not have my boyfriend jump to conclusions."

"I'm trying not to."

"It's not what you're thinking. It was just a family argument. I promise. You can even ask my mom."

He took a moment before answering. "Okay. I believe you."

"Thank you."

He grabbed her hands again. "Not gonna lie. Sucks that I'll only get to see you in the hallway and at pickup."

She groaned, leaning forward and burying her head in his chest. "Yesterday was a bad day," she mumbled.

"Come again?"

She pulled back, taking a deep breath. "My aunt moved out, too. I have to take the bus now."

Marcus smiled. "My grandparents wouldn't mind giving you a ride. Would your mom allow that?"

Leah shrugged. "We could ask."

"She's got work, right? So, she won't even know who drops you off…"

The tardy bell rang, and Leah grinned. "You're supposed to be rubbing off on me, not the other way around."

He smirked. "I'd say…" He pressed his lips together, clearing his throat.

"What?"

"Never mind." He looked her over. "Better get to class." He snuck one last quick kiss. "See you at pickup."

***

Marcus was right; his grandma, Samantha, happily gave Leah a ride home. And Leah happily rested her hand on Marcus's thigh as they sat next to each other in the van. "Thanks again, Samantha," she said.

"No problem, sweetie."

They pulled up to Leah's place, and Marcus walked her to the door. "Hopefully you can talk your mom into being okay with this arrangement."

She played with the hem of his t-shirt. "She's depriving me of my study partner. So, if she wants me to keep my grades up, she should concede that I deserve to shorten my ride so I have more study time."

"I like your logic. And when you're off of house arrest, I vote we have a big date." He slid his hands to her waist. "Dinner, movie, all of it."

She frowned.

"Or not?"

"It's complicated. Maybe we'll just hang out at your place."

He felt her forehead. "Are you okay?"

"Yes…"

He put his hand on her waist again, pulling her closer. "You'd rather be supervised at my place than spend time at the theater alone?"

She gave him a half-smile. "It's…" She wrapped her arms around his waist as well. "Free is good. I won't have an allowance for a while."

"I don't mind paying."

She bit the insides of her cheeks. "Giving me rides is more than enough. I don't need you always paying for me. I don't want your charity."

He scoffed. "Since when is any of that charity? Because I want to spend time with my girlfriend? If anything, you're doing me a favor."

She rolled her eyes. "We'll see."

He leaned down, kissing her and sliding his hands lower, into the back pockets of her jeans. He then studied her face. "Is this okay?"

"Your kissing? That's more than okay."

He squinted. "Not what I'm asking about."

She grinned. "You know where I stand on that kind of thing when it comes to you."

"Just because you wanted it once, doesn't mean I can just assume."

She gazed into his warm brown eyes. *This one. He's a keeper.* "I usually like to handle things myself. But it's safe to say I'm alright with you handling me this way."

It was his turn to roll his eyes, though he grinned while doing so.

"Pretty bold, though." She wiggled her eyebrows. "With your grandma in the van."

He stole a glance over his shoulder. "She can't see from this angle. And if she's parked, she's reading a book."

"Thanks for asking. Did you take some sort of gentleman's class back home?"

He laughed. "Yep. Private class. My brother and I. My dad was the teacher."

"I really look forward to meeting him."

Marcus wore a hesitant frown. "Is this going to jeopardize our chances of you coming to the wedding?"

Having analyzed the situation, Leah figured her punishment was probably more about her mom being stressed, than angry. Hopefully this wouldn't have any further repercussions.

"We'll make it work."

Chapter 17

AFTER LEAH'S WEEK OF in-school-suspension, she was over the moon to spend lunch with Marcus and Jake again. Luckily, her mom consented to allow her to also get rides from Marcus. After a couple of days of lunch with Jake, Leah and Marcus agreed to leave early, allowing for some private planning and talking time.

"How are things going at home?" Marcus asked as they strolled across the school lawn.

Not fantastic. Her mom hadn't been able to pick up extra hours yet. "Not bad. And we talked about going to the wedding."

"Really?" His face lit up.

"Yeah." She smiled. "I told her it's in Detroit, and that we'll be supervised the whole time. She's still thinking about it." Her stomach twisted, revolting at the lie. She'd tried the Detroit story. The answer had been a resounding 'no.' She wasn't surprised. But Leah wouldn't take no for an answer. And even if it ended up being the final answer, she might fudge the truth anyway.

"I'll take it." His happy expression faded. "One problem, though. You'll have to be able to make your own rift."

"I thought you said they do it for you at the cave."

He winced. "Yeah, well, I wasn't thinking about the fact that you're not a Boman. We can pretend you forgot your passport, and have you present your vines, but we're not going to have a good reason why you can't make your own rift. All regular Ivies and Seeders are expected to."

She frowned. "I… I could pretend I'm a Boman?"

He shook his head. "My grandparents will be there and know you're not."

Why is this so complicated? "How hard is it to learn? You don't think you or Jake could coach me through the theory of it?"

He shrugged. "We don't know what it's like."

She couldn't really expect more of them, since they'd been born without powers. Leah swallowed hard. "Then I'll talk to Tanner."

Marcus scowled. "No."

"What other option do I have?"

"*Any* option that's not him."

"Which is none."

"Just … let me think about it. We've still got two and a half weeks."

***

Leah's anxiety was building. It was just a wedding. She was just going to meet Marcus's family. But it was so much more than that. She wanted to see her homeland. She wanted to size up the woman who had destroyed her family.

The next day, Leah approached Tanner's locker between classes. "Tanner."

He looked past his locker door. "Stay away from me. I wasn't the one who got you in trouble."

She rolled her eyes. "I know. Not that you obviously said the truth, either."

"Leave me alone, psycho."

"I need help."

He laughed. "I don't care what it is. The friendship shop closed up a while ago."

"Please." She whispered, "I need to learn to rift."

"So, you are crazy, then? Even if I liked you, I told you—it's illegal."

"A cave rift."

"And yet I still don't care." He shut his locker.

"Please! I'm begging you."

His attitude exuded arrogance. "Begging, huh?"

She rested her hands on her hips, glaring. "Yes. What do you want, a blow job?"

He grinned. "Is that a genuine offer? I don't think Marcus would be okay with that."

"No." She clenched her teeth. "You owe me for not talking about what you've done."

"Not like there were witnesses."

She balled her fists. *This was a bad idea from the start.* "Why are you such a dick?"

He leaned against his locker, crossing his arms. "Why do you want to go so much right now? Doesn't your mommy still have you on a tight leash?"

She huffed. "If you must know, I'm going to the wedding. And my mom gave me permission."

He savored a deep breath with an air of triumph. "Leah… You might have Marcus fooled that you're a reformed citizen, but not me. If your mom gave you permission, why doesn't she teach you herself?"

Leah wanted nothing more than to wipe that smug look off his face. "You don't know me as well as you think you do." Thoughts of her parents came to her mind. She could have, *should have,* rightfully been a princess. Real royalty. Over him. "And someday, you might regret that."

His eyes grew wide. "Maybe you need a therapist. But seriously. Heard of a restraining order? Touch me or threaten me again, and maybe we'll look into that."

Out of nowhere, Marcus appeared, placing a hand on both Tanner and Leah's shoulders. He smiled disingenuously at Tanner. "Tanner, buddy. Next time you mess with Leah, I'm going to break your face." He released his grip as Tanner rolled his shoulder, throwing daggers with his eyes at Marcus.

Clearly enunciating, Marcus added, "I think we both know this could get *much* worse for you."

That vague threat stole all the color from Tanner's face.

Marcus faced Leah. "You, me, let's go to class." He grabbed her hand, yanking her away.

"Why the hell did you talk to him?" Marcus scolded.

"I really want to go." She scowled at the ground.

"You will! But you couldn't give me just a couple of days to get it sorted? Maybe put a little faith in me?"

She met his gaze. "Fine. It was stupid. He said 'no' anyway."

He stopped walking, holding her hands. "I found you a teacher."

"What?" She read his face. "Who? Where?"

He grinned, looking around to make sure no one could hear him. "A sophomore Ivy at another school."

Her eyes lit up. "That's great!" She gave him a huge hug. "You're amazing!"

"Well … don't thank me yet."

She backed up. "Why?"

He scrunched his face. "She lives two hours away, and is only willing to meet us halfway. I don't know that your mom is going to be cool with us driving that far out with the way she keeps tabs on you."

Leah gnawed her lip, thinking. A light bulb flickered on. "I'm off of house arrest on Saturday. I have a plan."

***

Leah, Marcus, and Jake sat down at their usual spot for lunch. The couple exchanged a glance, and Marcus cleared his throat. "So … Jake. What are you doing Saturday afternoon?"

Jake shrugged. "Emily and I are probably doing something. Not sure what yet."

"How would you feel about a double date?" Leah asked. "Except … not actually doubling?"

He raised his eyebrows, taking a swig of soda. "I'm not following."

"You know how my mom is crazy about tracking my phone and everything?"

"You've mentioned it."

Leah nervously stirred her applesauce. "We kinda need my mom to think we're out for dinner and a movie while we're doing something else for three hours. We were hoping you'd take my phone?"

Jake bunched his eyebrows. "Three hours? What are you guys even—" He held up a hand. "Never mind. I don't think I want to finish that question."

Leah smirked. "Oh, you better believe it. I mean, three hours is *impressive* stamina. But Marcus is pretty amazing." She seductively bit a knuckle in challenge to Marcus's disapproving glare.

Jake closed his eyes, turning every shade of red. "Leah, I never want to hear those words from you again."

Leah busted out laughing. "Fine. Whatever."

Marcus rolled his eyes. "You know me, Jake. Would I ask you to do something like this if it weren't important?"

Jake sighed. "Just take the phone with me to dinner and a movie?"

"Yes," Leah replied. "We'll meet you at the restaurant for the handoff. Then you'll text my mom as me when you're leaving there and arriving at the theater. I'll have it typed up; you just have to hit send. We'll meet you there after the movie."

Jake hesitated, looking between the two. "Fine. But what if she calls?"

"That's why it's at a movie theater and not just leaving a phone at Marcus's place. She won't call."

***

Marcus texted Jake from the restaurant parking lot once he and Leah arrived. Not knowing all the details, Jake wanted to leave Emily out of it, so he intentionally left his wallet in the car, giving himself an excuse to leave her momentarily.

Leah handed Jake the phone out of the truck window. "Thanks a million!"

He looked down at it, making sure it didn't require a passcode. "Sure."

She couldn't help herself. "Don't worry. We have plenty of water, snacks, and protection."

"Seriously?" He glanced past Leah to Marcus. "Got a muzzle for your girlfriend?"

Leah smirked. "Hmm … I packed the whip and handcuffs, but a muzzle?"

Marcus started to roll her window up from his side, and Jake turned, walking away.

She yelled out the window before it closed shut, "Thanks again!" She faced Marcus, still smiling.

He shook his head. "Why are you doing that to him? Are you really that horny?"

She giggled. "Come on! You can't tell me that's not a satisfying reaction. And you—I've already told you how cute you are when you're frustrated or blushing." She winked.

"You'll be the death of me," he said in that same exasperated tone he always used when she teased, the one that had a hint of a smile to it, like he secretly enjoyed it. "Let's get on the road."

She grabbed his free hand after he shifted into drive, ready for their first mini road trip.

***

Marcus and Leah made good time arriving at their rendezvous point, which was just shy of an hour's drive. They parked at a diner and went inside, texting the Ivy girl they'd arranged to meet. Leah was a ball of nerves, more anxious with each minute that ticked by. She was excited to meet another Ivy, but terrified of having to let someone in on her secret. Or at least the tip of the iceberg that Marcus knew about.

A tall girl with short blonde hair approached their booth. "It's Marcus, right?" She squinted.

"Yes. Kara?"

The girl nodded, sliding in. She didn't even acknowledge Leah, instead intently focused on Marcus. "You're *the* Marcus, right? I didn't realize that's who I was meeting today!"

Leah glanced between the two. Kara was positively giddy, mouth agape, fangirling over her boyfriend.

Marcus looked uncomfortable. "Just Marcus."

Kara closed her mouth. "But I'm right, right? You're Sir Guillen's son?"

'Sir'? What's that supposed to mean? Is that like 'Mr.' in the Green Lands? Or is that some kind of proper title?

Marcus cleared his throat, sitting straight. "Yes. But I'd rather not discuss my family, if that's okay."

Kara swallowed. "Yes. Of course. Sorry, I'm being rude."

The waitress dropped by. "Would you like to add to your order?"

"We already ate on the way here, but I've got the bill. Did you want to eat anything?" Marcus offered.

Kara pointed at the lemonades they'd started sipping. "I ate too, but I'll take one of those."

Marcus smiled at the waitress. "We won't be here long, so if you could bring the check with it, that would be great."

Once she left, Kara perked up, placing her hands on the table. "So … what's up?"

Marcus slid his arm around Leah. "This is my girlfriend, Leah." The girls exchanged 'hellos' before Marcus continued quietly in the noisy room. "She's like you. And we need help on something I can't do, because, well … if you know who I am, then you understand."

"Right. Yeah." Kara furrowed her brow. "But what can I possibly help with?"

The waitress brought a lemonade and their check.

Leah shredded her straw wrapper, tying it into knots over and over. This was all so awkward.

"It's a little unconventional," Marcus said. "So, we'd need you to be discreet, and keep this between us."

Leah leaned forward. "My parents have some weird rules, is all. It's not a huge deal, it's just embarrassing, you know?"

Marcus gently rubbed Leah's back. "Can you teach her how to rift?"

Kara raised an eyebrow, taking a sip of her drink. "You don't know how to rift?"

Leah bit her lip. "Like I said, kinda stupid and embarrassing. I know how to use, you know," she held up her wrists, "for other stuff, but they didn't let me learn rifting."

"But why?" Kara appeared thoroughly confused. As Marcus had taught Leah, any other Ivy would have learned a decade ago, at the latest. And wouldn't likely be in the human world without having created their own rift to get there in the first place.

"Just trying to keep things simple. It's not like we're asking for help with the *illegal* kind," Marcus stressed. "And we have a tight deadline. We've got today and next Saturday."

Kara nodded knowingly. "The big wedding?"

Marcus confirmed with a nod of his own.

Kara shrugged. "I've never taught someone before, but I'll do my best. We better get going."

They took a final sip of their drinks as Marcus left a few crisp bills on the table. Having scouted the location with online maps beforehand, they left on foot for a nearby walking trail.

"How are you liking your foreign exchange year?" Leah asked.

Kara smiled. "It's fun. I'm really glad I got to come. What about you guys? And did you meet here, or back home?"

"Loving it here." Marcus squeezed Leah's hand. "And we met here."

"Neat. What region are you from, Leah?" Kara asked.

"South. Not far from the palace." Marcus had already drawn her a map showing her roughly where major landmarks were, so she wouldn't be in the dark.

"Cool. I'm way north," Kara said.

"How about your Garden Club? What's it like at your school?" Marcus asked.

Kara swung her arms. "It's really nice. Two guys, another girl. I'm the only Ivy. The other girl's a Seeder Boman, and the guys are standard Seeders."

Leah cringed. "How does it feel to be outnumbered?"

Kara chuckled. "I don't know? It would be cool to have another Ivy, I suppose, so it's fun to make a new friend." She gave Leah an encouraging smile. "What about your school?"

"Just a couple others," Marcus said. "Another Ivy Boman, though he's a permanent resident on this side. And another Ivy."

Kara's eyebrows scrunched as they cut off of the path, out into the woods. "She wouldn't teach you?"

Leah rolled her eyes. "He. And he's a jerk."

Kara reached for one of her dangly earrings, straightening it. "It happens. I'm glad to help."

Chapter 18

ARRIVING AT AN AREA WITH fallen trees and large boulders, the group stopped for the training session.

"Since I'm not much use with this part, I'm going to patrol and keep an eye out for any humans who might stumble off the path and see something they shouldn't," Marcus said. He gave Leah an encouraging squeeze on the shoulders before heading off.

Kara and Leah sat down on fallen logs. "So, you said you know other Ivy stuff, just not rifting?" Kara asked.

"Yeah." Leah carefully extended a vine, glancing around. It was so foreign to show it off without being scolded or fearing being caught. "I've got down maneuvering them." She grasped a pebble, picking it up and chucking it to the side. "And flexing the leaves to be sharp." She did as she'd practiced, flexing and swinging her vine with enough force to have a couple of leaves stick into the log next to her. "And then, you know, the chemical stuff."

Kara nodded. "Okay. Just not rifting?"

Leah shrank with embarrassment. "Yeah."

"Right. No problem." Kara moved, sitting next to Leah. "I'm right-handed, so I always use that vine. And the rifting channel is the central one."

Leah froze, her heart beating faster. It was like meeting the Garden Club all over again. Terminology she'd never heard, trying to pretend she wasn't completely in the dark. "Right. That makes sense. The central channel for rifting?"

"Yeah. Between the numbing and growth channels."

Leah stared blankly at the ground.

"Um… Well, maybe we should talk more about that…" Kara addressed the elephant in the room. "What chemicals have you been trained on?"

Leah frowned, meeting Kara's gaze. "Please don't judge me. Or say anything. I … guess you could say I'm homeschooled on Ivy stuff. And I didn't have a very thorough teacher."

Kara chuckled. "It can be our secret. Does Marcus not know about that part, either?"

Leah shrugged. "We don't really talk about the abilities like that."

"I've never dated a Boman, but I can see how that might be tough."

Leah furrowed her brow. "Why would it be tough? You wouldn't date a Boman?"

"Oh, no. I'd date one. I've never actually had a boyfriend. But, you know, just the differences between you."

"Do people care that much about Bomen not having vines and green-folk energy?"

Kara grinned. "I guess it depends on who you hang out with. And if we're talking about PG topics or not."

Leah remembered her and Marcus's close call in the intimacy department. Marcus had admitted there was a difference, but had never elaborated. "What's different?"

Kara blinked, a look of embarrassment crossing her face. "That's probably a conversation to have with Marcus. And we should focus on rifting, right?"

Leah straightened her posture. "Right."

"What do you know about the chemical arts?" Kara asked.

"A poison? Haven't really practiced, though."

"Basic self-defense poison?"

"I guess so?"

Kara rubbed her hands together. "Alright. Imagine a multilane highway between your mind and the vine you're trying to activate. There are different lanes, or channels, we'd normally be trained on. Things like numbing, coagulation, various levels of poisons, fertilizers, and so on. Of course, some are really advanced, and everyone has different skill sets, so don't feel bad if you don't know them all."

Leah appreciated her kind reassurance.

"The one we really care about right now is the central channel. In a way, it's hidden under what you know for the self-defense poison. That kind of poison is a crude combination of the others. So, if you reach underneath, there's a central channel that's easy to find for rifting. That's the one that goes both ways, working in tandem with your target to open the space."

Leah closed her eyes, imagining all of these channels. She thought she maybe, perhaps, could sense it. "What do I do with it?"

Kara pointed to a small mushroom. "Extend a vine. See if you can detect the connection between that channel and the mushroom."

Leah followed her direction, feeling a hint of warmth, or clarity. It was amazing to awaken this part of her. "I think I get it."

Kara smiled. "Great. From here, it's pretty tricky. My understanding is tree rifts are a lot more intuitive because you can pull that energy from the tree. Cave rifts are a different thing altogether."

Leah choked down her anger. *The stupid murderous queen took the more natural route from her people. Sure, that makes sense.* "Right. A rock isn't living … so how does that work if we can't connect?"

"It takes a lot more concentration, but it's not supposed to be as draining as it used to be, since all modern caves in the network are jade-enhanced."

No idea what that means, but okay… Leah drew a deep breath. "Just tell me what I need to do."

Kara coached Leah on connecting to a few more small plants. They moved to the downed trees, which were no longer alive, but still had wisps of that living energy. Touching a rock did nothing for Leah; it was literally like trying to communicate with a brick wall. She tried time and time again. Frustrated and feeling a real energy drain for the first time in her life, Leah took a short break.

"You know Marcus's family?" Leah took a swig from a water bottle she'd brought.

"No, I've never met any of them."

"But they're a pretty big deal, right?" Leah tried her luck.

Kara gave her the same almost-incredulous look Jake had given her before. "Do you really not know who his parents are?"

Leah swallowed hard. "Of course I do. Sir Guillen, right? I guess I was just curious if you knew if they *acted* like a big deal, you know—stuck up."

Kara fiddled with her earring again. "Not from what I've heard. But you never really know with public figures, right?"

Right… Public figures. Important enough to have a queen attend their son's wedding. Leah kept the other thousands of questions to herself, having already given away too much about her lack of training and Green Lands knowledge.

They got back to practicing with boulders, Leah trying to push her energy down her extended vine. Marcus checked in on them. "How goes it?"

"I think she's promising." Kara smiled.

Leah threw a discouraged frown at Marcus.

"Anything I can do to help?" he asked.

"Actually, do you keep your personal jade on you?" Kara asked. "Maybe we can somehow use it to enhance her training, like the caves do?"

"Couldn't hurt to try." He sat on a large stump, pulling off a shoe and working off an anklet with a square green stone strung in the middle. "Just be careful. Make sure I get that back." He handed it to Kara while looking at Leah. "I checked with Jake. Everything's fine, but we should probably leave in the next fifteen to twenty minutes."

Leah's heart dropped into her gut. She was nowhere close to accomplishing anything worthwhile. "Okay."

Marcus left to go patrol the perimeter again.

"What are we supposed to do with that?" Leah asked.

Kara studied the stone. "Honestly, I don't know. I just figured it wouldn't hurt? Let's put it around your wrist and keep trying."

They tried for another fifteen minutes without any notable progress. Marcus returned, marking the end of their training session. He came up behind Leah, massaging her shoulders. "So, what do we think?"

Leah sighed. "Kara's been doing great. I just don't even know what it's supposed to feel like."

He wrapped his arms around her from behind, resting his chin on her shoulder.

Kara frowned. "Sorry. I tried my best."

"Could you meet up again for another hour next week?" Marcus asked. "I can pay you, pay for your gas money, all that."

Kara waved a dismissive hand in the air. "I don't need your money. But I can make some time next week, no problem."

Leah felt a smidge of hope. "Thank you so much, seriously."

The group walked back to their parked vehicles, finalizing plans for the next week. Kara encouraged Leah to practice what they'd been covering before their next meeting. Marcus and Leah hopped in his truck, getting on the road without delay.

"You seem pretty frustrated," he said.

"Yeah, well, I am." Her head was swimming, and she genuinely didn't know if it was from frustration or Ivy energy drain.

"Was it helpful at all?"

She leaned her head back. "Maybe. It's humbling, that's for sure."

"You could try to look at it as an exciting new step? Pretty cool to learn to master your powers, taste your potential."

She appreciated his sweet attempts to reassure her. And it wasn't like she had much room to complain about learning to use her powers, when he hadn't been born with any. She still felt defeated. "What's our backup plan? Are there any other options to open a rift if I can't get it?"

"The only thing I can think of … is the employed gatekeepers would understand if your energy was too low. But that's a stretch, considering how little it takes for someone who's rifted for half their life."

"How would my energy be used up?"

"If you used up several strands of vines and expended a lot of chemicals."

She laughed. "So, our backup plan is to make me look like a serial killer that ties people up and poisons them?"

He chuckled. "Yeah, I guess so." He reached out his hand, and she took it. "Things will work out."

She looked down at her wrist; his anklet was still there. "I'll do my best." She smiled at the stone. "Is this like wearing your boyfriend's letterman jacket?"

He stole a peek. "Not quite. I'll want that back as soon as we return."

"No one's mentioned this. What's special about it?"

"It's used more in Seeder culture, and by Bomen in both nations. Regular Ivies rarely use jade, other than in the boosted caves."

"What do you use it for?"

"Even with help, I can't get through a rift without it."

"Oh." She gently stroked the stone, noting the swirl carved into it on one side. "Then I'll definitely make sure you get it back. When are other ways it's used in the kingdom?"

"Community coordinators use jade, and if you're in the palace."

She glanced at him. "Have you personally been in the palace?"

His mouth hung open for a moment. "Yes."

"You really don't like talking about your family and their connections? Not even with me? Kara called your dad 'Sir Guillen,' what was that about?"

He sighed, checking his blind spot and switching lanes. "I'd just like you to meet them first."

"That's kind of … odd, though. That you're keeping that from me."

He frowned. "I'm not keeping it from you. I just… You don't like accepting help; I don't like talking about them."

Fair enough. Not like I'm sharing important details about my own family. "Would you at least explain why the queen will be at the wedding? That's pretty intimidating, to be honest. You said your dad had connections to help us get through the caves. Kara acted like your family's famous. I don't want to look like an idiot."

He hesitated. "Whether people like them or not, my parents played a big part in the war. My mom does a little of this and that now, but my dad still does a lot of work in policy and Bomen rights. He reports directly to the queen."

Leah's eyes grew wide. "Does he like his job?"

"Yeah. He likes helping people. He's done a lot of good for Bomen. Both of my parents have."

"Does that mean they're politicians?"

He huffed. "Tip of the iceberg of why I don't like talking about this kind of stuff. It's not like they're corrupt human politicians, you know. They're good people. And even though the war ended almost two decades ago, there's still a lot of mixed opinions. Just like how some people don't agree with my parents being in a mixed-race relationship, or my Seeder mom being allowed to adopt Ivy Bomen." He shook his head. "It's complicated. I just want you to get to know them for who they are without any preconceived notions. Is that so bad?"

Marcus had explained Seeders and their limitations, that it wasn't possible, even back then, for Marcus's Seeder mom to flee the Green Lands with his Ivy Boman dad. Seeder women, after their powers came in during their teenage years, 'rooted' in the realm, and couldn't survive in the human world long-term after that. Now, Leah was even more excited to meet this 'Sir Guillen' who'd chosen not to flee the Green Lands like Jake's parents had. It wasn't just for his love of his wife; he'd been brave enough to stay behind in the chaos brought by Queen Kaylah's reign, to fight for his people's rights.

Leah squeezed Marcus's hand. "They raised you. You love each other. And if they're making things better for Bomen, then I'm a fan." She paused, wanting to reassure him she wasn't trying to be a social climber. "But not a creepy superfan." She winked at him when he glanced over with an appreciative smile.

Chapter 19

MARCUS AND LEAH ARRIVED AT the movie theater just in time as the movie was ending, getting out of the truck to stretch their legs. Leah handed Marcus back his jade anklet, and he slipped it on as a bracelet.

Jake and Emily emerged from the theater. "Hey, what are the odds of seeing you two?" Emily said. "What movie are you guys coming to see?"

Leah did her part to distract Emily as Jake slipped Leah's phone to Marcus. "We haven't decided yet. It looked like there's a couple of good ones."

Emily adjusted her glasses, smiling. "We should double sometime!"

"Yeah," Marcus said. "We were going to see if you guys wanted to do dinner and a movie together next Saturday."

"I'll have to check with my mom first. But pencil us in, you two." Leah smiled as Jake pointedly narrowed his eyes.

"I'm free," Emily said.

Jake glanced between Marcus and Leah. "We'll talk."

Jake and Emily drove off, and Marcus turned to Leah with a smile. "It worked."

She pulled him into a hug. "Our plan to get training worked. The training, not so much. All the other steps, I guess we'll see."

He stepped back, holding her at arm's length. "One step at a time. How about you text your mom and let her know we're capping off our date night with some ice cream?"

After driving to a nearby ice cream shop, Marcus parked in the far corner.

Leah smirked. "Are we actually getting ice cream?"

He grinned. "We can get some to go, can't we? It's been two weeks since we've had time to just chill together. Is that so bad?"

"I won't argue with that."

They ordered shakes to go and reconvened in the back seat of the truck. "I missed you," she said, leaning against him.

He set his shake down in a cup holder, wrapping his arms around her, caressing her neck with his lips. "I missed you too."

She giggled. "Not wasting any time."

"How do you feel about hickies?" he asked.

She faced him, surprised. "Really?"

"Yeah." He bit his lip.

She studied his face. "I'm actually not a fan."

Marcus blushed. "That's fine."

"Why do you want one?"

"Just kind of thought it was sexy. You know, if we each had one."

She wrinkled her nose. "I don't love the whole 'marking your territory' or bragging kind of stigma that comes along with it."

He furrowed his brow. "No. I didn't mean it like that. It wouldn't be visible. I wouldn't want you in trouble with your mom or anything."

She set her shake down, wearing a mile-wide grin. "Not visible? Where were you going to ask to put it?"

He tapped on his knee, looking down. "I don't know. I, um …
just…"

She lifted his chin. "Sometimes, you are so shy."

He let out a breathy chuckle. "I thought, like, under your shirt,
but you know, you'd still have your bra on."

She beamed. "I *am* corrupting you, aren't I?"

He rolled his eyes. "No. I'm just happy with you."

She took his hand. "How about this? When you decide you're
ready for *everything*, we'll revisit those hickies."

He nodded with a shy smile. "Okay."

She swallowed, ready to add to his awkwardness. "What's
different about a Boman in the sex department?"

His knee nervously bounced. "I'm not a green-folk sex-ed
teacher … but I guess you deserve to know."

She'd already learned a little of this and that, but not too many
specifics. "Yeah … I mean … I don't think there's anything different
about me from a normal girl, 'cause…" Their eyes met.

"Because you've been with a human guy, and he didn't freak
out?"

She looked down, her face warming. "Yes."

"Then you know what it's like to be with a Boman. In those
essentials, we're the same. Though … um, even if the person you
were with didn't say anything…" He dodged eye contact this time.
"Well, they say Ivy girls are better than human girls. But that could
just be talk."

She bit her lip, nodding slowly. She'd never had complaints from
the guys she'd slept with, but she didn't want to dwell on them right
now, and she was perfectly happy with Marcus assuming it had only
been one. It wasn't like the count reached the dozen Tanner had
flippantly accused her of.

Truthfully, though, there had been far more regret and pain with
each of them, than happy memories. Each of them had started with
hope, or at least a desire to numb some part of herself. Each had
soured in some way—earning her a reputation, trauma, a bucket of

distrust, a stalker, or the inability to look her mom in the eyes for a month. There was an irony somewhere there, that her relationship with Marcus had only started to help her reach a goal, that she never would have pursued him if she hadn't come up with a harebrained idea to assassinate a queen in another realm.

But Leah *really* didn't want to focus on past experiences right now. Not now. Not ever. "But you admitted there's something different between regular Ivies and Bomen in that regard."

He scratched the back of his neck. "Ivy guys are different. Let's just say … normal green-folk guys…" Even his ears were turning red as he cleared his throat. "Well, guys talk. Either stuff is really great, or if they're trying to do things so a human girl doesn't recognize … it's just not very enjoyable … to hide what you really are. And Ivy to Ivy, like Seeder to Seeder, there's even a difference, because your body recognizes the compatibility."

She wanted to know more, but it was obvious he wasn't comfortable. "I guess I don't need *all* the details. I'm not dating any of the other kinds, right?"

An embarrassed but relieved smile crossed his face. "Right."

She twisted her lips. "Is it weird at all for you? The differences? 'Cause girls really don't care about that part of it. They care about who it's with and how it's done. And I think you're perfect the way you are."

He gently tucked her hair behind her ears. "I think it's normal to compare yourself, but I'd like to think I'm confident in myself in that way. And I appreciate your vote of confidence."

She moved over, sitting on his lap. He wrapped his arms around her.

"In what ways *aren't* you confident in yourself?" she asked.

"Hmm. The usual stuff. Or maybe there's no such thing. But fear that I won't be successful. Fear that I won't be judged on my own merits. What about you? Where would you say you lack confidence?"

She looked into the distance, out of the truck window, turning inward. "That I'll make stupid decisions. That I'll disappoint people." She frowned. "I'd say I do a good job at proving both of those are legitimate shortcomings."

He squeezed her tighter. "We're all works in progress."

She gazed into his soft brown eyes. "Yeah, we are." She leaned forward, caressing his lips with her own. He slid a hand up to the nape of her neck, reciprocating. His lips met hers time and time again, in perfect synchrony. Eventually, Leah's phone pulled them apart.

Leah calmed her breathing before answering. "Hi, Mom. Yes, we're just finishing up at the ice cream shop."

Marcus grabbed his shake and noisily slurped up the partially melted portion of it.

She winked in appreciation of the background noise. "Sure, we can do that. Okay. Love you."

Leah hung up the phone. "Mind if we swing by the grocery store on the way home?"

He squeezed her knee with his hand. "Fine with me. Do you know if there's train tracks between here and there?"

"I don't know."

He grinned. "Then maybe she won't know, either. How long does it take to get stuck behind a train?"

Leah giggled. "I guess a few minutes." She leaned in, kissing some more.

***

Leah returned home with eggs and a gallon of milk. She took them straight to the kitchen to put them away before stopping by her mom's room. "I'm back." She leaned in the doorway.

"Thank you for swinging by the store. You were good?"

Leah rolled her eyes. "You should assume I'm being good for as long as I date Marcus. He's a good guy. I feel like a broken record."

Her mom sat on her bed, patting a space next to her. Leah joined her, sitting cross-legged and leaning back against the headboard.

"You really like this one, huh?"

Leah grinned. "Yeah. How did you know it was love with my dad?"

Her mom's eyes grew wide. "Love? Marcus?"

Leah's cheeks warmed. "I'm not saying that. I'm asking about *you* guys."

Her mom hummed softly. "It's so rarely in one instance that it happens, or that you know. At least that's what I think. When is it flattery or infatuation? And when is it the real deal?"

Leah smiled; she loved hearing about her dad. About her parents together. "Was he your first?"

"Yes, he was."

"Were you his?"

"Mmm, no."

"Did that bother you guys?"

"Are we talking about me and your father? Or you and Marcus?"

"I can't just ask questions?"

Her mom gently poked her arm. "Just because a guy doesn't sleep with you, doesn't mean he's perfect."

"I wasn't bringing up Marcus. We talked about Marcus. I changed the topic to my dad." Leah rolled her eyes again. "And it's a bit hypocritical of you, you know. It's not like you waited until you were married."

Her mom sighed. "Not hypocritical. Wanting you to learn from my mistakes."

Leah turned to face her mom, brow furrowed. "He was a mistake?"

"No! I didn't mean it that way. Your father wasn't a mistake. Becoming sexually active so young just complicates things."

Leah raised her eyebrows. "You never specified *how young* you were when you started."

Her mom cleared her throat. "That doesn't really matter for either of us at this point."

Leah looked down in thought. "Was I an accident?"

"Why would you think that, sweetheart?"

Leah shrugged. "I don't know. Just a question. If you knew he was going to die, would you have held off on getting pregnant?"

Her mom shook her head. "Never question that. You weren't an accident. And you're that piece of him I have left. I would never give you up." She smoothed the bedding. "It wasn't the best timing; I'll give you that. We were just starting our reign, and our family, in a chaotic war. We didn't realize it would end so soon."

Leah scooted closer to her mom. "What's it like in the palace?" She thought of what Marcus had said about the palace using the jade stone, whereas most Ivies didn't use it for anything. She wanted to ask more about it but couldn't think of any questions that wouldn't give away she knew too much.

"Mmm, the palace. So beautiful. I loved the stained glass windows. A lot of fond memories in that place from our dating." Her voice faded off in a melancholy whisper. "Until it all ended."

Leah felt a pang of guilt. "I'm sorry about Cheryl leaving. Did you guys reminisce about the Green Lands much?"

"Not really. Not for a long time." She nudged Leah. "I like talking to *you* about it now."

Leah smiled. It truly did sound so foreign, so majestic there. The realm was eternally spring.

"Oh yeah, and my favorite room." Her mom perked up. "It's called the Queen's Room. So unique, vines everywhere. Very peaceful."

"Is there a King's Room too?"

"Mmm, no."

"What happens in the Queen's Room?"

Her mom smirked. "What did prior generations do? Or what did your father and I do?"

Leah arched an eyebrow. "For the love… I appreciate that we can have mature conversations, but I think we're stepping over the parent-child line here."

Her mom chuckled. "We were newlyweds. Don't judge us!"

Done with all the sex talk for the day, Leah was ready to move on, focusing on something that had genuinely bothered her earlier. "You taught me that poison stuff, with my vines. Is there anything else I can do?" Kara had described *several* channels. Why would her mom be keeping them a secret? What else was she hiding?

"Not that I'm aware of. Of course, I wasn't a nurse or soldier. It was just standard training. And I'm sure I'm a bit rusty."

It sounded like an honest reply; Leah would ask Kara more the next weekend. "How's it going, trying to get more hours at work?"

Her mom averted her gaze. "I'll figure it out."

"I mean it when I say I could get a job to help."

"No. It's my responsibility to take care of you."

Leah looked her mom in the eyes. "I'm old enough. I'll be eighteen next year. You know I'm practically an adult, right? And that someday you'll have to let me go?"

Her mom frowned again, looking down into her lap. "I'll take care of things."

Leah studied her, frowning as well. What would her mom be, if left alone? She'd had her husband, homeland, and all the rest of her family and friends taken from her. She didn't deserve it. Leah also feared her mom might never really be able to let her go.

Chapter 20

MARCUS WENT TO LEAH'S HOUSE the next day, because her mom had asked for Marcus to come over more often. Since Leah's house was so much smaller than that of his grandparents, they did a lot more whispering and cuddling than having open discussions and kissing. Marcus let her know he'd confirmed with Jake that they'd repeat the phone exchange the next weekend. Jake wasn't excited to be involved in keeping secrets, but he begrudgingly agreed to help his friends one more time.

"I'll need to spend as much time as possible practicing trying to rift," she said as they snuggled in her living room.

"Does that mean I won't be seeing as much of you this week?" Marcus asked.

"I still have homework to do. And I'm pretty sure your place is a better option for concealing activity." She smiled. "But if you want to go hang out with other friends, I get it. I'm sure it would be boring to watch me try to figure it out."

He squeezed her hand. "We'll see. I don't know if you've noticed, but I like spending time with you."

Her cheeks warmed. "Okay. How are we feeling about everything else?"

He rocked his head back and forth. "We'll see about the rifting. The biggest thing other than that is making sure your mom lets you go. I think we can count on my dad understanding." He scrunched his face. "At least I hope so. I *really* hope this works out. I'm getting pretty excited."

"Me too. But I'm going to be relying on you to help make it look like I'm not a complete noob over there." He'd explained the wedding would be taking place in Capital City in the Green Lands—neutral territory crawling with Seeders, Ivies, and Bomen from both nations.

He leaned closer, nuzzling her neck. "I've got your back."

She giggled.

***

Leah loved learning her new abilities. Being able to sense the life in simple vegetation around her was nothing short of astounding. The evening before their second meetup with Kara, Leah and Marcus had an after-school picnic at a little park. With the area empty, Leah did some practicing. She almost wondered if she was at a level where she could attempt a tree rift, able to sense a balance in living things. Touching her vine to a rock still felt useless.

"Want to borrow this, m'lady?" Marcus handed her his jade anklet.

She smiled, taking it from him. "M'lady?"

He made a silly face.

She was about to put it around her wrist, then decided to try something different. "If the caves are jade-enhanced, maybe having it in contact with the rock is more helpful than in contact with my skin." She wrapped the anklet around the rock she'd been practicing on, then extended a short tendril, trying to push her energy down the lower central channel in her mind. She physically and mentally poked at the rock. The rock blocked her energy, stubborn and immovable.

She sighed. *This is a waste of time. If I knew the locations for tree rifting and how to get around...*

Marcus knelt behind her, holding her in his arms. "We've still got a week. Don't stress so much."

Leah closed her eyes, allowing her muscles to relax. She savored the warmth of his embrace, and envisioned the warmth of the energy of the Green Lands as Marcus had described it. Not just a temperature warmth, but a richness that flowed in the realm, the source that fueled all green-folk powers. Extending her tendril again, she touched the rock, exerting pressure and focusing on the path her energy was taking. The energy hit the rock, but didn't immediately bounce back. Like a spark of flint over a campfire, a trace of energy jumped past.

Her eyes shot open. "Something happened!"

"Really?" he whispered excitedly.

"Yeah, let me try that again." She sat straighter, this time doing it with her eyes open. There was no visible spark or glow, but something passed from her. It was just an inkling, into the unknown void. It had no direction or destination, but there was *something*. She grinned, her heart beating a mile a minute. "I don't know if it's enough, but something's definitely different."

"That's awesome." He squeezed her tight, his arms still around her. "You're amazing."

She leaned back in his arms. "I think you were right. That some of it was in my head." She blew out a puff of air. "Now the question is, will you be able to hold me like this so I'm calm enough to do it at the cave?"

He gently kissed her cheek. "I wish. But every second before and after that, I'm there for you."

She tried a few more times. Pushing out the stress of lies. The worry of her mom's job. The pain of her family problems. And it seemed to work. Further attempts didn't yield anything bigger, though she wasn't disappointed—she'd hardly expected a giant rift to open with beginner techniques using the enhanced equivalent of a caveman's power saw that she'd created by simply strapping the jade to the rock.

Taking a break from her exertion, she lay on the picnic blanket with Marcus, pointing out shapes in the clouds as they drifted by.

"I'm really proud of you," he said.

"Thanks." She smiled. "I think we should be optimistic … but also realistic. This is going to take a lot of things to line up to get me over like we're planning."

He sucked in a long breath and let it out slowly. "Like your mom's approval?"

"Actually… I wanted to surprise you, but I guess I don't know why I was waiting…"

He rolled over to face her. "She said 'yes'?!"

Leah grinned wide. "Yes. She agreed I've been doing good, that I've earned it." She rolled onto her side and gave him a peck on the lips, moving a hand up and playing with one of his curls. "And she's seen how good you are. And how good you are for me."

He smiled, then it faded. "Kind of makes me feel worse, knowing we're lying to her."

She frowned. "She lied to me my whole life, and is keeping me from there, though, right?"

He pursed his lips. "You're right. You told her it's in Detroit?"

"Yeah. Don't worry. I've got everything worked out. My phone will have an 'unfortunate accident' so she can't track me. And I have an old friend who's going to fake some emails to keep in touch."

He furrowed his brow. "Is it enough? What's going to happen if you get caught in this lie?"

"A decent grounding. But it's worth the risk."

Concern was painted on his face. "But you said before that you moved here because she didn't approve of, well … stuff in your past. You don't think she'd lose it and make you move again, do you?"

"No. I've lived all my life with her. I can gauge her reactions. Just trust me, okay?"

He interlaced their fingers. "Okay."

Leah forced a smile as her stomach knotted tighter. That was all a lie. Her mom, of course, had said no. But that didn't mean Leah hadn't come up with a plan. A plan that *had* to work. "Everything will fall into place."

He gazed at her lovingly. "It will." After a moment, he sat up. "Do you want to go back to your place?"

"No. Let's go to yours." *Have to keep them apart to prevent the stories from unraveling. One more week.*

***

The next afternoon was a repeat of the previous Saturday. Jake gave a stern reminder at the initial phone handoff that he wasn't doing any more favors like this, and Leah decided to keep her teasing to herself. The drive to the rendezvous was nice, and Kara was right on time. Leah explained her practice and progress to Kara as they walked to a well-concealed training area.

"That's brilliant," Kara said. "I hoped the jade might help, but it makes more sense to put it on the element you're using. If jade was capable of magnifying our powers, I'm sure every Ivy out there would be wearing it."

Leah nodded thoughtfully, a question coming to her mind that she tucked away for later.

They reached their training spot, and Marcus surrendered his jade for them to practice. "I'm going to go make sure no one wanders down this path. Probably for the best you practice without me." He winked.

It took Leah a while to clear her mind properly and get back to the place she had been the day before. "How do I even know this is the right thing? How will we know when I'm good enough and doing it right to open a cave rift?"

Kara winced. "Honestly, I'm not sure. This is kinda hypothetical." She furrowed her brow. "Let me try what you're describing and compare it to how a rift feels."

Kara extended a tendril, pressing it against the rock with the jade strapped to it. She stared off into the distance; it didn't look like she was even doing anything. After a moment, she nodded, facing Leah with a smile. "I see what you mean. That's kind of cool. I think you're on the right track."

Leah's heart lit with hope. "You think I could make it?"

Kara shrugged shyly. "I want to say yes. But you won't really know until you go to try it in the right place."

Leah glanced around, making sure Marcus wasn't approaching to check in. "I don't want you to take this the wrong way, but I was wondering about tree rifting. It doesn't seem like such a big thing to me."

Kara's eyes grew wide. "That's illegal."

"I know. Don't get me wrong. I guess I was thinking … like a trial run. I didn't think it was such a big deal." She was getting increasingly annoyed by everyone's shock at such a simple request. It wasn't like she was asking for help robbing a bank.

Kara shook her head. "It's legal if it's on your own private property. But most people still don't do it. And you'd have to know the name for your departure and arrival points. I'm assuming you know your arrival point, but…" She gestured at the trees around them. "I couldn't tell you how to do it from a random place like this. They say it's intuitive, but I had to have the program coordinator help me with the names of places around my exchange-host home and school, for an emergency exit. I don't know how to do that myself."

Leah sighed. *Why can't this be easier?* She didn't know departure *or* arrival names. You couldn't rift without these names, the GPS code words associated with each rifting location in the human world and Green Lands. "Thanks for explaining. Please don't mention that to Marcus or anyone else. It was just hypothetical, you know?"

Kara read Leah's face. "Yeah. No prob."

Leah decided to push her luck a smidge more. "You know the jade thing, how it amplifies energy in some ways?"

Kara nodded.

"I've heard there's some in the palace. Do you know what it does?"

Kara looked surprised. "That's kinda cool. Didn't know that. Did Marcus tell you that?"

Crap. Worse than Marcus finding out, would be a royal fangirl gossiping about a politician's son's know-nothing girlfriend blabbing about something the public didn't know. Leah didn't need a spotlight turned on her. She shook her head. "No. Don't remember where I heard that. Maybe it's just a rumor."

Kara nodded like she bought it. "I could see it being true, though. Maybe it amplifies the energy at the palace in some way."

Leah's eyes rested on the jade. *Energy meaning power.* If the palace was somehow enhanced, was that part of why her dad had died? Along with his throne, his sister had decided it was something worth killing for?

At the end of the training session, they returned the jade to Marcus, and Kara offered to stay in touch in case they needed more help or to hang out another time.

Marcus stressed how proud he was of Leah as he started the truck. Leah's mind was focused elsewhere. Web of lies? It felt more like a *tornado* of lies—a messy whirlwind that would someday spit her out without an ounce of mercy. She stared out the window on the ride back home, listing them all. Lies to her mom, to Marcus, to Jake, and maybe even to herself, just to name a few.

"Leah?"

She blinked, looking at Marcus. "Yeah?"

He raised his eyebrows. "You okay?"

"Yeah, just kind of out of it."

"I asked if you wanted to meet up with Jake and Emily for ice cream after we get back. A thank you to Jake. A celebration for you." He smiled.

She squeezed his hand. "Yeah, let's do that."

"Are you worried?" he asked.

"About what?"

"Creating a rift? Going over?"

She adjusted her seat. "Maybe that's what's bothering me. What are we going to do if they realize we're lying at the cave? What kind of trouble can we get in?"

"Don't stress so much. My dad will either cave, or he won't." He laughed. "Pun not intended. Anyway, I doubt he'd know we're lying." He huffed. "Gosh, I sound like a horrible person. He's not naïve, you know. He's just trusting, and likes to give people the benefit of the doubt. And coming from me…"

She frowned. "I'm sorry I'm making you lie to your dad."

He glanced over. "Are you twisting my arm? If it ever came out, I think he'd understand in the long run why we're doing this. He definitely believes in sticking up for people who've been wronged."

Leah nodded with a half-smile. His dad was standing up for Bomen rights during Leah's aunt's corrupt regime. Of course, he'd understand that her mom keeping her from her home realm was wrong.

"As for the cave employees," Marcus continued, "I think at most, they'd be confused as to why you couldn't properly open a rift alone. They wouldn't jump to any conclusions about you being some sort of outlaw or something." He chuckled. "Are you good at fake crying?"

"Um… I could practice?"

"Couldn't hurt to say you hit your head or give them some tears about being so stressed out your powers weren't working right. You know, like getting out of a speeding ticket. Just as a backup plan." He squeezed her hand. "And … if worse comes to worse, and you get denied, we'll survive. It would really suck, but you could apply for your passport on your eighteenth birthday. You don't need your mom's signature or approval at that point."

True. It wasn't ideal, though. "What's needed for a Green Lands passport?"

"The standard stuff. Parent names, place and date of birth to prove green-folk heritage. Maybe a background check?"

Leah's heart dropped. Her eighteenth birthday didn't matter. She'd *never* own a passport. The corrupt regime would never allow that. She'd only be putting a neon sign over their heads announcing where she and her mom could be found. She literally had to rely on their plan for the wedding, or—someday, somehow—figure out tree rifting if she wanted to experience the Green Lands for herself.

Her mind wandered, remembering something Tanner had once said. Her mom hadn't talked much about other family beyond Leah's dad. But Tanner had mentioned other siblings to the queen. "The queen has two younger brothers, right?"

Marcus furrowed his brow. "Where'd you hear that? Was Kara gossiping?"

Why does he get so worked up about it? Just because his dad's a politician and deals with the royal family, now I can't ask about anyone remotely related to the queen?

"No. Actually, Tanner mentioned it a while ago. Forever ago. I don't know why it even popped into my mind. I guess I was just wondering about all the people I'm going to meet at the wedding and if they'd be there, too." She gave him a warm smile. "But I promise, I'm not a weirdo like Tanner. I won't kiss the royal family's feet or anything."

Marcus made a comical disgusted face. "I usually avoid kissing *anyone's* feet. Rather unsanitary."

She chuckled.

"Umm, yes. She does have two younger brothers."

"Will they be there?"

He shrugged. "It's not my wedding. I haven't tracked the guest list or RSVPs. I'd imagine they were both invited, but I'd only give it a fifty-fifty chance either would show."

"Why is that?"

"Well…" He rocked his head back and forth before changing lanes. "I guess I don't know how much of our history you've gleaned, but things got real ugly with the royal family. Between the queen and her older brother, their parents. The two younger kids got mixed up in all of it. They were pretty young. They're not exactly living in the limelight these days."

"Do they like the queen?"

Marcus laughed again. "I get that you and your mom are pretty close, but you know most adults don't go around confessing their struggles and feelings to teenagers, right? I've met them, but I wouldn't know how close they really are."

Leah nodded. Maybe she'd been looking at this all wrong. Maybe she wasn't just yearning for justice for her dad. Maybe, like her mom, she was yearning for that connection to family. She hoped she would get to meet her uncles at the wedding. Marcus, her uncles, her homeland—that could be enough.

Since they were on the topic, Leah figured she could safely push a smidge more. She didn't remember her mom bringing them up. "The queen's parents, are they still alive?"

"No. They were assassinated in the war."

She struggled to hide a frown. Queen Kaylah had taken her dad *and* her grandparents from her. "Guess that's some serious family drama, huh?"

"You could say that again."

Several miles down the road, Leah still couldn't shake the fact from her head—her aunt had also murdered her own parents. "This Kaylah, she didn't agree with her parents' policies, did she?"

"What? Oh, no. Definitely not."

Chapter 21

LEAH AND MARCUS ARRIVED AT the movie theater on time, discreetly getting Leah's phone back from Jake, and heading over to their favorite ice cream joint. It was nice spending normal time with normal people. Though, Leah almost let some green-folk talk slip. She'd gotten so used to being free around the Garden Club that she forgot Emily was a human not in the know. Even as expats like Jake, green folk didn't easily give up their identities and secrets to humans.

After dessert, Leah and Marcus lingered at her doorstep for a few minutes, enjoying each other's company. Leah smirked internally; grateful creepy Cheryl wasn't around to watch them from the window. Leah's mom at least respected their doorstep drop-offs more tastefully, and both Leah and Marcus appreciated those last few minutes together.

Marcus pulled back from their kissing, catching his breath. "One week. Can you believe it?" He tucked her hair behind her ears. "I'm going to have to remember to not steal the focus from the bride and groom by showing you off too much."

She grinned. "I can't even believe this is all real. Less than a year ago, I didn't know that place even existed." She gazed into his eyes. "Or that I could find someone so amazing in every way possible."

After another short smooch, Leah went inside the dark house, turning on lights as she went. She popped into the bathroom to clean up for bed. She paused, listening carefully and furrowing her brow when she heard what sounded like sobbing ... coming from her mom's room.

Concerned, she knocked on her mom's door, then turned the knob. Her mom sat on her bed, now quiet, sopping up her tears with tissues.

"What's wrong?" She'd never seen her like this before.

"Nothing. Don't worry about it." Her mom looked down, blowing her nose.

"This is not nothing." Leah approached the bed, sitting by her mom.

Her mom moved a pillow to make space for her. She had puffy eyes, and wet hair as if she'd just showered, and was already in her silk pajamas for the night.

"Is this about work? Do we have to move again?"

Her mom sniffled. "No. I got that all taken care of."

Leah tilted her head. "That's good, right? You'll just be working later?"

Her mom averted her gaze, shaking her head. "No. I, uh... I asked for a raise. We'll be okay."

Hmm... "Really? Enough to make up for losing Cheryl's income?" That seemed like it would be a significant increase for only having worked there for a few months...

Her mom took her hand. "You let me worry about finances, okay? It's *my* job to take care of us."

Leah nodded. "I love you."

Her mom pulled her in tight, laying her head on Leah's. "I love you too, princess."

Still confused, Leah asked, "If work and money are okay, then why are you crying?"

Her mom finally responded after a long pause. "You know me. I just get too sentimental sometimes."

"My dad?"

"Yeah. Him. Other family. All of it. But I'll be okay. Sorry you had to see me this way."

Their relationship was complex. Sometimes, her mom was her best friend, other times her warden. Sometimes she was ready to go to bat for her daughter, other times she was in denial, or too depressed to handle more. "I'm a good listener, I think."

Her mom kissed her head. "I know, sweetheart."

When her mom didn't start sharing anything, Leah carefully crafted a related inquiry. "I'd love to hear more about your family, and dad's. Would you tell me about them?"

Her mom gave her a gentle smile before obliging. "I had three sisters. I guess I should say *have*… Last I heard, they're all still alive and married with kids."

More family Leah would never know. Aunts, uncles, cousins.

"Sometimes I imagine what it would be like for you to have grown up around cousins." Her voice grew cold, from nostalgic to hurt. "Last time Cheryl checked, my parents were still alive, but not in great health."

Leah frowned, wishing she could check in on them or somehow inquire. "Do you still keep in touch with Cheryl? Even if she doesn't want to live with us, would she be willing to go check things out for you?"

"Let's not count on Cheryl for anything."

Leah's guilt grew. If she'd been better behaved, better tempered… She hadn't thought about how Cheryl was the main go-between for news from the Green Lands. Being an aide to an exiled queen had to make it far less risky to show her face than the actual queen.

"What about my dad's family? His parents? Any other siblings other than the one that … killed him?"

"His parents died in the war, too. He had two younger brothers."

"What were they like?"

Her mom took a deep breath. "Truthfully, I didn't know his brothers well. Around the time we got engaged, the boys were being taken care of full-time by staff. And his parents… They were interesting people. I don't know that they wholeheartedly approved of me, but they were pleasant."

"Why didn't they approve of you?"

"This and that. I'm sure it didn't help that I was just a lowly peasant. Not exactly lowly, my family had some status. But you know, not close to the royal line."

Leah poked a pillow. "Oh. Then maybe they weren't so great. 'Cause I think you're a fabulous mom."

Her mom wiped her nose again. "Don't think badly of them. They were pleasant to me. I hold no ill will against them." She let out a breathy chuckle. "And they had good taste. Your dad was their favorite, after all."

Leah smiled. "Maybe it's a good thing I'm an only child. I don't have to worry about my parents picking favorites." She loosed a breath. Every moment of warmth and wonder that she enjoyed while learning more about her dad and family was tainted by the bitter taste of the betrayal they'd all suffered. "I still can't believe she killed her brother, uncle, *and* her parents."

After a moment of silence, her mom spoke up. "I'm pretty tired, sweetheart. How about we head to bed early?"

"Okay." Leah gave her a big squeeze.

***

Sunday passed.

Practice rifting.

Keep the lies straight.

Monday passed.

Focus on school. Practice rifting.

Keep the lies straight.

Tuesday passed.

Focus on school. Garden Club. Practice rifting.

Keep the lies straight.

Wednesday passed.

Double-check every aspect of the plan. Focus on school. Practice rifting.

Keep the lies straight.

Thursday passed.

Doubt every aspect of the plan. Double-check every aspect of the plan. Focus on school. Practice rifting.

Keep the lies straight.

Friday passed.

Try not to freak out. Doubt every aspect of the plan. Double-check every aspect of the plan. Focus on school. Practice rifting.

Keep the lies straight.

And Saturday morning arrived.

***

Leah woke early. She needed to get things right. She picked out her cutest clothes that wouldn't make her look too conspicuous. Listening intently for the sound of the shower, she began to pen her letter.

I'm sorry to do this to you. I love you. Please, PLEASE don't worry. I'll be safe. This isn't Marcus's fault—I lied to him and his grandparents. They bought the ticket for me already, and it was nonrefundable. I just really wanted to go to the wedding. I know it's wrong to leave like this, but I'm not a little kid. I hope you can forgive me. I'll be back by the end of spring break, and I'm willing to face the consequences, even being grounded until the end of the school year. It means that much to me. I hope you can understand that someday. You know I've been doing so good for MONTHS. Please allow me this one thing. I love you. ~Eleana

She folded the letter, letting out a long exhale. She couldn't have her mom risk her life by frantically coming to the Green Lands in search of her. It would be better this way, thinking she'd gone to Detroit. And hopefully the way she'd written the letter—framing her reasons, justifications, and hinting at a lesser punishment than she feared—would help on her return.

As she stared at the folded paper, a darkness overshadowed Leah's mind. This was the right thing to do, right?

She resolutely set her pen to a new piece of paper and forged a second letter, tucking it away in case it would be needed later.

The bathroom door closed, and Leah jumped up—this part was crucial. Picking up a large glass of water she'd already prepared, she quietly crept into her mom's room as the shower started. Finding her mom's cell on the bedside table, Leah plunged the phone in, taking it back to her own room to soak.

Leah pocketed the few items on her checklist and put the letter to her mom under her pillow for now. She perched on the edge of her bed, her knee bouncing up and down.

Marcus texted. <Still on?>

<Are you sexy?>

<LOL. I'm guessing that's a yes.>

< :D >

Leah took her mom's phone from the glass of water; it should be damaged by now. She clicked the button. *Crap.* It was an older phone. It should have worked already. Her heart beat faster as she plunged it back in, and the shower turned off.

She shot off a text. <Stall a half hour?>

Panicking, she shoved her cell in her pocket, leaving her mom's to soak. Stepping into the hallway, Leah was met by her mom in a robe with a towel on her head.

"Good morning, princess. Why are you up so early?"

Leah shrugged. "Just woke up and couldn't fall asleep again. Craving bacon. Wanna make breakfast together?"

Her mom's smile was warm. "Yeah, I'll be right in."

"Cool, I'll get it started." Leah turned down the hall, her heart thumping in her chest. She hurriedly threw a pan on the stove, then yanked bacon and eggs from the fridge. Her phone chimed.

<Sure. See you then.>

She let out a sigh of relief. Leah ripped the bacon package open, slapping strips haphazardly into the pan. As they began to sizzle, she pulled bread out and ran back to her bedroom to check on the phone.

You've got to be kidding me. DIE!

She plunged it back in, a little water splashing on her dresser. Her mom's bedroom door shut.

"Eleana, have you seen my phone?"

UGH!

Leah left her room, heading to the kitchen. "No. Where did you see it last?"

Her mom reached into a cupboard, grabbing breakfast plates. "On my bedside table."

Leah dropped slices of bread into the toaster. "Did it fall under your bed? Or between the bed and table?"

Her mom sighed. "Maybe." She finished setting the table, then went back to her room.

The toast popped up; Leah feverishly buttered the slices, considering alternate options with the phone. She flipped the mouthwatering bacon and dodged a wild pop of grease from the pan.

Her mom returned, scrunching her eyebrows. "Still couldn't find it." She pulled a container of strawberries from the fridge. "Could you call it for me?"

Leah's eyes grew wide. "Sure. Take care of the eggs? I've got to go to the bathroom first."

Her mom kissed her on the forehead. "Yes. And thanks for the breakfast idea. We should do this more often."

Leah summoned her most authentic forced smile. "I agree." Pacing herself to not run, she casually and quietly stepped into her room, retrieving the phone.

Still working.

She huffed, crossing the hall to the bathroom. Hoping the sizzling of breakfast in the works could mask the sound, Leah held the cell under the bathroom faucet and turned it on high and hot, directly into the charging port.

Please. Please. Please. Please. For. The. Love. Please!

She turned the phone off and on a few times, flushing the toilet after a while. She got on her knees, still holding the phone under the running water, trying to figure out what to do. Leaning her forehead against the bathroom cabinet, she considered using a bobby pin in the charging port. If her mom's phone worked, she could track Leah's phone. She could call Marcus or his grandparents. Marcus's dad or the officials at the cave could try to call her to ensure Leah had permission to travel. This *needed* to work.

Leah stood and clicked the phone on.

It didn't light up.

She clicked a couple more times. *Nothing.* She turned off the water and dried the cell with a towel. Leaning back against the bathroom counter, Leah closed her eyes and let out a long, slow breath.

I will spend the rest of my life rescuing puppies and kittens and hugging trees. Thank you.

She double- and triple-checked that it was out for the count. Luckily, it showed no water damage behind the screen—it just wouldn't start up.

Leah left the bathroom, strolling into the kitchen. She held up the phone, shaking it playfully. "Forgetful in your old age? You took it to the bathroom."

Her mom was visibly perplexed. "I really don't remember taking it in there." She took the phone back and set it down on the kitchen table. "Grab some juice from the fridge? I think that's all we're missing."

Leah did as asked, then sat down at the table, trying not to stare at the phone. Her mom soon joined her, and they dug into their breakfast.

"You're all dressed and everything. Very cute, might I add," her mom said, scooping eggs onto her toast.

Leah smiled. "No shoplifting. No cheating, stealing, plundering, murdering, or anything else. *And* I got dressed early on a Saturday morning." She puckered her lips, nodding. "I see Ivy League colleges knocking down our door without me even applying."

Her mom chuckled. "My little princess—all reformed." She tilted her head. "All joking aside, I *am* proud of what I've seen in you lately."

Leah choked down the lump in her throat. "Thanks. I've been really trying."

Her mom frowned. "And I know you're not too happy with me for not letting you go to that wedding."

Leah pushed around the strawberries on her plate. "I'll survive. I know you're worried about me." She glanced up, raising an eyebrow. "Even if I think it's overkill."

She pointed her fork at Leah. "I'm a mom. Even normal human moms worry, you know." She picked up a strawberry. "But I was thinking about having a girls' day so you weren't just bumming around the house. Kick off spring break with something fun. Go out to lunch? Some shopping therapy?"

Leah winced. "Marcus and his grandparents are taking a later flight. He's coming over any minute to pick me up. We're just going to hang out for a little while."

"Hmm … when is his flight? We could do dinner instead?"

Leah's phone chimed.

<Be there in ten.>

"Yeah, dinner sounds great," she said while texting her reply. <See you in ten. Text when you're here. Mom = bad mood, best to stay out there.>

"Seriously? This piece of junk won't even turn on?"

Leah looked up. The dead phone refused to resurrect, despite multiple attempts by its owner. "Did it run out of battery?"

"No. I charge it every night." Her mom kept jamming the buttons. "I've had it for a while, anyway. I swear they make phones sturdier, but at the same time make them so you feel like you have to replace them every six months."

"Good thing you got the raise, right?"

"Yeah…"

Leah rushed to finish her breakfast and went to brush her teeth, opting to not have bacon breath for today's momentous occasion. Wanting to put on her best face, she included a coat of her favorite kissproof lipstick and stared at herself in the mirror. As she gazed into her own bright green eyes, her heart sank. She wasn't a great person. Not like Marcus. She wasn't even a good person. She was a liar, through and through.

Leah bit her lip, pushing past that truth. It wasn't the *only* truth. She was a caring person. She loved her mom, and even though this would hurt her, it was right. Leah deserved to see her homeland, to see the place her dad had ruled. He had shared her bright eyes. He would have wanted her to see what she could have been the heir of, before she became the heir of exile. The heir of nothing—nothing but pain.

She shook her head. She also cared for Marcus. He was just as elated as she was to have her attend the wedding and meet his family.

Leah's phone chimed.

<Here.>

She looked in the mirror one more time. *You can do this.*

Leah popped into her bedroom, pulling the letter to her mom out so it was visible on her bed. She turned off her phone, leaving it in a dresser drawer. The scene was set. Her mom had no reason to go in there for a while.

She left her room, finding her mom back in her own room. "I'm headed out." She gave her mom a hug. "Love you."

Her mom squeezed her tight. "Love you too, princess."

As Leah passed the doorway, her mom called out to her.

Leah turned back, itching to leave. "Yes?"

"You have your phone, right?"

"I'm a teenager. A teenager that knows her mom tracks her phone. I think that's a solid yes."

Her mom smiled. "I'm going out to get a new phone while you're gone. I'm trusting that you're following the rules and you're only going to Marcus's place? I'll text you once I have my new one set up."

Leah cocked her head. "I haven't been murdered while going to the movies or lunch with him yet, but yes, we'll stay at his place. His grandparents will be there. We'll be good."

"I'm trusting you this time," she emphasized again. "I love you."

Leah's heart dropped. Things would never be the same between them after this. "I love you too. Bye."

Chapter 22

LEAH LEFT THROUGH THE FRONT DOOR, making a dash to Marcus's van. She hopped in and gave him a quick smooch. "Let's go." She buckled up.

"Everything okay? Your mom's still cool about this?"

"Yeah, of course. I told her the flight was delayed. She's fine."

"Should I," he shrugged, "go thank her for letting you come?"

She furrowed her brow. "No. I told you—she's in a mood. Let's go before she changes her mind."

Marcus laughed. "Fair enough." He put the van in reverse. "You okay? Anxious or excited?"

She stopped biting her nails. "Both."

"Ditto." He backed out of the driveway, heading to his house.

"Just remember to follow my lead," he said. "And I'll try to whisper hints along the way for customs, and stuff we may not have gone over. In a lot of ways, it's really not all that foreign over there."

She bounced her knee. "Great. Will do. As for following the other person's lead..." She cleared her throat. "I've had a lot of time to consider possible problems. And it's not something to brag about, but we both know I'm a better liar ... so, let me take the lead on that kind of stuff, okay? I'll squeeze your hand twice or something if I need your backup."

"Maybe that's for the best." He threw her a quick glance. "It's okay what we're doing, right?"

She faced him. "I thought we agreed on this. That we both want it."

"Of course we do." He grinned. "We both want other things, too. But we're waiting on that."

Smiling, she grabbed his free hand. "We have the rest of our lives for that, right? Your brother's wedding only happens once."

He squeezed her hand. "You're right."

"Happens on occasion."

After a few minutes, they pulled into Marcus's driveway. He turned the van off. "Crap! We're going to need to swing by your place on the way there."

Her eyes grew wide. *No. No. No. No. No. We need to flee. Not return.* "Why?"

"You didn't bring a bag. You think your mom is going to believe you flew to another state for a week without so much as a carry-on?"

Her heart froze as she thought up an answer on the fly. "She didn't see me leave. She won't notice. And I'll email her from your phone at the cave to let her know I forgot it but it's too late and I'll just buy new stuff there."

His face twisted with hesitance. "Are you sure?"

His grandparents came out the front door, locking it behind them.

"Yeah. Let's not delay this any more than we have to. I think my heart might give out from anticipation if we wait any longer."

He chuckled. "Okay. If you think she'll buy it."

"It's better this way. Going back now would only raise suspicions with your grandparents."

"Ooh, you make a good point!" They unbuckled and crawled into the back seat.

Marcus's grandparents got in the van.

"Thanks so much for letting me ride with you guys," Leah said. "My mom wanted to take me but had to go into work."

"No problem at all," Samantha said.

Marcus scooched closer to Leah, slinging his arm around her. She rested her hand on his thigh, and he reciprocated with a wink.

"Of course, we offered to just swing by your place on the way," Brad said. "Would have been easier."

Marcus and Leah shared a glance, and he grinned. "What can I say?" Marcus asked. "Part of Marcus's foreign exchange year in the human world means getting to drive as much as possible."

Samantha and Brad reached over the center console, holding hands. "Plus, sweetheart, I believe we were young once," Samantha said. "Teenagers need a few minutes to *properly* greet the person they're dating without their fuddy-duddy old grandparents peeping in on them."

Leah laughed. "You're the coolest grandparents I know. You're not so bad."

"High praise. We'll take it," Samantha said as they got on the freeway. "But what about your own grandparents? Won't they be jealous if they find out you gave us that title?"

Leah hid her hurt. The grandparents who had been assassinated by their own daughter, Queen Kaylah? Or the ones in poor health who she'd yet to meet? "Fair enough. Coolest grandparents I'm *not* related to."

"Shouldn't have pointed it out to her," Brad said playfully. "I don't think they make a coffee mug for 'coolest grandparent I'm not related to.'"

Marcus leaned over, whispering in her ear, "You're going to fit right in."

They drove far from the city limits into a more forested area. Leah's heart skipped a beat when she saw the Green Lands cave building. A bit uncharacteristic-looking, it was disguised as a nature preserve, complete with a legitimate human-friendly set of displays. It was overpriced and in poor shape—the online reviews were atrocious. Good enough to keep away any smart human, but still available for the poor saps willing to fork over the money and contribute to the poor reviews after their visit.

The building was nestled into the side of a tall hill, providing covered parking for green-folk patrons, and disguising the cave within.

Marcus handed Leah his phone once they parked. "She needs to text her mom that we got here safe. If you guys want to head in, we'll be right behind you."

Samantha grinned. She'd caught them kissing and cuddling enough in her house to make plenty of assumptions. "Lock up and don't keep us waiting too long."

Marcus smiled as they left. "Decided to email about your forgotten luggage?"

"Yep." Leah turned the screen so he couldn't see it. <I love you. Look on my bed.> She sent it off. There was no going back. Her mom couldn't call Marcus or his grandparents—all of their phones would be left behind in the car. And their house would be empty. But she couldn't just leave her mom hanging, in case it took her forever to look in Leah's room. The moment she got a new phone synced, that message would come through and she would *freak*.

Leah turned off Marcus's phone, leaving it in the seatback pocket. "Is there anything else I should know?"

He rubbed his chin in thought. "Um … I feel like you've got the basics down. You've done great so far." He cringed. "Well, I guess one thing: my parents don't know I'm dating anyone. I, uh … didn't tell them about you over Christmas Break."

Nodding, she pressed her lips tight. "I get it. You weren't sure you wanted to date me anymore."

He kissed her on the forehead. "I was just mad. And I figured it was better to say nothing rather than something I'd regret." He gave her a half-smile. "But being away from you, and not being able to talk about you… I'm pretty sure all that did was make me want to see you more."

A soft smile grew on her face. "Then I'll take it."

He furrowed his brow. "One last thing—my dad. I suppose I should correct what Kara said. You can call him 'Sir.' Or 'Guillen.' But don't call him 'Sir Guillen.' He hates titles."

"Okay, I'll remember that." Skipping the copious kissing Samantha probably assumed they were doing, they headed in, hand in hand.

They left the parking garage down an elevator to the ground floor. Striding past the dumpy little displays of dusty, poorly labeled taxidermy animals and bugs, Marcus guided Leah down a winding hallway, past the bathrooms, and into a door marked 'Employees Only.' They crossed the back room and passed through another door marked 'Restricted Access.'

And then they were there.

Leah took in the crazy view. A well-lit, simply decorated lobby was occupied by a couple dozen people. The main focus at the end of the room: a cave opening twice as tall as Leah. On the left stood a pair of guards, reviewing passports and guiding guests through an abbreviated customs. No one packed baggage due to the inability to carry much when rifting, but there were still items restricted from the realm for the safety of its inhabitants—fauna and flora one might be able to tuck into a pocket. To the right of the cave, small groups of people trickled in, greeted by loved ones there to pick them up.

Near the door where Leah and Marcus had entered, his grandparents stood chatting with a tall man Leah recognized from pictures hanging on Marcus's grandparents' walls. Leah's heart raced. There really was no going back. Well … technically, the worry was mostly about *having* to go back. Either way, she and Marcus were at a pivotal point they'd been working toward for a month, and for Leah, really, it was five months of preparation. In some ways, her whole life.

Marcus ushered Leah forward with a supportive hand on her back.

"Hey, buddy!" His dad smiled, a brunet in his lower forties.

Marcus gave him a hug and stepped back, eyebrows lifted. "Buddy?"

His dad cleared his throat, lowering his voice. "Right. Not cool or manly." He faced Leah. "And this is the infamous girlfriend I heard about five whole minutes ago."

Leah smiled and extended a hand. "Leah. Nice to meet you, sir." She noted his pale blue eyes and a large scar on his temple. She had expected a politician to be bald or round, and less approachable, but he really hadn't changed much since the photos she'd seen had been taken.

He wore a charming smile. "Sir or Guillen. Just not Sir Guillen, please."

Leah grinned, and Marcus took her hand.

Guillen rubbed his hands together. "Hope you're ready for a lot of nonstop family chaos. We all ready to go?"

Marcus squeezed Leah's hand as she focused on hiding her panic. "Could we talk for just a second, Dad?" He glanced at his grandparents. "We shouldn't be long."

Samantha and Brad seemed confused, but obliged. "We'll be on the other side, waiting."

As they walked toward the cave entrance, Marcus took the lead. "Well, um… We kind of have a small problem."

Leah's grip tightened on his hand.

"What's that?" Guillen asked.

"Leah couldn't find her passport this morning."

Leah frowned, as did Guillen.

Marcus shifted his weight from one foot to another. "We were hoping you might be able to help with an exception."

Guillen sighed.

"I'm really sorry, sir. I hate to put you in this position. I thought I knew where it was, but then I went to grab it, and…" She laid on another frown. "I understand if you're not able to help."

"We were just really looking forward to Mom and everyone getting to meet her," Marcus added.

Guillen rubbed the back of his neck, wincing. "I'm sorry, Leah." He shook his head. "The wedding isn't for another couple of days. Would you be able to take some time to look for it and meet us before then?"

Marcus gripped Leah's hand even tighter.

"I'd say yes, but we just moved," she said. "And my mom is kind of horrible at organizing. It could be buried under dozens of unmarked boxes."

Guillen pursed his lips. "My in-laws said you're Ivy?"

She raised her free hand, extending a short vine tendril. "Yes, sir." She was definitely starting to sweat.

Guillen gave them both a disapproving look. "I don't appreciate being ambushed like this." He focused his gaze solely on Marcus. "You know I wouldn't normally make an exception of this kind."

Marcus cocked his head. "Everyone knows the security checks are mostly for human control in and out, anyway."

Guillen huffed, tucking his hands into his brown trousers. "We shouldn't expect to be above the law, Marcus."

Leah's stomach was in tight knots. *This isn't going to work.*

Marcus looked down. "It means a lot to me, to have her come."

Leah gnawed on her lower lip, wondering if she should just concede, not sure how else they could appeal to him. This part of it all was reliant on Marcus's guess that his dad would cave. She was an idiot for sending that last message to her mom. If she'd never done that, if their cave strategy didn't work out, she might have had a chance to take a cab home and hide the letter, and the truth, before she was discovered. But she'd burned up that lifeline.

Guillen focused on Leah, then glanced at their tight hand-holding. "I'd feel better if your parents had come here so I could meet them. Taking a minor through a rift with this kind of exception makes me extra uncomfortable."

"I only have a mom." Leah laid it on thick, fishing for any sympathy she could garner. How many times had she *not* gotten in trouble for shoplifting, after all, because she could tell a half-decent lie? "And she had to go into work today."

"Humans can fly anywhere in the United States at our age without parental approval," Marcus said.

Guillen pointed at Marcus, his face still disapproving. "Going between realms and between human states are very different things." He turned again to Leah. "How about we call your mother?"

Bingo. "She's not allowed to answer her phone at work, so it's turned off." She hoped and prayed he wouldn't still call and leave a voicemail that pointed to the Green Lands. Marcus had explained that a lot of green folk were cautious about leaving any sort of electronic or paper trail pointing to their true identities. "But she wrote me up a permission letter." Leah pulled out her second folded letter, forged that morning.

Guillen read the note. "She knows where you'll be? If she needs to come over and reach you?"

"Yes. Of course."

Guillen bobbed his head in reluctance. "One time only."

Marcus instantly beamed, releasing Leah's hand and giving his dad another hug. "Thank you. Thank you. Thank you!"

Leah relaxed her muscles, relieved at having cleared a giant hurdle. "Thank you so much, sir. We've been talking about coming to this wedding for weeks."

Marcus wrapped his arms around her, kissing her on the cheek.

Guillen smiled. "Let's not make your grandparents wait any longer."

The relief of his permission was quickly replaced by crushing anxiety about the most unpredictable part—her rifting skills were unproven. The trio walked over to the departure line, waiting for their turn. Leah played through her mind the many facts Marcus had relayed to her. She thought of the jade he and his dad had on their person at all times. His grandparents had gone through the rift with a different kind of jade, specifically made for humans.

Their short line progressed slowly as groups of people came through the incoming side at intervals. Departure and arrival coordinators staggered groups to avoid any type of backup or crowding in the rifting spaces.

Her heart beating harder and stomach tight, Leah paced her breathing as they approached the guard for their turn.

"Sir Guillen." The man nodded without asking for a passport.

Guillen nodded back politely, gesturing at Marcus. "My son."

Marcus pulled out his passport, a small green booklet. A decorative symbol had been embossed in gold on the front—A flower blossom, surrounded by the outline of an ivy leaf, resting on the background of a handprint. He presented it to the guard. The man did a quick look-over, handing it back. "You have your token?"

"Yes, sir." Marcus tucked the passport in his pocket, wrapping his arm around Leah again.

"Last in our party," Guillen said. "Name's Leah. Ivy. No passport. I'll be vouching for her under a diplomatic visa for the week."

'Diplomatic visa.' That sounds so formal, so official, so big.

The guard nodded, pulling a notebook from his podium. He clicked a pen, ready to take down details. "Last name?"

Leah swallowed. She and Marcus had created a bit of a cover for her, including what region she came from, picking an obscure rural one. But Marcus didn't suspect her mom of being in hiding—Leah couldn't lie in front of him about their names. She trusted her mom had changed her name as part of their cover in exile. "Edwards."

The man jotted it down. He asked for her parents' names, kingdom address, and duration of travel. Leah had already casually asked Marcus about common names in the Ivy Kingdom, and had picked a fake one for her dad that would fit in. Guillen provided his home address as where she could be found in the Green Lands for the duration of the visa. The man tore off a copy and handed it to Guillen. "She'll want that for the return." The man then looked at Leah. "Ivy? Vines, please."

She showed her vines, and he allowed them to pass.

"Thank you for your assistance," Guillen said as they moved into the cave entrance.

The final phase—the one that relied *solely* on Leah.

A few yards into the artificially lit cave, the small group met up with a couple chatting in front of them. They waited while a group of incoming rifters came through on the other side, separated by a rope divider. The couple recognized Guillen and greeted him, starting up a conversation about recent mundane policy changes.

Marcus held Leah from behind, whispering in her ear. "You'll do great. Just breathe."

Leah focused on the floor, and the warmth of his embrace, as she tried to calm her rapidly building nerves. She readied herself to observe the couple in front of them, hoping they were also Ivy so she could witness it for herself. It was so odd to not know—they could be anything.

Almost as much as Leah wanted to see an Ivy make a rift, she was curious to see a Seeder rift, and how rifts were made for Bomen and humans. Only Seeders could make cave rifts that others could go through.

The departure coordinator—the first person Leah *knew* to be a Seeder—informed the awaiting group that they were set to go. The first two people approached. Leah watched with bated breath.

The coordinator stepped forward, swiping their hand in the air, and a shimmering rift opened.

Two Bomen or humans, incapable of making their own rifts. Great... I don't get to watch anyone make an Ivy rift. Her chest rose and fell with anxiety.

"Should we go first, Dad?" Marcus asked.

"No. Leah's under my supervision now. I've got to make sure she gets through."

Leah appreciated Marcus's attempt to lessen her audience. Which they now had—a couple more people were now behind their group.

Marcus squeezed Leah tight one last time before releasing her.

As important as her ability to make this rift work was her ability to make it look like she'd been doing it for years. Her heart thumped in her chest as she gnawed on her lip. She stepped forward, spotting a line of jade embedded in the floor.

Focusing her mind, Leah thought of the words, the coordinates Marcus had given her. *Selen to Boloru.* She held her breath and extended a vine, exerting pressure, and trying to connect to the stone. *You've gotta do this on the first try.*

Feeling something there, she swiped her vine along the jade in the floor—not too fast, not too slow—the energy pulling with her. Somewhat hesitantly, but there. She dragged the energy from left to right, as if unzipping a seam between the worlds. As she finished her stroke, a surge of energy ran down the channel from her mind. A barely visible rift shimmered before her. Only *imagining* the look on Marcus's face, she retracted her vine and did her best to casually walk through.

Chapter 23

EVERY INCH OF LEAH'S SKIN was caressed with a warm hug as she strolled through the rift. Her view changed from the back of a cave, to a flash of warm light, to the natural daylight of a new room on the other side. She hadn't expected to be emotional, but she instantly fought tears. This was the biggest moment of her life. She drew a deep breath and tried to compose and orient herself.

"Please move on, ma'am," the receiving employee said.

"Oh. Yeah. Sorry." She rushed along.

This cave looked different, artificially carved out instead of naturally formed. Large skylights allowed daylight to fill the area. Leah was met by Samantha and Brad, and their warm smiles. She joined them, peering back into the cave. She beamed. Matching her gaze and smile was Marcus, approaching right before Guillen. Leah wanted to cry. She wanted to run up and kiss Marcus, and thank him, and gush over the experience. But she bottled it up. This was normal. She'd done this before, obviously.

He still gave her a quick hug, whispering in her ear, "You're amazing."

"Sorry about the wait," Guillen said to his in-laws. He turned to Leah, holding her folded temporary visa. "Don't lose this."

She nodded and happily tucked it into her pocket.

It would be a half-hour walk from the cave to Marcus's house. Electricity didn't work the same way in the Green Lands—something about the rich energy and its magnetic properties disrupted human technology like cars.

Marcus and Leah lingered at the back of the group, holding hands and whispering as Guillen got caught up with Samantha and Brad.

"Your first time. How was it?" Marcus asked.

"Terrifying!" Only now was her heart calming, her skin cooling.

He chuckled. "But you did it. I'm seriously proud of you." He kissed her on the cheek again.

She grinned, feeling the unique energy of the realm soaking into her body as Marcus had previously described. There was an instant sense of home to this place, something she'd never experienced in the human world. She understood why her mom and Cheryl longed for this place.

The charm of brick streets and stone buildings with lush plant growth added to the brightness of the day. A hummingbird buzzed nearby, drinking nectar from a creeping vine with orange and yellow flowers. It truly was a paradise here, a whole other world. Much of the flora and fauna mirrored what could be found in the human world, though some were uniquely present in this realm.

The air was warm, just right. The Green Lands existed in a perpetual state of spring.

Without warning, the truth collided with Leah's joy. She'd run away. She was hurting her mom. There would be consequences. She was jeopardizing her own safety.

Forget that. Enjoy it for what it is. Live in the moment. You're going to be fine.

"I know we're going to have tons of your family around, but we will be able to have some time alone, right?" she asked.

Marcus smirked. "Oh yeah. We'll make time."

She bit her lip. "Good."

He pulled her in tight, sliding a hand in the back pocket of her jeans as they walked along, whispering about the agenda of the week.

"Come on, now," Guillen called back to the straggling couple ten minutes into their walk. "If Marcus is going to surprise us with a girlfriend, I've got to get to know her."

Marcus slid his hand up to her waist, and they picked up the pace to join the adults.

Guillen asked how they'd met, for details about Leah and her family, her interests, hobbies. Leah shared partial truths she and Marcus had worked out.

As they approached the two-story home, Guillen gave a warning. "Take a deep breath now. Lots of chaos between now and the wedding, and you might not find the time to catch your breath along the way."

Leah smiled. Everything was so foreign. She still had so much to learn. And she wasn't the biggest fan of crowds, but there was something endearing about a large family after growing up with only her mom and an abusive fake aunt.

"I'll add to that," Marcus said. "Lots of huggers. You've been warned."

Leah laughed. "I'll try to survive."

They walked into the beautifully crafted home, which was constructed from a combination of raw wood and stone. Warm spices filled the air, as well as the chatter of a few people. From the entryway, they moved past a stairwell and a kitchen, into a large living room where a few people were talking. The home, like everything else Leah had seen so far, was a lot more primitive than what she was used to in the human world, but not quite as caveman as she'd feared.

A charming brunette in her late thirties smiled and hopped up at the sight of the new arrivals. Guillen reached her with a hug and a kiss. She hugged Samantha and Brad, then Marcus. She looked at

Leah, who was hanging back, fidgeting with her hands. "Looks like you picked up a spare along the way," she said playfully.

"Mom, this is Leah," Marcus said. "My girlfriend."

Leah stepped forward, extending a hand. "Nice to meet you, ma'am."

The woman grimaced. "I might be in denial, but I refuse to believe I'm old enough to be a ma'am, yet. Please call me Rachel." She shook Leah's hand.

"Okay." She examined Rachel, taking in her brown hair and eyes, but knowing her hair could glow yellow and her eyes green, with her Seeder powers. And under the skin on her arms, sharp green blades hid, a dormant weapon any Seeder with powers possessed.

The adults sat back down while Leah's focus turned to the younger adults.

"And the bride and groom," Marcus introduced them. His older brother, Tobias, had straight hair a darker brown than Marcus's, and a much wider nose. Camry—his bride—had chestnut hair that extended just past her shoulders, subtle freckles, and wore a light purple-pink lipstick. Leah shook their hands before she and Marcus sat down near the couple on a long couch.

"Well, now the wedding's *ruined*," Tobias drawled.

Camry raised her eyebrows. "Why's that?"

"The count's off. No one could have imagined Marcus being capable of bringing a date," Tobias razzed.

Marcus glared.

"None of that," Rachel warned.

"Be nice to him." Camry lightly punched her fiancé in the shoulder.

Marcus sat straighter, his arm still around Leah. "You wanna get started already?"

Tobias flashed a crooked grin. "Five rounds."

"You're on." Marcus stood.

Tobias got up. "Are you ready for Leah to see you cry?"

Marcus shook his head. "She knows how good I am." He squeezed Leah's shoulders. "I'll be right back."

"Boys!" Guillen raised his voice. "I think we need to talk about the big problem here."

The brothers exchanged a glance.

"I'm not even invited?" Guillen said, his hands in the air.

Tobias laughed. "You and Marcus can be a team, old man. You'll both need the help."

The boys left the room, turning down a hallway. "I do not," Marcus protested.

Guillen got up, releasing Rachel's hand. "But I might." He followed after them, his voice trailing off. "Old man?"

The room fell silent, just the three girls and Rachel's parents left behind. "I have no idea what just happened," Leah said, wide-eyed.

"A house ruled by boys." Rachel chuckled. "Welcome to my world."

Camry faced Leah. "You must not have brothers."

Leah shrugged. "Only child."

"I have brothers. No matter how old they get, they stay the same."

"What are they even doing?"

Camry nodded at the large glass windows in the living room providing a view of the enormous backyard. "You'll see."

"Do you guys want any tea?" Rachel offered her parents. "Leah?" They all accepted.

The steam curled up from Leah's cup as it cooled down enough to drink. She took in the room—the simple construction and décor. Natural. No human electronics. Unadulterated, basic, peaceful.

"Well, we certainly didn't get much of an introduction before they stormed off like that," Rachel said. "Tell us about yourself, Leah."

Leah glanced out the window at the boys. They lined up on the lawn near the window, all barefoot by now. They crouched in runner's stances and took off, racing down the yard. "Um … what do you want to know?"

"Anything and everything."

Leah introduced herself. Most of it was true. There were obvious omissions. Some things were outright lies—either to protect her and her mom's identities, or bending the truth as she'd agreed upon with Marcus to avoid any judgment on their characters as 'the wrong type' of Ivies that had left when the war was ending.

"You're not just there for a foreign exchange year?" Rachel asked.

"No. My mom and I move a lot. She likes variety. A little here, a little there," Leah said.

Rachel sipped her tea. "Well, that's nice. If you're able to travel and you like it, then why not?"

Leah gave her a polite smile. Marcus had explained that his Seeder mom couldn't leave the Green Lands anymore. She could still travel anywhere *within* the Green Lands, and was even capable of flying, but she was confined to the realm as a matured, fully-rooted female Seeder.

Leah glanced out the window again; the guys were on the fourth lap of their game. Once they ran to the end of the yard, they stopped and threw knives at a target, having to land them well, then ran a lap of the yard, retrieved the knives, and aimed at the targets again.

"Marcus said you guys have been able to do a lot of traveling around the realm, right?" Leah asked.

Rachel's face was kind and gracious. "Comes with the territory of our work, but yeah."

"That's really cool." Leah looked at the other people around the room. "I've been excited to get to meet Marcus's family. He talks about you guys often. I hope it's not too much trouble, me just showing up like this."

"Not at all," Rachel insisted. "Did you have arrangements for somewhere to stay, or will you be staying here?"

Leah pursed her lips. "We were planning on me staying here, if that's alright."

"Sounds good to me. Same rules as at my parents' place—no young couples in bedrooms."

Leah nodded. "Yes, ma'am."

Rachel lifted her eyebrows.

Leah smiled. "Yes, Rachel."

"Speaking of," Samantha said, "where would you like us to stay?"

"Mmm." Rachel's cup clinked as she set it down. "We just finished the upgrades on the guest house. Let me show you." The three got up. Before leaving down the hall, Rachel turned to Leah. "Whenever you're hungry, feel free to raid the kitchen. I've got all sorts of platters in the cooler and on the counter. I know the time change on rifting days can be a bit odd, so we'll probably just graze here and there today."

"Okay. Thank you."

Leah wrung her hands as the group left, staring out the window. The boys approached the house at a sprint, until Tobias tripped Marcus and they started to wrestle. She grimaced. "Are they going to be okay?"

Camry chuckled. "Yes. And if they break an arm, it's mighty handy having a Seeder for a mom."

Leah had forgotten that part of Rachel's powers—healing. She had a million questions to ask the woman, but couldn't really go there, needing to pretend Rachel *wasn't* the first Seeder she'd really ever interacted with. "Right. Yeah. This is kind of weird for me. First time meeting a boyfriend's parents so formally."

Camry waved a hand dismissively. "Don't be nervous on account of their positions or connections. They're really down to earth. I think you'll fit right in."

"Thanks." Leah realized she might be able to relate to Camry more than perhaps anyone else here. Camry was human. "How did it feel for you, when you found out about the Green Lands and everything? You met in the human world when Tobias was an exchange student, right?"

"Yeah. It was a bit of a shock. I kind of didn't really believe him until he brought me here. You know, Bomen can't exactly show the extra stuff like the vines to prove they have green-folk heritage." She sighed, playing with her engagement ring. "They really welcomed me. My personal token was made with Rachel's blood. It's a pretty special sacrifice, you know? She couldn't come meet me. I couldn't come here to meet her. But she knew how much Toby loved me, so they went through the process of having it made up."

Leah smiled, recalling a conversation she'd had with Tanner ages ago. Allowing humans in posed a risk to green folk. But if it was the right humans, like Camry, maybe it wasn't so bad. "She sounds pretty awesome for a Seeder."

Camry cocked her head. "I don't know about awesome for a *Seeder*, but awesome for a mother-in-law."

"Have you met many Seeders?"

Camry shrugged. "Some of her family, employees at royal functions and at caves, really."

So, not many… She also remembered something about Marcus's parents choosing to live in the Ivy Kingdom because the Seeder nation wasn't safe for Bomen. Exceptions like Rachel obviously existed, but any group of people that were hostile toward people like Marcus, and his dad and brother, weren't the type she could ever associate with. She hid a frown. Her dad had understood that. He'd tried to stop the war with the Seeders. *Without* giving in to their demands like his murderous sister.

That's not why you came here. Enjoy the moment.

The brothers came bursting into the room from the hallway they'd originally left down. Tobias stood in front of Camry, arms wide open. "My love! A hug for the victor?"

She giggled at his mud-smeared shirt and face. "Not a chance. Go clean up."

A set of hands rested on Leah's shoulders, and she looked up at a less muddy but very sweaty Marcus. "Victor?" he scoffed. "You tripped me!"

Tobias feigned innocence. "I don't know what you're talking about. I'd love for an impartial judge to decide." He gestured to the girls. "And I don't think they're going to help."

"Toby cheated," Camry coolly declared.

Tobias's jaw dropped as he gasped. "My heart!"

She snickered. "Go get cleaned up, and we'll see what we can do about fixing that heart of yours."

Rachel returned, sitting back in her original chair. "Who won?"

Guillen came in, breathing hard and clutching his side. "I'm pretty sure I did." He plopped down next to his wife.

"Sure, Dad. Whatever you want to believe," Marcus said. He squeezed Leah's shoulders. "I'm going to hop in the other shower if you're alright out here."

She looked back up. "Yes, please."

Marcus took the stairs near the entrance. Guillen slumped in his chair, facing his wife. "I think he might have had a point, calling me an old man."

Rachel grinned. "Yeah. I think I saw another white hair the other day."

He put a hand over his heart. "Et tu?"

Rachel playfully poked his shoulder. "Maybe you should shower too."

Guillen pulled himself up with some grunts and groans, leaving the three girls alone.

"So, Leah," Rachel said. "Let's talk clothes and shopping."

Chapter 24

LEAH RAISED HER EYEBROWS. "Are you trying to tell me I can't wear these clothes for the whole week, wedding included? I've always worn human t-shirts and jeans to important events."

Rachel picked up on her sarcasm, chuckling. "It might be frowned on."

"Leah can use some of my visiting clothes for regular days," Camry said. "You guys still have them, right?"

"Of course," Rachel said, then turned her focus back to Leah. "And as for your dress, we could carve out some time tonight, or there are a couple of openings tomorrow."

Leah's schedule was pretty much a blank slate. "Um … whatever works for you guys. It's not like I have a set schedule."

Rachel bobbed her head. "Let's say tomorrow morning?"

"Deal. I didn't bring any Ivy money on this trip, so we'll need to exchange my human money before we go shopping." Leah had brought the rest of her savings, hoping it was enough.

"Don't stress about it. My treat."

"Thank you, but I'd like to take care of it myself," Leah said.

Rachel took a deep breath, smiling. "We'll see tomorrow."

"Do you want to take a look and see if my stuff will fit you?" Camry offered.

"Sure."

"In the same room, Rachel?" Camry asked.

"Yes. And we'll have Leah stay in that room."

Leah followed Camry down the hallway, past a bathroom and patio door. At the end, they took a right and opened a door to the small guest bedroom.

"I've stayed here *many* nights on visits," Camry mused, opening a small chest. She knelt down, pulling out some clothes. "They're all green-folk style, but I think they're comfy and cute."

The simpler cuts with intricate designs mirrored the styles Leah had seen worn by most of the people they'd passed that day. Everything was made of natural fibers. "I really appreciate it. I think those should work fine. You're sure you don't need them?"

Camry flashed her a guilty look. "I might have enjoyed too many shopping trips on previous visits. I already have a stash at the inn my parents and I are staying at." She took the clothes and put them back in the chest. "Obviously, we can pick you up some underthings of your own tomorrow morning, too." She stood back up. "That's the nice thing about prices here. In a society where you can't take much with you when you travel, they make it affordable to rent or purchase the necessities." She shook her head. "Of course, you already know that." Blushing, she added, "You're from here. I keep forgetting that."

"No worries." Leah took in the room. It was simply but tastefully decorated. A blue tatted curtain draped across the window. A small vanity with an ornate oval mirror was pushed up against one wall. Aside from the closet and chest, the only other thing in the room was the bed. On the vanity sat a large ceramic bowl; Leah decided to empty her pockets of the things she'd stuffed in there earlier that morning.

She pulled out her human currency, placing it at the bottom of the dish. In the same pocket was the lipstick she'd brought.

Camry laughed, pulling out a tube of her own. "I do the same thing. Gotta bring the trusty stuff with you."

Leah smiled. She reached into her other pocket, taking out the temporary visa and her forged letter from her mom. Falling out of her pocket and onto the ground was a single condom packet. Her eyes grew wide. She snatched it up and shoved it under the pillow, then placed the papers on the top of the bowl. She faced Camry, mortified.

Camry grinned, eyebrows raised. "So, you and Marcus are pretty serious."

Leah sat on the bed, biting her lip. "No. Well, I mean… We haven't … yet. Please don't tell anyone about that."

Camry shrugged. "I'm not here to judge or lecture or tattle. Marcus is a good kid, a smart kid. I don't know you that well, but you seem smart too." She crossed her arms. "If you were Seeders, you'd likely already be considered adults."

Leah almost made a snide remark about that having to be the reason they had so many kids—because they started so young—until she remembered they actually *didn't* have children super young and had no choice as to how many they had, if they chose to have them at all. Twenty-four kids or none—Seeders were a weird bunch. *You really need to shut up, and not comment or ask questions that will give away that you're a noob!*

"Right. Well…" Leah fidgeted with her hands. "I hope it's not weird that I'm crashing your wedding."

Camry waved her hand dismissively. "No. Definitely not. Things are just different here. I've accepted that. It's … not exactly what I've grown up with in the human world, you know? The family structure, a kingdom, all of it. Heck, I had to buy the dress here." She frowned. "And only my parents are able to come to the ceremony."

Leah mirrored her frown. "None of your siblings, other family?"

Camry wrinkled her nose. "You know the laws. None of the rest of them are in on the secret." Her smile recovered. "But then again, how many girls get to have two weddings? When we return, we'll have a full one there, too. And they're both equal in my eyes."

Leah nodded. She wanted to ask if they were being forced to live in the human world after the wedding, or if they just didn't prefer being here with the current state of affairs. But again, she realized she might give away some naïveté.

"Actually, no pressure…" Camry perched on the wooden chest. "How would you feel about being my maid of honor? I have local bridesmaids, but I never picked a maid of honor for this wedding, and Marcus is the best man."

Leah swallowed hard. "You're sure? I've never done it before. What would I have to do?"

Camry leaned back against the wall. "Really not a big deal. Hold a bouquet. Walk up the aisle with Marcus. It's a bit of a human-Ivy combo theme on how we're doing things. It's not like you have to give a speech or anything crazy."

Leah considered the request.

"Hey, Cam." Marcus poked his head in.

Leah got up, greeting him at the door with a hug. She then surveyed him; it was so odd seeing him in more traditional Ivy garb. His hair was extra curly, still wet from the shower.

Camry stood. "Is Toby out of the shower too?"

"Yeah."

She glanced at Leah. "No pressure. Just let me know?"

"You know what? Why not. I'd be honored."

Marcus wrapped his arms around Leah's midriff, squeezing her tight and kissing her cheek. "What's that?"

"I guess I'm going to be the maid of honor."

"Thanks, Cam," he said with a soft smile in his voice.

"No. Thank you," she said.

Marcus pulled Leah backward into the hallway so Camry could exit in search of Tobias. Once Camry was out of sight, Marcus left a trail of kisses down Leah's neck, making her giggle. She turned around with a smile as he held her hips.

"I have been informed that I could work on my manners and not abandon you like I did earlier. Sorry." He pouted. "And that I should give you a tour of the grounds as a proper gentleman."

She couldn't resist digging her fingers into his curly locks. "I really didn't mind. And I don't always want you to be a proper gentleman with me."

He smirked. "Either way, let me show you around."

Marcus gave Leah a tour of the house. It was an odd configuration, but she liked the unique layout. As strange as anything else she'd seen were the bathrooms and kitchen. They were primitive by her usual standards, but familiar enough that they wouldn't be too hard to get used to. Instead of normal faucets, they used water pumps. Replacing light bulbs, they used skylights for daytime and candles for the nights. The occasional clear-quartz and jade lightkeeper hung on the wall, but only Rachel could use those; only Seeders could channel the energy that made those devices work.

In the kitchen, they used an old-fashioned coal stove for cooking, and without electricity, had to access underground cellars for cool storage.

Marcus's bedroom was upstairs; Leah only got a brief sneak peek from the doorway. It was pretty tidy for a teenage guy's room, compared to what she'd seen before. A nature painting hung on the wall, as well as pictures of family.

Heading out into the backyard, he showed her the guesthouse, a swimming pond, a large garden, and a water pump. He stopped at a flower bed and pointed out a patch of fire-orange flowers. "This is one of the plants that aren't found anywhere else but the Green Lands. They're named Guenjalis, and they're actually related to Seeders."

Arching an eyebrow, Leah studied the flower. "*Related* to Seeders? Is that your mom's great uncle or something?"

He laughed. "I told you before—they're a floral race. In exchange for their support in the war, the queen helped them with research, and they discovered there's some kind of symbiotic relationship between Seeders and this flower."

Nodding, Leah tried to smile and act intrigued. She didn't want any more history lessons. No more mentions of the queen and what she'd done—betraying her own people by giving in to Seeder demands and slaying Leah's father.

Marcus led her to one last thing on the grounds—a large tree house.

"Let's take a look," he said, climbing up the ladder first.

Leah followed, daring to be free enough to use her vines along with her hands to pull herself up. They looked out over the property, and Leah felt more at peace. It was vibrant and well-cared for.

Marcus sat down, and Leah cuddled up on his lap.

"Mmm, some *us* time." She smiled. "You didn't use up all your energy playing earlier, did you?"

"I'll *always* save some energy for time with you." He gazed into her eyes. "How are you liking it so far?"

Her heart was full. For him. For this place. "I love it. Your family's awesome. The energy here is awesome. You have no idea how much this means to me."

He gave her a contented smile. "You have no idea how much *you* mean to me." He stole a quick peck on the lips. "Sounds like you're getting along well with Cam."

She nodded. "I really like her. I wish we had a girl like her in the club." She leaned into him. "Do you and your brother get along?"

"Yeah. We get along fine. We tease. We fight. Normal sibling stuff. He was older than I was when we were adopted, so I think he might remember some stuff, and he can get kinda sensitive. But it's the typical older kid thinking the younger one gets whatever they want, and the younger one getting stricter rules because of mistakes made by the older one. You know how it goes."

"Actually, I don't," she said wistfully.

"Right. Sorry… Do you wish you had siblings? That your mom had remarried?"

"Maybe? I guess I don't know about siblings. It's always kinda been us against the world, and I love that part of us. Even when I screwed up, we were a team. But she deserves to be happy; she just can't get over my dad." The hurt dug deeper with every mention of him. "But he was a great man that died too young. I guess I can't blame her."

Marcus held her tight. "I'm sorry."

"Thanks." She hesitated, considering how beautiful and peaceful everything had been thus far in the Ivy Kingdom. They weren't exactly walking through the slums that likely covered the map under a tyrant's rule. "Are your parents ... well-off?"

"We're ... comfortable," he answered, as though he *hadn't* been comfortable with the question.

She stroked the creases in the sleeve of his shirt. "That probably came off all wrong. I guess I just mean that I'm not sure what's considered a normal home or neighborhood here. Obviously, your parents have important positions, so it makes sense they would be." She smiled. "Your mom is taking me dress shopping tomorrow. She told me she wanted to pay for it. It didn't seem like she's going to take 'no' for an answer."

He kissed her on the cheek. "Let her buy it."

Leah shifted to better look at him. "I can handle it."

He grinned. "You won't win this one. You don't know how stubborn she is."

Leah shrugged, ready to take on the challenge. "I guess we'll see."

He chuckled. "Yeah. *You'll* see."

She stuck out her tongue.

"Oh, really?" He stole a kiss. And then another, and another.

Leah happily, gladly, giddily enjoyed some alone time with him after a phenomenal adventure, only possible thanks to him.

After what could have been a mere minute, or a healthy hour, Leah pulled back, getting lost in his warm brown eyes. Her heart was swelling. Nothing in her life compared to this experience. Nothing. She shifted, straddling him.

He smiled, keeping eye contact.

"I…" she started. Somewhere in her heart, she had to let it out. But fear choked her back.

Leah glanced down, rubbing the linen fabric of Marcus's shirt. "I, um…" She'd never said those three words to anyone but her mom.

After another moment of hesitation, Marcus spoke up. "You know, the last time we were in this position, *I* was the one incapable of forming complete sentences."

He wore another handsome grin, and she blushed.

"Hey, Marcus! Stop making out!" Tobias called from below.

Leah slapped a hand to her mouth, stifling a laugh.

Marcus nudged her off of his lap. He leaned over, looking out the entryway. "We're capable of holding conversations, you know."

"Don't lie. We all know teenagers only go up to tree houses to make out," Tobias said.

Camry's voice came next. "Be nice. Don't pretend we didn't do the exact same thing."

"You're proving my point."

"What do you want?" Marcus scowled.

"We're heading out for the rest of the day," Tobias said.

"Okay. Cool. Thanks for letting us know," Marcus said. "Anything else?"

"I thought … you know … I'd remind you that a dozen or more people will be in and out of the house over the next couple of days. And they'll all know you're out here swapping spit with your girlfriend if you're up there all the time hiding away."

Leah couldn't stand it any longer. She stood up and leaned against the railing, grinning without an ounce of shame. "You're right. And I'd give it four out of five stars for a make-out spot. It could use some pillows to be more comfortable."

Tobias glanced from her to Marcus. His face barely cracked a smile as he pointed to Leah. "I like this one. She's honest."

Marcus rolled his eyes. "Glad you approve. See you tomorrow."

Camry smirked knowingly and grabbed Tobias's arm, nudging him along. "Later, Leah."

Marcus and Leah popped back into their hiding place with a chuckle and a couple more stolen kisses.

"I suppose he's right. I *did* say I was going to show you off, and I can't do much of that from up here."

She rubbed his hand. "True. Before we head out, can we go over more of the details for this week? We spent so much time preparing to get here, but I'm starting to get more nervous about what it's all going to look like."

They discussed the rest of that day's agenda. Mostly visiting—family and family friends dropping by in preparation. Marcus might see if some of his friends in the area were free and he could introduce them. The next day, Leah would shop with Rachel, and then it was more family. They would want to be available for any last-minute tasks they might be asked to do as maid of honor and best man.

And then it was the wedding day. A close family breakfast in the morning, but a large luncheon in the early afternoon. The official ceremony would begin at dusk, followed by a reception. The rest of the week would be a lot more casual and laid back.

"I'm still nervous about being around royalty. When will we be around them?"

Marcus puckered his lips. "Royalty is a broad spectrum. But if you're talking about the queen and king … they'll be at the luncheon, and obviously the wedding. She's officiating it."

Leah sat straighter, surprised. "Officiating it? Not just a guest?"

He grabbed a twig and poked at the tree house floor. "Yep. And then the queen- and king-in-waiting will be at both of those events, too."

She furrowed her brow. "What are a queen- and king-in-waiting? Like, their kids?" It was obvious by now that Marcus wasn't a prince in hiding or anything like that, just a politician's son. She'd initially made sure to rule out the possibility that Marcus could be some unknown cousin, wanting to avoid a creepy romantic connection with her big plan. But Tanner had confirmed Leah didn't have cousins on her dad's side. And her mom didn't come from royal lineage.

Marcus shook his head. "No. Next in line. They're actually set to officially take over in just over a month." Marcus cleared his throat. "The queen-in-waiting is the current queen's cousin."

Leah's mind ran a mile a minute at the news. "Why? Are the current ones getting kicked out?"

He laughed. "No. Why would you think that?"

"You know the replacements? Are they good people?"

He gave her knee a squeeze. "They're the best kind. I'll introduce you."

That at least gave Leah some comfort. But less than a month left with Queen Kaylah being in her position… "What are the current ones doing after they're replaced?"

"Dunno. I suppose they're going to take a nice long vacation."

Leah's very core ached, her patchwork reality of a life unraveling. The queen had murdered Leah's dad for the power, just to turn around and give it all away seventeen years later? Queen Kaylah wasn't even that old! And she was stepping down to go on a 'nice long vacation'? *Nothing like murder and betrayal to reap the benefits of a cozy early retirement.* "I'm nervous I'll do or say the wrong thing. Will there be a ton of guards? I don't want to get in trouble."

He intertwined their fingers. "Don't stress it. I mean, don't lunge at them, but they're pretty approachable. And yeah, there'll be guards to make sure everyone's safe. Just pretend it's a normal wedding."

She nodded, trying to conceal her concerns. Could she really be in the presence of that woman? Be within mere feet of her during the ceremony? Or was the universe trying to tell her something about her original plan?

Chapter 25

MARCUS AND LEAH WENT BACK inside the house, greeted by visitors from all parts of the Green Lands. Many more would gather in Capital City territory on the day of the wedding, which would be a short cave trip away from where Marcus lived.

For the rest of the evening, they socialized with visitors, and Marcus took Leah around the neighborhood, introducing her to friends. She tried her best to enjoy it, but old pangs of hurt and rage began to fester. How could she be near that woman—the queen? Leah was finally witnessing the smallest inkling of the life she and her mom could have enjoyed—full of family, friends, the warmth of the Green Lands.

She went to bed with a heavy heart, trying to override her frustration. She was there for the experience, for the wedding, for Marcus. But this might be the only chance she may ever have to be here. What mattered most?

The next morning, Leah had an early wake-up call. It would be just her and Rachel walking to a dress shop. They shared pleasant conversation. Leah got to hear all sorts of stories about Marcus growing up. She tried to hide the pain, hearing happy stories of a whole family. The queen had taken that from her.

With the first shop in view, Rachel finished another story, this time about what it was like sending both of her boys off to the human world for their foreign exchange years. "You know, you look kind of familiar, Leah."

Leah stiffened. "Really? I don't have any family in the area. I've never actually been this far south..." No one in this realm should recognize her. She hadn't even been born when her mom fled. She *did* look a lot like her parents, but that was actually fairly uncommon for green folk. Seeder families looked nothing alike, something about their genetic makeup. Most Ivy children bore a faint resemblance to their parents, but it also depended on which ancient clan they descended from. In very rare instances, Ivies known as 'whispers' were born, the trait seemingly random. They had exceptional gifts, and their offspring tended to share a closer resemblance.

Marcus and Leah had discussed all of that a while ago when talking about Ivy powers. Leah had wondered if one or both of her parents had the special gift, but there was no way of knowing, and no way to safely bring it up with her mom.

Rachel shrugged. "I'm sure I've just seen your doppelganger somewhere."

At the first shop, they picked up the basic necessities Leah needed for the rest of the week. Leah fought off her old demons, the itch to take a memento from the shelves. Perhaps her mom had been right about that point, that Leah's shoplifting habit was partially connected to her stress level.

The second destination was a dress shop, filled with a wide variety of styles and colors. A third of the store was solely dedicated to rentals. Rachel made casual references about how impractical it was to go by foot and pack much when traveling in the Green Lands. No beasts of burden resided here, no electronics worked. And the few steam engine trains they utilized were always overcrowded. And rifting constraints didn't allow more than what you could easily have on your person—carrying more volume that wasn't an actual part of you was either draining, or impossible.

"That works fine for me. I can afford a rental," Leah said.

Rachel steered her toward the new dresses. "No. Let's get you something of your own. Like I said, my treat."

Leah frowned, staring at the dresses. They didn't even matter.

"It's not hard to see how much you two like each other." Rachel smiled softly. "I'd imagine we might see you back here for a visit later? We wouldn't mind storing the dress for a future visit."

Leah hugged herself. "I'd still rather buy it myself."

"It's not charity, you know." Rachel drew a pensive breath. "My husband and I adopted two boys, and I love them to death. But once Camry came along, I realized how fun it could be to have a daughter. We just met—I get it. I'm not your mom. But let me treat you, okay? It would be a favor to me."

The more Rachel talked, the less Leah wanted to allow her to buy the dress. Leah didn't deserve it. Not with the dark thoughts running through her mind. A heaviness had set in when Rachel mentioned keeping the dress for Leah. That was the problem—Leah would never be back. She'd never get a special visa like this again. She could never qualify for a passport. She didn't know when or if she could ever learn to tree rift to come back. This might be Leah's first, last, and *only* visit to the Green Lands.

Rachel stood there, waiting for an answer.

Arguing over who bought the stupid dress was the least of Leah's concerns. "Okay."

Rachel's smile brightened. "Great! Since you're the maid of honor, we'll want to pay attention to the color scheme. Something in light green or lavender."

Leah scanned the dresses in a daze. A dress didn't matter. Or maybe she should take care to pick out a nice one, with this being her only shot here. She leaned toward a cute simple one with thin straps until she looked past it at a rack mounted on the shop wall. Long sleeves.

There hung a floor-length, lacy lavender dress with long sleeves. "Is that too fancy?" she asked, pointing at it.

"Nope. Anything in here would work."

Leah took the dress into a changing room. It hugged her just right, with a beautiful scoop neck. She tugged at the sleeves. It was crazy, absolutely crazy. *What are you thinking?* She looked at herself in the mirror. Her dad's eyes looked back at her, framed by her mom's nose and hair. *Who are you? What's your past? Nothing worthwhile. She stole that from you. What's your future? Nothing worthwhile. She stole that from you.*

Her eyes filled with tears. Her mom was home, hiding in exile. Terrified, panicked, livid. Alone. Leah was selfish for leaving. *But not as selfish as the queen.* What could Leah's legacy ever be? What would the man with matching eyes tell her if he were there today? He had died for what he believed in. Could Leah do the same?

Leah sniffled and wiped away her tears. She wasn't committing to anything. It was just a dress. A dress with sleeves.

The kind she might be able to use to help conceal a weapon.

Leah exited the dressing room with dry eyes, the dress draped over her arm. "Let's get this one."

Each holding a bag of purchases, they hit the road to walk back home. "You okay?" Rachel asked.

"Yeah. I guess I'm just nervous about meeting the queen for the first time." She felt like a broken record, but it was the easiest and vaguest truth to tell.

Rachel slung her arm around Leah. "Don't be. She doesn't bite."

No. But she murders to get what she wants.

"Yeah. I think I'm also just tired. Must not have slept well last night."

"I know that feeling all too well. And weddings are crazy. Especially with *our* family. But no one would judge you if you snuck a nap sometime today."

Leah smiled. "Thanks. Maybe I will."

***

Leah took Rachel's advice to lie down. She didn't need sleep as much as she needed clarity of mind. Her mom's comments cycled through her mind. *'Sometimes you have to know when to give up hope.' 'You and I—we don't belong anywhere!'*

Why had Leah even come? She was hurting her mom for what? A guy? A vacation? Her mom didn't deserve this. *What is your life really worth? Where do you really fit in? You're here talking about buying dresses and BSing your way through a week of fun instead of trying to get justice and honoring your dad's memory.* Maybe Cheryl was right about Leah: she was a disgrace. She'd never amount to anything.

The more she thought of her mom, the more Leah's heart hurt. What had Leah really ever done to make her mom proud? Her mom wasn't stupid, either. Could Leah spend the rest of her life keeping this visit a secret? Did her mom *already* know she was in the Green Lands, instead of in Detroit? Even if she didn't know that part of it, her mom *absolutely* knew Leah had run away. For a week. With her boyfriend. *My life as I know it is over.*

Leah knew, without a shred of doubt, that the moment she came home, they were moving. The boxes were probably already half-packed. No more Garden Club, or green-folk lessons. No vine training. No Marcus.

She fought tears unsuccessfully, each drop imbued with pain as it soaked into the cream pillowcase. When she returned home, she was going to lose Marcus. Trying to take out the queen—and in the process ruining his brother's wedding—she was going to lose Marcus. Either way, she was going to lose him.

I love him.

We're only teenagers. It's not love. And even if it was, how could it last? That's stupid. You've had a good go at it, but just like every other relationship, it has an expiration date.

The only constant had been her mom's love. Other than that, and more important than any other relationship in Leah's life, was the memory of her dad and his lost potential. His people would never see his dreams come to fruition. His wife would never have her husband back. Leah would never know her dad's love. Or even her grandparents' love. Or aunts, uncles, cousins. Yes, she liked Marcus's family. But compared to her own, what did she really owe them?

The queen deserves to die. It's not a question of if I'm crazy *enough to do it. It's a question of whether or not I'm* brave *enough to do it.*

Leah took a shaky breath and wiped away her tears. It wasn't a question of whether she could live with such a serious decision. Perhaps the question she should have been asking the whole time was whether she could live with herself if she *didn't* take action. Maybe her life had been preserved in the first place for this event. And how could she really deny it when it had fallen right into her lap?

A soft tap sounded on Leah's bedroom door. It slowly opened. "Leah?" Marcus whispered.

The decision isn't final until I'm there. Leah quickly and subtly wiped up any remaining tears, then sat up. "Hey." She forced a smile.

"You okay?" he asked, peeking his head in.

"Why wouldn't I be?" She got up, reaching for him in the hallway and soaking in a long warm hug.

"Just worried since you've been in there so long," he said.

She smiled a little more genuinely. "Maybe just overwhelmed. You know how much I *love* hanging out with tons of people. The girl that has a flock of friends at school."

He chuckled. "Fair enough. Want to come see something fun?"

Enjoy him while you have him. You're going to lose him either way. She grabbed his hand. "Lead the way."

Marcus led her down the lane from their property to a little stone cottage a mile away.

"And what is this?"

He gestured at the cottage with wide arms. "A wedding gift."

"That's … quite a gift."

"Let's take a look." Marcus led her around to the back, pulling a key from its hiding place under a large rock. They stepped inside the quaint one-bedroom setup, which was fully furnished.

"This whole place is really a wedding gift?" she asked.

"Yep. That way when they come to visit, they always have a place they can call home."

A place to call home. A place in each world to call home. And I don't belong anywhere.

"That's really cool," she said.

"Want to see our gift to them?"

"Who is 'our'?"

"From you and me. Hope you're okay with it. My dad and I went to the market while you were out with my mom." He pulled her to the front entrance. "This painting." He rocked his head back and forth. "Do you like it? Maybe I should have waited."

She wore a melancholy smile, taking in the colorful brushstrokes of an abstract painting. It was framed in a striking striped wooden frame that was delicately hand-carved. "It's beautiful."

"Wanna sit down for a while?" he asked.

"Sure."

He claimed one end of a couch, and Leah lay on her side, her head in his lap.

"What's wrong?" he asked.

"Nothing's wrong."

He sweetly moved her hair from the side of her face. "I would definitely disagree."

Marcus was kind, and loving, and smart. What was Leah? A liar. A thief. A subpar person. She was going to lose him anyway, and she'd never deserved him in the first place.

"Just … I guess a little jealous of your family." She rolled over, looking up at him. "You have both parents, and lots of grandparents, and aunts, uncles, cousins. Everything. I have my mom."

He frowned. "I'm sorry." He played with her hair, smiling. "They'd happily adopt you. The more the merrier."

She flashed a half-hearted smile. "I'd love a family like this. They're all really nice."

"You have a good relationship with your mom, though, right?"

She nodded, gazing into his eyes. "What's the hardest thing you've ever had to do?"

He pursed his lips. "I can admit I've had an easier life than some. But I guess it's just … trying to figure out who I am. Or at least who I want to be." He shrugged. "But maybe that could be said of every teenager. What about you?"

She pondered her own question. The last several months had been some of the hardest of her life, and also the greatest. Her choices had never mattered as much as they did right now. "I agree with the way you worded it. Who I am. Who I'll be. It's tough. And we don't all have the same journey."

Was there any chance he could ever understand hers? What if she just told him her secret? If anyone could understand, Marcus would, right?

It wasn't that simple. It was *far* from simple. His parents worked for the woman who had murdered Leah's dad. Having met the lot of them, Leah had tried to ignore one important truth. It wasn't like anyone had gushed about the queen like Tanner had, but it certainly didn't seem like they were plotting something against her either.

Leah was alone. No one in either world could fathom how this felt. She trusted Marcus with everything, except maybe this truth. With her and her mom's lives in the balance… He might overreact and turn them in, for all she knew.

After some silence, Marcus attempted to coax Leah from her somber mood. "If you could pick, which realm would you live in, now that you've been here? You'll be able to choose once you're eighteen, and your mom would have to accept it if you came here and only visited there sometimes." He winked. "Like I'll visit you until you turn eighteen."

I'll never have that choice. "I like it here." She looked away, considering his pronouncement. If she assassinated the queen at his brother's wedding, they were done. She probably wouldn't even survive the attempt. Either way, they were done—he wouldn't be visiting. If she cowered from the task, she'd go home, and her mom would move them and deny contact—he wouldn't be visiting. But if she warned him ahead of time that she would be moving … he'd still come see her in the human world, and they'd find a way to make it work, right? "What about you? Do you want to live in the human world, or here?"

"Guess that depends a lot on who I'm with at the time." He grinned. "Tobias moving there for Cam makes more sense with her being human. I think I'd have a harder time moving away from family. But I'd be willing to, under the right circumstances."

She had a glimmer of hope. Maybe she'd been thinking about this all wrong. He'd be willing to come see her, to be with her. But after tasting the energy of the Green Lands, could she so easily give it up? And in reality, how long would he stay with her? He hated her lies. More would come out eventually. It was inevitable. And what would happen the next time she screwed up? What if her shoplifting habit picked back up when she got stressed? She'd already been sorely tempted just earlier that day.

I'm going to lose him one way or another.

"Do you think your parents are proud of you?" she asked.

"I hope so. I think so…"

Her mom wasn't. Her dad wouldn't be. And she'd done nothing to earn their pride. But maybe she could. She could make a difference, make a statement, have a purpose more grand and noble than a regular teenage human could even fathom. After all, she wasn't regular, and she wasn't human.

***

Leah and Marcus didn't linger long at the cottage. After heading back to his house, it was more of the same—meeting new people, visiting and helping with the wedding preparations. Leah did her best to appear as though her mind weren't running a marathon. As though she wasn't contemplating the unthinkable the next day.

They gathered for a small quiet dinner with Marcus's family, bride and groom included. Leah glanced around the large wooden dining table. Tobias and Camry were glowing. Rachel and Guillen complemented each other so well. Samantha and Brad had a natural chemistry. Leah wanted that with Marcus. And in a lot of ways, they had that. But she was going to lose him anyway. And it was all one woman's fault that Leah would never sit at a table like this with her own parents. She caught Marcus's eye with a sweet smile. *I wish.*

Leah pondered the agenda for the next day. The queen would be there at both the luncheon and the ceremony, officiating the latter. If she could muster the courage, Leah could try getting to the queen at either event. The luncheon would be less public, so perhaps there would be less security detail. But at the wedding, she'd be literally tasked with walking right up to the woman. Surely, she wouldn't have a dozen guards standing right beside her then.

Camry announced they couldn't stay for long after dinner. They were going to spend the rest of the evening with her parents on final preparations.

"Oh, I almost forgot." Guillen frowned. "I got word that Catrina might not be able to make it to the luncheon, but she *definitely* will still make it to the wedding."

Rachel frowned as well. "How come?"

Guillen shrugged. "She's plenty busy. She sent her apologies."

Camry nodded. "It's okay. Thanks for letting us know."

Marcus leaned over, whispering in Leah's ear. "Catrina's the queen-in-waiting."

"Oh. Cool." Leah gulped. That made the decision easier. Assuming both women had security detail, with one less queen in attendance at the luncheon, she stood a much better chance.

After a short discussion with the bride about her duties the next day, and a few hours hanging out and playing card games with Marcus's family, they called it an early night. Leah went to her guest room. Despite the warmth of Green Lands energy, it felt cold. Despite the busy, welcoming family, it felt lonely.

Leah lay in bed, imagining the next day a thousand different ways. She wasn't sure she could actually do it—take a life. But she made her list, and it felt less wrong than she'd imagined it should. It wasn't just about her family. The entire Green Lands could benefit.

She rolled around in bed, restless, unsure. There was only one thing Leah was certain of: she couldn't trust herself.

Chapter 26

UNABLE TO SLEEP, AND UNCERTAIN where the next day would take her, Leah got out of bed. It was wrong to go see Marcus, given she might hurt his family the next day. But maybe spending time with him would help calm her, help clear her mind.

Leaving behind the beeswax candle and striker she'd been provided, she relied on the moonlight streaming in through windows around the house. She tiptoed out of the guest room, walking down the hallway as stealthily as possible. Climbing the stairs, she quietly made her way to Marcus's room. Only one of the steps scolded her with a muted creak. She stood at his door for at least two or three minutes, contemplating this decision. What was she going to accomplish?

Taking a deep breath, she gently knocked on the door. She waited a minute, realizing she might have to knock louder if he'd fallen asleep. But she couldn't risk waking others. As she went to turn the knob, it opened from the other side.

The room was pitch black. "Yeah?" Marcus said, barely above a whisper.

She lunged forward, holding him tight. She hadn't anticipated the amount of flesh she'd be touching. He wasn't wearing a shirt. She slid a hand down until she reached a waistband. Even if he slept commando, he probably wouldn't have opened the door that way.

He let out a breathy chuckle, resting his chin on her shoulder. "Can't sleep either?"

She soaked in the warmth of his embrace as his hands rubbed her back. "No. Can I come in?"

"Um… Well… You know my parents' rules. They'd kill me if they found out."

She frowned. "I just want to talk, and cuddle."

Silence. What else could she say? 'I'm trying to decide if I should ruin your brother's wedding?'

"Sure. Just for a little while." Marcus pulled Leah in. The door clicked softly behind them. He led her by the hand to his bed, where he lay down.

She joined him, cuddling up next to him. After a minute, she shifted positions, instead facing away. He followed her, spooning her with his arms around her.

"What's up?" he asked.

She sighed. "I guess it's just nerves about tomorrow. First time being a maid of honor. First time meeting a queen. A lot could go wrong."

"Mmm, feel you there. My first time being a best man. My mind's playing everything I need to remember on a loop. And imagining myself doing something embarrassing like tripping and face-planting." He chuckled, then squeezed her tighter. "As for the queen, you *really* don't need to worry about her. It's not like this is some official royal function all about *her*. This is Tobias and Cam's wedding."

Leah calmed the smallest degree with his reassurances. Just the feeling of Marcus's chest rising and falling behind her gave her the tiniest spark of hope in the sea she found herself drowning in. He was good for her. She wished she could say the reverse.

His voice softened. "Maybe it's good to just rip off the bandage tomorrow. Introduce yourself to her; then you can finally let go of these nerves." He kissed her bare shoulder. "And she's going to love you."

Leah internally scoffed. *Not likely.*

His lips placed another kiss on her shoulder. "Just like I do."

Her entire chest ached as she fought back tears, unsuccessfully. That was not what she'd come to hear.

"I mean, I don't know if it's love. I guess … just … I really care about you, Leah. You're special to me." He kissed her shoulder a third time.

Tears streamed down her face onto his sheets. She couldn't breathe. Couldn't speak. She wanted to reciprocate. She loved him too. But she couldn't say that. She might do the unthinkable the next day. She was going to lose him either way. "I care about you, too."

They both lay still and silent for another moment. Maybe he deserved to hear it. As a goodbye? Maybe it wasn't a goodbye. She might chicken out.

As much as she needed something to shut up the nightmare in her mind, she needed to show him she really *did* care.

Leah rolled over, feeling his face and finding his lips. She caressed his lips more sweetly and softly, more intentionally than she ever had before. It was slow, intimate, deep. It was 'goodbye.' It was 'I love you.' It was 'thank you.' It was everything she felt for him, all rolled up into one.

He reciprocated perfectly, gently, passionately.

Her heart pounding, she came up for air. His lips grazed her neck, his thumbs slipping under the waistband of her pajama bottoms.

"I, um…" he whispered as he caught his breath. "I'm ready. I want to. Do you?"

Leah pressed her lips together, her heart breaking completely. She wanted it. He wanted it. *Why now?* "No."

"Oh. Um… Okay," he whispered in obvious confusion. "I, uh … have protection. Or … we could do something else."

She stared into the darkness that obscured his face. "No." Her mind was spinning, her heart faltering. Maybe she owed it to him, knowing what she might do to his family. Maybe she owed it to him as a goodbye. Maybe she owed it to herself, to enjoy one last special thing with him before putting herself in danger.

She couldn't. She knew Marcus. It would only hurt him more. "I should go."

"You're sure?" The hurt in his voice only made things worse. "We can just go back to cuddling if you want."

"No. We both need our sleep. This was a mistake. I'm sorry." She rolled over and quietly left his room, closing his door with a soft click. Back downstairs after climbing into her own bed undetected, she wetted her pillow with fresh tears, hating the unfairness of every aspect of her life.

You're going to lose him either way.

*****

How do you pretend to be happy and normal on the most important, and possibly last, day of your life?

Despite taking forever to fall asleep, Leah got up fairly early and helped Rachel make breakfast. Rachel flipped sunflower oatcakes on a griddle over the coal stove while Leah stirred a bowl of granola.

"I appreciate the help," Rachel said. "I usually don't mind cooking; it helps me focus on my to-do list. But today's going to be a bit crazy." She folded her arms with a spatula in her hand. "I'm so old."

Leah smiled. "You guys don't seem that old to me. And I'm happy to help." *It's keeping me busy, distracted, calm.*

Footsteps descending the stairs to the right announced Marcus's approach. Leah clung to her facade. He joined them with a hand on her back.

"Hey, handsome," Rachel said.

"Hey." He flashed Leah a hesitant, shy smile.

Leah bit her lip and looked down, her resolve breaking. "I, uh… I should go shower." She spotted a frown in the brief moment she dared to glance at Marcus as she left.

She hurried in the solar-heated shower and got ready, everything in place but her fancy new dress. Marcus avoided eye contact as much as she did during breakfast. Their awkward silence wasn't noticed amongst the excited chatter of other family members. Leah trained her eyes on a large painted family portrait on the wall. Rachel's old friend and mentor—another Seeder—had painted it for their family. What if Queen Kaylah hadn't murdered Leah's dad? There could have been just such a painting hanging in the palace of her own family that Leah would now kill to see.

"Is it okay if Leah and I go for a walk?" Marcus asked his parents as they finished up.

Rachel glanced at a pendulum clock ticking in the corner. "We leave for Capital City in an hour."

"Just along the canal."

"It's up to you. An hour. That means both dressed and heading out the door."

He looked at Leah, pleading with his eyes.

"Yeah. I'm sure we can be back in plenty of time," Leah said with a forced smile.

They left out the back door. Leah frowned as they walked past the tree house. *How did things change so fast?* Exiting through a side gate, they turned down a dirt path alongside a canal. They walked side by side for a couple of minutes without a word.

"Are we going to talk?" he asked.

She focused on her feet. "You're the one that wanted to go for a walk."

Stopping, he took her hand. "You won't even look at me?"

She looked up briefly to meet his gaze. "I'm just tired."

He huffed. "You're a better liar than that." He drew a deep breath. "Did I freak you out by saying I love you?"

Biting the insides of her cheeks, she shook her head.

The hurt in his voice cut deep. "What did I do wrong?"

She studied his face. "Why would you think you did anything wrong? You're perfect."

His mouth hung open as he grappled for words. "You… Have you just been teasing all these months? You were the one who said when I was ready … that you would be, too." He threw his head back, running a hand through his hair. "I realize how much of a dick I sound like when I say that out loud." He sighed. "I'm not trying to guilt you into it. I just… I'm confused about what changed."

"You didn't do anything wrong. I'm not mad. It wasn't you. I'm just…" All she could manage was another shrug.

He narrowed his eyes. "Are you seriously pulling an 'it's not you, it's me'?"

She gave him a half-smile. "I guess I am. It's the truth."

He scrunched his eyebrows. "Are you breaking up with me? On today of all days?"

"No!" *But maybe I should.* She fought back tears. "I don't want to lose you."

"Why would you lose me?" He studied her face. "What don't I know?"

He wouldn't understand. He couldn't.

Better to give a less shocking truth. "I just worry. Thinking of back home. If this didn't go off perfectly, and my mom makes us move when I get back."

He squeezed her hand. "So, we'll have to work harder to see each other. I'm up for the challenge. Because I *do* love you, Leah."

Her lip quivered as she broke into tears. He pulled her close.

"I don't know what's going on with you, but I'm here for you, okay?" he whispered. "I know the lies to our parents are bugging you. And you're sad about family stuff. And nervous about today. And I shouldn't have put any extra pressure on you last night when you just wanted to talk. I get it. I'm not in a rush."

He released her, holding her at arm's length. "What can I do?"

She gnawed on her lip as he wiped away her tears. She was thinking about this all wrong. She needed to live for today. "How about another hug?"

He obliged, not letting go until she first started to. He studied her face again. "Are we okay? Are you okay?"

She nodded. "You're right. Just too much going on, I guess."

"That's what's nice about being a team." He kissed her hand. "Sometimes, when one person is down, the other can help lift them up."

"Yeah. We should get back."

He wrapped a reassuring arm around her as they returned to his house to get dressed.

***

Marcus looked sharp in his medium-brown slacks and vest over a cream button-up shirt. Leah felt that much better after their walk and chat. This wasn't about her, or them, or anyone else. This was a wedding day. She liked Tobias and Camry.

"You look amazing." Leah wore a genuine smile at seeing Marcus dressed up in this more traditional Green Lands formal attire.

"You're stealing my lines now?" He winked.

The family headed to the cave they'd first rifted into. Confused, she whispered to ask Marcus how that would work for his mom—she couldn't rift anymore. He clarified that it was only interworld rifting mature Seeder women couldn't do. They could still rift within the Green Lands because of the energy on both departure and arrival.

Still plenty nervous, but with a successful trip under her belt, and more energy coursing through her veins here, Leah opened her own rift to make it through.

Capital City was a bit of a misnomer. It was the name of the city, but also the colloquial term for a wide chunk of territory, what was left of neutral territory after the war ended. Leah wondered if it would be better or worse for her, if she did go through with her suicide mission. But she looked down at her hand, held firmly by someone she genuinely cared for. Genuinely loved. Someone she actually invested in and had allowed into her life. Who'd helped guide her to her true identity.

***

Leah had thought Marcus's family property and the surrounding homes were breathtaking—but the manor for the wedding was beyond words. It was massive. She couldn't believe it wasn't a palace.

After touring the picturesque grounds for a while—complete with a dozen flower gardens, and likely twice as many chiseled statues—and getting instructions on her part in the ceremony, Leah and Marcus went back to meeting and greeting people as they trickled in. The luncheon was only supposed to be family and close friends. Leah's opinion soured a bit at the thought of them also inviting the queen and king, no doubt as a show of status. *They worship her.*

As an 'intimate' gathering involving a Seeder family, there were over three dozen attendees. Leah nervously eyed the people she assumed to be Seeders. They looked just like Ivies, just like humans. But beneath their skin, they were lethal. Sharp blades could extend on their forearms, between their wrists and elbows. Some of them could shoot darts—wooden stakes—from their fingertips. The women were able to easily harness two to three times as much energy as Leah could.

The hairs on the back of her neck stood at attention, her pores clamming up at the thought of being so surrounded by her parents' enemies.

The moment Queen Kaylah and King Eric entered the room, everyone stood. She was gorgeous, thin, elegant. He stood next to her with broad shoulders, his handsome face accentuated by a sharp jawline. The queen and king gave off quite the air of authority as they politely nodded to the room, then sat at the end of a huge banquet table.

Leah was sick to her stomach. Just the sight of this woman bombarded her with so many emotions. Between Marcus and Samantha, Leah sat down when everyone else did. *Stupid, murderous bitch needs to have people worship her at a wedding. It all has to be about her?*

"You okay, Leah? You're looking pale," Samantha remarked.

Leah choked down her hatred, focusing on her food. "Yeah, fine. Thank you." She forced a smile.

Marcus placed a hand on her knee, rubbing sweetly. "See, not bad so far, right?"

"Yeah. It's great." *Why is it so much easier to lie about shoplifting than to get through a simple lunch?* She took a bite of food, looking up when a cackle of laughter traveled down the table. *She even has a stupid laugh.* The queen had jet-black hair, intricately braided, with a tiara to finish it off. It was simpler than the tiara Leah had back home. Wearing bright red lipstick, the queen kissed her husband, then carefully wiped away a smudge of transferred lipstick with her thumb.

Leah's heart became hollow. Had she *ever* seen her mom that happy?

Queen Kaylah had murdered Leah's dad for this throne. A throne she shared with a human. The throne she was stepping down from like it hadn't come at a precious cost.

Leah's mom's words played through her mind. They didn't belong here. They didn't belong in the human world. They didn't belong *anywhere*. Leah would never meet the man who'd given her the bright green eyes she loved. Her mom wouldn't date again. They'd never be whole again. Leah wasn't supposed to even be here, alive.

Leah stared more than she ought to, her reality crashing down around her. The room was caving in, and no one else could see it, could feel it.

A servant approached the queen and whispered something. The queen's gregarious expression vacated the scene immediately. The exchange was short, but telling. The servant shrank in size as the queen's face turned stern. She jabbed a finger at one of the doorways, her jaw set, her nostrils flaring, as she made some type of demand. The servant timidly bowed and left the room.

Something in Leah snapped.

"I'm going to use the restroom." She set her napkin down on the table, heading through the dining hall exit into the hallway. Leah hugged herself in the bathroom, trying to control her breathing as her face heated. *Can I seriously do this?*

Planning an assassination and actually carrying it out were vastly different things. *Could* she really do this?

There had to be more to the story, right? Yes, Leah's mom had lied to conceal the Green Lands and the horrible truth of her husband's demise, but she hadn't lied about anything else. *Everything* Leah had ever heard from the Garden Club and Kara backed up the fact that this queen *wasn't* a good one. But maybe, perhaps, there was a tiny sliver of something redeemable? Something Leah had missed? Maybe the queen had changed? Then again, look how she treated her servants...

Leah ticked off a list with each of the queen's offenses.

She'd murdered Leah's dad and grandparents, and others.

She'd destroyed her people's way of life, leaving many jobless, devastating their economy, and outlawing some of their natural abilities.

She'd taken the coward's way out of the war by giving in to Seeder demands and forfeiting Ivy lands.

She'd created an unhealthy atmosphere for Bomen, at least in other parts of the kingdom, or for those not employed by her for her own agenda.

She treated her servants like crap.

How many offenses did the queen need before taking her out became the right thing to do? Like Leah's mom had once said— people had become complacent in accepting her rule.

Leah splashed her face with water and toweled off. She tucked a stray hair behind her ear, gazing in the bathroom mirror. Those green eyes. "This is for you, Dad."

Leah returned to the dining hall with a carefully crafted smile. Marcus grinned, likely proud she was so well composed. The room buzzed with excited chatter and the scraping of silverware against plates. Everyone here was happy; maybe the queen wasn't so bad? Hadn't ruined things as much as Leah's mom had let on? But Leah's time in the Green Lands was hardly representative of the whole of it. These people were royalty, politicians, the enemy of her father. They were well-to-do. They were there for a wedding. Of course *they* were happy. The room pressed in on Leah, suffocating her.

Once Leah sat down, she leaned over, daring to broach the topic as she hadn't dared before. "We talked about the queen having two younger brothers, but I was wondering about the older one. She killed him, right?"

Marcus furrowed his brow, whispering in return. "Yeah. Not really the best conversation with her or this group, though."

"Why did she do it?"

He looked annoyed at the impertinent topic. "He was bad news. I can tell you all about it later."

"That's what they teach in schools?"

He took a sip of white grape juice. "Of course."

A numbness took hold of her, her heart teetering at the edge of a precipice. "You believe it?"

"We really shouldn't talk about this right now, okay?"

She stared at him. "It's a yes or no question."

He tilted his head in warning. "Yes. I believe it. Where is this even coming from?"

And with that confirmation, Leah had her answer—what she'd known all along. Her dad's memory was being tainted by his murderer. And Marcus believed it.

She'd screw up eventually. He'd break up with her eventually. And his belief in this fake queen's propaganda meant he didn't truly love the real Leah. How could he? *I was going to lose him no matter what.*

She shook her head dismissively, chomping down on a grape.

Later during the meal, she glanced down the table at the woman responsible for all the pain in Leah's life. All the pain in her family.

The queen had to die.

Chapter 27

BEFORE THE LUNCH PLATES WERE cleared, Leah needed to make use of those dress sleeves. She needed to use her old skills to stash a knife.

"Who are all those people down there?" she asked Marcus to distract him. He began naming everyone at the far end of the table. Shoplifting when no one else was in the same aisle was one thing. Tucking a knife up her sleeve amidst dozens of people, guards included, was a whole nother feat. Luckily, there was plenty of conversation—and eyes focused on their tablemates and not on the table—as plates emptied.

Leah placed her napkin on the knife, then rested her hand at the end closest to her. Not that different from a store shelf, really. She slowly, carefully extended her vine just enough to touch her mark under the napkin as her eyes darted around the room.

Servants began to clear the plates at the end of the table; she panicked. Swiftly grasping the blade, she reeled it in faster than she'd meant to. One of the serrated teeth caught on the end of her lace sleeve. She tried to tug it free.

With every second that passed, a servant grew closer to clear Leah's plate. She focused on freeing the knife, making it quick, and pretending to pay attention to Marcus's ramblings about who was who.

The queen stood up.

Leah set her free hand on the napkin to hide the wiggles and apply pressure. She yanked her vine free. "Is the queen leaving?"

She looked to her left; the servant was almost there. She extended her vine under the napkin again, carefully angling the knife to scrape against her skin and not the dress.

"No. She'll be around for a bit. It's probably the best time to meet her now, before the hordes show up for the actual ceremony." He smiled.

Leah successfully tucked the knife up her long sleeve, retracted her vine, and moved that hand onto her lap. The servant reached for her plate. Leah put the napkin on it, and he whisked it away.

One heart attack down. One left to go.

"How about I introduce you to her?" Marcus offered. "Not too many people swarming around her right now."

Leah glanced around the room. People were just barely starting to get up. Many sat in place. Some approached the bride and groom.

Now or never. The actual ceremony will have more guards, will be more public.

"I'm afraid I'll be nervous, and her guards will tackle me or something." She tried to sound genuinely anxious in a lighthearted way.

Marcus chuckled. "I mean, don't lunge at her or anything. Otherwise, you're fine." He reached for her hand. "Let me introduce you."

Leah moved her other hand to cover the one hidden under the table so he wouldn't feel the knife. "I want to go alone."

He raised his eyebrows playfully. "Really? You look terrified. I know her. It's not a big deal."

She swallowed hard, answering too curtly for a good show. "I want to do it alone!"

He raised his hands. "Fine. Whatever. Just … go say hi."

She filled her lungs to capacity, gazing into his eyes. "I need you to know it wasn't your fault."

His face grew pink as his eyes darted around. "You're bringing *that* up right now?"

He didn't know what she meant. He soon would.

"Never mind. Just in a weird mood."

He kissed her on the cheek. "I can confirm that." He chuckled again. "It's all family here. Just breathe. If you want to go meet her on your own, go for it. Then I'll tell you something fun, okay?"

She nodded. "Thanks."

Leah stood, concealing the knife under her sleeve. She crossed her arms to further hide it as she approached the front of the room where the queen stood. Each footstep closer required twice the effort to mask Leah's rage, her terror.

The king—a handsome tall blond—stood a few feet away, busy speaking with someone else. No one really talked about the king much. Leah hadn't asked. But it just now dawned on her that the humans had probably played as significant a role in helping the queen in the war as the Seeders had. What resources had *he* brought to the table? That was why kings and queens from different kingdoms and lands paired up, wasn't it? To combine resources, to conquer.

The room wasn't filled with wedding guests prattling on. It was filled with ghosts, with screams only Leah could hear. The human world—the majority of the Earth—was *massively* larger than the little tucked-away Green Lands realm. Her dad's troops had really never stood a chance, not when the queen had paired up with Leah's father's enemy *and* the humans.

Red clouded Leah's vision. She sweat, her breathing shallow.

The queen chatted with a couple of people. Leah stood close, waiting for her chance. She assessed the room and spotted only two guards nearby. They weren't that close. If Leah could get within striking distance, this whole thing could be over before anyone even knew it began.

It felt like a decade waiting for her turn to talk to the queen. Leah was tempted to look over her shoulder, but she knew she'd catch Marcus's attention. She couldn't look at him again. They were over. Everything was over.

Queen Kaylah acknowledged Leah with a warm smile, no doubt an expert at charming everyone she was around. She'd duped Marcus's family. The two other women walked away, and the queen invited her to approach.

Leah shuffled forward, her feet each weighing a ton. She clutched the arm with the knife to her chest, ever so slowly moving it down in front of her. Almost forgetting, she dipped into a half curtsy.

Queen Kaylah gave Leah a wider smile, tilting her head to look past her. "Marcus's date, right?" She narrowed her eyes playfully. "I thought I heard girlfriend."

Leah couldn't find her voice. She didn't need one.

Cupping her left hand under the other wrist, she allowed the blade to slide down. Past the serrated edges, Leah let her vines push it out enough to grasp.

In a swift and decisive motion, she raised the knife and aimed for the queen's throat.

The blade barely meeting skin, the queen grabbed Leah's hand, quickly wrapping her vine around Leah's arm.

"Your Majesty!" someone yelled.

In the split second it took the queen to recognize the attack, Leah launched her vine from her other wrist toward the evil woman's throat, the queen's eyes boring into Leah with fury.

The queen caught the vine with her free hand, wrapping her second vine around Leah's other arm.

The whole thing happened within the blink of an eye, and now Leah's arms were numb. Panic, defeat, and rage warred within her as her heart pounded, useless emotions that wouldn't change her fate now. She was done.

"Everyone stay where you are!" someone boomed.

"Leah!" Marcus yelled.

The queen's jaw was clenched, her nostrils flared. Two guards—Ivies—came up to Leah, securing her with vines as the queen released her own.

"*Marcus?*" Rachel called for answers.

"I… I don't know!" he replied.

"Take her," the queen seethed.

"*I hate you,*" Leah said. "I HATE YOU!"

The guards yanked Leah to the side, pulling her toward the back exit. Her last view of the room showed a multitude of shocked faces.

Worst of all was the soul-wrenching look of shock and betrayal on Marcus's face. "Leah?"

Leah's jaw clamped shut. A river of tears cascaded down her face as the guards pushed her out of the room.

The guards weren't gentle, even though she wasn't resisting. They swiftly shoved her down the hallway. Leah was a jumbled mess of adrenaline, still unsure of what she'd just done. Still unsure of whether or not she regretted it. Opening a door at the end of the hall, the guards moved her inside the small sitting room, securing her to a chair with more vines.

Leah said nothing. They said nothing. One stayed in the room while the other exited, shutting the door behind him.

Leah's eyes fell to the marble floor as she tried to process what she'd done. She'd just tried to kill someone. But her life was a messy web of lies and failure, anyway. She was calmer than she'd expected to be.

Until she thought of Marcus. She began to cry again, and hated that she wasn't able to do more than wipe her moist cheeks on her shoulders. Marcus was good. Even if he bought the lies about Leah's dad, he couldn't help it any more than she could have helped her mom hiding the truth from her most of her life.

Her mom. This had been far too rash. Leah had promised in her runaway letter that she would come home. That was never going to happen. You didn't try to off a murder-happy queen, or any queen for that matter, and get let go.

This whole predicament could have been prevented. Choose Marcus and deny her true self, or not allow herself to fall for him in the first place. She never could have had it both ways. *Why did I waste so much time caring about Marcus? If I had focused, I could have done it.*

The door opened, and Leah looked up. The queen stood before her, entering and grabbing a chair to sit across the room. The door clicked behind her as she sat down, crossing her legs, straightening her dress, and staring at Leah.

Queen Kaylah took a composed breath as the remaining guard watched on. "Leah, right? Or is that name a cover?"

Leah glared into the woman's dark brown eyes. "It's Leah. Eleana, actually." She instantly frowned. "Please don't hurt Marcus. He had nothing to do with this. I promise. He didn't know anything!" She was downright desperate, unsure how corrupt the queen was. She'd killed her own brother, so why not her employee's innocent son?

Queen Kaylah raised her eyebrows. "I believe you. Marcus is a good kid. But maybe a little too trusting. I would never hurt my favorite cousin's son."

Leah's eyes grew wide. "Wait. What?"

The queen smirked. "I have a hard time believing you didn't know Guillen is my cousin."

Leah read her face. She had to be lying. Marcus had never mentioned he was actually *related* to royalty. *But … back in the dining hall, he just said something about it all being family in there.* She'd thought he'd meant it as a generalization, with the obvious exception of the queen and king.

The queen examined the injuries on her hand. As she'd caught Leah's flexed vine, she'd sustained some cuts. The serrated knife had done enough damage to draw blood on her neck, though not much.

"But I want to talk about you, Eleana. Who sent you? Why do you want to kill me?"

"No one sent me. You *deserve* to die."

The queen rocked her head back and forth, far too casually for the mood. "Some people think that. Comes with the territory." She pointed to Leah. "But why do *you* think so?"

Leah looked her dead in the eyes. "Because you murdered my dad."

Queen Kaylah bowed her head, frowning. "I'm sorry if that's true. Whether by my hand or my orders, many lives were lost in the old war." She looked again at Leah. "I assure you, I took no pleasure in any of them."

"Oh, I think you took pleasure in this one." A sapphire necklace around the queen's neck gleamed in the daylight pouring in through several windows. "Seems to have done you a lot of good."

"No."

"No pleasure? Not even when you killed your own brother?"

The queen's head twisted slightly as she sat straighter. "What do you mean by that?"

Leah twisted her head to match, trying to figure out her game. "Kill more than one of them? Did you lose track?"

The queen's eyes narrowed. "No. I only killed one. What is your father's name?"

She proudly spoke it. "King Soren."

Queen Kaylah went pale. "And your mother?"

Leah shook her head in confusion at these stupid questions. "Who else? His wife, the queen." She didn't even know her mom's real name, since she'd adopted an alias in her self-exile, and hadn't yet shared it.

The queen remained silent, studying Leah's face. "You look like her," she whispered. "Where is your mother?"

Leah swallowed hard, looking down. This was bad. This was exactly why her mom never wanted them to return to the Green Lands. And in her stupidity and anger, Leah was leading them right to her mom. She could only pray her mom's careful, watchful eye could help her elude them. If not, Leah would never be able to forgive herself. "I'll never tell you."

The queen's voice rose. *"Eleana! Where is your mother?!"*

Leah met her gaze in loathing, her eyes clouded with a coat of tears. "I'd rather die."

Without another word, the murderous queen got up from her chair, leaving the room without even trying to deny her part in the assassination of Leah's dad.

Chapter 28

KAYLAH GOT LESS THAN TEN steps out of the room before leaning against the wall and sliding down. She stared at the floor, trying to find her breath. She couldn't breathe, couldn't formulate a coherent thought.

Soren?

Her breath became rapid as she grew numb to the world around her.

"Henry, go call for him," one of the servants said.

"May I please heal you, Your Majesty?" someone asked.

Kaylah remained on the floor, dazed, focusing on a pattern in the marble that resembled a little tree with its leaves stripped from the branches.

Soren?

"Kaylah, sweetheart." Eric crouched down, visibly concerned. "Are you okay?"

She didn't answer, her mind playing back a memory from so many years ago.

He said she was pregnant.

Eric rubbed her arm. "I'm here for you. You'll be alright."

Kaylah blinked, fully registering her husband's voice. "Soren had a daughter."

Eric's eyes searched hers. "You're sure?"

She nodded slowly. He knew better than to ask that question. Soren wasn't a name she uttered casually. Not after the horrible things he'd done to so many people, to her.

Eric's throat bobbed. "Will you please let the healer clean you up?"

Kaylah held out her hand, and the Seeder healer stepped forward. The hand and neck injuries took barely any time at all, then she began cleaning up the blood.

"What do we do?" Eric asked.

Kaylah took calming breaths. In and out. She needed to collect herself. She was a dignified head of state, not a fragile teenage girl. She'd had years to grow even thicker skin. But this had completely blindsided her. She looked at a guard. "Three guards for the girl. She says she acted alone, but keep things under lockdown." She stood, Eric aiding her. "We need to talk to Marcus."

Guards led Kaylah and Eric to a larger sitting room where the bride and groom and their closest family members were being watched over. Tobias and Camry huddled in a corner with her parents. Rachel and Guillen stood on either side of Marcus. Sitting, he stared at the floor, his head bowed, still in shock. The moment Kaylah walked through the door, he frowned, tears forming. "I promise. I don't know what that was about. I'd never be part of that."

"I know." Kaylah matched his frown, hurting for the kind-hearted boy. He'd spent so much time in the palace growing up. She didn't doubt for a second his innocence in all of this.

He went back to staring at the floor. "I don't know why she did that."

Kaylah knelt before him, gently placing her hands on his knees. "Look at me, Marcus."

A tear rolled down his cheek.

"I don't blame you. She told me you weren't involved."

He shook his head. "Why did she do it?"

Kaylah bolstered her courage. He wasn't ready to hear it yet. "Tell me about Leah's home and family."

He furrowed his brow. "She just lives with her mom. Her dad died in the war before she was born. Her aunt moved out earlier this year, but I don't know where she went."

Kaylah nodded. "I need her mother's address."

He looked back down. "Why?"

"Marcus!" Rachel chastised. "This is serious."

He remained silent.

Kaylah needed that answer, and there was no time to waste. "I'm asking as your family. I'm ordering as your queen."

He met her eyes in shame. "720 West Ash."

"Thank you." Kaylah nodded at the guards, and one left. She stood, surveying the group. Eric lovingly rubbed her back. All eyes other than Marcus's were on her, waiting for an answer. "She's the daughter of Soren and Beata."

Rachel gasped, clutching a hand over her mouth. Guillen's eyes grew wide. Marcus looked up, losing all color in his face.

"No," Rachel said.

"You're *absolutely* certain?" Guillen asked, reaching out to hold Rachel's hand.

Kaylah nodded. "His eyes, the rest looks like her mother. If we'd known she existed, we would have been idiots not to see it. And the age is right."

"I thought she looked…" Rachel wore a familiar crestfallen expression. "I had nightmares last night."

That was a gutting confession to hear, though no surprise to most in the room.

"He told me she was…" Rachel whispered. "I thought he was lying."

"Me too," Kaylah offered.

"Soren? That's that guy, right?" Camry asked Tobias.

He glared at Marcus. "Yes." His voice was hard. "That's the one."

Guillen ran his free hand through his hair. "This is my fault."

Kaylah furrowed her brow in confusion.

"I…" He glanced at Marcus. "She showed up at the cave without a passport. She said she'd lost it in a move. I issued a temporary diplomatic visa. Any security checks would have led to me. I'm so sorry."

Kaylah shook her head. "No. No one here is to blame. Her mother put it in her head that I murdered 'King' Soren."

Marcus got up from his chair, stomping to the door. A guard stood in his way, and Kaylah nodded to allow him to leave.

Rachel let out a heavy sigh, glancing between her two devastated sons. "What now?"

Kaylah frowned, addressing the bride and groom. "I'm sorry, but we're going to have to cancel today. We're in neutral territory, and I can't be sure it's safe with all the people coming. And it's … a sticky family situation and political nightmare." Her frown deepened as the bride's eyes filled with tears, and she nodded in understanding. "I'm so sorry. This wasn't the best time for this to emerge." She turned to a guard. "Send notification to the cave network to intercept guests where possible. Ensure they're discreet."

"Yes, Your Majesty."

Rachel squeezed Guillen's hand. "I'm going to check on Marcus."

"I can stay here," Guillen said.

"I'm going to talk to the girl again," Kaylah said.

"I'll come with you," Eric offered.

She pursed her lips. "I'd like some time alone."

Eric wrinkled his nose. "You're sure that's for the best?"

She nodded. "They know where to find you. Stay with the family, please."

He returned the nod, sitting down on a settee.

Kaylah turned to head out.

"Are you okay?" Guillen asked.

She looked back with a forced smile. "Of course I am. I always am."

He gave a sympathetic frown.

She grinned, shaking her head. Guillen may have only been a cousin, but he was more of a big brother than Soren had ever been. Both Guillen and Eric always had her back. "Don't you two gang up on me now."

Chapter 29

THE UTTER SILENCE MADE IT feel like decades passed in the room where Leah was held captive. All she could do was look around at the expensive decorations and the guard. The tingling in her arms announced the queen's numbing poison was wearing off. *How could I completely forget she has vines and that there are these different chemical channels I haven't learned?* She huffed. Even Tanner in his idiocy had described the queen as 'badass.' Leah was beyond stupid—and that stupidity had earned her this fate.

The door opened, and the queen came back in—she didn't have a scratch on her. *Of course she'd have a Seeder healer on hand to take care of her every need.* The lack of blood soured any satisfaction Leah had felt. But she hadn't been able to see herself trying to live a 'normal' life anymore, and she certainly wouldn't be able to now. Her life was anything but normal.

The queen sat down with the poise of a ruler this time. "I think we should talk about your parents, and find out what your mother taught you all of those years in hiding."

Leah scowled. "You admitted you murdered my dad already. That's enough for me."

"Executed. Not murdered. That's an important distinction."

Leah rolled her eyes. "The victor always gets to label things and tell the story the way they want."

Kaylah continued. "You called your parents the queen and king. They never had that legal title. They were frauds."

Leah glowered, her face heating. "I trust my mom more than I ever could the bitch that stole their place. I've seen her tiara, and I've heard enough from outside sources to know the truth."

"Why do you think they had the right to the throne?" Kaylah asked coolly.

"Because he was the oldest. Obviously."

Kaylah cocked her head. "We're matriarchal. Did your mother teach you about the Mother Vines?"

Leah clamped her mouth shut. She'd never heard that term. "It doesn't matter."

"Leah, *none* of my brothers are eligible for the throne. It's not just tradition. It's a dictate of the way our powers work. That's why the next heir is Marcus's aunt."

Leah read her face. *The queen-in-waiting is even more closely related to Marcus?* "Tradition or not. Powers or not. You shouldn't be ruling if you're nothing but a tyrant."

Kaylah scoffed. "What could your mother say about me being a tyrant? She ran away before my coronation."

"*She* never mentioned that. I have it on multiple accounts. You strip your people of their rights and give extra to the horrible Seeders. All you did to stop the war was pacify the enemy."

Kaylah almost seemed amused. "What rights have I stripped?"

"Tree rifting."

"It's been limited, yes. It's forbidden in the human world. Each tree rift requires a tree sacrifice. That's not our world to ravage. It's severely restricted in our own realm. Between previous generations of selfishness in the royal line, and irresponsible rifting in our own lands, we *decimated* our entire kingdom. It was necessary to get it under control. And tree rifting became a waste once we got our cave networks up!"

Leah rolled her eyes again. All lies, excuses, and justifications. If any of that was true, her mom or the guys in the club would have mentioned it.

"What else did you say?" Kaylah asked. "Oh yeah, horrible Seeders. How many Seeders have you met? Was Marcus's mom horrible?"

"There are exceptions," Leah grumbled. "She chose to move here because she married Guillen. I know they did it because it wasn't safe for him as a Boman over there. I can't believe you're related to Bomen and tolerate Seeders that would harm them." She mumbled about how family obviously didn't matter to Kaylah anyway.

Kaylah buried her face in her hands. "How is it possible you have *everything* wrong? Yes, once the war ended, it wasn't safe for Ivy Bomen in Seeder lands. Part of that is because it took a lot of hard work to get to where we are right now, having peaceful relations. But the bigger part is because *we* literally poisoned those lands! Did your sources talk about how the Ivy Kingdom tried to wipe out the Seeder nation for almost two centuries? Guillen, Marcus, Tobias—they would have died over there because the land wasn't survivable for them."

Leah gritted her teeth with annoyance. Kaylah had an argument for each point of proof Leah had. Why were they even having this conversation? "I have no reason to believe anything you say. You stole my dad and made my mom and me live on the run. *And* you killed your own uncle and parents. Who knows how many more innocent people?"

Kaylah's eyes narrowed. She wasn't amused by *this* accusation. "Is that what your mother told you? That I killed my own parents?"

Leah tilted her head. "So, this one you'll deny?"

Kaylah was stone-cold sober. "I will absolutely deny that. Categorically. Your parents killed them. They both had a hand in it."

Leah shook her head. *Proof of her lies.* "My dad was their favorite child."

Kaylah gave her a wry smile. "You're right. He was. We'll look past the fact that parents shouldn't have favorites, or at least not let their children know it." Kaylah stood, clasping her hands in front of her. "Soren was the oldest and the favorite. But he didn't have a right to the throne, and he killed his own parents for more power. That's as simple as it gets. I'm sorry if that's hard for you to hear, but you'll need to accept it sooner or later."

"Shut up!" Leah belted. "Why are you even telling me all this? My dad was a *good* man! My mom is a *great* mom!"

"Does a *good* man rape, Leah?" Kaylah threw daggers with her eyes. "He was younger than you when he started ordering servants to his chambers, and I know damn well it wasn't always consensual!"

"He would never!"

"Does a *good* man torture his sister in a dungeon for days, Leah? I happen to be that sister!" Kaylah's face grew more fierce with each offense she spat. "Does a *good* man kill his own parents to get gain? Does a *good* man take countless lives without a single regret?"

"SHUT UP!" Leah screamed. "I don't believe a single thing you have to say!" She'd heard enough. Her mom was a good mom. A great mom. They both loved her. This woman had no reason to tell the truth.

Kaylah stood tall. "I'm not going to mince words with you, Leah. You're old enough to think for yourself. Ask yourself why we're having this conversation, and why you haven't already been carted away to a dungeon. I'm well within my rights to order your execution posthaste for an attempt on my life. But why are we talking?"

"I don't know. I don't know how it works inside a killer's head."

Kaylah quietly scoffed. "Says the girl who tried to kill her own aunt before getting the facts straight. I'm throwing you a lifeline. Don't waste it." The murderous queen shook her head, leaving the room again without further comment.

Leah's thoughts turned back to her mom, hoping more than anything she was still safe.

Chapter 30

KAYLAH RETURNED TO THE SITTING ROOM. Tobias and Camry had moved to another room with her parents to talk. Kaylah sat next to Eric, leaning against him as he threw an arm around her.

"How are you?" Eric asked.

She closed her eyes. "She's in complete denial. She thinks her parents are saints."

"What are you thinking?" Guillen asked softly.

She looked down at her hands. "I'm not sure how objective I can be about this. We'll see how things work out when her mother's brought in, and when Catrina gets here."

Rachel returned to the room, taking a seat next to Guillen. All eyes focused on her.

"Well … his broken hand, I could heal. His broken heart is a completely different issue." Rachel winced. "There might be a couple more broken things in that guestroom I can't fix, either."

Kaylah imagined there might be a dented wall in whatever room he'd found to let out some steam, but that was the least of their concerns right now.

"He really fell for her, didn't he?" Eric asked.

Rachel nodded, biting her lip. "He thought he loved her. Completely blindsided." She took Guillen's hand. "He admitted to knowing she didn't have a passport."

Guillen shot up. "You're kidding me!"

Rachel spoke in a calming voice. "He understands now how serious that was, what his lies have caused."

Guillen scowled. "But does he *really* understand? The *only* reason people respect our family is because we don't abuse our privileges. I *explicitly* told him I didn't appreciate what they were asking me to do. He went too far!"

Rachel stood next to him, holding his arm. "I remember a handsome young man willing to do *anything* to rescue a girl he loved."

A smile crept onto Kaylah's face at that response. Guillen had been Kaylah's first recruit in the revolution, and one of her elite spies selected to help rescue her best friend, Rachel. In a lot of ways, these two had saved each other.

Guillen glanced down, shaking his head. "That was different. I never got anyone hurt. I wasn't being manipulated."

Rachel gently lifted his chin to meet her gaze. "He thought he was helping a girl in need. Don't fault him for having a big heart like his dad."

Guillen's shoulders dropped. "Should I go talk to him? Is he okay?"

Rachel pursed her lips. "Give him some time." She faced Kaylah. "But I'd like to talk to Leah, with your permission."

Kaylah raised her eyebrows, unsure how that would go. Rachel had more reason to hate Soren than anyone in the Green Lands—and now Leah had hurt her son. "What's your plan?"

"She hurt my family. I don't really have a plan. But I deserve to have a word with her."

Kaylah hesitated. "She doesn't understand who her parents really were."

Rachel's tone dripped with anger. "Then I'll help clear that up."

Kaylah slowly nodded. "Be my guest."

***

Leah had known the dangers of trying to take out the queen. Somehow, she hadn't envisioned the part that could involve years in prison, or nonstop silence while tied to a chair. The queen's lies replayed in Leah's mind. What was her point? Why would she say such things? What did she hope to accomplish? Leah would *never* join her ranks. If anything, that would only disgrace her dad's name more in the public eye.

The door opened again, and Leah expected a third round with the queen. Prepared for more indoctrination, Leah went numb—Marcus's mom now stood in front of her.

"I never meant to hurt Marcus." Her throat was sore from screaming at Queen Kaylah.

Rachel's eyes shifted from brown to a terrifyingly unnatural neon green—a Seeder trait tied to their energy, powers, and sometimes emotions. "Let's not start with lies."

"That's not a lie. I'm sorry I ruined the wedding. And that I hurt Marcus. I … love him."

"You came into my home. You broke my son's heart. You destroyed my other son and future daughter-in-law's big day. You lied to my husband and jeopardized his respectability. You can't tell me you didn't intend or predict those consequences!"

Leah sniffled. No one would believe her. They wouldn't understand that she really did love him. Love them. They wouldn't understand how hard the decision had been. How much she'd fought with herself over it. "I'm sorry for all of that, but what she did to my family is something I couldn't live with."

Rachel shook her head. "What Kaylah did to *your* family? Let me clear something up for you. It was the other way around. Kaylah is one of the most selfless people I know. And I know her better than anyone else."

Leah shrugged. "Even horrible people can be nice to their friends."

"Your parents earned themselves multiple death sentences. It's not just about me thinking Kaylah is a good person. It's also about me knowing your parents *weren't*."

Leah scowled. "Did you even know my parents?"

"Your mom, Beata? No. But her crimes are well documented. Your dad, *better than most*." Rachel swallowed, looking away. "You're sad your dad died. I get it. But you didn't know him. He was a monster."

"Stop it!" Leah yelled. Each lie aimed at her parents was like a punch to the gut. "Stop talking about them like that!"

Rachel looked her squarely in the eye. "You deserve to know the truth. Your dad destroyed my family. My human parents, the ones you've spent countless hours with at their house? He and his uncle put them through *hell*." She paused. "And the things he did to my people…"

Leah pursed her lips. "War's messy." *Good or bad, winner or loser, no one comes out unscathed.*

"Yes." Rachel cocked her head. "But Soren *enjoyed* it! That's what separates us. Ugly things happen in war. But he was sadistic."

Leah rolled her eyes. "The woman I was raised by is a great mom and law-abiding citizen. I don't believe anything you say."

Rachel paced the room. "You don't believe me because you don't *want* to believe. But I don't give a shit about what you believe, Leah! Facts don't change based on someone's belief!"

"Then maybe you got your facts wrong!"

Rachel stared into Leah's eyes again. "You say you care about Marcus? How would you feel if he was a slave?"

That was a horrible thought. *What is she talking about?*

"That's what he would be, if your parents had it their way."

Leah frowned. "No! Kaylah made things worse." She shook her head, distinctly remembering that Jake's parents had fled when the war was over. His mom had been pregnant with him, scared for him.

Rachel pulled up her dress sleeve, pointing to a faded tattoo—an Ivy leaf outline surrounding the number five. "Kaylah stopped this. This is the kind of mark my sons would have been forced to take. Bomen were considered worthless, disabled disgraces, better used as slaves. By fourteen, they were taken from their families, not considered worth educating, forced to do manual labor, and had their rights stripped from them. They weren't even *allowed* to have children; it was outlawed. That's how it was for decades. Your parents wanted to continue that—actually, to make it worse."

Leah's heart ached at the description. *Why am I letting her get to me? It's not even true.* "My mom isn't like that. And you're not even an Ivy Boman—why would that tattoo be proof?"

Rachel's demeanor softened a degree, her eyes fading to brown again. "You really don't know much about our world and family, do you?" She stood with her mouth open. "I volunteered to take this mark in the war to go undercover with Guillen. We fought with Kaylah against your parents."

Leah felt hollow, Rachel's words piercing her. Leah clearly wasn't a good judge of character. She never would have pegged Marcus's family as being so involved in her dad's demise, in her parents' downfall. She stared at the ground, searching her thoughts. *What if … if I'm not a good judge of character when it comes to my mom? Or a man I've never met? Maybe only the parts about him are true, and my mom never understood? Maybe they're all true. Maybe none of them are.*

Rachel reached for the door, glancing back. "I liked you, Leah. And so did Marcus. But I've had to kill for my family. I won't let anyone hurt them. Your dad did his best to destroy my life and that of my family. Don't take on that legacy."

<h1 style="text-align:center">Chapter 31</h1>

LEAH SAT IN SILENCE FOR much longer, stewing over the things Rachel had said that cut deep. The things she and Kaylah had said about her parents, about her dad, were unfathomable. Leah ached, particularly at the thought of Marcus living as a slave. It couldn't be true. But if it was… Her stomach churned.

The door opened again, and Leah's heart shattered. It was the last person she wanted to talk to at the moment.

Marcus slid in, shutting the door behind him. "Can we talk alone?" he asked the guard.

The guard, who'd been standing silent the whole time, shook his head. "Sorry."

Marcus glanced at Leah. "Does she have to be tied up that way?"

The guard nodded.

"I'm sorry," Leah whispered. "Why didn't you tell me you're related to the queens?"

Marcus frowned, shrugging. "Why should it matter? Would that have made a difference? Do you only murder people who *aren't* related to the person you're dating?"

She met his challenge with a faint scowl. "Tell me, Marcus, if you knew who my parents were, would you have given me a chance?"

It didn't take him long to consider her question. "No."

It was like a knife in her heart. Why hadn't she just kept up the lies? Or told him she'd loved him? "Then doesn't that make you a hypocrite? If family relationships don't matter?"

He threw his hands in the air. "That's different! I'm told you won't accept the truth about your parents. What all did my mom tell you about her relationship with your dad?"

"That she knew him well. That your parents fought against him."

Marcus huffed. "Your dad dated my mom at our age. For *three* years."

Leah's eyes narrowed. "I know that's a lie. He started dating my mom when he was fifteen!"

"I don't deny that. But he *also* dated my mom. The difference was my mom didn't know he was cheating on her. She didn't know what he was, that he was manipulating her." He looked Leah dead in the eyes. "Until he kidnapped her. And tortured her. And…" He looked down, wringing his hands. "There's stuff she won't talk about to her own sons, but you hear things." He shook his head. "The irony of me worrying about what Tanner did to you. What other guys did to you. When your own dad did all of it and worse to other women. He hurt women. He didn't respect life. If that's the man you're worshipping, you're no better than him."

Her lip quivered. If she could believe anyone, it would be Marcus. He could be misled, manipulated—she knew that. But he was good at heart. He loved his family. Why would he lie about that? "I don't know what to believe," she whispered.

Marcus's eyes filled with tears. "Tell me, Leah, have you ever witnessed your mom having a panic attack? Or been woken in the middle of the night by her screaming? Because I have. And that was all because of *your* dad."

A tiny squeak of regret rose in Leah's throat. She couldn't bear to see him cry.

"I guess the apple doesn't fall far from the tree," he said. "Manipulating me. Using me."

She frowned. "It's not what you think."

He shoved his hands in his pockets. "Then explain it to me. *Convince* me you had no idea who I was, and that you didn't use me for revenge."

Leah swallowed the lump in her throat. "It wasn't all a lie. I…" She searched her thoughts and memories. "I really did like you. I really didn't know who I was when we met."

He raised his eyebrows in disbelief. "Then when did you find out?"

"You were the person that taught me about green folk and the Green Lands. That was all true. I was so lost. But then … it wasn't much later that I found my mom's journals and learned they were a king and queen, that he was murdered by his sister."

"*Fake* king and queen. *Executed*. Not murdered," he clarified. "So, the entirety of our relationship was a lie geared to me bringing you here."

Her chest tightened. "It… I… Sometimes, yes. But most of the time it was just me being me! I talked myself out of this a dozen times!"

He scowled. "Should have done it a dozen and one."

Tears welled up in her eyes. "I love you."

"Don't you *dare* say that to me."

"But I—"

"Don't, Leah!"

"I'll say it because it's true!"

He glanced at the guard before returning his attention to her. "So true that you wouldn't sleep with me? Teased me for months, and then when I finally thought we were on the same page, you realized you couldn't go through with it? Why bother? You were already getting what you wanted."

"No. I didn't do it *because* I love you. I... I knew I couldn't trust myself. I didn't want to hurt you more."

"Then you failed miserably. How many times did you lie to me, Leah? How many times am I supposed to believe you and be disappointed?"

"You lied to me too! You should have told me about your family!"

"*I never lied!*" His face reddened. "You want to know why I didn't tell you more? Why I'm so private about my family life? You're living proof of why! I'm related to royalty. Everyone in the Green Lands knows my parents' names. They're in the damn history books, Leah!" He jabbed a finger at his chest. "Why the hell would I choose to keep that close to me?"

He stared into her eyes, tears forming again. "I'm proud of them. I love them. But I didn't want to be *defined* by any of them. Hate me or love me, I wanted to be judged for *me*. Not them. I wanted someone to love me for *me!*" A tear rolled down his cheek. "I thought I found that in you." He wiped away his tears. "I was going to tell you my relationship to Kaylah when I offered to introduce you. I was going to tell you *everything* this week, but you ruined that."

She looked at the floor. "I'm sorry. I'm sorry I screwed up everything."

He paced the room. "Sorry doesn't fix things. My brother won't even speak to me right now. I ruined his wedding. Do you know what kind of drama this could cause? What kind of old battle scars... What kind of outrage this is going to stir up? How much trouble my dad might get in, because you convinced me to lie to him!"

"I lied to my mom, too." She met his gaze. "She never would have agreed to me going *anywhere* overnight. She didn't say I could go to Detroit. I ran away from home! She's sitting at home, worried out of her mind."

Marcus averted his gaze.

No! "What did you do? Please don't tell me you..."

He wouldn't look at her. "I didn't have a choice. What did you expect me to do?"

She sobbed. "She's a good mom! She loves me! She liked you! She was nice to you! She didn't know my plans!"

"She's a war criminal," he muttered through clenched teeth.

Tears streamed down Leah's face. "She's a good person! What are they going to do to us?"

Marcus opened the door. "I don't know." His voice shook. "And I don't care."

The door clicked closed, leaving Leah to her heartache and the silent guard in the corner of the room.

Chapter 32

GUILLEN FROWNED, TALKING TO HIS wife with Kaylah and Eric. "He won't say much. He's still pretty hurt about it all."

"Do you think he helped get through to her?" Rachel asked.

Guillen shrugged. "I don't know. But from what you two have said, she's pretty brainwashed."

Kaylah sighed. "I'm not so sure. I saw the doubt and confusion on her face. We're going to have to see if we can bring back her mother and go from there."

Eric held Kaylah's hand. "I think we've done enough to assess the threat here. It's time for all of the luncheon guests to go home. You guys should be with your family."

Rachel frowned. "You guys are family too." She took a deep breath. "But you're right. Tobias and Camry need us right now. Her parents have to be pretty rattled, too. And I expect Marcus will still want to be alone, but his room back home will be more comfortable."

Kaylah forced a smile. "We'll send an update when we have one."

Rachel and Guillen stood. "Send word if you need anything from us," Guillen said.

"Will do," Eric said.

Kaylah dismissed the guards as Rachel and Guillen left the room.

"Hmm… I like it when the guards go away." Eric grinned.

Kaylah flashed him a genuine smile and gave him a sweet kiss on the lips.

He gazed into her eyes. "I'm sorry this is stirring up a lot of rough memories. What can I do to help?"

That was always a hard question to answer. She tried to push down flashbacks from almost two decades prior. Rachel and Guillen had almost lost their lives to save hers. Many others loyal to her had made the ultimate sacrifice. The entire Seeder nation had honored their alliance with her to end a war more than two centuries old. And risking his life for the cause, putting his life on hold for her, had been a loving high school sweetheart, a human.

She looked down at their hands, giving his a squeeze. The day she'd been able to figure out how humans could make it through a rift, and the day she first saw the love of her life in her homeland, right before her coronation—those were days that gave meaning and hope when the weight of the realm felt too heavy to bear.

And right now, Kaylah's heart was heavy. *That poor girl.* The idea of Soren being a father was a nonstarter. Leah was better off without him, no matter how confused she was. Kaylah was physically ill, imagining the sick pleasure Soren would've had about this. She'd sent him to the grave all those years ago, but he was still able to reach out and hurt people, long after he was gone.

"Babe?"

"Yeah, um…" She hadn't had episodes like this in years. "What?"

He asked again, "What can I do to help?"

"Today? Just be here for me."

He raised his eyebrows, giving her a gentle smile. "Am I being reduced to a pretty face today?"

She chuckled softly. "You're more than a pretty face. You're my rock."

He pulled her in tight and kissed her head. "I feel like I cuddle better than a rock would."

***

Kaylah stood outside the door, ready for a whole new round of lies and bad memories. This time she wouldn't be rattled. Straightening her posture, she opened the door.

She stared into the face of a woman she hadn't seen in almost two decades. Black hair, cut shorter than Kaylah had seen it before. She wasn't that same young girl, following Soren wherever he wanted.

Beata wasted no time. "Where is my daughter?!"

Kaylah kept her composure. "I know you've been hiding in the human world for a long time, but you're out of touch. We haven't used teenage assassins for as long as you've been gone."

"Where is she?!" Beata seethed.

Kaylah tilted her head. "And to send her so untrained."

Beata glared. "I didn't send her. I kept her safe from *you*. And if you hurt a hair on her head, I will rip out your heart myself. *Where the hell is my daughter?!*"

Kaylah remained calm, reading Beata's face. They both claimed Leah had acted alone. With Kaylah in the human world so much during the years Beata and Soren had dated, she hadn't known Beata that well. What she did know of her, from their limited interactions, hadn't impressed Kaylah.

Beata was an enigma. Seemingly kind at times, but capable of cruelty. Strong in her own right, but often willing to submit to Soren's demands or whims.

Soren had loved mind games, and Kaylah knew how to play them, too. She chose the higher road. "Leah's fine. Only one of us in this room is a murderer." She rocked her head back and forth. "Then again, she's fine … for now. We haven't decided what will become of her. Attempted assassination of the queen—you know what kind of sentence that carries."

Beata didn't skip a beat. "I'll take her place."

Kaylah raised her eyebrows. "It's hard to die twice. Your crimes have already earned you a death sentence."

"Leave her alone. She's innocent."

Kaylah sat down. "See, that's what we're trying to figure out. It seems someone has filled her mind with all sorts of bullshit fanfare about the outstanding character of her parents."

Beata scowled. "You're too close to this. You always hated Soren. You were always jealous of him."

Kaylah scoffed. "Jealous? Of what?"

"Your parents loved him more than you," Beata stated matter-of-factly.

Kaylah leaned forward in her chair. "I didn't need their love. I wonder how much they loved him when the two of you murdered them."

Beata sat straight, defiance in the set of her jaw. "I'll never admit to that. And any crimes you put on me were under his orders. I didn't have a choice."

Kaylah pointed a threatening finger. "Don't mess with me. We have plenty of witness accounts of the types of things you knowingly allowed to happen. Entering the Queen's Room is just one of *many* crimes listed under your name. I don't need to prove them all."

Beata swallowed. "Soren named me queen when we married. I had a right to be there."

"*You had NO right!* You were never a legitimate queen, and you damn well know it!"

"You weren't up for the task. And you would have killed your own parents, anyway, if we hadn't beat you to it. Don't pretend you're morally superior!"

"You're probably right. But we'll never know. I would have done it to save lives and bring peace, if negotiations had failed. You did it because you were greedy."

"He did it because he had big dreams! He did it because he loved me!"

Kaylah narrowed her eyes. "But *did* he really love you? You and I both know how it works. The moment he caught me, he could have killed me and the next five heirs down the line. That's how he would have made you a *legitimate* queen with power over the Vines. But he didn't do that, did he? He kept me in the dungeons," Kaylah's eyes betrayed her, misting at the memory, "torturing me, and servants in front of me, while you lived in the lap of luxury higher up in the palace. Don't pretend you weren't aware of the kinds of things he was doing."

"He did love me. And I loved him! I'll never forgive you for taking him away from me!"

Kaylah took a breath to recompose herself. "I'll never ask for your forgiveness. I did what needed to be done. And I'm prepared to do it again."

Beata whimpered. "Spare Eleana. She didn't know what she was doing."

Kaylah sat back in her chair, a million questions running through her mind. "How did you even get by all these years?"

Beata sneered. "By working harder and living more simply than someone like you could ever understand."

"Marcus told me you had a 'sister' living with you? I know that's not true."

Beata's expression changed to a look of confusion and surprise. "Marcus?"

Kaylah smiled. "You really didn't know Leah's plans, did you?"

"Her name is Eleana. And no. I told you I didn't. What does he have to do with this?"

"Tell me about your aides. We were told four went missing with you. We only captured one."

"You'd be surprised how loyalty wanes when the hidden funds of the assassin networks dry up," Beata muttered bitterly.

Kaylah nodded with a small grin. "We knew we missed some of those accounts. The human world is a lot bigger than here, isn't it?"

Beata sighed. "Just let us go, and you'll never see us again. We haven't bothered anyone."

"Out of the question. You'll be sentenced for your crimes."

"It was a long time ago! All I've done since I left was try to be a good mother!" Beata frowned. "I'm only guilty of anything because of Soren. He already paid the price. Why can't that be enough?"

"Don't pretend you were under his thumb. You, my parents, and my uncle were the only people who had any sort of say with him. You followed him around like a lovesick puppy. You're not innocent!"

"He loved me, dammit! And I loved him! And he would have loved our daughter! War is ugly. Making my daughter an orphan, or worse, won't fix it."

Kaylah stood, clasping her hands and putting them to her forehead. "You're right. War is ugly. But that excuse can only go so far." She eyed Beata. What should she say to her? She could destroy her. Soren had never planned to make her a proper queen, not the way she seemed to think. She could also tell Beata about his last moments. About how he'd screamed for her. About how he'd been tortured for information. She could do *a lot* to hurt Beata before she ordered her death. And she *wanted* to hurt Beata.

But pity grew within Kaylah. Soren had only ever used people as tools. Beata's parents hadn't won any awards for citizenship. Was Beata just a product of her upbringing? Her surroundings? At what point did a victim become responsible for their actions?

Kaylah rolled her shoulders, choosing compassion. "If Soren was even capable of love, I believe he might have loved you. I saw the way you two were. And in his last days, he never gave you up."

Beata cried.

Kaylah searched her face again. *This isn't about getting a confession. I have evidence enough. Her fate is sealed. This is about Leah.*

Kaylah sat back down with a sigh. "He told us you were pregnant. We didn't believe him."

Beata frowned, nodding. "He ordered me to leave so she would be safe."

"Was she planned?"

Beata gnawed on her lip. "What couple doesn't talk about having kids?"

"In the middle of a war? When your resources are stretched thin?"

"He wasn't ready," she softly confessed. "But he didn't get mad when he found out."

"Does Leah know?"

"No. She doesn't need to know that. He was happy to have an heir on the way!"

Kaylah nodded, processing everything she'd gleaned from the conversation. As it often did, her need to balance justice and mercy weighed on her. "There's nothing you can say or do for your case. You know our laws, Beata."

"But—"

Kaylah held up a hand. "However … Leah still has a chance. If she has *any* shot at living a decent life, she needs to know the truth. If you love her, tell her the truth. Think of *her* for once."

Beata stared into Kaylah's eyes for a full minute before responding. "I'll answer her questions. But I will *not* admit to my daughter that I had any part in taking away her grandparents."

"I've already told her as much. And she'll hear about it as she learns history. It's a matter of public record."

Beata clenched her teeth. "She *won't* hear it from me."

"Suit yourself. Just remember when I bring her to see you that *you're* the one determining what the rest of her life will be like."

Chapter 33

LEAH WAS MUCH MORE COMFORTABLE at the change of guard. They allowed her to use the restroom and hydrate. She splashed her face with cool water to wash away dried tears. The mirror reflected a stranger. Could it be true—what they were all saying? What would that mean for her? Lies stacked on top of lies. Who was she?

A pair of guards escorted her back to the room she was being held in. This time, they secured her wrists with a wide band, something that prevented the use of vines. But they didn't strap her to the chair. What was going to happen next? The guards wouldn't say anything. But she knew one thing—she dreaded each time that door opened.

And soon enough, it did… Kaylah again.

"What now?"

Kaylah slid her chair closer and sat down. "How are you doing? Do you need anything?"

"To go home?"

Kaylah frowned. "Sorry, kiddo. No can do."

Leah pressed her lips together. "Why should I believe any of you? How am I supposed to know what to believe?"

Kaylah blew out a puff of air. "It's complicated, right? I can vouch for the honesty of myself, and Rachel and Marcus. But I understand that might not hold much weight for you." Kaylah leaned forward, resting her elbows on her knees. "I want to talk to you as your aunt, okay? Not the queen. Not the enemy."

Leah shrugged, studying the bands on her wrists. "The only aunt I've ever known wasn't even my aunt. And she was horrible. Then I learned I had a different aunt, but she killed my dad before I was born. I doubt it'll do you any favors."

"I'm sorry you didn't get to grow up with family. I truly am. No one deserves that. But I know your mother loves you very much."

Leah's eyes shot up. "You have her, don't you?"

Kaylah nodded. "We've talked."

Leah hated herself, and wanted to cry, but she had cried all of the tears she could. All she wanted now was to turn back time.

"I'm going to allow you to see her before we discuss consequences for either of you," Kaylah said.

"Okay."

"Before I take you to see her, do you have any questions for me?"

Leah ran through all of the information thrown her way in the last few hours. "Is it true they used to treat Bomen like slaves? That Marcus would have been taken from his family?"

"Yes."

Leah was instantly sick to her stomach. "But my dad didn't start that, right?"

"No. That became law long before him. But he had no agenda to stop it. He was unkind to Guillen because of his differences. He had … plans to further exploit Bomen in the long run."

Leah nodded. "Marcus said my dad hurt his mom and other girls."

"Yes."

Leah felt dirty by association, if it was true. "I never knew him. I can admit that. And if he was as bad as you all say he was, then … it sounds like my mom isn't guilty of anything. I'm sure he forced her to do anything she had to do. She shouldn't be punished. She's a great mom."

Kaylah took a deep breath, then slowly let it out. "She loves you. And I don't doubt she did her best with you. But that doesn't make her innocent. We have witnesses. We have confessions. And I know her well enough to understand the dynamic they shared. She wasn't forced to be with him. She wasn't *forced* to do anything."

Leah was numb, trying to sort through all the allegations. "Like help kill my grandparents?"

Kaylah bit her lip, giving a single nod.

Leah searched her face. Her mom's reactions would help her make sense of it all. "I want to see her."

***

Leah followed Queen Kaylah into another room, her wrists still bound. It killed her to see her mom strapped to a chair.

Her mom tilted her head, frowning. "Sweetheart. You shouldn't have come. Are you okay?"

Leah nodded. "I'm sorry. I really am." She glanced at Kaylah. "Does she have to be tied to the chair like that?" She realized she was now in Marcus's position, asking that question. She hated seeing her mom tied down—so captive, so undignified. And she almost wanted to hug her, but she also couldn't imagine doing it right now.

"Sorry. She'll stay as is for right now," Kaylah responded. "Let's take a seat."

Two chairs had been set up opposite Beata. Leah moved hers a little to be more in between the two, but off to the side.

"I was told my dad dated someone else at the same time you two dated," she started.

Beata sighed. "It wasn't like that. Don't let them put a wedge between us. He wasn't cheating on me. I knew all about the mission he had to do."

Leah read her face. "*Every* detail about it?"

Beata raised her eyebrows in chastisement. "We weren't even engaged at that point. I doubt he told me *everything*."

"But you knew he was dating another woman. A Seeder. And that he kidnapped her and tortured her?"

Beata took a moment before responding. "War's ugly, Eleana. I don't expect you to understand. I told you not everyone agreed with his tactics."

Leah's gut twisted. "That woman is Marcus's mom."

Beata's eyes grew wide, looking to Kaylah for confirmation. Kaylah gave a tiny nod.

"Marcus is a Seeder?" Beata asked, unable to hide her disgust.

Leah had never seen that expression on her mom before. "No. He's an Ivy Boman."

Beata glanced away, her face still unhappy, as though that wasn't much better.

Leah's mouth hung open. "You're the one that always told me our physical differences didn't matter!"

Beata shook her head, looking at her daughter. "I meant that about *you*, sweetheart! What was I supposed to say to my daughter? My daughter deprived of a normal life and hating her own vines? Hiding and dating humans who would *never* be worthy of her!"

Leah swallowed a lump in her throat, remembering a previous discussion. "You never dated again because you didn't think humans were good enough, either. It wasn't just about missing my dad."

Beata looked away again, not answering.

Dismayed, Leah kept her voice soft. "I love Marcus. And I've ruined things with him because of you and the pictures you painted in my mind."

"You don't understand everything yet, Eleana. Don't let them turn you against me. You and I, we're the same."

Leah shifted in her seat. "You really think my dad would have loved me?"

"Of course!"

"What about my grandparents? Would they have loved me? The ones you killed?"

Beata threw a quick glance at Kaylah. "They would have loved you more than you know. I'm sorry you won't get to meet them."

"Sorry because you killed them?" Leah intently looked into her mom's eyes.

Beata was an expert at dodging eye contact. "I told you your father was ambitious."

Leah's eyes narrowed. "Answer the question. Did you kill my grandparents?"

Beata met her gaze. "There's a lot of tragedy in your family. Your father didn't like taking no for an answer. That's all I'll say on that."

That was as good as a confession in Leah's eyes, but she still didn't fully know what to make of her grandparents or their deaths. "But Kaylah didn't kill them?"

Beata shook her head.

But ... she told me Kaylah killed them. Didn't she? Leah searched her memories. The truth of the matter tore into her very soul. *No. She didn't.* Marcus had mentioned they were assassinated, but hadn't named the assassin. Leah had only *assumed* it was Kaylah, and when she'd mentioned her shock about that news to her mom...

The memory was now strikingly clear. Her mom hadn't responded. Hadn't confirmed or denied the claim. She'd allowed Leah to believe what she'd wanted to believe, that Kaylah had been to blame. Her mom's silence, her every denial right now, screamed her guilt.

Leah gathered her composure, pressing further. "My dad didn't like taking no for an answer. How many women did he not take that answer from?" Leah balled her fists. Maybe her mom didn't know as much about this. Maybe this one wasn't true.

"He didn't do that as much once we were engaged," Beata defended.

"You knew he raped women, and you stayed with him?!" Leah shouted in disbelief.

"No one understood him like I did! It wasn't that simple. And it wasn't always like that. There were plenty of sluts happy to spend time with a prince or king. Sweetheart, you didn't grow up with a life of privilege. It's complicated."

Kaylah spoke up. "Don't you dare blame it on privilege! He understood the meaning of 'no' as well as I did! He hid his escapades from our parents. And when he got caught by our uncle, he had his ass handed to him. Your weakness in accepting his behavior doesn't excuse his actions."

Leah closed her eyes, trying to process her thoughts. Her mom was strong and brave. How could she also be this other woman? She opened her eyes, focusing on her mom's face. "Did he ever hurt *you*?"

Beata only shrugged slightly. "He could be rough; I told you he wasn't perfect. But it wasn't like that. I could take care of myself. I wasn't some weak, battered wife."

"Which makes it worse." Leah's eyes burned with anger. "You let Cheryl hurt me. If you knew he hurt other women, and he hurt you, why the *hell* do you think I would have ever been safe with him as my dad?!"

Beata shook her head fervently. "I never would have let him lay a finger on you!"

Leah frowned again, wishing she could take back the last day, wishing she could have made the right choice. "I love Marcus. I never would have made either of you proud. And if my dad loved me at all, it would have been because he was proud that one of his sperm performed its most basic function." She found her tears again. "We were never in hiding to keep *me* safe. We hid for *you*."

Beata spoke softly. "I've made mistakes, Eleana. We both have. But I love you."

"It's not possible to love both him and me. Which is it?"

"I wouldn't have had to choose. I love you both!"

"Then you choose him."

Beata sobbed. "No. No! You don't understand what I've had to do for you. Especially after Cheryl left. I've broken... I..." Her eyes glazed over. "I chose you. I always have. I always will."

While Leah found comfort in her mom's profession of love, her heart filled with terror at her confession of having needed to do something for them. "What did you do?" She imagined more bodies, blackmail, any number of things.

Beata shook her head, defeated. "It doesn't matter anymore, does it?" She looked up at Kaylah with a scowl. "Nothing associated with our lands or people that you can add to your list."

Kaylah shifted in her seat. "I think we've heard enough. Is there anything else you need to know, Leah?"

Leah stood, her heart heavy. She hugged herself, grappling with all the chaos of the day. "No. That's enough."

Kaylah walked to the door; Leah followed her.

"I love you, Eleana!"

Leah stopped in place. Despite everything, she couldn't turn her back on her mom. "I love you too." She faced Kaylah. "What's going to happen to us?"

Kaylah glanced between the two. "It hasn't been decided yet."

Leah had nothing left. No parents. No family. No friends. No Marcus. No trust. No self. Her heart and hope were gone. "If you kill her, you should kill me too."

"No!" Beata screamed.

Kaylah furrowed her brow. "Why would you say that?"

Leah exhaled. "Because I never would have been born if you'd caught my mom when you did my dad. Why should it be any different now?"

Kaylah spun. "Is that what you told her?! No wonder she tried to kill me!"

Beata returned her anger. "You would have put me right next to Soren. Don't deny it!"

Kaylah balled her fists. "I would like to think I'd have given you the benefit of the doubt, to confirm whether you were pregnant first!"

"So, what? I'd give birth. You'd take her straight away and make her an orphan then? That's better, right?"

Kaylah narrowed her eyes. "Did you get knocked up hoping for a pardon?"

"No!"

Leah trembled, the last ounce of her identity crumbling before her. "Can I please go?" she begged.

"Yes," Kaylah said curtly, escorting her out of the room.

Halfway down the hall, a guard walked up to Kaylah. "Lady Catrina has arrived. She's in the sitting room."

"Thank you."

Kaylah returned a tear-filled and silent Leah to her room. "You'll be the first to know what we decide."

Chapter 34

KAYLAH ENTERED THE SITTING ROOM, a raging headache engulfing her. She rubbed her temples and plopped down next to Eric. Lady Catrina—her cousin, Guillen's younger sister, the queen-in-waiting—and her husband sat opposite them.

"Sounds like quite a day," Catrina said. She had always been a more proper lady than Kaylah. Soft-spoken, dainty, logical, kind.

Kaylah cleared her throat. "Eric and Stephan, can you please give us some time alone?"

The men nodded and headed out. Kaylah didn't usually shoo them away. She and Eric were a team, even if he was 'only' a human, married to an Ivy queen, as some would say. And Catrina and Stephan often sat in with them when discussing policy, in preparation for handing over the crown. But legally, it was Kaylah's call on what Beata and Leah's fates would be.

"A nightmare." Kaylah blew out a long breath.

"I can't believe all of this. Imagine Soren as a father…"

"Like I said—nightmare."

Catrina tilted her head. "What's she like?"

Kaylah frowned. "She has his eyes. Other than that, I still really don't know. She tried to kill me today, but I just saw her devastated by the truth of who her parents are. The dust has to settle."

Catrina matched Kaylah's frown. "I heard Marcus took it pretty hard."

Kaylah nodded. "That poor boy. He's so sensitive."

Catrina picked up a goblet of water from a side table. "So, what are you thinking at this point?"

"You know the limits of the law."

Catrina's jaw dropped. "You could do that to her? The girl?"

Kaylah rolled her eyes. "No. Not the daughter. I'm just saying, it's within my rights. Soon enough, you'll be having to make this kind of call."

Catrina pressed her lips together. "I know it's been a hard reign for you. But Stephan and I are hoping we have significantly fewer threats and attempts on our lives."

"And we're lucky we didn't have to get your mother out of the way."

Catrina looked down, rubbing her thumb along the goblet stem.

"Sorry, that was insensitive. You know, well…" Kaylah's aunt, Catrina's mother, would have been next in line before Catrina. That woman had been stubborn. She'd loathed nearly everything about the changes Kaylah had worked so hard for. Right up to the day she died.

Catrina nodded. "I know full well your meaning. I think it's possible to love and forgive someone at the same time you hate their actions."

Kaylah sighed. "Right. So—the girl. She didn't understand what she was doing. Of course I won't execute her. But…" Her heart reached out to Leah. *That last outburst.* "I worry about how things will go for her… She said she wanted to die if her mom dies. They were pretty close."

Catrina bit her lip. "That's not great. Do you think she'd be serious about it?"

"I have no way of knowing. And … I don't feel right about changing her mother's sentence."

"Let's go over that one." Catrina took a sip of water, then set down the goblet. "You mean execution?"

Kaylah nodded. "Her crimes are proven. The trial held in her absence still holds."

"She entered the Queen's Room," Catrina said. "That's a death sentence. But really? When was the last time someone was actually put to death for that? And you yourself wrote that out of law, even if it's still forbidden by tradition."

Kaylah scowled. "She did it while it was still in law."

Catrina gave a slight nod. "And she helped assassinate your parents. Which you were also prepared to do."

Kaylah's jaw dropped. "You're defending her?! That was both illegal *and* for the wrong reason. Don't put me on her level!"

Catrina raised her eyebrows. "I'm laying out the facts. I'm not trying to justify her crimes. We're just talking." She crossed her legs. "We still don't fully know how culpable she was for that crime. Unless you know more than I do."

Kaylah's annoyance flared. According to all accounts, the only people who had made it out of the room her parents had died in were Soren and Beata. No one could confirm who had done the actual killing. "I don't."

"Okay. Then that leaves us all the other crimes Soren committed. Which we're only aware of her being a part of in the sense that she's condemned as an accomplice."

Kaylah crossed her arms. "So, we should let her walk away? Full pardon? Slap on the hand?"

Catrina's voice wavered from its gentle nature. "Will you calm down? Maybe you're too close to the situation to make an objective decision."

Kaylah glared. "Too close? Was I too close when she was upstairs screwing Soren while I dripped blood on the floor down in the dungeons?"

Catrina swallowed. "I know this is bringing up a lot of horrible memories, okay? I'm not unsympathetic to that. You know I love you. And I know they were wrong. But thinking about that girl, and more importantly our kingdom and treaties—that's more important." She gestured with a hand in the air. "I'd say life in prison."

Kaylah pinched the bridge of her nose, frustrated at herself for letting her emotions get carried away. It had been years since she'd even heard Soren's name, then to have this all crashing back into her life again… What was best for the kingdom? And peace with the Seeders? This had happened in neutral territory. Would Seeders demand Beata's life? Or even that of the girl? Would they need that satisfaction to appease old anger easily stirred up? What about the Bomen?

What about her own people? There was peace, and so much had changed in the last eighteen years of her reign. But that didn't mean there weren't still die-hard Soren dissidents out there, or those who agreed with at least some of his vision. Would the appearance of the girl and her mom cause an uprising? If Leah and Beata lived, would it give their cause hope? Would Kaylah's people see her as weak if she didn't execute them? Or ruthless and vengeful if she did?

These were not simple policy decisions or mundane social displays. These were deep wounds reopened.

Kaylah needed fresh air. She walked to a window in the sitting room. The early sunset sang the very definition of beauty and peace. She gripped the windowsill, waiting for inspiration to strike her. She wasn't always the best with words, or considering others' feelings, but she wanted to be. Sometimes she relied too much on logic or on anger. But she was blessed in her station—she didn't have to call the shots alone.

She strode to the door, addressing a guard in the hallway. "Call for our husbands, please."

"Yes, Your Majesty."

The men shortly rejoined their wives.

Kaylah took Eric's hand. "Beata's crimes remain as we once knew them. Nothing has changed. There's no statute of limitations on them." She and Catrina shared a glance. "Catrina thinks life in prison would be best for Beata, for the sake of her daughter. I agree. I'm still not sure what's best for the kingdom, however. I'd like your input."

"I agree with Catrina," Stephan answered.

Eric nodded, looking down in thought. "I feel like ending our reign with an execution that could be seen as a personal dredging up of old family issues isn't the way we want to go."

Kaylah's heart fought it. "Fine. And what about the girl? What are we supposed to do with her? She has a lot to learn about her own people. She has a lot of healing to do."

"You're thinking of keeping her in the kingdom, right?" Stephan asked.

"Of course!" Kaylah replied. "Her days with the humans are over. We're not just shipping her off. I just … don't know where is best. A good family willing to take her in? I wouldn't dare put her with anyone in Beata's family."

Eric squeezed Kaylah's hand. "But she should be with family. I know we never planned on kids, but it's not like we didn't help raise your brothers."

Kaylah's little brothers had only been eight and ten at the time of their parents' assassination, and their older brother's coup. Once Kaylah had regained control of the palace, she'd also had to fill the role of mother for brothers she had hardly known growing up. And with all the trauma of their childhood, and the stress of being in the public eye, neither had really turned out to be the ideal citizen, or member of the royal family. Kyas was nothing short of a social recluse now, and Rian had a known drinking problem.

But this wasn't about them. This was about Leah, and what was best for her. Kaylah's eyes welled with tears. "I want to say yes. But … I—I don't know if I'm strong enough to look into those eyes every day. And I don't think she could stand living with someone who took away her parents. I'm sorry. I know it's selfish."

Catrina frowned, rubbing her barely showing belly. "Not selfish. We all have different things we struggle with." She glanced at her husband. "Maybe we could take her in?"

Kaylah shook her head. "A two-year-old, one on the way, *and* a troubled teen? All while you're moving into the palace and taking over?"

"We're up to the challenge," Stephan answered confidently. "Like Eric said—she should be with family."

Catrina clasped her hands together. "Let's not look at her like a burden. She can be seen as someone to bridge the gap of our reigns. From war to peace. Hope in the new generation? I know I haven't met her yet, but … do you think that's possible?"

"Hope in a new generation?" Kaylah repeated. "That's hard to say. We can't parade her around like propaganda. But it seems like everyone loved her … until she showed her true colors."

Catrina's voice and smile were ever calm. "We'll treat her like she's worth believing in, and she might just rise to the occasion. Plus, once we move into the palace, I think it's a sign we're willing to move on from our family's past."

Kaylah smiled weakly. "And Soren's followers might be pacified, seeing her in there."

Eric looked around the room. "Then we're all agreed?"

The nods were unanimous.

Chapter 35

SHE HAD BEEN IN HER new home a week. Leah lay in bed, still struggling to grasp the reality of her situation. The family was welcoming and kind, but this wasn't home. It might never be. Granted, in two weeks it would quite literally not be her home, or theirs. They were moving to the palace.

She rolled over, hugging a pillow. What was that going to feel like? She'd be in the place her parents had always wanted her to be, but without any title, not that she deserved one.

Staring at a stack of books on an ornate vanity, Leah sighed. They didn't force Ivy history down her throat, but they'd assigned her a tutor and made it abundantly clear that she was free to ask any questions. She'd perused, though it was hard to do so.

The first couple of days following her assassination attempt had been the worst of her life. Before her mom was moved to an official Ivy prison, Leah had been given one more chance to talk with her, this time all alone. Despite the multiple witnesses against her mom, and even her mom's own confessions, Leah had worried the confessions had been coerced out of her.

In full shame, an absolute wreck, her mom had sworn over and over that she'd tried to do right by Leah. She'd admitted she hadn't been forced to say anything that day. She'd begged for Leah's forgiveness. Leah didn't know if she could give that.

Thoroughly devastated, Leah had cried so hard that night that she threw up. After telling Kaylah she'd be willing to die with her mom, and being in such bad shape, they'd put her on suicide watch, regularly checking on her.

Sometimes, she found it in her to leave her room to dine with the family, or to sit in the sunny library to read from these books, but most of the time she still stayed in her room, trying to make sense of it all.

A knock sounded on her door. "It's open," she answered, despondent.

A servant peeked inside. "You have a visitor, miss."

Leah rolled her eyes. "It's not 'miss.' It's Leah."

The servant nodded once. "My apologies, Leah. It's Marcus."

She shot up out of bed. "Really? I'll be right out." She grabbed clothes from her closet, quickly changing out of the pajamas she'd been sulking in all day. She looked in the mirror, regretting doing so due to the disheveled mop of hair disgracing her head. She bounded to the front sitting room, her heart lit with hope and aching all at the same time. "You came."

He stood, hands buried in his pockets. "Not by choice. I'm on my way back to school. What do you want?"

She frowned. "Just to talk."

He shrugged, not meeting her eyes. "Then talk."

"I'm sorry. Very, very sorry."

His expression was blank, his voice soft. "You've said that already."

Her heart sank. "I love y—"

"Don't! We're not together anymore. You can't seriously think I could forgive you after what you did."

She'd cried more tears in the last week than in her whole life put together. "I didn't understand."

"You understood enough." He shook his head. "And you're going to move into the palace. Sounds like you got what you wanted in the end, anyway."

"I never wanted that! I don't care about servants or titles, or any of that! I cared about my family." She looked down in shame. "I just didn't understand who they were."

"If you want my forgiveness, I… I'm not ready for that. I don't know if I ever will be."

"You're my best friend," she whispered. "You're my only friend. I guess … not even that, anymore."

"You don't stay with someone because you pity them. You stay with them because you have mutual respect. And that ship has sailed."

Leah met his gaze. "Who even am I? Tell me that. My dad was a monster. My mom's in prison for life! Who am I, Marcus?"

He glared. "I'm not your crutch. Figure out your own damn life."

"Please. I'm begging you." She frowned in desperation, wiping away fresh tears.

"I get that you didn't win the parental jackpot. I really do. I didn't either, Leah! Why do you think I was put up for adoption? The day my birth parents realized I was *defective*, they wrote me off, tossed me away like scraps in a compost pile. Same happened to my brother. We don't get to *choose* our parents. Learn to deal. Make a name for yourself that *you* will be proud of."

She fidgeted with her hands. "It's not the same. Your birth parents aren't infamous. And you have amazing adoptive parents."

He narrowed his eyes, his hands gesturing at the large room around them. "I'm sorry. Is my aunt's generosity not good enough for you? You have family willing to give you a chance. And you're right, my birth parents are some nameless nobodies out there. That just means you have more eyes on you. Maybe it will help keep you in line. Maybe you'll snap under the pressure. Maybe you'll tell the doubters to suck it, and move on with your life."

"Marcus," Catrina scolded at the door, her toddler breaking away from her side, hugging Marcus's leg. "She's trying. Go easy on her."

Marcus picked up the toddler with a huff, then faced Leah. "You have choices to make, but that doesn't invalidate that I get to make my own choices." He gave the toddler a hug and set him down. Marcus stalked toward his aunt, about to pass her. He stopped with a sigh, giving her a hug, too. "Good luck with your coronation preparations."

Catrina gave him a gentle smile. "Thank you. Good luck with school. Love you."

"Love you too." He left the room with Catrina standing at the doorway.

Leah sat, biting her nails and sniffling. "I don't know why I even tried."

Catrina frowned. "Do you want to talk?"

Leah shook her head.

Catrina picked up her little boy, holding him on her hip. "Just give him more time."

Chapter 36

Ten Weeks Later

LEAH STROLLED DOWN THE LANE, lost in thought, a guard trailing a few paces behind her. She still had so much to learn. About her homeland, culture, family. About herself. Eventually, she'd had to come to terms with the truth. And as much as she hated her mom's actions, she understood some of them.

Beata had never had a good influence like Marcus in her life. Her parents had been in charge of the old Bomen communities, not that they used any nice names for their quasi slaves back then. Leah still didn't know how much she could forgive her mom for her twisted prejudices and perspectives, despite the home she'd grown up in. Was *any* level of leniency just giving her an undeserved free pass?

Leah still held a special place for her mom in her heart, and suspected she always would. On a recent visit to the prison, she'd come to understand her more, and had been grateful for her mom's frankness. Beata swore up and down that Soren hadn't always been so brutal, so horrible, even if Kaylah disagreed on that point. Beata had believed he was a good man when they'd first met, but over time, he had started doing more things she found hard to stomach. She hadn't protested his actions as much as she ought to have. She'd been too taken with him. He'd talked her into too many things she hadn't been comfortable with. And once she'd lost him for good, her grief broke her, and she could now admit she'd remembered things with rose-colored glasses.

Leah stumbled on a rock in the path, almost twisting her ankle, but catching herself. She should pay more attention, but her mind still played back her previous conversation with her mom.

Her mom still wouldn't confess what she'd done in the human world to earn them money, not fully. She had opened up some about that, though, too. Losing Cheryl and her income had pushed her over the edge in desperation to watch out for Leah. The same day Leah had found her mom sobbing in her room, she'd done something that earned them a healthy sum. She still wouldn't give specifics, but it had something to do with a promise she'd made to Leah's dad years ago.

It was hard to hear her mom confess that she realized she hadn't been putting her daughter first, that she'd been clinging to Soren's memory for far too long, to an old promise. But that day, she really had chosen Leah. In her heart, she'd let him go in a way she'd never imagined. Even confessions like that were heartbreaking for Leah. It had been too little, too late.

Since Cheryl had abandoned them, and Beata knew her current address, Beata had given it to Kaylah in hopes it would help her and Leah. Cheryl was brought in, and just like Beata had blamed Soren for her actions, Cheryl swore she'd never wanted any part of it, but had been forced to help Beata as her aide back at the palace. Leah didn't buy a word of it, still fully believing she'd just been a bitter old maid hating the life of exile in the human world, and taking it out on Leah. Where Beata had let Leah down, Kaylah didn't. She heard her out. She believed her.

Cheryl was sentenced to thirty years in prison for child abuse, and aiding and abetting a war criminal. Leah never wanted to see that woman again, and was promised she wouldn't have to.

Leah took a pensive breath as the breeze rustled leaves high above her head. A chipmunk scurried up a nearby fence post, and Leah plucked up a long velvet grassweed, swishing it in the air. She still obsessed over her mom, unable to reconcile her behavior of the past and present.

Ironically, the fact that her mom *hadn't* blatantly lied more was somehow frustrating to her. Her mom hadn't taught her more of the chemical arts—the other things she could do with her vines— because she hadn't actually known them. Like cave rifting, Kaylah had been the revolutionary to lead her people away from war, to a better understanding of their own powers, and to a more sustainable way of life.

Most of the real lies and misunderstandings were taking shape for Leah over time. It took her a while to wrap her head around why Jake's parents would have fled at the beginning of Kaylah's reign, because Bomen hadn't even been physically capable of travel to the human world until Kaylah and Rachel had discovered that option. Queen Catrina had helped clear that one up for Leah. Like Jake's parents, many Bomen, especially ones like his mom—illegally pregnant with him—had fled once Kaylah made it possible to, fearing she would be deposed. Kaylah's parents and then brother were all assassinated or ousted in less than a year's time. It was understandable that the most vulnerable population took the chance they were given to flee in a time of uncertainty.

Leah shook her head. *Everything* had been twisted. She'd chosen to hear and believe what she'd wanted to. Now, she was having to carefully reframe her every decision that had led up to the failed assassination, and every decision after that. She'd written a long letter of apology to Camry and Tobias. *What a horrible and public way to ruin their special day.* With Leah having lost her mind, her hope, and even her faith in Marcus's family, the couple's wedding had felt like the smallest consideration, as collateral damage.

Turning the corner at the end of the street, nearing her next destination for the day, Leah sighed. Queen Catrina and King Stephan were nice. And despite being so busy, they made an effort to ensure Leah was as comfortable as possible. Leah felt guilty for tainting Catrina's special day, her coronation. Leah was the black eye the Green Lands hadn't seen coming.

Leah chuckled to herself. She'd once asked Marcus if Catrina was taking over because Kaylah was being kicked out. It was far from the truth. Kaylah and Eric had served their best, but it had been a rough reign—trying to redesign a kingdom that had spent centuries oppressing Seeders and their own citizens. And unable to have children together, with Eric being a human, they could produce no heir of their own. Once Catrina's awful mother had died, and Catrina was married and having kids, she was in a good place to rule. Catrina had always been a proper lady, immensely helpful, yet barely even part of the old war. Her name and reputation held no negatives in the public eye.

The guard still walking behind Leah broke the silence of their travel. "Her Majesty wanted me to remind you of this evening's state ball, miss, and to allow extra time for one more dress fitting."

"I know, thank you. I doubt this will take long," Leah replied. She'd given up on fighting Catrina's staff calling her 'miss,' and she was growing even more fond of the pretty dresses.

Out of nowhere, Leah's mind went back to her journal entry from the day before. As horrible as it was that Leah's dad had slept around, Leah had been holding out hope that maybe it meant she had a half-sibling out there somewhere. *What kind of person wishes that on a kid, anyway? Especially if the mother is one of the women he forced himself on...*

But Soren had been careful to ensure he didn't have illegitimate children floating around. Leah was still alone as his only living offspring. Living, because records indicated she wouldn't have been all alone. When prevention hadn't worked, he'd had things taken care of. He hadn't just taken Seeder lives, or servants' and soldiers' lives, he'd taken some of his own children's lives. That was the shadow Leah lived under. That was the shadow she was fighting every day to break away from.

***

Rachel poured tea for herself and Leah before sitting back down, tucking her legs underneath her. "How are the lessons going?"

Leah smiled, sipping her tea. Rachel was actually the hardest person to look in the eyes, after how much Leah and her parents had hurt her family, but she was more understanding and forgiving than Leah could have hoped for. "Thanks again. You make the best tea. Even better than at the palace."

"High praise. Do I need to share my secret blend with Catrina's cooks?"

"Yes please. As for lessons, um … I mean … having to be tutored during the summer sucks. But I get it." She set her teacup down. "But if we're talking powers, I think I've got down numbing real well." The history lessons were kind of a given.

Rachel smiled. "Nice. I understand that one can be tricky."

Leah rocked her head back and forth. "I'm just doing local numbing, really. There's still lots more to learn."

"Hey, Mom, what's with the extra guard out—" Marcus stopped once he walked into the room. His eyes swept over Leah. "Oh." He turned and headed past the kitchen, upstairs.

Leah sighed. "I thought he was ready."

Rachel returned a sympathetic frown, shrugging.

Not a minute later, footsteps came back down the stairs, and Marcus peeked around the corner. "Go for a walk?"

"Yes." She looked at Rachel. "Thank you again for the tea, and everything."

"Anytime."

After a few paces in silence along the canal, Leah decided to get the conversation started. "I know I sound like a broken record, but I'm sorry for everything I've done. And I say that without any expectations."

He nodded, looking straight forward.

She swallowed. "How was the rest of school? How's Jake?"

"It was good. Well … it was alright. Jake's good." He met her gaze out of the corner of his eye. "I could see Jake being up to a visit next time he's in-realm."

She furrowed her brow. "Do you mean visit me? Or you?"

"Either. Both. He's pretty forgiving. And doesn't really delve deep into Green Lands politics."

Leah smiled fondly, wishing she'd spent less time planning and plotting, more time getting to know Jake better. "Is he still with Emily?"

Marcus smiled as well. "Yeah, he is."

"Did, uh… Well, I know word doesn't always travel fast between the realms, but did Tanner give you any problems?"

Marcus smirked, rubbing his hand. "Not after I broke his nose."

Her jaw dropped. "You didn't!"

"Oh, I did. He had it coming."

She wrung her hands. She couldn't assume it had anything to do with her. Tanner was a jerk, plain and simple. "I'm sure he deserved it."

"You know him well enough." Marcus paused. "Have you gone to see your mom in prison?"

"A couple of times. At what point do you stop loving someone because of their mistakes? Or I guess … at what point do you keep loving them, despite them?" She meant it as much about herself as her mom.

"You're not her. And you're not him. You made your own mistakes."

"Yeah. And I learned from them."

Silence hung in the air. *Next topic... Um...* "I hear Wedding Two-Point-Oh went off without a hitch. No crazy murderers on the guest list."

Marcus frowned. "It was really nice. They still kept their human-world wedding date, so they were already legally married over there. That one was nice too." He rocked his head back and forth. "I think Cam would be up to seeing you next time they visit."

She smiled. "And Tobias?"

"Yeah … we're still working on things. He knows how to hold a grudge."

She nodded. "I don't blame him. I'm surprised the rest of your family has been so nice to me."

He raised his eyebrows. "They're your family too."

She blushed. "I know. Did that make things weird, when you realized that? It took me a little while to process it, with how we … well…"

He stole a glance but didn't stop walking. "We're kinda related. Heavy on the kinda, light on the related. It's not like we're cousins. Our dads were. And I'm adopted, anyway." He looked back at Leah. "Is it weird for you?"

Her heart still clung to hope. "Not really."

Marcus reached into his pocket. "This is what I went up to my room for." He handed Leah a bottle of red nail polish.

She scrunched her eyebrows, accepting it. "Nail polish? This is why you asked me to visit?"

He rubbed the back of his neck. "Yeah, um. Well, no. I think they threw away the receipt, but when they were clearing out your old place, they asked if I had any input on what you'd want that could be taken back."

She looked at the almost-full bottle. "You can bring back anything that will fit in your pockets through a rift, and you brought me this? They gave me my childhood photos weeks ago."

He opened and closed his mouth a couple of times. "Yeah, well. I don't know." He pointed to the polish. "If I remember right, that was the first one you bought with your own money. I thought it was a nice reminder for your new life."

She smiled, her heart warming. "Thanks. I've been doing loads better. You'd be proud of me." She tucked the bottle in her pocket.

He nodded. "I've heard. And, um … I also brought your throwing knives back home. I just didn't bring them for the walk. I figured you could take them when you leave to go back to the palace." He glanced over his shoulder at the guard walking several paces behind them. "Assuming they'll let you have them?"

Leah rolled her eyes. "I'm assured she's around for *my* protection, not to protect the world from me. I'm still allowed to eat with a full set of cutlery at the dinner table, thank you very much."

A look of embarrassment flashed across his face. "Sorry, I didn't mean—"

"No, Marcus." She stopped abruptly, facing him. "You don't need to apologize. For anything. Ever." She hadn't expected her eyes to mist, but her heart couldn't handle skirting around the topic. "I was in the wrong. I know that. Completely. And I don't expect you to take me back. I don't deserve that. I know that too." A tear rolled down her cheek. "But I hope you can give me another chance at being your friend. I miss you."

He wiped her tear away. "I'm pretty sure I'll do something over the course of my life that requires an apology." He smiled. "At least one." He studied her face. "I can do friends." His smile grew to a grin. "I think my parents would prefer we started there."

Her heart leapt. *Started?*

Marcus's cheeks took on a shade of pink. "It was an … *interesting* discussion with my parents about why my girlfriend came prepared with a condom stashed under her pillow."

Leah's eyes grew wide, her face burning. "Oh gosh. I'm sorry! I really didn't think things through. I didn't exactly do an inventory when they returned my clothes and lipstick." He was still smiling, but she felt horrible about adding to the stress he had to have gone through after she was taken into custody. "You didn't get in too much trouble, did you?"

He chuckled, looking up at the sky. "Let me see if I can remember what they said. Something to the effect of 'You are not to, under any circumstances, ever even *consider* sleeping under the same roof as any girl that you are dating, or considering dating, or even think is pretty, unless you're fifty years old or married to her.'"

Leah did a poor job of stifling a laugh. "I'm really sorry."

He got more serious, gazing into her eyes. "You don't have to keep apologizing. I've … forgiven you. Don't say you're sorry anymore."

A huge weight lifted from her shoulders as she lunged forward, hugging him. She was about to pull back, realizing things were still touchy, until he reciprocated with one of his tight squeezes. It felt like home.

Leah leaned back, searching Marcus's face. She was acutely aware of his hands lingering on her waist. "I don't have to apologize, *ever*? Because I'm pretty sure I'll do something over the course of my life that requires an apology." She smiled. "At least one."

"Then try to make it something only needing a small apology. For my sake?"

"Deal."

He slid his hands down, grasping hers.

She looked at their hands, her heart racing. "What does this mean to you?"

"It means I missed you, too. And I care about you. And I want to get to know the new, real you. And give you a chance to know the full me, family notoriety and all. We'll go slow."

"Yes."

He grinned, squeezing her hands, then turned, dropping one of them and continuing on their stroll. After another minute of Leah's heart overflowing, Marcus cleared his throat. "Will I see you at the ball?"

"Yeah. Save me a dance."

"I'll save you two." He pressed his lips together. "You know that if we had kids, they'd be like me, right? All Bomen."

Her jaw dropped. "Kids? We have a year left of high school!"

He chuckled. "I didn't mean to give you a heart attack. That's years in the future. I'm just saying… I want to make sure you understand that about our people. That you know what you're signing up for … if things lead down that path someday. A lot of people around here still care about that, still consider Bomanism a curse."

She stopped him, gazing into his warm brown eyes. "I understand how it works. And I might still be figuring out who I am, but I know who *you* are. And the world could use *a lot* more people like you."

Epilogue

THE BALLROOM GLITTERED AS CANDLELIGHT bounced off chandelier crystals, and reflected off the gilded wainscoting. Glassware clinked, girls giggled, and adults everywhere mumbled in greeting.

Leah sat at her table, alone, sipping grape juice and trying her best to mind her posture. Marcus and his parents had been busy conversing when she'd entered, and she hadn't wanted to bother them. After slinking to her designated table, she people-watched as the room continued to fill, as the violins played upbeat tunes, as the gaze of literally every person in the room rested on her at some point.

It was lonely in the corner. In part because she didn't really know many people yet, other than the servants who occasionally swung by her table to check on her. In part because her personal guards were doing a more-than-sufficient job of gatekeeping her company that night. They wouldn't take any risks at Leah's first ball. Everyone here at the palace was theoretically pro–Queen Catrina. That meant they should respect her wishes to welcome Leah and help their kingdom move on. That also meant they might despise Leah for being the daughter of Soren, one of the most hated men in the history of the Green Lands. Leah hadn't done herself any favors either, by attempting to assassinate their much-beloved Queen Kaylah.

The whispers and glances were hard to ignore. Leah knew what it felt like to be slut-shamed. She knew what it was like to be the topic of perverts in the locker room. None of that compared to this experience.

Closing her eyes and taking a deep breath, Leah forced herself to repeat Catrina's pep talk. She'd only ever be able to clear her name, to claim her future, by showing she was above the gossip, above the hate. It probably would have been easier if it was just her peers throwing looks of disdain her way, but the adult eyes on her made things that much worse.

"How are you doing, miss?" one of the guards asked, leaning close.

Leah forced a smile. "Doing well."

"Good… Would you like to dance?"

Arching an eyebrow, she turned to face him better. He had to be more than twice her age. "What?"

He nodded to his right. "Jaxon Withers, son of Governor Withers."

She almost giggled when she realized the guard had meant a boy her age wanted to dance, not that the guard had intended to ask her himself. She eyed the governor's son. He stood tall, holding his hands in front of him. His straight black hair hung below his ears, and his suit was as sharp as any of the other men's in the room. He looked at her with a smile and a small nod from a few feet away. The fact his request was even being passed along to her meant he was on an approved list of some sort, that the queen's security team felt this boy could be trusted. Leah didn't know whether to be annoyed with him or grateful he was attempting to rescue her from her island of solitude.

"He can ask me himself," she told the guard.

The guard waved Jaxon over. He glided over to Leah's table, bowing. She remained seated.

"My name is Jaxon."

She gave him a nod. "I'm Leah, but I guess you already knew that."

His smile grew.

Leah took a sip of her water. "How can I help you, Jaxon?"

He looked confused, glancing at the guards. "Oh, I thought they told you. I want to dance."

She wore a grin. "They did tell me. But I wanted to hear it from you."

"Oh." He rested his hands on the back of the chair across the table from her. "Well, I'd love to dance."

Studying his face, she figured she might as well have a little fun. "Then I'd say you came to the right place. I hope you enjoy your evening."

He narrowed his eyes. "So … that's a no?"

"I can't say yes or no to a question I haven't been asked." She folded her napkin. "All I know from you is that you hope to dance tonight."

His mouth hung open. "Yeah. I came over to invite you to dance with me."

She opened her eyes wide in mock surprised shock. "Aha. I didn't realize you were asking *me* to dance."

He smiled again. "Yes. That's why I'm here."

Straightening her unused utensils, she matched his smile. "Why do you want to dance with me?" She was trying to be playful, though she genuinely was curious. She hadn't expected many approved suitors would even try socializing with her that night.

Losing his cool, Jaxon squinted with a frustrated expression. "Why do I want to dance with you? It's a ball. That's what people do. If you don't want to, you can just say so."

She sighed. Her sense of humor was lost on this boy. She knew she shouldn't toy with him, and that Catrina would likely already disapprove of their conversation—it hadn't been 'gracious.' Sparing a glance in Marcus's direction, Leah yearned for him to be the one asking her, but he was busy talking to a row of dolled-up girls.

"Yes. I'd love to dance." She rose and took Jaxon's outstretched arm, and he led her onto the dance floor.

Luckily, he eased her into the dance with simple steps. She'd taken lessons at Catrina's urging, but hadn't practiced as much as she ought to have in preparation.

"So, how are you enjoying the Green Lands?" Jaxon asked.

Leah puffed up her cheeks. "Um… Good? Yeah, it's good." How was she supposed to have a conversation with anyone? 'Yeah, pretty good. Minus that whole bummer thing about finding out my parents are murderers, and I almost joined their ranks. How about you?'

"You like it at the palace?"

"Uh… It's," she glanced at the room around them, "shiny."

"Shiny?"

Another awkward question. What had he hoped she'd say? 'I'm glad to have lost both parents and am now being forced to live in the lap of luxury, at the same palace my dad's death sentence was decreed from?'

"It's beautiful." She forced a gracious smile.

"I understand you'll be touring the kingdom soon?"

"Yep."

He nodded. "How do you feel about that?"

Was he a therapist in disguise? "Why did you want to dance with me?"

His mouth was agape. "Do I need a reason?"

A diplomat, she was not. "*Need* one? Nah. But you *have* one. There's always a motivation behind what we do, right?"

"I just … wanted to dance with you."

"Hmm…" Catrina would not approve of the words about to come out of Leah's mouth, but it wasn't Leah's fault she hadn't developed a filter overnight. "Well, I'd say you either asked me to dance because you think I'm pretty, and you like the way this dress looks."

His eyes wandered over her deep plum dress for the shortest of moments before he blushed.

"Or you're doing this as an aspiring politician, like your father."

Jaxon studied her face skeptically. "It's just a dance."

"Or…" Leah bobbed her head. "You're one of those sick fan club people that fall in love with serial killers and write to them in prison."

He was not amused. "Excuse me?"

"Just call it like I see it. Which is it?"

He glared, but didn't miss a step in the dance. "You have no culture or manners. If I was less of a gentleman, I'd walk off of this dance floor right now."

Should she be ashamed of herself? Yes. Was she? Not really. She laughed loudly, playfully nudging his shoulder. She wore a giant toothy smile as if he'd told a great joke. "But it's all about appearances, right?"

He wasn't smiling. Instead, he ignored her for the rest of the dance. Leah was okay with that, for the most part. Her guilt grew a little with each step. She didn't even know this guy, but if there was something Leah was good at, it was burning bridges. And it was hard to imagine *anyone* not having an ulterior motive, given her story, given her precarious place in society.

Without conversation to occupy her, Leah watched the people who were watching her right back. A pair of soft brown eyes caught her attention. Marcus was watching. And then a girl rested a hand on his bicep. *Ugh.*

As the music slowed, Leah allowed her guilt to prompt her to speak again. "Sorry, Jaxon."

He didn't respond. As the dance came to an end, he released her, bowing.

"I really am sorry. That was rude of me."

He scanned her face. "Thank you for the dance."

"Did someone ask you to dance with me?"

He squinted. "No. I thought you could use a friend, and a kind introduction. But perhaps, Miss Eleana, you ought to get more help before you come out in proper society again." He gave her another bow and then turned on his heel, gliding off the dance floor.

Yep. She was an uncultured swine, alright. One that happily skulked off to her familiar corner.

Couples were already dancing away to the next song by the time she returned to her table and accepted a pastry from a passing servant carrying a tray. Marcus danced with a girl wearing a pink dress. Leah was green folk, alright. Very green. Jealously green.

She picked at her pastry, eating tiny crumbs, constantly stealing a glance at Marcus and his partner. The girl was striking. Her long blond hair cascaded straight down her back to where Marcus's hand held her. Her smile was perfect, her footwork graceful. And that dress—it was like a custom-fit beaded wonder with strips of fabric flowing away from her as she spun.

Leah guzzled some water. *This is going to be a long night…*

At the end of the dance, Marcus bowed to his partner, and she curtsied. Leah looked away. She was the epitome of an obsessed ex-girlfriend right now. What she didn't need was gossip about how she'd gawked at the queen's nephew all night, how she was probably plotting the assassination of every girl who stood in her way as she pined for him.

Instead, she stared at her nails, trying to not pick at or bite them. It was a messy habit.

"Free for this dance?" Marcus asked.

She looked up. He'd already reached her table, not needing to be approved to approach.

Leah glanced around the room. Couples took to the floor, but more eyes than usual were on them right now. The entire kingdom knew what had happened, the entire realm.

"Are you sure?" she asked, her pulse quickening.

"Of course." He extended a hand.

So many eyes rested on them both. And now that she had really learned more about Ivy society and Marcus's place in it, this felt risky. It wasn't surprising he'd been upset to find out his girlfriend had shoplifting and lying problems. He was the most eligible bachelor their age. His family had a reputation of being saints. People had expectations of him.

"I… It probably won't be great for your reputation," she said.

"You let me worry about that." He extended his other hand as well. "You promised me a dance. And right now, the only reputation you're giving me is that of a guy being royally shot down by the prettiest girl in the room."

She bolstered her courage. "Yeah, sure." She took his hands, and he led her to the floor. He rested a hand on her waist, leading her in the dance. Leah furrowed her brow at the song being played by the orchestra. "Is that human music?"

He gave her a charming smile. "I asked them to play our song."

"We have a song?"

"I don't know. I remembered us dancing to this once."

It was undeniably sweet. "Thanks. It kind of makes it feel a little more like I'm home…" That was a depressing confession. She *was* literally home, in her new home, in the palace.

"Are you enjoying it at all?" he asked.

She gripped his hand tighter. "I'm enjoying this right now."

"Jaxon's a better dancer than me."

She smiled at his fishing. "I figured you were too busy with your fan club to notice."

"Hmm…" He spun her. "Is that a hint of jealousy I detect?"

"Yes."

He wore a triumphant grin. "It would be hard not to notice you tonight."

"Hmm. That might be true. Jaxon probably thought so, since he claimed the first dance."

Marcus's eyes narrowed a bit. "He's kind of a nitwit."

She batted her eyelashes. "Is that a hint of jealousy I detect?"

He pulled her closer. "Yes."

"Good."

They took a few more steps in silence. She couldn't resist stealing a peek at the others in the room. Rachel smiled when their eyes met.

"That really is a … stunning … dress," he breathed.

She blushed, focusing on him. "Thanks. I had to fight Her Majesty and the seamstress to let me wear it the way I wanted."

He didn't say anything. He didn't need to. Queen Catrina was genuinely very kind, but could be a bit strict. She'd insisted Leah should try harder on showing a good face to work on her respectability. It wasn't like anyone in the Green Lands knew the kind of reputation Leah had left behind, but a young lady trying to prove herself ought not to show so much cleavage.

Leah had wanted a breathtaking sweetheart gown, or to not go to the ball at all. They'd compromised. Leah attended, and had a shawl. A shawl she took off and draped over her chair the first moment she could.

Leah lifted a hand, wiggling her fingers. "You didn't compliment my nail polish."

Marcus spared a glance at the red polish, the one he'd just returned to her, then smirked. "It's your color. You'll have to forgive me for not noticing it. That dress doesn't accentuate your nails."

She stood taller, puffing out her chest. "Tell me, Marcus … what *does* it accentuate?"

He shook his head. "You're going to make this hard on me, aren't you?"

She feigned confusion. "What?"

"Dancing with other guys. Wearing a dress like that. You're going to make it hard on me."

She looked him dead in the eyes. "I heard what you said the first time. I just wanted to make sure. You said I was making something on you … hard?"

His face bloomed red. "Leah!" He stole glances around them, not that anyone would have been close enough to hear her say it. He would never *not* be cute when he blushed. "You can't just say stuff like that in public."

It was a playful moment, like those they'd shared before. And his response was more shock than censure, but it threw her into a melancholy mood.

They continued to sway. She swallowed. "If we're going to do this… Friends, or more than friends… Even if we didn't, and we just saw each other at royal functions and awkward family gatherings, because there's really no escaping those anymore… I need you to know I'll never be the girl they want me to be."

He searched her face.

"I'll practice the dance steps. I'll do the curtsying. I'll attend the right royal functions. But I'll still be me. I'm going to spout off gosh-awful puns, and fight with the seamstress about what I wear, and make *wildly* inappropriate jokes while dancing in the middle of a ballroom filled with people watching and waiting for me to fail. That's what you're in for."

He nodded, pensive. Disappointment painted his face.

But then an almost sinister grin overtook his lips. "Do you promise?"

She matched his grin, her heart melting completely.

"I know you don't love being the center of attention," he said. "I'm used to this. You'll get used to it too."

Doubtful.

"But … if they're all going to stare and spread rumors, what do you think about giving them something to sink their teeth into?"

"Um… What are you thinking?"

He wore a cat-that-ate-the-canary smirk. "Hold on."

"What?"

His hands gripped her tighter, and yanked her into a wild spin. She let out a short scream, then giggled as they spun around and around. She quickly became dizzy, and almost lost her grip, but shot out vines behind his back to secure herself.

When he slowed, the song was coming to an end. She was still laughing, but almost out of breath. He was laughing, too. They helped steady each other, and she leaned her forehead against his chest. "Yeah, people might talk about that…"

He chuckled a little more.

After taking a second to recompose herself, she stood straight. "Well, that was a dance."

He bowed graciously, and she curtsied. "Still saving me another one?" he asked.

She almost grabbed his hand, but held herself back. "Yeah. Of course. I can't wait to see what we'll do next."

They lingered a moment.

"Well…" He fidgeted with his hands. "If you want, I could introduce you to a few people…"

She glanced past him at the group he'd spent time with earlier. She recognized a few faces he'd introduced her to weeks ago, but several were new to her. A cute blonde stared right at her—and then her pupils flashed an unnatural green, Seeder green. "No. I think I'm good in my corner right now." Leah forced a smile. "Baby steps."

"Okay. We'll chat?"

She nodded, and started walking away. The Seeder girl's eyes were no longer neon, but they followed her back to her table.

The next hour or so, Leah sat at her designated spot. She took more than one bathroom break, and chatted with guards and servants. She festered over the situation, and over the Seeder girl. Had she been jealous that Marcus made a scene with Leah? It was public knowledge they'd dated. It was obvious to everyone now there was still something there. But it might not have anything to do with Marcus at all. It might have just been Leah's parentage.

A couple of guys even inquired about dancing. Leah declined. She wasn't in the mood anymore. And she couldn't handle much more of being a wallflower, either.

Needing a break from the noise and crowds, she sauntered to one of the open balconies, escorted by her security detail. They kindly gave her some space and waited just inside.

Leah looked out over the expanse of the kingdom before her. The moonlight lit giant mountains in every direction, and landed on the sea of treetops surrounding the palace. It was positively ethereal, but it only helped a little.

"I shouldn't be worried, should I?"

Leah glanced over her shoulder. "No, Your Majest— I mean, Highness."

Kaylah smiled. "The titles are confusing sometimes, aren't they?"

Leah blew out a puff of air as Kaylah joined her at the edge of the balcony. "Yeah."

"Of course, *you* don't have to use one with me."

Leah nodded. It was still weird. How could it not be? To just call her 'Kaylah' to her face? Or … 'Aunt Kaylah'?

"You're not enjoying the dance," Kaylah said.

"I know. I should try to at least look happier."

Kaylah adjusted a bangle around her wrist. "I don't know about that. I think people understand the position you're in."

Leah didn't really care for a heart-to-heart right now. She just wanted peace and quiet. She continued to take in the scenery.

"Well… I just wanted to make sure you were okay out here."

Leah gripped the balcony railing. "I'm not out here to fling myself off the edge."

Kaylah said nothing. They'd also put Leah on suicide watch those first few days because Kaylah's ruling hadn't been an official one. Kaylah had met with the Seeder and Bomen councils to address the issue of Leah's assassination attempt, and her very existence, during that time. It had taken a while for Kaylah to report that her decisions had been upheld.

"If you ever need a break from the palace, the invitation's always open to visit Eric and me at our place."

Leah nodded. She'd been there once already for tea. The grounds were expansive, and it was beyond serene. It was actually a tempting offer.

"Fewer servants," Kaylah continued. "And don't get me wrong, I love Catrina to death, but toddlers and babies, and dignitaries… Gross!"

Leah couldn't resist a tiny smile at that. "I'll give that to you. You're probably more fun, too." Perhaps that wasn't very generous of Leah to say. Queen Catrina was a sweetheart, but the rules upon rules… It was quite the contrast to what Leah had grown up with.

Kaylah splayed a hand on her chest. "I'm the fun one? I'm the fun one!" She balled a fist in triumph. "Yes! I didn't know if I'd ever be an aunt, but if I turned out to be, I for sure wanted to be the fun kind!"

Leah's smile grew. Kaylah admittedly had a decent sense of humor. And Eric was a fantastic listener. "Don't get too big of a head about it. Your tiara won't fit."

"That's why you get different sizes." Kaylah nudged her.

Leah chuckled.

"But I'm sorry you're not having more fun. Other than that rather unique dance you shared with Marcus."

Her stomach flipped at the mention of him. "Yeah. I'm sure I'll hear more about how wrong that was later tonight."

Turning to face the palace, Kaylah drew a deep breath. "You know, we Elonta women might be blessed to rule, but we kinda suck at fitting in sometimes."

"What?" Leah raised a skeptical eyebrow. Strictly speaking, she *wasn't* an Elonta, and had absolutely no place in the line of heirs to the throne, but that wasn't what Kaylah had been getting at. "I'm sure it's rough having millions of green folk adore you for fixing their problems. And from what I hear, Catrina's never even sneezed when she ought not to."

Kaylah grinned. "Okay. Way to call me out. Yeah, Catrina doesn't count. Maybe I just meant *this* Elonta struggled to fit in."

That was still hard to believe.

"We won't even mention the whole Seeder drama… Or Bomen. Or the family legacy I had to fight tooth and nail to disassociate myself from. Just me as a person… I'm not everyone's cup of tea." She straightened her gorgeous off-the-shoulder red dress. "I started my reign when I was just older than you. I wasn't properly prepared. I flubbed things left and right. I said stupid things that got people I love hurt. I didn't always have the best filter." She pursed her lips, then softly chuckled. "My friend, Saff, once described me as 'flippant and callous.' She wasn't wrong. And frankly, the list goes on. I dressed wrong. I wasn't a coy, proper lady. I was the monster who unilaterally decided to allow humans into the realm, and then, Lights of the Afterworld forbid, I married one." She pointed at Leah. "Mind you, his existence wasn't even public for almost two years until I announced it and refused to pick a sperm donor just to birth gremlins of my own."

Kaylah sighed. "Anyway, I didn't mean to make this about me. I'm just saying, people might not be ready for you yet. Yes, you'll have to accept some give and take. But they'll get there. And so will you." She cautiously wrapped an arm around Leah's shoulder, giving her a gentle squeeze. "Okay?"

Leah nodded. "Yeah." Kaylah could get a tad preachy, and as Leah had learned at the wedding luncheon, she could be fierce, but mostly, she was pretty down to earth. That was only one of a million things Leah had gotten wrong, had made assumptions on, and had felt like an idiot about later, once she'd learned the truth. She'd seen Kaylah's rough interaction with one of the servants at the luncheon as a sign she was a tyrant. That hadn't been the case at all. There had been royal wedding crashers outside of the manor causing problems, and she'd been curt, frustrated that her guards needed to barge into the family luncheon when they ought to have been able to handle the situation on their own.

Kaylah broke her reverie. "Are you too polite to tell me you want to be left alone right now?"

Leah smiled, averting her gaze.

"Alright. I can take a hint. Just know I'm here for you. Love you, kiddo."

Leah opened her mouth, but nothing came out for a moment. "Thanks." It was still too soon to go there with Kaylah, despite how much she tried.

Kaylah gave her a sad smile. "Good night."

Once the click of Kaylah's heels became muffled in the distance, it was just Leah, her thoughts, and the faint breeze. Tomorrow would be better. Things were better when she was busy with tutors, her counselor, and knife-throwing, and honing her skills, fine-tuning her powers.

Tomorrow would be better.

A warm hand caressed her back, and she sharply inhaled.

"Sorry," Marcus said.

She blew out a shaky breath. "I don't expect people to sneak up on me so much when I have a security detail watching my back."

He smiled gently. "You okay?"

She rubbed her forehead. "Did Kaylah send you?"

"No… Should she have?"

"No. Just don't need everyone checking up on me every two seconds."

He pursed his lips. "Sorry. Just hadn't seen you in a while. Though, I should learn my lesson." He cleared his throat, tugging on his vest. "I dated this *superhot* girl once, and she tried to teach me that girls don't always want to be saved. I wasn't the best student."

She grinned. "Maybe she was too stubborn to admit she sometimes *does* need saving."

"Yeah?"

Her smile grew. "Yep. You just have to be able to read her mind to know when and how."

He busted out laughing.

An owl hooted from a nearby treetop, and Marcus scooted closer.

"Are you only here with me, trying to work things out with me, because you feel bad?" She gazed into his eyes. "Or because this is one of those 'for the greater good' things where we show we can put aside our differences and make up for our parents' mistakes?"

He didn't answer right away, instead lifting a hand to her waist, then sliding it to her hip. "No. Not at all." He spoke softly. "Part of me…" He stared at his hand as he stroked her hip bone with a thumb. "Part of me wants to pick up where we left things … that night … in my room." He met her gaze, exuding passion. "The night I told you how I felt, before things went wrong."

She took his other hand, placing it on her other hip. "I'd be okay with that."

He panted an exhale. His look of wanting washed away as he removed his hands from her body entirely. "But part of me, the part that's been used before, even before I met you, *needs* to go slow this time." There was hurt in his expression. "Please don't rush me."

She nodded, gutted at that confession. He'd never told her that before, not that it likely would have made much difference when she'd been blinded by idiocy to use him in the first place. "I can be patient." Perhaps that wasn't the whole truth. She could *try* to be patient. They both still had healing to do. Unfortunately, she felt like her healing would best be done with the one she loved by her side, and his needed to be done with some distance.

"But I will say…" She wanted to lighten the mood. "Try not to take too long. There's only one of me, and frankly, every single day, the guards have to fight off *dozens* of sexy suitors trying to pound down the palace doors to get a chance to date me. So, I'm just saying, hot commodity right here."

He smirked knowingly. "They would be, if they knew you the way I do."

She blushed. "So, we're friends. Ish. Friend adjacent. Friends that have a look in their eye and a tenderness to their touch that friends ought not to have."

He pressed his lips together. "Sorry."

"It's okay. I want that. But I'm afraid we're going to be five years down the road and I'm still waiting for you to call me your girlfriend, just to find out you thought we were back together after a month."

"Trust me, when I'm ready to be exclusive again, you'll know. The whole realm will."

She smiled, a calmness settling in her heart. "Okay."

Marcus furrowed his brow, looking off into the distance. "Can I ask you something?"

"Of course you can."

He lightly ran his hand over the railing. "What do you like about me?"

"Really?" It felt like a ridiculous question, given she'd told him during their time together. But then again, it wasn't a ridiculous question at all… They were starting from square one again. He didn't know how much of anything she'd said during their time together was genuine. It was going to take a long time for her heart not to ache in situations like this. The old Leah would have moved on, would have protected herself by washing her hands of him. The new Leah knew she'd be an idiot to let him go.

Marcus didn't respond, didn't look at her.

"I love a ton of things about you. You're studious, and love your family, and you like to help people. You're … forgiving."

He gave her a cautious understanding glance at that mention.

"And I love your sense of humor, and," she lifted a hand to his bicep, its beauty wasted in the suit he was wearing, "you're strong, and talented, and have handsome eyes."

He smiled.

She slid her hand up to his shoulder, then the side of his neck, and ran her hand through his naturally curly hair. "And I love this, the curls."

His smile grew, and he stared at her. Her lips yearned to be kissed. Her heart nearly beat out of her chest in protest at the absence of his arms around her.

But he still didn't snatch her up, didn't draw her close. Didn't kiss hope back into her.

As the moment floated away, she stopped playing with his hair, and lowered her hand. "Anything I've ever said about why I like you has always been true."

"Thank you," he said softly. "Did I tell you what made me change my mind about you? About us?"

"No. You didn't."

"It hurt to hear you say you, well, that you loved me. For the first time, only *after* what you did."

Her heart was a pincushion. "I'm sorry."

He rubbed his chin. "It sucked. And I came to understand that you couldn't help yourself, given what your mom had said. You didn't know the big picture. And in part, I was to blame."

"No you weren't."

He side-eyed her skeptically. "How much history did I teach you?"

She frowned. "You were my boyfriend, not my history teacher." She poked his arm. "Plus, you taught me lots of valuable things, like how green folk earn good luck."

He instantly donned a toothy grin.

"Though I will say, the servants and guards all get *super* creeped out when I ask them to blow raspberries on my neck. I could use some good luck! Your aunt has forbidden me from chasing them around the palace asking them to do it, and I can't figure out why!"

Marcus's laughter was music to her ears. After a moment, he sighed, growing serious again. "Anyway, I guess I finally started to forgive you when my mom and Kaylah shared how you told them, and your mom—even after you knew she hated Bomen—that you loved me."

"I did," she whispered.

"I think that speaks volumes, what you say about someone else when they're not in the room. You had no reason to say that if it wasn't true. It did nothing to help your case."

"I said it because it was true. It *is* true." Her heart raced. Her lips and tongue still didn't know how to form the words properly, but she pushed through. "I love you."

He swallowed, silent. His hands slowly clenched into fists at his sides.

"It's okay." Tears rolled down her cheeks. "You don't have to say it again until you're ready. If you … ever…" She sniffled.

He threw his arms around her and pulled her in. No one could hug like Marcus could. "We'll get there," he whispered into her ear.

She stood there, relaxing her muscles, allowing the weight of her choices, the weight of the realm, to slowly drip from her conscience. She breathed in his cologne, calm, her heart beating to the rhythm of his.

After what had to have been several minutes, her tears had dried up. She let out a cleansing breath. "Thank you."

"Anytime. Are you ready to go back in?"

There was probably another hour left of the ball. As an official palace ball, it was going to be a long one. "Honestly, I'm pretty worn out. I might just head to my chambers."

He straightened one of her ringlets. "I wouldn't blame you. I'm sure it's been a long day. Maybe I'll rift over, drop by, sometime in the next couple of days?"

"I'd love that. Bring your throwing knives."

"I can do that."

"Or … I could ask one of the palace archers to give us lessons."

Marcus playfully squinted at her teasing. "Maybe another time…"

She let out a breathy chuckle. "Then it's a… Well, not a date."

"Okay. Anyway, I won't hold you hostage for that second dance. I'll take a rain check."

"Actually," she stood taller, "I'd like to take you up on it now. It would be a good way to end the night."

He held out his arm, and she hooked hers through it.

"Maybe let's dance a little less conspicuously this time..." she suggested.

He winked. "I can manage that."

As they passed her security detail, who had no doubt witnessed the entirety of their conversation, Leah breathed deeply, holding her head high. She could do this. She and Marcus could do this.

They sauntered to the dance floor, nodding politely to others along the way. With impeccable timing, the orchestra struck up the next tune. Marcus held Leah's hand, guiding her to the floor.

And they danced. He wasn't a prince. She wasn't a princess. But they glided across the floor of the palace, light on their feet, peacefully gazing into one another's eyes.

In her heart, in so many ways, she was still searching for a sense of self, a sense of home. In many ways, in his arms, she was already there.

The scrutiny of the onlookers melted away in the background, hidden by the harp and the violin playing nearby. The anxiety of the evening was swallowed up altogether, replaced by hope. Hope in friendship. Hope in love. And, with the support of those who mattered most, hope in family.

~**Please consider leaving a review!**~

On Amazon, Goodreads, StoryGraph, and/or anywhere else this book can be found.

This goes a long way to support authors!

Don't forget to sign up for J. Houser's newsletter for publishing updates, promotions, and bonus content!

JHouserWrites.com

Also, connect with the author here:
YouTube, TikTok, Facebook, Instagram, and Twitter under:
JHouserWrites

Order Book 5 Now!

Leah is the black eye the Green Lands never saw coming.

Born to two of the most hated rulers, she didn't earn any points with the people by trying to assassinate their most beloved queen.

Now, she's forced to build a new life, an uphill battle with all eyes on her. Two years after the failed assassination attempt, she's making great strides in learning her powers, improving her reputation, and forging a new future.

All until a tiny little accident makes her question her family ties and her goals.

A teenage pregnancy was never part of her plan, and now she's faced with the reality of starting all over again. Can her relationship with Marcus survive the scrutiny of the royal family, and that of the entire realm?

Author Q&A

Where did you get the idea to write *The Heir of Exile*?

Many of my ideas are a mix of real-life experience and crazy dreams. This entire Seeder Wars series started from a tiny spark of inspiration when I woke one day. Leah's story, however, all started with my curiosity about her mother. What kind of woman was Beata? What kind of person marries the villain? We only knew her by name in the central trilogy. Was she forced to marry Soren? Naïve about his true nature? Just as bad as him, or worse? And how would their daughter in exile turn out?

What should I read next?

Leah and Marcus have more to their story. The villain's daughter will most definitely have a tough road to walk as she tries to find her place in the Green Lands. Check out their story in the next book to see their relationship unfold.

If you jumped into this series with *The Heir of Exile* as your first book, I would highly recommend going back and reading books 1–3, starting with *Seeder Shadow Wars*. You know some spoilers from Leah's story, but there's still a lot to discover and enjoy on the journey!

Interested in other books in this world? If you sign up for my newsletter, you'll be updated on new releases. More books are in the works, including Guillen's story as Kaylah's spy.

More on the author & her books!

More by J. Houser

THE
SEEDER WARS TRILOGY

THE
HEIR'S DUOLOGY

Also available in the

Seeder Wars world!

Magic in the Match is a
series of standalone
Adult Fairy Tale
Sweet Romances.

Magic in the Match
**Fairy Tale
Romances**

A selection of premium book journals. They each accommodate entries
for 250 books and have individual aesthetic touches.

For more information, go to JHouserWrites.com!